# Megan O'Mally

## HEARTS OF THE OZARKS
### BOOK 3

## AVA MacKINNEY

# What Readers Are Saying About
# Eliza Long

-A great work of historical fiction! It had me from beginning to end. Now I'm anxiously anticipating the next book!

-What a fun read! I read it all in one night and stayed up way too late. Engaging storyline and I loved all the history about Springfield, Missouri, where I used to live. There was so much I didn't know. Nice to read a good fiction book for adults and not feel nervous about the content... Super clean but still engaging and real. I am excited for the next books to come out!

-If you enjoy an adventurous story, that's difficult to put down, then the book "Eliza Long" is for you. From the first to last page, it holds your attention. This historical fiction book, that is set during the "War Between The States" has characters that are full of emotions, faith & suspense. Ava MacKinney is an excellent writer & I can't want for her second book to be released.

-I'm really enjoying this book! I'm halfway through and only received it yesterday! I like Eliza's personality and the fire in her, also really enjoyed the portrayal of the time period! Makes me travel back in time every time I open the book. Good job Author!

-Loved it - the characters, the story, the history, and the romance. I was able to get a pre-publication copy of Maddy Malone as a beta reader and I love it even more than this one. I also was a beta reader of the third book in the series (Megan O'Mally) and love it as well - more humor and more variety in the story.

-I JUST finished this book! Read it in less than 24hrs! I loved it!! Excellent story! Deeply engaging! Fun read!

Since I live in the area it was even more intriguing. Can't wait for the next one!!!!!

-Well written, great story, and historically accurate!

-This book has a great storyline and is well written. You can tell the author studied the history and area. Buy this book!

-Loved, loved your book! I read it in 2 days! Couldn't put it down!

-I read your book this week and LOVED it! Excellent writing, gripping story, history of Springfield that I didn't know - what's not to love? THANKS!

-Your first book was super engaging... I read it all in one night! I'm excited to read the next one. Way to go!

-I am reading your book!! Wow and wow!!! I am impressed. The book starts out with a bang. There is no good place to stop. So much going on. I can't put it down. I love the historical setting. You are an amazing writer and I do read mostly historical novels.

-It was so enjoyable to read your book, **Eliza Long.** You truly wrote a great book and I didn't want to put it down to get something else done. I am looking forward to your next book and next book and next book!!

Publishing Coordinator – Sharon Kizziah-Holmes
Cover Design – Jaycee DeLorenzo

Paperback-Press
an imprint of A & S Publishing
Paperback Press, LLC

ISBN -13: 978-1-960499-92-9

# DEDICATION

I dedicate this book to my parents, Russell and Elin Batten, who always encouraged me to read and to dream. Our cozy farmhouse in Vermont was stocked with books of every flavor, which my siblings and I freely indulged in. Often, my dad would entertain us by reading a novel to the six of us around the supper table. Days were spent roaming the farm among the woods and streams, playacting our much-exaggerated versions of the latest stories or tv shows.

*Wagon Train* was the show that inspired Megan O'Mally, a story that was birthed in me decades ago. In fact, this is the first novel I wrote. After many edits and rewrites, it's a story that I love. I hope you do too.

# ACKNOWLEDGMENTS

So many people have helped me along this journey and I appreciate them immensely. My beta readers, editors, proofreaders and my readers that kept asking if I was done yet, and why in the world was this taking so long. Thanks guys, I needed that.

I especially want to thank my publishing coordinator, Sharon Kizziah Holmes, who has patiently guided me through the publishing path of all three of the books in this series, answering all my questions and providing her expert advice.

Thanks also to my two professional editors, Addison Williams and Nanette Sipe who kindly and patiently helped me craft a novel that is way better than the original.

# PROLOGUE

*Southwest Missouri, August 12, 1861*

The farm wagon hit another rut. Megan grabbed the splintered side and braced herself. As far back as she could see were soldiers and citizens in every kind of conveyance imaginable, with cows, pigs, sheep, and chickens being herded along. They were running for their lives. The Confederates were close behind, and what they planned for them, one could only imagine.

Megan was too numb to be afraid. Her secure world had been snatched from her just two days ago. In less than an hour's time, after she had sent her students home, she packed everything she could and fled the city, traveling northeast toward Rolla, along with half the city of Springfield.

"The Secessionists are coming! They've beaten our troops and they're on their way to Springfield! Send the children home to their families and get out before it's too late! Hurry! They're already raiding the south side! There's not much time!" An unknown man had screamed the words and fired his rifle into the air that fateful afternoon then left, riding fast to alert their neighbors.

Megan was covered in dirt from the top of her head down to her worn black boots. When the driver pulled the horses over to rest, she jumped down from the wagon and stepped back from the road to sit for a while in the shade of an old sycamore. Wiping away sweat that had trickled down her forehead into her eyes, she started worrying about her friends, Maddy and Eliza. Were they among these refugees? Were they safe? Her heart ached with fear. Squinting toward the back of the column of travelers, she looked for any sign of them.

Yesterday, she'd heard the rumor that a large shipment of gold had been smuggled out of town and was hidden somewhere in their midst. Also, valuable military supplies had been taken out of the city to keep the Confederates from finding them. That alone gave the Confederates reason to pursue them. It bothered her to think the Federal troops would risk the lives of civilians to hide their precious cargo.

When she reached Rolla, she planned to telegraph Uncle Chester to let him know she was on her way. Uncle Chester, Aunt Eleanor, and their daughters, Julie and Emily, had offered their home to her months ago when the first rumors of war were stirring. St. Louis was fairly stable under the control of Federal troops. It would be a safe haven until the war was over, she hoped.

As she sat under the sycamore, she prayed desperately for the safety of her fellow refugees, especially for her two friends and her students. Tears came unbidden as she thought of them. Only God knew where they were and if they were safe.

The sight of a wagon with several wounded soldiers interrupted her thoughts. She had seen many on this trip. It was almost too much to bear. Guilt washed over her at her selfish weakness. She had tried to help, but she was exhausted to the point of despair. *This is war and I despise it!* She buried her face in her skirt and wept.

# CHAPTER ONE

*Almost four years later*

A warm, rainy Friday in April 1865 was the beginning of a weekend that would forever change the course of Megan O'Mally's life.

Raindrops drizzled slowly down her classroom window. She stacked her books and threw her cape over her shoulders, fastening it under her chin. What a week it had been! The week before had rocked with ecstasy with the news of Lee's surrender then plummeted into despair at Lincoln's murder. This week was spent putting pieces back together. The children at Robberson School were confused and frightened, thinking maybe the fighting would continue. Most had been touched closely by the war. Megan, too, had been perplexed by the implications of this hideous assassination.

Megan passed the telegraph office on her way home. She, along with several others, crowded to read the latest news posted on the bulletin boards outside. To her great delight, the terms of surrender were still being worked out, with the South cooperating to bring an end to all fighting.

"Thank God," the lady next to her uttered, tears streaming down her plump cheeks. She turned and squeezed Megan's hand, sharing her relief. Megan squeezed back and choked back tears. The crowd dispersed as others tried to shoulder their way to the front. Cheers erupted at the news.

Megan tightened her cape and continued her way home. In spite of the rain, she was in good spirits. She looked forward to the coming evening. She was going to accompany her cousin, Emily, to another celebration ball, this one hosted by Major and Mrs. Barkley, longtime friends of Megan's Uncle Chester and Aunt Eleanor Parsons. Despite Lincoln's death, the festive air was in full swing in St. Louis and Megan delighted in it.

When she walked through the front door of the Parsons' large house, she glanced up and caught her uncle's eye as he sat sorting paperwork in his study. She blew him a kiss and he winked affectionately at her. Megan was deeply grateful for his family taking her in when she needed a home. The last four years living in St. Louis had been relatively stable in spite of the war. Her life was safe, routine, rich in relationships.

She adored Chester even though he seldom had time to spend with his family. He was present at family meals and dispensed hugs and smiles freely on his beloved family, but beyond that, he was unaware of how they spent their time. He left that to his wife. Their daughters, Julie and Emily, were very content with their father's indulgence and pursued their interests and lifestyles with abandon.

Exhausted, Megan made her way up the long stairway, deposited her books on her desk, and threw herself across her bed. Her fingers fumbled with her hairpins as she struggled to untangle them from her long hair. Finally loosened, it fell across her face and over the comforter. She loved teaching but she always felt drained by the end of the day. Heaving a sigh, she forced herself off the bed and made her way to her desk to look over her students' work. A small envelope, addressed to her, lay on top of her Bible. "Mail! Oh, how nice!" she exclaimed with delight. Quickly flipping it over, she saw it was from her sister, Elizabeth.

*April, 1865*
*My dearest Meggie,*
*Thank God this horrible war is almost over. Now, hopefully, traveling will be safe in Missouri again.*

*We all miss you very much. I hope things are still going well with you. You won't believe how much the girls have grown. Suzanne just had her twelfth birthday! Lucy is 10 and our baby, Abby, is 7! You'd just turned 17 when we saw you last, and you still looked like a little girl to me. Don't be angry, Meggie, you'll always be my little sis no matter how much of a beautiful woman you might grow to be. Have you grown any taller?*

*I must apologize for rambling like this; I just want to see you so badly. I'm afraid that might not be possible since Charles has decided that we are pulling up roots and moving west. It's something he has wanted to do for a long time and I've finally given in. I'd much rather stay here, but the plans have already been made.*

*We'll be leaving in early May with an outfit that has experience. That doesn't leave enough time to visit you since we still have much work to do to prepare for the journey. I'm not sure if we'll ever see you again and I'm deeply distressed by that. We will keep in touch by mail. You may send mail ahead of us to any of the locations listed on the back of this letter, or send them to the land office in Oregon City.*

*Better yet, pack up your belongings and join us. That would be an answer to many prayers.*

*With all my love,*
*Your sister, Elizabeth*


Tears coursed down Megan's cheeks as her hands dropped to her lap. "No, Elizabeth. No! Please, don't go." Hugging the letter to her chest, she walked to the window. Charles and Elizabeth were the last of her immediate family. Even though they had lived far away from Megan for the last several years, Megan had maintained a strong emotional tie to them. She swallowed hard and brushed her tears away with the back of her hand, gaining her composure just before Emily came breezing through the door.

"Hi, Meg. Mother said dinner will be a little early because of tonight's ball. She bought a new dress and wants a little extra time to put herself together." She let a little giggle escape before she chattered on. "She also informed me that two handsome officers dropped by to ask permission to escort us. How does that sound to you?" she asked with wide, teasing eyes.

"Lee and who else?" Megan asked. Lieutenant Lee Johnson had been showing quite an interest in Megan for several weeks and had been her companion for many rides and picnics to the country, various teas hosted by officers' wives, and the few balls they had recently attended.

"Lieutenant Jonas Parker," Emily announced as she danced over to the window next to Megan. Emily's blonde hair was pulled up and back with golden ringlets cascading down to her neck. She was more than beautiful, Megan thought as she watched her. Her skin was as smooth as porcelain and her blue eyes were wide and expressive, surrounded by long curled lashes. Everywhere she went, men stopped to stare. It was almost uncomfortable to be with her. And Emily shamelessly delighted in every minute of it. She knew she was beautiful and flaunted it, but in such a childlike, teasing way, it was hard to take offense.

Megan found her quite amusing, although a little
embarrassing at times.

"Who's the letter from?"

"Elizabeth," Megan answered with a shaky sigh. "Here,
read it."

"'My dearest Meggie,'" Emily began in a theatrical
voice. She continued reading aloud as she paced the floor.
"'You'd just turned seventeen when we saw you last and
you still looked like a little girl.' Oh Megan!" she burst into
laughter. "Doesn't this make you furious?"

Megan shrugged and gave her a weak smile. "Not really.
Read on."

Emily launched into the next few lines as if she were
reading a melodrama while Megan rolled her eyes and
waited. Then she abruptly lowered her voice and finished
the letter.

"Oh, Megan, I'm so sorry." Emily's eyes met Megan's
and, for the first time since entering the room, she seemed
to realize that Megan was hurting.

# CHAPTER TWO

The rain continued to come down in a slow, dreary drizzle as Megan placed her hand in Lieutenant Lee Johnson's. He held on longer than necessary as he assisted her into the barouche he had hired for the evening. Megan pulled free and struggled to gather her skirts together on the seat to make room for him.

Emily had again encouraged Megan to choose a gown from Emily's abundant wardrobe. Megan was never sure how Emily managed to afford that many expensive dresses. But at least she was generous with them, and since Megan was only slightly smaller, she helped herself from Emily's wardrobe quite often.

For this evening, Megan had chosen a rose-colored evening dress with short sleeves and a neckline that was fashionably low. Too low, Megan thought, but since most of the young ladies there would be similarly attired, maybe no one would notice. Her skirt was slightly trained and had three over-skirts all draped over her cumbersome crinoline. This made it particularly difficult to find space to sit on the narrow seat.

Lieutenant Johnson grinned down at her after he hoisted himself into the vehicle. He deftly moved her skirts over and swung his tall frame into place beside her. Stretching his arm across the back of the seat, he leaned and murmured in her ear, "You look lovely tonight, Megan."

"Thank you." She smiled at him and turned to look out the window at nothing in particular. "This is a beautiful hack. It was nice of you two to get it for the night."

"Maybe we can sneak away from the ball for an hour and go for a little ride."

"Oh, that would be nice! I'll ask Emily."

"No, I meant just the two of us," he said softly, his fingers gently playing with her sleeve.

"I'll have to ask Aunt Eleanor."

"Megan, You're twenty-two years old and an independent working woman as well. Why in heaven's name do you need permission to go riding with a gentleman?"

She laughed and flashed him a big smile. "It makes me feel safe."

"Safe? You can feel safe with me. I just think we need some time alone so we can get to know each other better. I may not be here much longer, you know."

"Oh, really?"

"Really. Now that the war is over, we're being assigned to different posts. It may be a matter of weeks or even days before I get a new assignment."

"So, you're staying in the Army?"

"I didn't train at West Point for nothing."

They heard Emily and Lt. Parker laughing their way down the walk. With a squeeze on Megan's shoulder, Lee whispered, "Try to arrange some time for our ride tonight, alright? Is that asking too much?" Before Megan could answer, the door swung open and Emily entered with her voluminous skirts.

Major and Mrs. Barkely lived in a large colonial house. When Megan stepped down from the barouche, she was struck by the sight of large black swaths of cloth draped over the tops of the doors and windows in the front of the house. The flag in the front yard was at half-mast, all to commemorate the death of their beloved president.

Once inside, Megan was dazzled by the festive atmosphere. The ballroom was decked out with red, white, and blue streamers and tablecloths. People were talking, laughing, and dancing. The war was over! The Union had won! They couldn't help but continue the celebration.

Halfway through the second dance, Megan saw her aunt and uncle walk in with Julie. She had never seen her older cousin look so lovely. She broke away from Lee and made her way through the crowd to speak to them.

"Julie, you're beautiful! That green gown makes your eyes sparkle!"

"Thanks, Megan," Julie answered with a slight blush.

"I'm glad you found time to come. Are you going over to the hospital tomorrow?"

"Maybe later in the day," Julie replied. "I need to spend some time over at the Union Aid Society Office to get caught up on some bookkeeping first."

"Sounds like fun," Megan commented wryly.

"Would you like to come along?"

"Not really. I have lessons to work on. Maybe I'll join you later, when you go to the hospital."

"Good, I'd love the company."

"Good evening, Miss Parsons." Lieutenant Johnson took Julie's hand in his and gave her a short bow. "You certainly are lovely tonight. May I have this dance?"

They walked together onto the dance floor, a bashful smile planted on Julie's face.

"Oh, Megan, you sure know how to pick a man. He seems like such a gentleman, to say nothing of that handsome face of his." Aunt Eleanor slipped her arm through Megan's and gave her an affectionate squeeze.

"He is handsome, I'll admit that, but I can't take any credit for picking him."

"He'd be a fool if he bypassed my gorgeous niece."

Megan laughed. "Stop, Aunt Eleanor. I'm afraid your perception of me is a little biased. I love your new dress, by the way. I didn't get a chance to see you before we left."

A man dressed in a uniform interrupted their tete-a-tete with an invitation to dance.

"I'm sorry," Megan said. "I don't believe we've been introduced."

Uncle Chester stepped up and offered the officer his hand. "Robert, how are you? May I do the honors?" He turned to his niece. "Megan, this is Lt. Robert Shaw from Illinois. And Lt. Shaw, this is my niece, Miss O'Mally."

"My pleasure, Miss O'Mally. I hope you'll excuse my forwardness and accept my offer." He gently took her hand and gave a low bow.

"Certainly," Megan replied. They walked away and were quickly swallowed by the dancing crowd. Just as Megan put her hand on the man's shoulder, the music stopped and the crowd dispersed.

"I'm sorry, Lieutenant."

"Will you dance the next one with me?" he asked with pleading eyes.

"Of course, I will," she quickly reassured him.

Lt. Shaw stood only a couple of inches taller than Megan. His face was pockmarked, but otherwise very handsome with kind eyes and a mouth that was quick to smile. He had looked so terribly disappointed when the dance ended that Megan didn't have the heart to say no.

The music started so the Lieutenant took her in his arms and skillfully led her around the floor. As they danced, he told her hilarious stories about life at the barracks. In the middle of her laughter, Johnson moved to Lt. Shaw's side.

"Cutting in, Lieutenant," he said with steel in his voice. He towered over Lt. Shaw who turned back to Megan and said politely, "Thank you, Miss O'Mally. I hope you'll honor me with another dance later tonight."

"I will, Lieutenant. That's a promise."

Lieutenant Johnson waltzed her over to the edge of the crowd. "Well, I leave you alone and you're dancing with every Tom, Dick, and Harry in the place."

Megan gave him an icy stare. "I wasn't aware you had any claim on me. If you think bringing me here gives you that claim, then I'll find other means of transportation from now on."

Lee held his hands up in mock surrender. "OK, OK, don't be so touchy! I'm sorry." He leaned in close and lowered his voice. "Have you talked to your aunt about our little ride?"

Megan turned and walked away with Lee on her heels. "No, I haven't had a chance," she said over her shoulder.

"Well, are you going to?"

"I'm not sure I want to."

"Megan, stop!" Lee clamped his hand around her upper arm and turned her around.

"Don't treat me like this," he implored.

"I'll go with you if you promise you'll act like a gentleman and won't treat me like you own me."

"You have my word."

"And," she added with emphasis, "if you'll get me back here in plenty of time to give Lt. Shaw the dance I promised him."

Lee sighed and rolled his eyes. "Alright, anything you say."

A soft breeze blew gently on Megan's face through the open window of the barouche as the horses trotted down

Fifth Street toward Walnut. She saw the Presbyterian Church where she had faithfully attended these past four years. A few months before she had arrived in St. Louis, there had been a very tragic skirmish between Union soldiers and civilians here on this corner. A crowd of southern sympathizers had mocked the soldiers, and someone had fired a shot. When a soldier fell dead, his comrades opened fire, killing two civilians and wounding several others. Megan shuddered as they drove by. *Thank God it's over.*

As they headed toward the waterfront, Lieutenant Johnson slid across the narrow seat, closer to Megan. He put his arm around her and whispered close to her ear, "It's beautiful out tonight, isn't it?"

"Mm-hmm," she murmured softly, her face still turned to the window, enjoying the breeze and the sights.

"Look at me, Megan." He gently cupped her chin and turned her face toward him. "You're beautiful, you know," he said huskily, softly placing a kiss on her forehead. "You're the most beguiling woman I think I've ever known." He moved his lips down and gave her a quick peck on the tip of her nose then moved farther down and caressed her lips with his own. She relented and let herself enjoy the feel of his strong jaw and gentle mouth. He let his hand drop from her face down to her waist and pulled her closer as the intensity of his kiss increased.

Megan pulled away and breathlessly asked, "Could we take a walk along the river?"

With both arms still around her, he asked, "Why? It's so much more comfortable in here."

"I, I just want to get outside. It's such a beautiful night and I love all the sounds and smells down by the docks," she said with a little too much enthusiasm.

Lee sat back and ran his fingers through his hair. He looked at her for a moment then said, "Fine, Miss O'Mally. If that's what you want, that's what we'll do."

The moon was in its third quarter and reflected every wave and ripple. Seagulls flew around the docks scavenging for remnants of food. Despite the late hour, there were still many men at work, loading and unloading barges, mending nets, repairing boats. One big showboat was at dock upstream, and Megan could hear loud music and raucous laughter pouring out.

Lee kept his arm around her shoulder and walked with her, listening to her chatter about everything she saw, heard, or smelled. She chattered about everything that popped into her head just to pass the time. After they'd walked several hundred yards, he turned her around and she continued her prattle, this time filling him in on all the antics of her students.

She knew she was boring him, and frankly, she didn't care. If she could keep talking long enough, maybe he'd restrain himself. She wasn't ready for commitment to a man she'd only known a couple of months. And to be honest, she was a little frightened by how quickly she had responded to his advances and how much she'd enjoyed it.

Just before they reached the barouche, Lee guided Megan to a small cluster of oaks. He turned her toward him, bent down, and gave her a quick, gentle kiss on her lips. "Don't you ever stop talking, Megan?" His voice was deep and husky and as Megan's heart beat wildly, a little voice in her head told her she was a fool for not falling for him. Lee put his hand behind her head and kissed her once then slowly a second time.

"Lee," Megan whispered.

He ran his hand down her back and pulled her closer, kissing her with more intensity.

Megan had to struggle to break free from his unyielding hold. "Lee," she said with more firmness in her tone.

"What, baby," he cooed as he buried his face in her hair.

"Lee, please listen to me." She shook herself free and stepped back, her face flushed. "I'm sorry. I'm not ready for this, yet."

"Well, how much are you ready for?"

"I...I don't know. I'm confused. Can't we just enjoy each other's company without this?"

A look of annoyance narrowed his brown eyes. For a moment, he just stared down at her. Finally, he asked, "Would you allow me to hold your hand as I escort you back to the hack, miss?"

Exasperated with his impatience, she wryly answered him. "Of course, you ninny."

They rode in silence most of the way back, getting there in plenty of time for Megan to dance with Lt. Shaw. As the evening wore on, Lieutenant Johnson's irritation seemed to melt away and he again warmed up to Megan, bringing her punch and little cakes, dancing, and making small talk.

When he delivered her to her uncle's house that night, he guided her up the short walk with his hand on the small of her back. At the top of the steps, he turned, bowed slightly, and whispered, "I'm so sorry if I've been rushing you, Megan." He slowly brought her hand up to his lips, kissing the back of it. "You are too precious to be trifled with. I'm afraid the years of military life have made me forget how a gentleman should conduct himself." Gently he turned her hand over and planted a kiss in her palm.

Then he walked away, leaving Megan on the porch with her fingers clasped over her palm and her heart beating with pleasure.

# CHAPTER THREE

The sunlight broke through the new elm leaves outside Megan's window and danced across her eyelids. She savored its warmth as she lay sprawled across her bed enjoying that dreamy, half-sleep state that comes before waking. *No need to rush today.* She let out a long, contented sigh.

Her door opened slowly and Julie came tiptoeing across the room to her bed.

"Megan," she whispered.

Megan stretched and rolled away from her.

"Megan."

"Hmmm?"

"Are you coming with me?"

"Mmmmm."

"Megan, I'll be leaving for the hospital soon." She waited for a response. "Are you going with me?"

Julie walked impatiently to the window, looked down on the street, and counted to ten. Turning around, she hollered, "Megan! Wake up!"

Megan sat straight up, her eyes wide open with fear and confusion. "What's wrong?" she croaked.

Julie tried to stifle a giggle but lost the battle and collapsed on the foot of the bed in a fit of laughter.

"I'm sorry, Meg, but you looked so funny."

"What's going on?" Megan asked, still trying to make sense of her morning.

"I'm sorry, but you wouldn't answer me. Everything's fine. I just want to know if you're going to the hospital with me."

"Get out of here," Megan replied, throwing a pillow at her. She lay back down and pulled the blankets up to her chin.

Julie stood, smoothed the wrinkles out of her skirt, and headed for the door. "Well! If that's the way you want it," she sniffed. "You told me last night you might go with me. Just thought I'd check."

Before the door closed on her, Megan rolled over and called, "Julie? Julie, come back!"

Julie cracked the door and stuck her head in with a faint smile tugging at the corners of her mouth.

"You said you weren't going to the hospital until you were done with the bookkeeping down at the Union something Society."

"I already went there. I'm done."

Megan plopped her head down on her pillow and stared at the ceiling. "What time is it?"

"Ten."

"Heavens, Julie! How can you already be done at ten o'clock in the morning on a Saturday?"

Julie shrugged. "It's not too difficult if you get to bed at a decent time."

"Please, spare me." She rolled over and threw the blankets aside. "Can you wait long enough for me to get dressed?"

❦

Megan had very mixed feelings about going to Jefferson Barracks Hospital. When she first started visiting the hospital three years ago, she couldn't bring herself to enter the ward where the most serious casualties were. She tried. The first time she walked through the door, the combined smell of chloroform, ether, and rotting flesh caused her to gag and run outside for fresh air. After that, she limited her visits to the men with minor wounds or those who were well on their way to recovery. Even then, it was difficult to deal with their pained expressions, the incredible homesickness they suffered, and the broken spirits she saw so often.

The knowledge that she was doing something to help in the middle of a messy war overcame her negative reactions. The expressions of gratitude on the men's faces gave her all the affirmation she needed.

She hadn't come to the hospital since the war's end, so when she and Julie walked through the front door, they immediately sensed a difference. The men were joking and laughing. Some were sitting up and playing cards. Two men in a corner were playing checkers. In the midst of raised heads, smiles and greetings, the two young women made their way to Ward C.

"Howdy, Miss O'Mally, Miss Parsons! I wondered if I'd see you ladies again," one man in a bed to their right said. "Remember me?"

"How could we forget?" Megan answered with warmth. "You're Josh Pickens. How are you? Can I do anything for you today?"

"Sure can! Well, not 'xactly for me, but fer a buddy o' mine."

Megan's eyes followed the direction his finger pointed.

"Down there, four beds down." He lowered his voice. "He's new in here, recovering from a bullet in his back.

The doc dug it out, but he don't seem to have much movement in his arms and legs yet and he's pretty down."

Josh's voice had dropped to a whisper and Megan had to lean in close to understand him.

"He don't talk much, but I bet if you offered to write a letter home fer him, he'd shur appreciate it."

"I'd be happy to. What's his name?"

"Jonathan Walker. He's a long way from home an' missin' his folks pretty bad."

Megan walked over and introduced herself. The soldier looked younger than her by several years. He glanced at her when she spoke then turned away. Megan was saddened by his hopeless expression. She'd seen it before; too many times to count. She sat and gently took both his hands in hers.

"Jonathan, can you feel my hands?"

"Yes, ma'am," he answered in a slow monotone.

"Can you squeeze my hands?"

"No, ma'am."

"What have the doctors told you?"

"Not much. They're pretty busy."

"Well, Jonathan, I'm not a doctor. I'm not even a nurse, but I'm pretty sure if you have some feeling in your hands, you have a good chance of recovering the use of your hands and your arms. The same goes for your legs. Do you have any feeling in your feet?"

"Thank you, ma'am. But, I've been told by others that prob'ly know more than you, that there's not much hope."

Megan was struck by his despondency. "Jonathan, could you please try to squeeze my hand?"

"No, it'll hurt." His voice held no emotion.

"How do you know if you won't try?" she asked tenderly.

"I've already tried and it hurts."

"You might have to make yourself hurt if you want to get better."

He replied by turning his head away from her. She placed his hands on his chest, wiped her tears away, and reached into her purse for some paper and a pen and inkwell.

"Would you like me to write a letter for you?"

He quickly turned his head toward her. "Yes, ma'am, if you don't mind. I'd like that a lot."

"You just talk and I'll write as fast as I can."

He pressed his lips together and started slowly. "Dear Pa and Ma, this here's Jon. I'm sorry I didn't write for so long, but I can't write. I can't move my hands or arms and I can't walk. I got a bullet in my back. I'm in the hospital in St. Louis. They tell me the war's over so I guess they'll be sendin' me home sometime soon. Don't expect much when you see me."

He stopped. Megan looked up to see him biting his lower lip and fighting the tears that were beginning to squeeze through tightly closed eyelids. She knew he'd wipe his sleeve across his face if he could. She was tempted to pull out her handkerchief and help him, but she suspected it would only serve to remind him again of his helplessness.

Jonathan cleared his throat and waited, cleared it again, and continued huskily, "I'm not the same. I'm not sure what the future holds for me. I'll be no use to you or anyone else. Please tell Clara..." He was silent again then struggled to get the rest of his words out. "Tell Clara, the engagement's off, and...and I'd rather she not see me."

Megan kept her head down as she, too, fought to control her tears.

"That's all. Sign it, 'your son, Jonathan.'"

In the buggy on the way home, Megan told Julie about Jonathan's letter. "You know, the strange thing is that I've written a lot of heartrending letters for soldiers and they always bother me, but this was different. I guess I expected everything to be so positive now that the war is over."

"That's pretty naïve," Julie responded.

"I know. I just want to be done with this whole ugly mess."

"That would be nice, but I have a feeling the war will continue for a very long time."

Megan looked at her older cousin. "What do you mean, Julie?"

"People in leadership have decided to stop the war, but that doesn't mean all is forgiven. There's bound to be deep animosity for years."

Megan felt too depressed the rest of the afternoon to get much done on her lessons. When Emily dropped by and asked her to go out for the evening, she jumped at the chance.

"Where are we going?"

"Well, I have a little surprise for you," Emily began a little slowly and, Megan noticed, a little slyly.

"A surprise? I don't know if I like your kind of surprises." Megan grinned at her cousin, so unlike her sister, Julie. Julie was interesting and dependable and witty, but predictable, oh-so predictable. Emily, on the other hand, was anything but predictable. She was afraid of nothing; not people nor new situations nor social convention. She did what struck her fancy at the moment. Countless times, Megan had been embarrassed by Emily's antics. Like the time they had gone on a picnic with two other young ladies and four officers. Emily had swung out over the creek on a rope and let herself drop in, fully clothed. The men loved it, the women were shocked, and Megan hid her face in her hands and laughed hysterically in spite of herself. And there was the time Emily showed up at a party at Major Day's home escorted by three young officers. And the countless times she would go out with no escort or chaperone to unknown, mysterious destinations.

Megan often wondered why Emily's parents didn't stand in her way. Uncle Chester was too busy to notice and Megan's very proper Aunt Eleanor worried about her daughter, but had always been overly indulgent with her youngest. She told Megan one day that time and maturity would tone down her daughter's flamboyant behavior.

"I want to take you to a party at a house north of the city," Emily said.

"Are we invited?" Megan asked suspiciously.

"Oh, I've been there several times and Miss Potter gave me permission to ask you to come."

"What's the party for and who's going?"

"Since when does a party have to have a reason behind it? It's just a party...for fun, and there will be other women and soldiers...officers mostly, Miss Snoot." Emily tossed her head and turned up her nose. "And you most certainly don't have to come."

"What if I most certainly want to," Megan answered, mocking her cousin by tossing her head as well.

Emily turned and grabbed Megan's hands. "Well then, let's most certainly get ready. And do I ever have the most gorgeous dress for you tonight!"

Despite Megan's protests that she could wear one of her own gowns, Emily managed to have her way. A half hour later, Megan stood in front of a mirror in shock. She quickly put her hand up to cover the exposed flesh.

"It looks bad to you because you're on top looking down. From here it looks entirely respectable."

"I'm beginning to seriously doubt your idea of what's respectable," Megan said, trying in vain to tug the material up over her bosom.

"Honestly, Megan, people will hardly notice. Besides, all the women are wearing dresses this way." Emily laughed at the expression on Megan's face. "Here, you ninny, wear this. It'll hide your precious bosom." She handed Megan a beautiful jeweled wrap that matched her magenta satin evening gown.

Megan adjusted the wrap and fastened the front. Begrudgingly, she checked herself in the mirror and pushed a few curls into place. Emily had insisted on doing Megan's hair in a different style. She'd pulled it up high on her head in a loose bun and let a cascade of little ringlets spill down around her cheeks and neck.

Megan put up a fight over the expensive necklace and earrings Emily selected for her, but she relented because they were both getting slightly giddy over the whole affair. She took one last look at her reflection, shook her head in resignation, and grabbed her tiny matching purse. *Where does she get all this stuff?* she wondered for the hundredth time.

"Maybe a crazy evening like this is just what I need to unwind, but I still think you're out of your mind. Aunt Eleanor would simply die if she saw me."

"Oh pooh! She'll get used to it," Emily laughed as she adjusted one of Megan's dangling ruby earrings.

"Get used to it? I'm not even planning on getting used to it because this is the last time I'll go anywhere looking like this!"

"You'll love it when you see how the men pay attention to you."

"I get all the attention from men I want, thank you!"

"Well calm down! You probably won't even see anyone you know."

"Let's hope not!"

Emily drove her father's buggy several miles out of the city. There were only a few scattered homes, many of them large Victorian houses. They slowed down as they approached a fancy wrought iron gate. A thin, old black man dressed in a faded coachman's jacket opened the gate.

He grinned a toothless smile up at them as they passed through. "Welcome, ladies. Welcome to Miz Potta's."

Emily thanked him politely and flicked the reins across the horses' backs. They descended down a long drive through thick woods.

"Emily, I'm feeling a little strange; dressing like this, coming way out here unescorted, and being let through the gate into these woods by someone like him."

"What's wrong with Jock?"

"Nothing's wrong with him. He's just not what I'd expect. Are you sure I'm invited? And don't you ever get scared coming here unchaperoned?"

"Stop worrying. Miss Potter is a wonderful lady and she has a gorgeous house and everyone dresses like this when they go to her parties."

"Wonderful." Megan sat back and folded her arms.

"Just relax and enjoy yourself."

"I'll do my best," Megan said ruefully.

The lane they drove down was unkempt and longer than Megan had expected. Finally, they broke through the bushes into a beautiful garden filled with dogwoods and magnolias. Neatly trimmed bushes lined a small stream. Through the dusk, Megan could see tulip beds that extended to the front of a huge white house with a roof lined with gables. A big porch with massive pillars wrapped around three sides. She saw tree-lined paths and several small white cottages nestled in among the trees and rosebushes behind the house.

"What a place!" she exclaimed as she was helped out of the buggy by a well-dressed stable boy. "Emily, why haven't you brought me here before? This is beautiful!"

A strange look passed over Emily's pretty face as she slipped a coin into the stable boy's hand. She looked up and gave Megan an encouraging smile. "It looks perfectly reputable, doesn't it?"

"Reputable? It's more than reputable, it's...it's

enchanting!"

Emily linked her arm through Megan's and walked up the wide, immaculate steps to the double front doors. She made several short raps with the knocker and was greeted by a tall, impeccably dressed butler.

"Welcome, ladies. May I take your wraps?"

Megan unclasped hers and handed it over, too entranced by the entrance hall and curving staircase to remember why she'd worn it. They walked through the hall toward doors on the right that opened to a lavishly decorated ballroom. As they passed the food and drink table, a strong smell of alcohol reached Megan's nostrils. She stopped dead in her tracks. Suddenly, the magic of her surroundings vanished.

"What's the matter, Meg?" Emily asked, looking back at her. She followed Megan's eyes to the punch bowl. "Oh, that? She only puts it here for the few soldiers who want it. Down there at that end of the table is punch with no liquor in it."

Megan gave Emily a withering glance before she walked to the other punch bowl. She helped herself to a small glass, carried it to an upholstered chair, and seated herself. Peering over the rim of her glass, she studied the room and its occupants very carefully. A few were dancing to the music provided by four very enthusiastic men who were playing a variety of instruments and happily taking requests from the floor. Several attractive young girls, dressed more extravagantly than she was, were standing in groups around the room carrying on light conversation with various enlisted men and young officers. She also noticed their dresses were far more revealing than hers. Almost choking on her punch, she glanced down and remembered taking her wrap off. *What was I thinking? Megan, you idiot!* She looked around at the women in the room and realized, somewhat regretfully, Emily had been right; everyone was dressed like this. Nobody will notice; surely not.

Several couples could be seen walking on the porch just

outside some French doors, and others were heading down the steps to the garden. A large, buxom woman with thick black hair piled on her head was talking to Emily and occasionally glancing Megan's direction. She started across the room toward Megan. Despite her size, she was truly elegant. Her face radiated warmth and charm. She held her hands out to Megan in greeting.

"Hello, you must be Megan. I'm so glad you've come. Your cousin speaks very highly of you. She said you were pretty, but I don't think the word 'pretty' does you justice. You're a real beauty!" Her voice had a rich, nurturing quality. Megan at once felt at ease with her.

"You make yourself at home, honey. If you enjoy your stay, come and see me and I'll plan on having you back often."

"Thank you, Miss Potter. You're very kind."

"Emily, why don't you show your cousin around, help her get to know the place." Miss Potter breezed away to talk to a woman who was signaling her from the stairway.

Megan thought Emily looked rather uncomfortable. "Don't worry, Em. I like her. Actually, I think she's quite charming. Take me outside and show me her garden before it gets too dark."

"Sure, but you won't be offended, will you, if I slip away to spend some time with a certain gentleman?"

"Who is it this time and where are you 'slipping' to?"

"I don't think you know him. He's a very wealthy widower. I met him here a few weeks ago and we just like to walk through Miss Potter's garden and talk. It's so pretty out there."

"In the dark?"

"She has lanterns along the walks and a lot of light from the house reaches across the grounds."

"Emily, I'm just giving you trouble. Since when did you start defending yourself? I'm not your chaperone; although heaven knows you need one!"

"Oh dear! Look who's here!" Emily grabbed Megan's arm and kept her from stepping through the French doors to the porch. "It's Lieutenant Johnson!" She pulled Megan back into the room. "If you'd rather he not see you here, I'll drive you home."

"Lee? Why should I mind if he sees me? We've made no commitment to each other." She walked through the door then looked down at her exposed flesh and froze.

"Megan, you really shouldn't…" Emily stopped mid-sentence as she watched her cousin step outside in full view of the lieutenant.

He and a fellow officer were standing ten feet from the doorway, drinking punch and talking with a young woman in a long green gown trimmed with white lace and hanging low on her shoulders.

He glanced up quickly as she stepped out then snapped his head around and gave her his full attention, an incredulous look in his eyes. Handing his punch to his companion, he placed both hands on his hips, his eyes narrowing to a severe glare.

Megan glared back, daring him to cast judgment. She knew it was because of the dress. Despite her shame, she stubbornly refused to let him dictate how she was to dress, especially since the woman he had been talking to was far less modest than she! She jutted her chin out and met his gaze, not letting a glimmer of shame show.

After an agonizing minute, his features abruptly softened to a sly grin. He chuckled softly and ambled toward her.

"I never thought I'd see the day you'd show up here."

"And why not? I have as much right to enjoy a place like this as anyone." She turned and walked toward the steps.

Lee shook his head from side to side and muttered, "I can't believe it."

"What's your trouble, Lieutenant?" his partner, Lt.

Gibson, asked.

"Oh nothing. I've just had my eyes blasted wide open, that's all. You never can tell about a woman, can you?" he said to his friend as he started down the steps after Megan.

He caught up with her on the lawn and grabbed her arm to stop her. "Whoa, sweetheart. Since you're here and I'm here, let's take advantage of the situation. I'm game if you are."

"You certainly didn't seem very happy to see me."

"Just surprised. I didn't expect you; that's all."

"I hope I'm not interrupting anything," she said, ice in her tone.

"If you were, I'm sure it will be well worth it."

"That's definitely a little friendlier." She placed her hand on his arm and asked, "Would you mind escorting me on a little stroll through these lovely gardens?"

"I'd love to. You lead."

Megan led him down a path toward the creek. The darker it got, the less self-conscious she felt about her immodest appearance. When they were out of the reach of any of the lights, Lee turned her around and backed her up to a tree.

"You are so beautiful, Megan." His hands reached up to caress her neck then slid down to her shoulders. Pulling her forward, he kissed her forehead, then her lips.

Against her better judgment, Megan forced herself to relax in his embrace. She let herself enjoy the feeling of his firm, warm mouth on hers.

"Where do we go from here?" he whispered.

"Follow me," she said impishly. Ever since she was a child, she had delighted in following paths as if they were mazes that would lead her to a secret place deep in the woods. Even though it was late, she could clearly see that the path ahead forked off in three directions. She grabbed Lee's hand and dragged him as if he were a childhood playmate.

"Which way should we go?"

"You should know, baby," he wryly answered.

"How about to the right?" She gingerly stepped over some roots and pushed a branch aside. "Oh, Lee! It's so beautiful! Look at the sky. See how the clouds are moving across the moon? It's so enchanting!"

She stopped by a fallen log and Lee pulled her down to sit next to him. "You're the one who's enchanting." He moved his hand to her waist and pulled her close for another kiss. "Aren't we going inside?" he asked.

"No, I like it out here," she whispered.

"Oh? It's not as comfortable, but if that's what you want, it's fine with me." He looked into her face and waited.

Megan turned her eyes to the ground then shifted herself away from Lee to look at the moon again.

"Oh, so you're one of those who plays hard to get, huh? You expect the man to lead? I'd be more than happy to oblige, darling."

Confused by his words, Megan quickly got to her feet. Lee stood also, wrapped his arms around her, and pulled her close. His mouth found hers again. One hand slid up her back to her neck. Slowly he slid her dress off one shoulder.

Megan backed away in shock, frantically pulling her sleeve up.

Impatience lit Lee's eyes. "Oh, come on! You can't play this game with me here."

"I don't know what you're talking about!" choked Megan.

He reached out, grabbed her, and pulled her tightly against his hard chest. "I know what you really want." His lips came down possessively on hers. Holding her tightly against him with one hand, with the other he again slipped her dress off her shoulder.

She struggled to pull away but he was too strong. He ran

his hand over the soft skin on her back and arm, bringing it around to the front to caress her throat. Gradually his hand lowered until with a quick jerk, he pulled her bodice down, exposing both breasts to the moonlight.

With enormous effort, Megan put both hands on his chest and shoved. Lee stumbled back and tripped over the log, cursing Megan as he went down. Struggling to pull her dress up, she staggered up the path, too shocked to speak.

Lee's angry expletives floated in the darkness behind her.

Megan pressed her hands against her hot cheeks, trying to suppress her panic before she stepped through the doors. The longer she stood, the more her anger grew, moving in to join her shame and bewilderment. *Emily, where are you?* She turned away from the door and walked along the porch to a large window, desperately hoping she could spot Emily in the growing crowd without drawing attention to herself. With mounting frustration, her eyes scanned the room. The fear of Lee catching up to her propelled her through a door into the ballroom. No sign of Emily! Quickly she crossed the room and headed for the stairway where Miss Potter was standing.

"Miss Potter, please, I need to find Emily!"

Miss Potter pointed to the top of the stairs, where Emily was standing holding onto the arm of a stocky older man.

"Megan?" Emily called down to her.

"Emily!" Megan blurted with frantic relief. She put her hand to her throat and swallowed hard. People were beginning to stare. In a controlled tone, she asked very politely, "Would you come here, please? I need to talk to you."

Emily lifted the front of her skirts and swept briskly down the staircase. "What's the matter, Megan?"

Megan grabbed her arm and marched her toward the front door. "Get me out of this place!"

"What happened?"

"Let's just go! I'll tell you on the way home." Her eyes stung with tears.

"I'll be back." Emily turned and ran daintily up the stairs to the scowling man, a high-ranking officer, Megan noticed. She whispered something in his ear that brought a devilish smile to his face and was back by Megan's side to quickly escort her out the door.

"Wait a minute, I forgot our wraps," Emily said.

"Forget them, Emily, please. Let's just get out of here." Megan pulled her toward the stairs.

Emily looked at her cousin with raised eyebrows. "This is more serious than I realized."

Once they drove past the front gate, Megan opened up and tearfully related the events of the evening. Her shame was so great, she felt as if she had been wounded some place deep inside her soul. She couldn't explain it; she could only beg Emily to tell no one.

Emily drove several minutes in silence. "Megan, I'm so sorry. If I'd known Lee was going to be there tonight, I'd never had taken you."

"What difference does it make where I see him? We've been together many times. If I had been smart, I would have seen through him from the beginning. What a lecher!"

In a very unladylike manner, she rubbed both of her white gloves over her tear-streaked face. She looked down and noticed a tear in the lace. She yanked her gloves off and stuffed them down the front of her bodice to cover the cleavage she had so shamefully exposed to countless people. "I hate this dress," she sobbed.

"The dress? Megan, settle down. It's not the end of the world." Emily sighed and shook her head. "I'm sorry I took you there. It's…it's probably better if you don't go back."

"You couldn't pay me enough to go back there," Megan said with vengeance, missing the flash of defiance in Emily's eyes.

# CHAPTER FOUR

**M**egan felt a stronger than usual urge to be in church the next morning. The Parson's had attended the Presbyterian Church at Fifth and Walnut for years. On this Sunday, the church was overflowing with civilians and soldiers, both still rejoicing in the last month's turn of events. Megan sat between Julie and the aisle.

"The Lord has been good to us," the Rev. Brown was saying. "Turn with me to Psalm 135 and follow along."

*1 Praise ye the Lord.*
*Praise ye the name of the Lord;*
*Praise Him, O ye servants of the Lord.*
*2 Ye that stand in the house of the Lord,*
*In the courts of the house of our God,*
*3 Praise the Lord; for the Lord is good:*
*Sing praises unto his name; for it is pleasant.*

Megan's eyes wandered across the heads of the people in front of her then across the aisle where she glimpsed a row of bluecoats two rows back. She turned her head to look at them and was appalled to see Lieutenant Lee Johnson sitting among them, staring at her with a smirk. Horror settled into the pit of her stomach when she realized it wasn't just the Lieutenant leering at her, but all the soldiers with him. Quickly she snapped her head around to face the front, her face hot with humiliation. Desperately she tried to block out the images of last night so she could focus on Reverend Brown's words.

"The Word of God says in Psalms 119, 'Blessed are the undefiled in the way, who walk in the law of the Lord. Blessed are they that keep His testimonies, and that seek Him with the whole heart.'"

*Undefiled?* Megan's heart pounded. Her head began to throb.

"'They also do no iniquity: they walk in his ways.'"

Sweat began to trickle down her forehead. She dabbed at it and tried to hold her head up and keep her attention on the pastor, hoping to hear something she could grab onto before she drowned in her shame.

"'Thou hast commanded us to keep thy precepts diligently.'"

*Diligently? I haven't even come close.*

Reverend Brown went on but Megan could no longer concentrate. She was filled with self-loathing. How could she have sunk so low? To ever consider going into public dressed as she had? To consort with the likes of Lee Johnson and allow him such liberties? She twisted her hankie between her fingers and almost suffocated with condemnation.

After the service, Megan wove her way through the crowd to the side door and slipped through. She made a beeline for Uncle Chester's buggy, but when she got to the sidewalk, the friendly greetings and chatter of the other parishioners hindered her progress. Finally, she broke free only to be greeted by a line of soldiers waiting near her uncle's buggy, the very men she was so frantically trying to avoid. Approaching them with as much dignity as she could muster, she kept her eyes averted and tried to work her way past them.

"Hello, Miss O'Mally," one of them said as he removed his hat. Another moved in front of Megan and offered his hand. She stopped and waited in perturbed silence.

"I'd be most honored if I could join you at Miss Potter's some night soon," he drawled.

Megan glared up at him, and then caught sight of Lee standing to one side laughing at her.

"Excuse me, please." Her voice was cold and hard as she pivoted and walked back toward the church and the security of Uncle Chester.

Another soldier doggedly stepped in her path. "Pardon their ungentlemanly behavior, Miss," he said in a distinct New York clip. "Allow me to introduce myself."

Megan tried to move past him, but he stepped backward and planted himself in front of her. "I'm Lt. Collins and I'd like very much to take you for a little drive in the country."

"I'm afraid not, Lt. Collins. Now if you would please excuse me, I..."

"Please, Miss. I'll treat you good."

"I'm sorry, Lieutenant. My answer is no."

He lowered his voice almost to a whisper and leaned in close to her. "What's the most you've been paid?"

"Paid?" Megan looked at him in astonishment. "That's none of your business!"

She brushed him aside and tried to move down the walk. The lieutenant took hold of her arm and whispered, "I'll make it worth your time, I promise. I'll see you out there."

Megan shook her arm free and frantically looked for Uncle Chester. *What's going on? I've got to get away!* As she picked up speed, the rude comments and snickers faded.

Uncle Chester and Aunt Eleanor were just then greeting

the reverend. With skirts swishing against her legs, Megan briskly walked over to join them. She tried to slow her breathing so she could speak in a normal tone. The reverend took her hand and shook it warmly in his. A smile crinkled the corners of his friendly eyes. She could barely make eye contact.

"And how have you been this week, Miss O'Mally?"

"Fine, just fine, thank you, Reverend," she lied and looked down to hide her shame.

Uncle Chester put his arm around her shoulder and added, "She certainly has been busy. I hardly see her anymore."

Again, Megan looked down to hide her face.

They said their good-byes and walked toward the buggy together. Megan could see the soldiers dispersing and mingling with the crowd.

"Uncle Chester, have you ever heard of a Miss Potter who lives north of the city?"

"No, can't say that I have. Why?" He looked fondly down at his niece.

"Oh, no reason. I was just wondering."

The day was hot, so when they arrived home, Megan changed from her Sunday best to something cooler. She dispensed with her corset and crinoline and instead wore a simple cotton chemise and drawers under a pink muslin summer dress.

After dinner, Megan confronted Emily in her bedroom. When she opened the door, she stood there for a moment and simply stared at Emily.

"Come in, Megan," Emily said in a tired voice, her usual gaiety gone. She shifted awkwardly in her chair and cleared her throat as Megan closed the door.

"Emily, you've got to tell me what's going on," Megan began. "Did you see those men at church? Did you hear them? What they were saying to me? What's happening?"

"What did they say?" Emily asked warily.

"They were all smirking like they knew what happened last night. And Lee, the snake, just stood there and smiled! He's obviously told them what he did to me, though it's hard to believe even he would stoop so low. But there's more to it, Emily, and I want a straight answer. They kept asking if I'd meet them at Miss Potter's. One man even asked me how much I was paid. Something's very strange and I think you know more about this than you're telling me."

Emily stared at her hands for a long time then said very quietly, "I do know what's happening, but I would rather not talk about it."

"Since it obviously involves me, I'm not leaving until you do talk about it. And I want the truth; all of it!"

Emily sat for a long time then stood and walked to the window, holding her head tightly between her hands. "Oh, Megan, I've really done it this time. I hope you can forgive me." She turned and faced her.

For the first time in years, Megan saw tears of remorse on Emily's face. With a voice filled with dread, she asked, "Emily, what have you done?"

"Megan, please, please don't breathe a word of this to anyone!"

"Tell me, Emily," Megan ordered severely.

"I swear by God's name, I never intended to do you any harm, Megan. I thought...I thought you might be ready for it." Emily's voice dropped. "I thought you'd like all that money."

"Ready for what?" Megan struggled to keep her voice calm as her eyes bore into Emily's.

Emily released a sigh of resignation. "Megan, Miss Potter's is a brothel; a high-class brothel."

Megan felt as if the floor was giving way beneath her. Everything but Emily's face faded into a haze. She couldn't speak, not even a word, as Emily's last words assailed her brain. Finally, she took a deep breath and managed to choke, "Say that again please."

Emily stared at the floor. "Miss Potter's is a brothel."

"And how many times have you been there?" She could barely get the words out.

"Many times. For about six months now."

"And you thought I might be 'ready' for it! How could you think such a horrible thing about me? Lee...those men...they thought I..."

Emily visibly cringed under the severity in Megan's voice. "I'm sorry, so sorry. I was wrong, Megan."

Megan still stood rooted to the floor. She stared incredulously at her younger cousin. "How could you, Emily? What kind of woman would do such a thing?"

"I guess there's no good reason for it. I enjoy the attention of men and I love the money." She looked up and gave Megan a tentative grin.

"You're a fool, Emily! A worse fool than I ever thought you capable of!"

Emily shrugged. "It's the men that are the fools. We're basically doing the same thing, but I'm the one getting the money. You'd be amazed at the women who are doing the same thing, just for all the extra money. Megan, if you knew how much I can make with only one man, you might reconsider."

"Dear, Lord!" Megan cried. Her hands flew to her ears and she paced across the room and back in fury. Whirling around, she pointed her finger at Emily. "You, Emily Parsons, are a whore! A common, no good, filthy whore!"

"Keep your voice down! This is different! This is not a whorehouse where the women live. I can go as often as I want or not go at all if I choose."

"You need to be exposed! For your own good, you fool!" She sat down hard on the bed and buried her face in her hands in time to catch her tears.

Through her fingers, she watched Emily walk to the window and stare down at the street below.

"Emily," Megan began to plead. "How could you stoop so low when you've been raised the way you have? What about your parents? What about church? What about God? Doesn't even He matter to you?"

"I don't know." Emily shrugged impassively. "I guess not much because I really don't want to stop."

"Oh, Emily." Megan felt drained. She wanted to find a hole, crawl in, and never come out. "Emily, I'd tell your parents except that it would kill them both to know this. I hope and pray that with God's help, you can turn your back on this filth before they find out what you're doing."

Megan looked at Emily, hoping she would see some sign of remorse. The remorse she'd seen earlier was for dragging Megan into the mess. But Emily showed not even a glimmer of regret for the role she'd played for the past six months. Megan finally said, "Good-bye, Emily," and walked wearily out of the room.

Megan feigned a headache to avoid facing the family at the supper table. The next morning, she got up early and slipped out the door for school before anyone else was downstairs. Being in the same room with Emily and her parents was something she wasn't sure she could deal with yet. She was also finding it very difficult to hide her own shame. Scenes of the past two days were tumbling chaotically through her head as she made her way down their street to the corner and turned toward the school. She felt so dirty, so tainted, asking herself over and over how she could have been so foolish. *What kind of woman are you that you could have been drawn into something like this? What kind of woman are you if your own cousin thought you were ready to be a whore?*

She stopped in her tracks at that question and almost dropped to her knees in anguish. *How can you blame Emily for thinking such a horrible thing when you've been so willing to be seen in public in scandalous attire?* Trying to shake the accusations, Megan forced herself to walk briskly and breathe deeply of the cool, spring air.

Mr. Barrows, the school headmaster, was at his desk, head in hands, as Megan walked down the short hall past his office. The other three teachers hadn't arrived yet. Megan deposited her books on her desk, turned, and started writing the day's lesson on the board. She had an all-girl class, ranging from three ten-year-olds up to a sixteen-year-old. The younger girls went to Miss Yarber's room and the boys were divided between the two male teachers.

Turning back to her desk, Megan's eye caught movement in the doorway.

"Mr. Barrows, I'm sorry. I didn't see you."

He cleared his throat awkwardly and said, "Would you please come to my office? I need to talk to you." He turned and strode away before she could answer.

Stopping just outside his door, Megan asked, "What is it, Mr. Barrows?"

"Shut the door and have a seat please." His forehead creased as he turned his eyes up toward her from his desktop.

Megan did as she was told then waited, watching him fold and unfold his large, beefy hands.

"This is not a pleasant job for me," he finally said with an uncomfortable sigh. He brought his eyes up to meet hers. "I guess the best thing to do is get it out straight and be done with it. Miss O'Mally, it has come to the board's attention that you've been frequenting a place of ill repute."

Megan drew her breath in sharply and covered her mouth with her hand.

"They met last night and voted unanimously to fire you. Unfortunately, it's my unpleasant duty to inform you." He stood.

Her heart pounding in her ears, she reached her hand

toward him in a desperate plea. "Mr. Barrows, I have nothing to do with that place. I had no idea what sort of place it was when I went. Please believe me!"

"I'm sorry. I find that hard to accept. And if I do, you can be sure the board will. Furthermore, no lady in a position such as yours should ever go near a place like that, accidentally or otherwise, and should never even associate with the people who do. In addition to this issue, there have been several complaints about the lascivious lifestyle you lead. As a schoolteacher to young ladies, you should be an example of a pure and moderate lifestyle. Instead, the board and I have been hearing reports of you gallivanting around from party to party in rather immodest apparel, seen in the company of a variety of men, riding around the city unchaperoned, being embraced and kissed in broad daylight on the walk in front of the home of one of your pupils? I could go on and on. And these, Miss O'Mally, are only the things that have been observed. I refuse to imagine what goes on elsewhere. This last episode was the final straw. These good people do not want a wanton woman like you teaching their impressionable young daughters. I'm sorry to have to be harsh with you, but you must understand the decision is final, based on numerous complaints. I'm powerless to change it."

Megan's mouth hung open in utter disbelief. Her mind groped for something she could say to redeem herself.

Mr. Barrows reached across his desk and grabbed an envelope. "Here's your pay for the last two weeks. Please pack your belongings and be gone before the girls arrive."

She stood and accepted the envelope when he held it out. He opened the door and held it for her as she dumbly walked through. She looked up at him and asked in a shaky voice, "Mr. Barrows, might I please stay long enough to say good-bye to my girls?"

"I'm sorry. The board requested you not be allowed to see them. They felt you've done enough damage." He cleared his throat. "It would do you much good, Miss O'Mally, to spend time in God's Holy Word. The board asked me to tell you to read Proverbs, chapter 7. They thought it would help you understand their decision."

In a stupor, Megan walked down the hall to her room and managed to put her few possessions together. She walked stiffly through the door and down the steps for the last time. The dam burst and tears began to course down her cheeks. Trying to sort out her thoughts and regain control of her emotions, she turned left toward the river instead of right toward home.

*How could this happen? What have I done? What sort of woman have I let myself become? My own cousin thought I was 'ready' for a brothel! Dear God, I've been so blind. How could I let this happen? A* wanton *woman? They don't even want me near their daughters!*

When she reached Walnut Street, she turned and walked until she came to the church. The stone steps led up to a row of massive pillars where Megan slumped in total confusion and discouragement. Laying her books down beside the pillar, she timidly tried the door. It opened. Inside, streams of sunlight poured through the windows onto the pews, illuminating floating dust in its path. A peaceful hush greeted her when she shut the door and closed out the noises of the street. She walked down the aisle, letting her hand trail along the arm of each pew as she passed.

*So holy, even more holy than on Sunday. What a beautiful place.* She dug out her hankie, wiped her eyes and took a deep breath. In a timid voice, she began to pray, "Lord? I'm not sure what I need to say to you, but…"

She paused long enough to allow the condemning thoughts to break in again. Shaking her head in frustration, she grabbed a Bible from the closest pew, sat down, and turned to Chapter 7 in Proverbs, the scripture the board had advised her to read. She scanned several verses before her eyes fell on verse 10. *And, behold, there met him a woman with the attire of an harlot, and subtle of heart. She is loud and stubborn; her feet abide not in her house: now is she without, now in the streets, and lieth in wait at every corner.* She read on, allowing every word to wound her deeply. *Hearken unto me now therefore, O ye children, and attend to the words of my mouth. Let not thine heart decline to her ways, go not astray in her paths. For she hath cast down many wounded: yea, many strong men have been slain by her. Her house is the way to hell, going down to the chambers of death.*

Megan shut the book and quickly put it where she'd found it, pulling her fingers away as if burned. Her face dropped into her hands in agony. *How can one such as I come into a place like this and dare to call him Lord?* Turning her back, she briskly walked to the door. Shutting it reverently but sadly behind her, she left.

Less than a block away from the church, she had resolved what must be done and made her way to the telegraph office.

## CHAPTER FIVE

"Megan, please, listen to reason. You can't just leave like this in the middle of the school year, and heaven knows the west is no place for a beautiful, young, single woman." Aunt Eleanor sat on the edge of Megan's bed wringing her hands and fretting like a mother hen.

Megan was sorting through the last of her belongings, trying to decide what else she might need and could squeeze into her two bags. She kept her eyes on her task in an attempt to avoid making eye contact.

"Megan, are you even listening to what I'm saying?"

"Auntie, I'll be with Charles and Elizabeth. I'll be fine. It's not as if I'm going to be alone. And besides that, I made up my mind a long time ago that as soon as the war ended, I'd go and stay with them for a while. It's been years since I've seen them. I can't let them take off for Oregon without me, can I?"

"That's no reason to pull up your roots and travel halfway across the country to the wilderness. You're a city girl, Megan. You thrive in this life."

Finally, Megan stood and faced her aunt. "You forget, Auntie, my roots are really in the country and definitely with my sister and Charles. You have been so good to let me stay here and I'll never forget your wonderful hospitality; but the war's over and it's time for me to move on." She walked over and wrapped her arms around her aunt.

"What about Lt. Johnson, Megan? You can't leave him. I thought the two of you were beginning to get serious."

Megan bit her lip and turned away. "Aunt Eleanor, Lt. Johnson is a soldier and always will be. I'd be a fool to want a soldier for a husband, living at forts all my life, being moved from place to place, entertaining officers' wives. Spare me, please."

"That hardly seems fair to the lieutenant, Megan. If I'm not mistaken, you certainly seemed to be encouraging his attention."

Megan's head dropped and she fiddled with the clasp on her bag. "He…he proved himself to be unworthy of my attention. He has shown himself to be anything but a gentleman and I never want to see him again."

Eleanor gasped. "Goodness, Megan, what has he done? Is it necessary for Chester to protect your honor?"

"No!" Megan said a little too forcefully. "It's best if the matter is dropped. Please, Aunt Eleanor, don't mention this to anyone."

"What about school, Megan? Doesn't this seem a little sudden? One day, you're teaching, the next, you're off to Oregon. Isn't that a little irresponsible? Why don't you take a week off to go see your sister before she leaves then come back and at least teach until the end of the term?"

Filled with dread, Megan sighed and turned to face Eleanor. "I'm so sorry to have to tell you this, Aunt Eleanor. I was hoping you wouldn't have to know."

"Know what, Megan?" her aunt's voice strained with worry.

"I was dismissed from my teaching position."

"Goodness, gracious, Megan! Whatever for?"

"If rumors travel as fast as I think they do, I'm sure you'll be getting the news from some well-meaning busybody. But I want you to know that whatever you hear about me, I'm innocent." She paused. "At least of the more serious charges."

"Megan, whatever are you talking about?"

"Some people have gotten entirely the wrong image of me because they saw me at a certain place."

"What place are you talking about?"

"I'm sorry. I can't say more without dragging..." She stopped and took a long breath. "I can't say any more, Aunt Eleanor, that's all. Just please don't believe any ugly rumors you hear about me, alright?"

"Megan, this is nonsense! Can't you explain yourself to the board?"

"No, I'd rather not discuss this any further. I'm sorry, Auntie, I really am. Besides, now that I've got my hopes up to see Elizabeth and Charles and the girls again, I don't think an army could stop me."

"But, Megan! A wagon train? Think about it. The heat and filth, sleeping on the ground night after night for months! And who knows what sort of people you'd be with?" Eleanor stood and put her arm around Megan's shoulders. "Megan, honey, don't do something you'll regret the rest of your life! Believe me; you won't make a good pioneer wife."

Megan grinned at her aunt. "Thanks for the vote of confidence. And whoever said anything about marriage? I'm done with men for a very long time, thank you! I'm not planning on being a pioneer wife. I'm planning on being a pioneer schoolteacher." For the first time, she felt a glimmer of enthusiasm and planted a kiss on her aunt's cheek. "Thank you again for so graciously taking me into your home. And trust me, Auntie. I'm sure I'm doing the right thing."

"Oh, Megan." Eleanor wrapped both arms around her niece and rocked her back and forth. "We'll miss you, you know."

"I'll miss you, too." Megan fought back the tears.

Eleanor abruptly dropped her arms and clapped her hands together. "Well, I'd better get busy if I'm going to find the time to pack some food for you and get you down to the station in time. It's not a short trip to Sedalia, you know. I do hope you find a seat near some decent folk."

Megan went back to packing. *Decent, huh? If they knew why I was leaving, they'd all sit as far away from me as they could. Thank God I'm getting out of here.*

"I'll go try to explain this to Chester and the girls. Hopefully they'll have enough sense to bite their tongues, unlike your nosy aunt." She winked at Megan as she walked out.

Huddled together in the buggy, the family rode in strained silence as the horses clip-clopped down the street to the station. Emily finally started babbling about the last time she rode on a train, while the rest of the family tried their best to hide the awkwardness of the situation. Eleanor kept reaching out to give Megan a reassuring pat on her arm. Megan loved these people dearly, but the urge to get away as soon as possible was overwhelming.

Chester bought Megan's ticket and led the ladies to an uncrowded corner of the station to wait. "Will Charles and Elizabeth be there to greet you?" he asked.

"I sent the telegraph yesterday, so I'm sure they've received it by now."

"If they're not there, do you know what to do?" Eleanor asked.

"I imagine the best thing would be to hire someone to

drive me out to their place."

"I don't think so," Eleanor said. "You have no way of knowing what sort of person might be offering his services. You'd better get a room in a hotel and send a messenger."

"It can't be that bad out there, can it? The war's over." Megan looked at her aunt then apprehensively up at her uncle.

Chester sat down next to her and put an arm around her shoulders, giving her a quick squeeze. Then turning to face her, he answered, "The war may be officially over, Megan, but not everyone is willing to lay down their arms. Since the surrender, there have been three battles that the newspapers have reported, and those are only the ones big enough to report. Calloway County here in Missouri refuses to surrender. There are a lot of bitter men out there and you need to constantly be on guard."

"Remember the massacre at the train depot in Centralia last fall?" Julia piped in. "Two trains and the depot were burned and almost 100 people killed."

"That settles it!" Eleanor threw her hands in the air. "You're not leaving! Not yet anyway! Chester," she demanded, "don't let her go."

"Settle down, ladies. Megan's not a little girl. She's a woman who has to make her own decisions. Megan," he said, looking her square in the eye, "I never intended to frighten you. I just want you to be careful. If you stay near the train and the depot in plain sight of good people, you should be safe. The train will be making eight stops before it reaches Sedalia; the longest one at Jefferson City. You should be fairly safe there if you need to stretch. Just don't wander too far. The whole trip will take about twelve hours, so you should be getting there about nine tonight."

"Are you sure about this, Chester?" Eleanor asked.

"Don't forget, Eleanor, this little lady traveled all the way from Springfield to Rolla in a wagon then managed to get herself on a train from there to St. Louis and the whole time, a war was in progress around her. I'm sure she'll do fine."

Megan noticed a strikingly handsome man with neat, blond hair, sitting across from them and obviously listening to their conversation. He was impeccably dressed in a beige suit with a black satin waistcoat and matching bow tie. Perched on his knee was a wide-brimmed hat with a flat crown. He noticed Megan looking at him and gave her a warm smile before looking down at his paper. She blushed slightly and looked quickly away. The last thing she wanted at this point was to encourage the attention of a man.

"How much longer before the train gets here, Uncle Chester?"

"It should get here within the next ten minutes. Would you like to move out to the platform?"

"Yes, please. If that's alright?"

Chester grabbed her two satchels and led the way through the growing crowd. Soldiers and people of every description were milling around, some sleeping against the wall, heads on their bags, waiting for trains to bear them on their journey toward home.

The power of a train never ceased to amaze Megan. It started as a dull roar and grew increasingly louder until she could see it barreling down on them from around a close bend. Black smoke poured from the smokestack. A stream of white steam shot straight up as the whistle let out a long, ear-piercing shriek. The train approached so fast she couldn't resist the urge to step back, although they were already a good twenty feet from the edge of the tracks. The platform shook as the brakes screeched the train to a halt then all was still. Passengers poured out of the train and before she knew it, the crowd started to propel her forward.

Emily grabbed her, gave her a quick hug, and stepped back. Megan saw tears in her eyes as they made brief eye contact.

"Megan, send us a telegram when you get there so we'll

know you're safe. I won't rest until you do." Eleanor hugged her protectively.

"I'll miss you, Megan." Julie reached out and grabbed her hand, giving it a squeeze.

Megan turned to find her uncle. They looked at each other for a moment before she threw herself into his arms with a sob. "Thank you so much for everything," she whispered.

"Good-bye, sweetheart," he whispered back. He held her at arm's length. "Take care of yourself. Give your sister and those three little ones a hug for me."

Megan scanned the car quickly and released a sigh of relief when she saw there were no soldiers. Settling herself in the first vacant pair of seats on the depot side, she waved her hand in the window and caught the Parsons' attention.

Chester stood with his arm around Eleanor, Julie dabbed at her tears and waved, and Emily...Emily stood behind them and sobbed into her hands. A lump rose in Megan's throat and she stifled a loud sob. *This will probably be the last time I ever see them.* The tears coursed down her cheeks and she pressed her knuckles against her mouth to keep herself from bawling out loud.

Just then, she felt the weight of someone settling into the seat next to her. Glancing quickly to the side, she recognized the well-dressed gentleman who'd been sitting near them in the station. He smiled that warm smile again.

"I hope you don't mind if I sit here, ma'am. The car's filling up quickly and this may be the only seat left."

She did mind, terribly in fact, but did she have any choice? She turned away to hide her tears and mumbled, "That's fine."

The train lurched forward then again, and again a third time before it started rolling smoothly. Black smoke clouded her view of the platform. Before she knew it, the Parsons were behind her, still waving. She tore her eyes away from them and tried desperately to compose herself, determined that this gentleman would not see her face until she did. She chided herself for not laying one of her satchels on the seat to discourage anyone from sitting there. *Oh well, he'll probably get off long before I do.*

Buildings flashed quickly by. Megan drew in her breath, startled by the speed. Her eyes tried to focus on the ground beside the tracks, but it soon became a blur and she started feeling dizzy. In no time, the train rounded a long curve and the buildings of the city began to shrink behind them. Soon, trees and bushes whizzed by close to the train. When she focused her eyes ahead, her dizziness went away. A feeling of relief and freedom settled like a blanket around her. She dabbed at her eyes, leaned her head against the vibrating window, and smiled. The train's rattle and hum droned on and on. Sunlight danced sporadically across Megan's face, breaking through branches and leaves wherever it could. Megan watched the telegraph wire swoop down and up again to the next pole. Down and up, down and up. She stifled a yawn and finally let her tired body succumb to the continuous rocking and swaying of the train.

"Dried apples? Hard candy? Licorice, ma'am?" Megan jolted awake. The sun was high in the sky and a boy with a basket in his hands was leaning across the blond gentleman, trying to show her his wares. "Only three cents, ma'am."

She tried to shake off her sleepiness to focus. With clumsy fingers, she dug into her purse for some coins. "Yes, candy, please," she muttered. He handed her a small bag as she dropped the coins in the basket.

"Did you have a nice rest?" the gentleman beside her asked.

Still not completely alert, she stammered, "Who, me? Yes...yes I did, thank you." She nervously smoothed the wrinkles in her skirt and tucked a few strands of hair into place then turned to the window to signal the end of their short conversation.

He was not easily put off. "I noticed your family back at the station. They seem like very nice people."

"They are," was her only response as she continued to look out the window.

"Did you grow up in St. Louis?"

She impatiently sighed and kept her eyes trained on the scenery. "No."

"I'm sorry. I realize we haven't been properly introduced. Believe me, if there was a mutual acquaintance on board, I'd have that taken care of in a hurry. But since there's not, I see no reason why two intelligent adults like us can't take care of the problem. My name is Dr. Andrew Cunningham. And you are…"

Megan turned and gave him a polite but cool nod. "My name is Miss O'Mally. I'm pleased to make your acquaintance, Doctor." She nodded again and turned back to the window.

"Miss O'Mally, if your icy attitude toward me is because you don't trust me, I can assure you I'm not one of those bitter, armed men your uncle warned you to stay away from. On the other hand, if your coolness is because I offend you in some way or if you have a communicable disease and you're trying to spare me, then I'll respect your wishes and not say another word."

Megan turned red and stared at her hands. She chuckled despite her best attempt to stifle herself. "I'm sorry," she said, finally looking at him. "I didn't realize how snooty I was acting."

"That's all right. I understand, under the circumstances, and I apologize for eavesdropping on your family back there in the station. I intended no harm. After hearing what they said, though, I can understand why you're so guarded. That's one of the reasons I sat here."

"But I thought you said…"

"The seats were full? A white lie, I'm afraid. Can you forgive me? I'm going all the way to Tipton, the stop just before yours. I couldn't resist the urge to…" He spread his hands out, trying to think of the right words. "To take you under my wing, so to speak."

"I appreciate your kind intentions, but I'm old enough and experienced enough to handle my own affairs."

He chuckled softly. "I'm sure you're perfectly capable. How about if I just stay close by so I can beat off any assailants, and in the meantime, we'll just be friends? Deal?" He held his hand out.

Megan laughed softly and shook his hand. "Deal." She found his humor and frankness to be refreshing and relaxing.

"So, where did you grow up?"

"Here in Missouri, just north of Springfield."

"Are you a farm girl?"

"Yes." she smiled. "Does it show?"

"Not at all. But it would certainly be no insult if it did. I grew up on a farm and I'm proud of it. What brought you to St. Louis?"

"The war. After the battle at Wilson's Creek, I didn't feel safe in Springfield. So, I left with thousands of others. My uncle's home was the logical place to go since St. Louis was relatively stable."

"So why are you leaving now?"

"Uh…I'm going to join my sister and her family. They're leaving for Oregon in a few weeks and I want to go with them. I haven't seen them in years and we've always been close."

"Is that a fact? Well maybe, if I'm lucky, I'll see you there."

"In Oregon? Are you…"

"That's why I'm here on this train. I grew up near Tipton and I just got word from my brother that he and a friend of ours are putting a wagon train together and leading it out there."

"They're leading it themselves?"

"There's no one I'd trust more. Since they were in their teens, they've been gallivanting all over the west; first, as part of a survey party to work for the Bureau of Topographical Engineers. Then after that, they caught gold fever and went to California, leading a small wagon train, and staked claims. I guess they made enough to live on and had enough left over to pocket for later."

"Sounds pretty adventurous."

"That's not all. After their search for gold, they hired themselves out as guides for hunting parties in the Northern Rockies and Plains. After two or three years of that, they came back to Missouri, put together a good-sized wagon train, led it to Oregon, then staked homestead claims in the Willamette Valley."

"I'm impressed."

"There's more. Are you sure you want to hear it?"

"Yes, please."

Doctor Cunningham went on. "Nick, my brother's friend, came back to join the Army, fought for two years, then got himself reassigned to Fort Klamath in Oregon in the middle of a sticky Indian situation. Then he resigned his commission and the two of them came back to Missouri last summer to see his sick mother. She died last fall, so the next thing I hear from them is they're putting a train together again and they want me to join them."

Megan couldn't help being drawn to this intelligent, humorous man. His deep blue eyes exuded kindness and warmth. She felt secure with him despite the fact she'd met him less than an hour ago.

"I've told you about myself, and you've told me all about your brother and his friend. What about you? You said you're from Tipton? Where are you coming from now?"

"Chicago." He started ticking off facts. "I got my medical training at Harvard, met and married a wonderful woman, started working at a hospital in Chicago, then the war broke out. Early '62, I was commissioned to work half-days at a prisoner-of-war camp. So, I got my taste of Civil War blood and guts. Pretty disheartening job, I'll tell you." He let out a sharp breath and shook his head.

"What about your wife?"

Cunningham gave a long sigh before he answered. "She died in childbirth last summer; the baby, too."

"I'm sorry." She instinctively put her hand out and touched his arm.

"That's the main reason I'm here. I made up my mind that as soon as the war was over, I had to leave and start fresh somewhere else."

"I really didn't mean to pry."

"You're not prying. I'm the one who's been prying. I'll admit, my wife's death was a very painful experience and it will be years before the pain goes away, if ever, but it's something I don't mind telling people about."

"Will you ever remarry?" As soon as the words came out, Megan realized her blunder. She blushed and stammered, "I'm sorry! I...I shouldn't have asked that. Don't bother answering me."

He laughed. "No, that's alright. Actually, I catch myself asking the same question quite often and the answer's always the same: no. At least not for a long time. Sarah was very precious to me and I'm afraid I'd be in no position to be a decent husband to anyone else. Frankly," he added slowly, "I'm still very much in love with her."

Strangely, Megan was comforted by his words. She had found herself growing more and more comfortable with the doctor but had also been vaguely bothered by the suspicion he was attracted to her. She could put that suspicion to rest.

The doctor stifled a yawn and settled back into the seat for a nap. Megan passed her time looking out the window at the constantly changing view. The Missouri River was swollen and muddy from spring rains. The banks were covered with trees in different stages of foliage, some elegantly attired in beautiful new blossoms. She drank in the freshness of it all. Being in the open country again caused her heart to quicken with joy. She found herself experiencing a sudden onset of spring fever, aching to get out in it and run through the green grass, pick bouquets of wildflowers, climb high in a tree and feel the fragrant breeze sway her with the branches. With a blissful sense of freedom, she rested her head on the window and drifted in and out of contented slumber.

"Will we be stopping soon?" Megan asked when Dr. Cunningham stretched and sat up.

He checked his watch. "Our first stop is Hermann, which is probably another half hour."

"I appreciate your friendship on this trip," she said. "It would seem terribly long without someone to talk to. I'd like it if we were traveling on the same wagon train to Oregon. It would be nice to know someone besides my sister and her family."

"I'll tell you how to contact me if you'd like to join us."

"No, don't bother. Charles and Elizabeth have already made arrangements with another party."

"Are you leaving from Westport or Independence?"

"I have no idea. I've only known for two days that I'm even going." Megan's eyes dropped nervously to her lap.

An uncomfortable silence followed.

"Why are you leaving?" he gently pried.

She swallowed before replying, "I already told you; I want to join my sister."

"Ah, yes. I'd forgotten."

Thirty minutes later, the conductor, in blue coat and brass buttons, made his way down the aisle announcing, "Hermann, Missouri; next stop. Train will depart at 2:15 sharp."

Andrew pulled out his watch. "It's not quite 2:00. We'll probably have time to get out and stretch our legs. Would you allow me to escort you?"

"Yes, please. Do you think we'll have time to go farther than the platform?"

"On a gorgeous spring day like today, it would be a shame not to."

The whistle interrupted his words with a long, loud shriek. The train slowed down and people around them began to gather their belongings. Suddenly the train lurched to a stop. Caught off guard, Megan threw her hands up to catch herself on the back of the seat in front of her. Eyes twinkling, Andrew stood and offered his arm for support.

It was truly a beautiful day. The sun was warm, the grass was green and soft with youth. Hermann was a small town. The effects of the war had been obvious for the last couple of miles; deserted farms, fallow fields, burned barns and cabins. It reminded Megan of her good fortune in being sheltered in St. Louis for the past four years.

"It looks we might have time to walk across the street to that field over there. See?" He gently placed his hand on her shoulder and turned her. "The field with the little grove of trees and all the flowers."

"Oh, it's beautiful!" Megan gushed with childlike enthusiasm. "Let's hurry." She took off down the steps and across the street with Andrew trailing behind. Before she was ten steps into the small field, she began to gather wildflowers of all colors, dashing back and forth as if on a treasure hunt. "Andrew, look, oh look! There are so many different kinds!" She held her bouquet under his nose and started to name each one. "This is periwinkle, or to be more specific, vinca minor, and you surely know dandelions and red clover. This bright pink one is called worm root because Indians used the roots as a medicine to get rid of tapeworms and roundworms. I wouldn't be surprised if you've used medicine with this in it."

She stopped for a moment, put her free hand over her mouth, and laughed. "I'm sorry. That's not the sort of thing a lady should be discussing with just anyone, is it?"

He chuckled and shrugged. "I'm not just anyone. I'm a doctor. I'm used to it. Although, to be honest with you, I knew nothing about this flower."

"And these delicate, pink flowers are called shooting stars because they grow wherever stars fall to the ground," she said with a twinkle in her eyes.

"You're quite an expert. I'm impressed. Where did you learn all this?"

"Most of it from my mother. She loved flowers, all kinds of plants, actually, and she'd take me on walks to collect them and press them. After I started teaching, my parents gave me a huge book about trees, weeds, and wildflowers from the Pacific to the Atlantic. I also have an old book of my father's called *Lindsey's Guide to Animal Species West of the Mississippi*. It's pretty fascinating."

"Did you bring them with you?"

"Of course. I'm planning on keeping a journal of all the different plants and animals I see on the way."

"That should be very interesting."

The train's whistle broke into their conversation and reminded them their time was up. Megan clung to her flowers and took off running toward the depot. Andrew caught up to her and grabbed her elbow. "Slow down. That's just the warning whistle." He drew up alongside her, still holding her arm. She was breathing hard. Looking down into her anxious eyes, he winked and smiled. "Don't worry; we'll be in our seats with time to spare."

He helped her onto the platform and up the steps to the train. After they were seated, Megan buried her nose in her bouquet and laughed. "I'm sorry. I must have looked like an idiot out there, running like a ten-year-old boy."

"I'll be honest. When I first saw you back at the St. Louis station, I had serious doubts about you ever making it on the frontier. But I'm beginning to believe you just might survive after all."

"I think it will be a welcome change after four years of city life."

"I hope so, Miss O'Mally. For your sake, I truly hope so."

The rest of the trip was very tiring, but thanks to Andrew, it was also interesting and delightful. At Jefferson City, they had a forty-five-minute stop, so Andrew took Megan to the nearest hotel for a meal. Two and a half hours later, the train reached Tipton. Megan had been scolding herself since Jefferson City for dreading to say good-bye to this man she'd only met a few hours earlier. When the train slowed and the conductor marched through announcing the stop, Andrew turned to her, reached out, and enveloped her hand in his strong warm clasp.

"Well, Miss O'Mally, this is it," he said without his usual sparkle. "Thank you for your delightful company and thank you again for allowing me to sit here." He continued to hold her hand while he spoke. "I'm glad I got to know you. Tell me your brother-in-law's name so I can look you up in Oregon."

The train jolted and the brakes screeched. Megan caught her breath and quickly answered, "It's Charles Batten, Charles and Elizabeth Batten. Oh, please do. At least try." She looked down and for a moment was at a loss for words. "Thank you, too, Andrew," she said just above a whisper. "And, Andrew? Please call me Megan."

His serious face broke into a big grin as he grabbed his bags and stood. "Thank you. I will. I'll see you later in Oregon, Megan. How's that?" He tipped his hat, turned, and was gone.

# CHAPTER SIX

**M**egan's eyes quickly scanned the crowd at the station in Sedalia. It was dark but the crowded platform was lit with lanterns hanging overhead. She heard Charles before she saw him.

"Megan, We're over here!"

Her heart beat with joy as all five of them pushed through the crowd. In a heartbeat, she was caught up in hungry arms and passed from Elizabeth to Charles and then to the girls. Only seven-year-old Abby held back. Elizabeth grabbed her again and they clung tightly to each other, both crying the silent tears of sisters who haven't seen each other in years.

Elizabeth slid her hands down to join Megan's and stepped back to look her over. "Megan, you are beautiful!" she exclaimed.

Megan gave a short, embarrassed laugh. "So are you, Elizabeth," she said with sincerity as she looked into her older sister's warm, blue eyes.

"No, Megan. I mean truly beautiful. You've always been

pretty, but you're a real head-turner now. Isn't she, Charles?"

Charles gave a hearty laugh and picked up Megan's two satchels. "She has surely changed in the last four years, but I've not had my head turned by anyone since I laid eyes on you, Elizabeth."

"Charles," Elizabeth said sweetly and reached up to stroke his whiskered cheek.

The three girls were all standing in a row watching Megan. She walked over to greet them again. "Suzanne, you're almost as tall as me. You were seven, Abby's age, when I saw you last, and now you're twelve. And you know what? Abby looks just like you did then."

Suzanne was beaming. She was old enough to remember Megan's last visit and seemed to be thoroughly delighted to add her beloved aunt to their family. Her hair was pulled back on each side and long, blonde strands fell to the middle of her back.

Ten-year-old Lucy stood bravely beside her. Although she was only two years younger than Suzanne, she was considerably smaller. Long brown pigtails hung down the front of her pinafore, tiny freckles spattered across her nose, and her cheek had a small dirty smudge on it.

Megan knew immediately Lucy was a kindred spirit. "And, Lucy, dear Lucy," she said as she hugged her tightly. "You look just like I did when I was your age." She laughed, held her at arm's length for another look, and glanced quizzically up at Charles and Elizabeth for confirmation. "Am I right?"

They both laughed and nodded. "Absolutely right," Charles said. "And she acts like you did then, too. I've come close to getting her out of as many scrapes as I had to get you out of. It's like living those days all over again."

Lucy grinned from ear to ear. "Does that mean I'll be as pretty as you when I grow up?"

Megan looked into her enormous blue eyes fringed with

long, black lashes. "You'll be much prettier, honey." Reaching down, she pulled a braid gently. "But don't be in a hurry to grow up. It's so much fun being a kid." She winked at Charles.

Finally, Megan moved over to Abigail, who clung to Lucy's dress and stared at the floor of the platform.

Squatting down to eye level, Megan softly asked, "You don't even remember me, do you, Abby? You were only this big when I saw you last." She held out her hand just above Abby's waist. "Look how big you've grown since then." Abby smiled, revealing toothless gaps. Her blonde hair hung in loose ringlets past her shoulders. She had a dimple on each cheek and one in the middle of her chin. Megan was momentarily taken aback when she realized both Abigail and Suzanne strongly resembled their cousin, Emily. *Maybe if they stay away from mirrors all their lives, they'll have a chance to grow up without being overly vain. No one should be this beautiful.* She gently coaxed Abby into a hug and from that moment on, Abby treated Megan like a long-lost buddy.

The next morning, Megan stepped out onto the porch and looked around in amazement. It had never occurred to her how much preparation went into a trip west. Charles and Elizabeth led her around their yard showing her the results of their hard work. They had been at it for months. They had two large, sturdily built wagons. Oiled canvas stretched tightly across rows of hickory bows. The wagon beds were waterproofed with a mixture of wax and ashes rubbed into every crack. On top of that, Charles explained, he had placed a layer of animal skins sewn together, which covered the sides and floor. They walked to the back of one wagon. Up each bow ran a series of hooks, some already holding milk cans, a sewing kit, various tools, and on one, a rag doll with a lopsided smile. Under each wagon hung a bucket full of grease for lubricating wheels and axles. And across the fronts were wooden seats, wide enough for the drivers and one other person.

"Charles has hired Ralph, a young man from Sedalia, to drive our second wagon," Elizabeth said. "He should be here soon."

In the corral next to their barn were twelve oxen. Five Jerseys stood in the field behind the house, two of them young heifers, two giving milk and one expected to calve on the way. Charles' five-year-old bay gelding stood by the fence, straining his neck through the boards trying to get at some spilled oats.

"I sold all but four of my chickens," Elizabeth continued. "I had to convince Charles that they would prove to be invaluable, especially late in the trip when our food supply dwindles down to a monotonous diet of dried meat and hardtack. He agreed and even told me to keep Rub-a-dub, Lucy's contrary rooster." She laughed. "He hopes to rebuild our flock when the trip is over."

Elizabeth, with three excited girls trailing behind, led Megan into the back lean-to to show her the supply of food they were packing. Flour, cornmeal, potatoes, rice, and beans were all in big sacks against the wall. Stacked in piles all over the floor were containers of crackers and hardtack, bacon, dried meat, and dried fruit.

"Goodness! There's enough here to feed an army!" Megan exclaimed.

"We'll be on the trail for five, maybe six months and we've got six people, no, seven people to feed."

"I'm so sorry, Elizabeth. I'm afraid I've been too busy thinking of myself this last week. I never even considered the extra work and expense..."

"Stop it, Megan!" Elizabeth grabbed Megan's arm and spun her around to face her. "If you could only have seen me when Charles showed me your telegram, you'd not doubt for even a second how thrilled we are to have you join us! Why, I made an idiot of myself in front of these girls, jumping up and down and crying like a baby. I didn't show it in my letter to you, but it about tore my heart out to think of going out there and maybe never seeing you again!" She choked back a sob and threw her arms around Megan. They pulled away, looked deeply into each other's eyes, then burst into laughter, wiping the tears away as they did.

Charles stuck his head through the door. "Looks like it'll be tomorrow morning."

"That soon, Charles?" Elizabeth quietly exclaimed, pressing her hand to her heart.

"When Ralph gets back from town, we'll get the rest of the furniture and food loaded. Looks like everything else is ready. I guess this will be our last night in this place."

"I'll get dinner ready," Elizabeth said quickly, wiping a tear away as she brushed past Charles into the kitchen.

Charles looked at Megan with an understanding smile. "I'm glad you're here, squirt. It'll make it a lot easier for her."

"I guess it's always harder for the women. At least you care, Charles. Not very many men would." She planted a kiss on his cheek and followed her sister.

After he left, Elizabeth turned to Megan and in low tones confessed, "For Charles, excitement for this big adventure overshadows any regrets at leaving home. For me…there's so much uncertainty of what's to come. And add to that my grief at leaving this home I dearly love." She paused and swept her hand in an arc through the room. She choked back tears. "Oh, Megan, it's so hard for me to be happy with our decision." She wiped her eyes with the corner of her apron. "But I love and trust that husband of mine, so I'm trying every day to find something positive."

Early the next morning after breakfast, the last cooking

and eating utensils were packed in a box attached to the back of the wagon. Suzanne, Lucy, and Abigail raced to claim choice seats. Before stepping out into the sunlight of the front yard, Charles and Megan turned to see Elizabeth walking quietly through the small house, trailing her hand over the furniture they had to leave behind.

"Uh, I'll go get settled with the girls," Megan said, leaving Charles alone with Elizabeth. She looked back to see Charles cradling her sister's head against his shoulder, his other hand stroking her back, soothing her with words only they could hear.

Megan and the excited, chattering girls climbed up over the drivers' seats and through the openings in the tightly stretched canvas. Settling herself on a folded blanket between the front edge and a barrel of flour, Megan noticed with gratitude that Charles had made four comfortable seats close to the front between the supplies and furniture. He'd even made a tiny place for sleeping way in the back and had spread a thick feather mattress across the tops of boxes piled almost to the canvas ceiling. When necessary, the family would sleep and ride in the wagon Charles drove. The other wagon, driven by Ralph, carried the supplies they would need on the trip. Most of it was packed on the sides, leaving a narrow aisle down the middle for easy access and more sleeping space. When the weather allowed, they would sleep outside under the wagons.

Ralph walked over and checked the oxen's yoke and harnesses. As his tall, skinny frame bent over, blue denim dungarees hiked up to expose skinny, white ankles above his boots. A long, bony nose with a bulb on the end hung over a mouth with too many teeth, all crowding each other for a place in line. He flashed a shy smile Megan's direction.

"Mornin', Miz O'Mally. Nice day for travelin', ain't it?"

"It sure is, Ralph," Megan answered, watching him check and recheck the buckles. He hadn't yet been able to look Megan in the eye, even though he often seemed to look for work to do where he could be near her.

"Hey, Ralph, Let's go!" Lucy hollered impatiently from the other wagon. She and Abby had both claimed seats on either side of him. All morning, Lucy had been making a pest of herself, following him around and asking questions. But Ralph seemed to welcome her attention. It was probably what the timid young man needed to feel at home.

"Lucy, you girls can't both ride up there! There's not enough room and I won't have you falling off under those big wheels on the first day of our trip!" Elizabeth called as she and Charles stepped off the front porch. Her good-byes were over and she was ready to enter into the spirit of their venture with typical motherly concern.

The day was perfect for their trip. Although it was sunny, a soft breeze kept them cool. The chickens cackled up a storm in a pen suspended under Ralph's wagon. Charles had arranged for two teenaged boys from a neighboring farm to ride along on horseback as far as Independence to help keep the cows moving in the right direction. It was chaos at first. None of the cows cooperated. Amid the giggling of the girls and the shouting of the two boys and the bawling of the five Jerseys, Charles finally decided to tie two cows to the back of each wagon and let the boys herd the pregnant one. He reasoned if she'd learn to be driven, the others would eventually follow her.

After he settled back on the driver's seat next to Elizabeth, he mopped his brow and commented, "They'll learn sooner or later."

From behind, Megan chuckled and poked him in the ribs. "Just think, Charles, this is only day one."

"Enough from you," he growled.

After their noon meal, everyone except the drivers decided to walk. The oxen plodded along so slowly, the girls ran wide circles around them, exploring and gathering flowers and interesting rocks. Elizabeth and Megan talked on and on, filling in all the gaps of the last five years, although Megan didn't mention the events of the last week. Life held exciting new prospects for her; being with her family again, meeting new people, seeing new places, living an entirely different lifestyle, and hopefully teaching again. The memory of her last days in St. Louis and her self-condemnation were still strong and threatened to stifle her enthusiasm, but as each day passed, she managed to bury them deeper.

That night under the stars, she tried talking again to the One she used to feel so close to as a child, but her image of God was replaced by the accusing, disgusted look she saw on the face of the school's headmaster as he listed one offense after another and refused to listen or forgive. The picture of herself as an immoral, lewd woman loomed before her until she buried her head in shame. Through tears she silently mouthed, "Thank you for helping me get away. Help me to change." Cold indifference was her answer. She gave up in frustration and tried to think of anything but God.

When they stopped for supper on the third day, Megan limped over to a stool near the cooking fire Elizabeth had started.

Charles' eyes squinted with disapproval as he watched her. "Why are you limping, Megan?"

"My feet are killing me," she answered, holding one tenderly in her hand.

"Take your shoe off and hand it over."

She unfastened it gently, eased it off her blistered foot, and offered it to Charles. He took one quick look and gave a grunt of disgust. Elizabeth glanced up from the meal with a twinkle in her eye as Charles started in on Megan.

"I can't believe you thought you could walk to Oregon in these things! When we get to Independence, the first thing I want you to do is buy two good pairs of comfortable boots; for walking, Megan, not for fashion. Save these silly little things for when we get there. Do you have enough money?"

"I have plenty, I think. I brought all my savings."

"Your dress, too, Megan," Elizabeth gently added. "It's not the most practical one for walking across a dusty prairie. You'd better pack it away for later and dig out something plainer."

Megan looked down at her burgundy calico dress scattered with white sprigs of flowers and lined with a row of dirty white lace along the ruffled hem. She turned red, laughed, and spread her hands out in resignation. "I'm sorry, this is it! This is the plainest, most practical dress I own!"

Elizabeth and Charles looked at each other in disbelief. Charles chuckled and demanded, "Then, what, dear girl, do you have packed in those two satchels I made room for?"

"Dresses mostly. I'm sorry. I packed what I had; what I thought I'd need the most. You should see what I left behind!"

"Megan, if this is all you have, they'll be ruined before we get there," Elizabeth said. "And besides, even after we get there, you won't be needing anything nicer than the one you have on now."

"If you can stand to part with them, I'd suggest trying to get some money for them at a dress shop in Independence. Then use that money to buy some clothes you can use," Charles said. He looked at her and shook his head good-naturedly as he walked away to check on the stock.

"I'm afraid we may have trouble finding dresses in Independence. It would make more sense to buy fabric and make them ourselves," Elizabeth said.

"Make them? There's no time for that."

"Do you have any shirtwaists?"

"Uh, three, I think."

"You'd be surprised how fast I can make a skirt," Elizabeth said with a reassuring smile. She stirred the stew and thought quietly for a moment. "If I can talk Charles into digging out the sewing machine for me, we could set it up right in the middle of nowhere and I could have two skirts made for you in less than two hours."

"Are you serious, Elizabeth? I'm amazed! I wish I could sew."

Elizabeth gave her a surprised look. "Megan, you can sew."

"No, I never learned. I can do simple mending and that's it. Ma taught me that before she died."

"Who made all the dresses you have now? Aunt Eleanor?"

"No, I had them made by a seamstress," she answered nonchalantly.

Elizabeth raised her eyebrows. "I'm afraid my baby sister has become quite spoiled by rich city living."

Megan shrugged. "Everyone I knew did the same. It sure made life easier. Besides, I was too busy teaching to have time for that sort of thing."

"Let me ask you; how long has it been since you've cooked a meal?"

"A whole meal?"

"Yes, a whole meal."

"Not since..." Megan's voice drifted off as she tried to remember. "Not since Pa died," she replied weakly. She flashed her sister a big smile and shrugged her shoulders in embarrassment. "I've baked a couple of pies," she offered.

Elizabeth sat down and stared. "Megan, Pa died five years ago. Did Aunt Eleanor do everything for you?"

Megan stared back at her sister then burst out laughing. "I guess I've been pampered all these years. Pitiful, isn't it? And here I am, twenty-two. What man in his right mind would want an old maid who can't cook or sew?"

"How about Julie and Emily? Are they as helpless as you?" Elizabeth asked with a mischievous twinkle in her eye.

"Julie's not but Emily's far worse. Come to think of it, I don't remember seeing her do any work in the four years I lived there. She could play the piano, knit, and do a little embroidery. That's it. Julie was a workhorse though. Both Uncle Chester and Aunt Eleanor treated Emily and me like we were their little princesses; never asked us to lift a finger and let us do whatever we wanted."

"It's hard to believe Uncle Chester and Ma grew up in the same family." Elizabeth shook her head. "Although, if my memory serves me correctly, I had the lion's share of the work around home while you went traipsing off through the woods all day doing who knows what."

Megan sat down beside Elizabeth and slipped an arm around her shoulder. "That's because you were eight years older than me. Remember, I was only nine when you got married and moved out. Believe me, I had plenty of work from then on."

"Not enough to keep you out of trouble though." Elizabeth threw her apron over her face and laughed hilariously. She pulled it away and used it to dab at the tears in the corners of her eyes. "Oh, Megan, the crazy things you used to do! I think Charles was ready to string you up by your toes a few times. Do you remember the time you, Carolyn Morris, and that Emhoff boy thought there was gold up in the creek behind Carlson's farm? You skipped school for two days and camped out up there. No one had any idea where you were."

"And Charles was the one who found us," Megan added with a sheepish grin.

"He wasn't too happy with you, was he? How about the time you put salt in the schoolmaster's coffee?"

"He had it coming."

"Five days in a row?"

"He was awful!"

"Oh, spare me, child! And wasn't it Charles who caught you red-handed?"

"I guess I was getting over-confident or he just knew ahead of time it was me, because he was just standing quietly in the corner watching. I never saw him. I did it every morning when the schoolmaster went out to ring the bell. I've never jumped so high in all my life as I did when Charles cleared his throat."

Elizabeth laughed and dabbed at her eyes again. "So, what did you say when you saw him?"

"Nothing. I stood there like an idiot with my mouth hanging open. Charles told me very quietly he'd walk me home after school then slipped out the back door."

"I never told you this, but I thought he'd die laughing when he got home."

"No! You're joking me, Sis."

"I swear it. I guess he thought you were pretty funny, but he liked to make you think you were in serious trouble."

"I probably would have been if he'd told Ma and Pa or the teacher."

Elizabeth's face grew serious for a moment. "I think part of the reason he stepped in so often was to save Ma and Pa from worrying about you. Ma was pretty sick then, you know."

Megan sighed. "Looking back, I realize that, but when I was ten and eleven, I was too busy in my own little world. I thought she was just getting old awfully fast. I had to grow up in a hurry after she died though. It would have been a lot easier if you and Charles had still been around."

Elizabeth patted Megan's knee. "I know, Megan, I know."

"Pa was never the same after that. He just kind of withered up inside, no enthusiasm for the farm or anything." Her face brightened a little. "So, for two or three years, I did all the cooking and cleaning. That ought to count for something."

"Oh, it does. I just hope you haven't forgotten

everything. Although cooking on the trail will be a tad different than at home. I'll sure be able to use your help."

Megan stood and magnanimously announced, "Elizabeth, I'll gladly be your servant all the way to the Willamette Valley. It's the least I can do to repay you for what you're doing for me."

"You've already repaid me, just by being here." She also stood and gave her little sister a hug. "Now let's get busy with this meal. You slice some of that ham while I dig the dishes out." She looked around, shielding her eyes against the sun low in the west. "Where did those girls run off to this time?"

# CHAPTER SEVEN

It was dark when the Batten's wagon pulled into a field outside of Independence. They had stopped for supper an hour before. They all got to work digging out their tent, feeding and watering the stock, and starting a fire for coffee. When Charles came back from helping Ralph and the boys with the cows, he handed a small bucket of milk to Elizabeth, then sat on the ground to stretch out by the crackling fire. The girls each grabbed a tin mug and eagerly held it out to their mother.

"Milk, Ma, milk," demanded Lucy.

"Lucille!" her father said sharply, "You'll get nothing if you've forgotten how to ask."

"Sorry, Pa." Her eyes dropped to the ground but she kept her arm extended with the cup.

"Apologize to your ma and you'll get yours last."

"Yes, Pa. Sorry, Ma." She meekly took her place behind her sisters.

Megan poured a cup of coffee and handed it to Charles.

"Thanks, squirt." He glanced up and gave her a tired

grin then held the mug between his brown hands, sighed, and stared dreamily into the fire.

Elizabeth brought three camp stools over and offered them to the other two adults. Megan gladly settled onto hers, and Charles declined, preferring to sprawl out on the grass.

"Tired, honey?" Elizabeth asked.

"You bet. Tomorrow morning, I need to meet with Webster at the feed store on Liberty Street. He'll tell us where he wants all the wagons for his train to gather so we can get organized." Charles' mouth stretched out in a big contented smile as he looked from the fire up to his wife's face. "This is it, honey. How do you feel?"

"I'm doing fine, Charles." She returned his smile with a confident one of her own. "I've made up my mind I'm going to take it one day at a time. With God's help, I'm determined I'm going to enjoy this as much as possible."

"That's my girl." He pulled her hand over and gave it a kiss. "I wish you could picture our farm in Oregon the way I do."

"I just know it'll be years of hard work before we see that farm you've got in your head." She patted his shoulder. "That's alright. You need to dream now and then. At least you're the kind of man that's willing to work to reach those dreams." She looked out to the western horizon. "I guess my main concern is the girls. If it were just you and me, I could face anything, but I worry all the time about our three babies." She paused and shrugged her shoulders. "I guess worrying won't get me anywhere. I need to learn to cast my fear at Jesus' feet and let Him do my worrying for me. He loves them more than I do."

The next morning after Charles had left and Elizabeth and Megan had finished cleaning up from breakfast, Elizabeth gave Ralph instructions to watch over their wagons and stock while they were gone. Suzanne helped

Megan dry the last of the dishes and Lucy and Abby jumped up and down, begging to go along.

"Why do you think we'd want to take two loud girls who seem to have entirely forgotten all their manners?" Elizabeth asked, looking at them out of the corners of her eyes.

Both girls settled down immediately and Lucy, wiping her hands down the front of her pinafore, cleared her throat and asked in her politest voice, "May we go into town with you, Mother? We'll walk, not run, and if we talk, which we promise we'll do very little of, we'll do it in the softest, quietest, most ladylike voices we own. And we'll stay behind you and we promise we won't touch the cloth or anything else we see, unless, of course, we happen to see a dog that wants us to pet it or a..."

"That's enough, Lucy," her mother interrupted. "I've already decided to let you come because I know that if you don't behave the way you've been taught, you'll be doing extra chores tonight. And please stay close. It's anyone's guess what type of people we may run into in a town like this."

"What's wrong with this town, Ma?" Suzanne asked.

"There's nothing really wrong with the town, honey. It's just that there are so many people from so many places passing through and it's hard to know what sort of people they are." She looked down at Abby's worried frown and added, "But I'm sure most of them are families a lot like ours. Don't worry, sweetheart," stroking a finger down her daughter's soft cheek.

They walked a half mile through a field and over a small rise before they saw the town. By the time they got to Lexington Street, they were surrounded by hundreds of people, all walking, running, riding in wagons and on horses, everyone moving, going someplace. Megan said, "Excuse me," in a nervous, quiet voice and they all moved around three Indian men who stood against a building and watched them with expressionless faces. Elizabeth was right. The majority of people were families like theirs, but mingled among them were a few Indians, some Mexican men with wide grins and loud clothes, men in Union uniforms, and many men with a brash, swaggering air. Excitement hung in the atmosphere and almost everyone moved with purpose.

Megan, Elizabeth, and the girls wound their way westward down Lexington toward the square. "There's the mercantile, over there on the corner." Elizabeth pointed. "I'll bet we find what we need there. Girls, stay up here on the walk. Half these people don't look like they're watching where they're driving. Abby, get your finger out of your mouth and, Lucy, stop staring."

"I can't help it, Ma. Everywhere I look there are people. Do you want me to look at the sky? There's no people up there. 'Course someone would have to hold my hand so I know which way to go or in case I start to bump into someone or fall down."

"Just look straight ahead. I think you can manage that," Elizabeth answered with mild irritation as she marched on toward their destination, missing seeing her daughter staring at the sky and groping around for support.

Megan giggled and grabbed Lucy's hand. "Don't forget those extra chores that may be waiting for you," she whispered.

They stepped through the entrance and closed the door on the noise outside. The store was bulging with supplies of every kind. Shelves were piled high with lanterns, shovels, cooking utensils, blankets, bolts of fabric, sewing supplies, boots, flour, sugar, eggs, crackers, hardtack and jerky, harnesses, bits, bridles, camp stools, just about anything a person might need on a long trip. The aisles were narrow to make room for the abundant merchandise. Business was good, very good, and the owner's delight was reflected in the loud, enthusiastic voice Megan heard at the counter in the back.

Megan found sturdy, comfortable boots that fit perfectly, picked up a couple of pairs of thick socks, then worked her way through the aisles to find Elizabeth. Two tall, broad-shouldered men turned into the aisle she was walking down. The one in front had his head turned, talking to his companion, and didn't see Megan. She turned sideways and backed up, making herself as small as possible between two buckets that jutted into the aisle. Banging his arm on the bucket, he turned just in time to see Megan's warning look. For just an instant, his steel-gray eyes locked with hers. Then he tore them away and in a cool tone muttered, "Excuse me, ma'am," and continued down the aisle.

His companion stopped, lifted his hat in greeting, and gave her a big smile. "Hello there. Don't mind the big klutz. He's got his mind on other things right now. The way you're tucked in there, I'd guess you were part of the merchandise. How much are gorgeous young ladies going for these days?"

Stung to her core, Megan glared at him and in her iciest tone demanded, "Move out of my way. I have business to attend to."

He stepped back as if stung by a bee. "Didn't mean to offend you, ma'am. You did look a little out of place between those buckets though." Megan heard him chuckle as she stalked away. "Nice to meet you. Hope we run into each other again sometime," he drawled.

Around the corner, Megan saw Elizabeth fingering some brown material. "Oh, there you are, Megan. How do you like these?" she asked, holding up the brown fabric and a navy-blue fabric, sprinkled with tiny rosebuds.

"They're fine," she answered distractedly, still fuming over the last words she heard that impudent man utter.

"Do you want two or three skirts? Since I'll have my sewing machine set up and I can cut all three out at the same time, it really won't be much extra work to do three instead of two. What color is your other shirtwaist?"

"Let me think... I have the ivory, the rose, and a pale green."

"How about this dark green with the same rosebuds that the blue has?"

"Sounds good to me. I could wear it with all three shirtwaists." Megan only glanced at the fabric. Her eye was drawn to the myriad assortment of items for sale. "You know, Elizabeth, I didn't ever take time to think about some of the things I might need on a trip like this."

"Don't worry about it. Charles thought of everything."

"But I can't depend on your family for everything."

"You're part of our family now, Megan."

"I know, but I'm an adult, an adult with a purse full of money. Surely there's a few things I could do to help out or at least take care of myself. You and Charles have enough responsibilities without having to worry about me, too. One thing I want to buy is a cow."

"A cow?"

"Yes, a cow. I've heard they may be in short supply in Oregon and if I buy one that's milking, I could share the milk, and if we run low on food by the end of the trip, we can slaughter it."

"Do you have enough money?"

"I do, unless they've gone up drastically in price in the last ten years. I also want to buy a gun."

"A gun, Megan? Why?"

"For protection mainly." She turned and headed for the back of the store. "I saw some back here near the counter."

"How long has it been since you've shot a gun?" Elizabeth asked, trailing along behind her sister.

"It'll all come back to me. Here they are, over here." She reached back and grabbed Elizabeth by the arm, pulling her up to the counter. "Tell me which one I should get."

"Tell you... What makes you think I'd know?"

"Well, do you think I should get a rifle or a pistol?"

"I... Megan, I'm still not sure why you think you need one."

"May I help you ladies?" boomed a loud, deep voice from the other end of the counter. A man of medium height with a huge stomach walked toward them, grinning like a Cheshire cat.

Megan cleared her throat. "I would like to buy a gun, sir, but I'm having a little trouble making up my mind."

"Well, I'm sure I can help you; after all, that's my job. I'll be with you two gentlemen in a moment," he said to two men that had just unloaded their purchases onto the counter.

Megan threw an apologetic look in their direction then stiffened when she saw they were the same men she had just encountered in the aisle.

"Are you interested in a rifle or something smaller?" the storekeeper asked.

Megan turned her back slightly to the men and lowered her voice. "I... I'm really not sure. I was hoping you could help me decide."

Totally oblivious to her embarrassment, he bellowed, "Well, it all depends on what you're gonna use it for. If it's for huntin', you'll need a rifle, but if you need something you wanna keep with you most of the time, you should get a pistol, but with a pistol you're sacrificin' accuracy."

Megan shrugged. "Well, I'm going to be traveling west with a wagon train and I thought I might need something for protection."

A deep male voice cut into their conversation just over Megan's shoulder and made her jump. "I've heard there are more deaths on the trip to Oregon due to accidental gunshot wounds than there are because of Indians." Megan jerked her head around and stared up into a strong, tanned face frowning down at her; the same man that had almost run her over a few minutes earlier. He continued, "It would be a lot safer for you and everyone else on the trip if you'd forget any ideas you have about owning your own gun." He gave her a hard stare, with no hint of amusement.

Megan exhaled sharply. "Excuse me," she said, her tone dripping with contempt. "This is none of your concern, whatsoever. I prefer to take care of my own affairs without interference from strangers." She turned back to the store owner. "Which of these pistols would you recommend?"

He cleared his throat and glanced nervously at his other customers. "Well, I have a pair of Dance Brothers .36 caliber Texas pistols and five Colts. If you want my opinion, I'd say a Colt would work best for you; easy to handle and I think they're a little more accurate, especially for someone with no experience."

She took the gun in her hand and turned it over. "I have experience." Holding the pistol at arm's length she squinted and aimed at the back wall." And after I practice, I'm sure my accuracy will improve."

Someone snickered behind her.

"I'll take this, thank you. Do you have ammunition?"

"Sure do, right over here." He handed her a box with 40 bullets.

"I'd like three boxes, please, if you have them."

By noon, Charles got back to the campsite in time to see both women working over the fire. It felt good to hear them talking and laughing. Elizabeth was handling the move far better than he had expected, and he was sure it was because Megan was here. Megan had a way of making people see the lighter side of things. He'd heard Elizabeth laugh more in the last week than in the previous couple of months. There had been enough women on the streets of Independence this morning with serious, worried faces to make him appreciate all over again the healthy camaraderie between these two sisters.

"Hello, pretty ladies. How'd your shopping go?"

They both looked up. "Hi, Charles!" Elizabeth walked over and gave him a quick hug. "Our shopping went very well, thank you. We found the cloth we needed and Megan bought a pistol and a cow."

"What?" He pushed her away so he could see her face. "A pistol and a cow?" The only answer Elizabeth gave was a smile, so he directed his look to Megan. "A pistol and a cow? Are you serious?"

Megan was in the middle of sampling the stew, so she just nodded her head and smiled.

"Whatever for?"

She shrugged. "For protection and food," she answered nonchalantly.

"Can you handle a gun?"

"You should know. You're the one who taught me."

Charles shook his head, walked over to a stool, and sat down. He let out a long sigh and started unlacing his boots. "I can't go on treating you like a kid. I suppose you know what you're doing. The cow, I have no trouble with, but I'm not exactly thrilled with the idea of you carrying a gun around, especially since it's probably been a while since you've even touched one."

Megan walked over and sat next to him. "I was hoping you'd have time to help me practice before we leave."

He studied her face. "You really think you'll need a gun on this trip?"

"I'd like to be prepared in case I do."

"Fine, Megan." He sighed again. "I'll help if I can find the time."

She grabbed his hand and squeezed it. "Thanks, Charles. I promise you, you won't be sorry and I'll be very careful."

She got up to leave, but he held on to her hand and looked sternly up at her. "Did you remember to buy a good pair of boots?"

Megan laughed, swung her foot up onto the stool, and hiked her dress up to the middle of her shin. "Does this answer your question?"

The next morning, they broke camp and headed to the Westport landing on the banks of the Missouri River. Charles and about thirty other men had met with the organizers of their train and they had been told to move on to Westport to accommodate those coming up the river. It would also save them a day of travel. They arrived in the afternoon to see about 100 wagons spread through a clearing next to the river. Two men on horseback rode across the field and waved their hands in greeting. Megan had walked most of the way. She and Abby, hand in hand, caught up to Charles' wagon in time to hear him say to Elizabeth, "That's McKay and Sanders. They were at the meeting yesterday morning. They're good men, you'll like 'em a lot."

Both men slowed their horses to a trot about 50 feet from the Batten's wagons, then rode up to Charles with hands extended. "Looks like you didn't have any trouble finding us, Charles."

"No, I sure didn't. Webster gives good directions."

McKay slapped Sanders on the back and roared with laughter. "He'd better be good. If he can't give directions from Independence to here, then I sure ain't trustin' him to get us to Oregon."

Megan decided immediately she would like these men as she watched them good-naturedly tease each other. McKay was of medium height, with light brown, curly hair and a ruddy complexion with eyes that twinkled when he talked. *Closest thing I've seen to Santa Claus.* Sanders was taller and heavier with dark hair, a bushy beard, gentle eyes, and the faintest hint of a grin always present on his face. They exchanged greetings with Elizabeth then turned their attention to her.

"So, this is the little school marm you were telling us about."

"This is the one. Megan, I'd like you to meet Dan McKay and Stephen Sanders. They each have five kids, and when they heard about you, they were both wondering if you'd be interested in doing a little teaching on the way."

Megan's face lit up. "I'd sure like to try. I don't have much in the way of books, but I'm sure we can manage something." She brought her hands up to her face with delight. "With these three girls and all yours, that's quite a classroom!"

"Except in this case, there's no room, no walls to hold 'em all in," McKay said.

"Yeah, I'm sure it'll be a challenge for you," Sanders added. "We're not expecting miracles or anything. Because of the war, our kids haven't had much of any schooling the last couple of years, so we'll be happy with almost anything you can work out. 'Course, my wife and I are gonna need 'em to help out with chores when the wagons aren't moving, so if you can possibly work it out so you can school 'em while we're movin', that would be ideal."

"I'll probably have to divide them up and take four or five at a time, but I think it'll work out fine. How old are they?"

"Well, mine range from a boy of 15 down to 5-year-old Amanda," answered McKay. "And I think Stephen's are about the same."

"Pretty close. My oldest is 16, a girl, and my youngest is a six-year-old, named after me," he said, making no attempt to hide his pride. "Come on down and I'll introduce you to them. Rebecca's gettin' anxious to meet some of the womenfolk she's gonna be spendin' the next six or seven months with."

Charles and Ralph guided their wagons in the direction

McKay and Sanders rode. Ahead Megan could see about forty to fifty wagons already clustered together near the river. Up the river, she saw another group of wagons, and across the meadow, two other groups.

"Webster said he wants to try to move out before these other trains get going," Megan heard Charles say to Elizabeth. "Says he doesn't want to ride in their dust and have our livestock get the leftover grass."

"How soon will we be leaving, then?"

"Probably two or three days if a good number show up. He'd like to get at least 75 wagons."

Before the Batten's wagons came to a stop, two women and a half dozen kids were swarming all around them. Lucy walked right up to two girls not much bigger than she and held her hand out. One of the girls grabbed the outstretched hand and the other girl reached out and claimed Lucy's other hand. "Come on! Let's take her down to the river. You have to see the frog eggs!" And they were off.

A woman with beautiful golden hair tucked into her bonnet laughed and introduced herself. "My name's Rebecca Sanders and those two are our twins, Rachel and Meggie. As you can tell, neither of them is very shy. This is Amy, our oldest. She's sixteen and this is 14-year-old Sarah and over there is Stephen, our youngest." Amy and Sarah smiled confidently up at Charles and Elizabeth, and little Stephen was too busy chasing a long-haired black-and-white puppy to realize he'd just been introduced.

A short plump woman with flour on her hands welcomed them enthusiastically and introduced herself as Caroline McKay. "This is Michelle, same age as Sarah, and my three boys are off tendin' the cows. And that's 5-year-old Amanda over there trying to catch up to Stephen."

Megan looked from one face to the next, trying to remember all their names. Elizabeth was beaming with joy and relief knowing the long trip ahead would be shared with such warm, friendly people. Charles pulled their wagon to level ground next to McKay's and they went about the business of setting up camp. That night, all three families ate around one big campfire sharing food and talking late into the evening

After everyone drifted off to their tents and wagons for the night, Megan and the three girls crawled beneath heavy quilts under the wagon. For a long time, Megan lay with her chin resting on her arms, gazing at the line of trees along the river silhouetted against the moonlit sky. There was no doubt in her mind that she had done the right thing, coming with Charles and Elizabeth. This was an entirely different world than the one she had just left; an easy place to forget. And the prospect of having students on the trip thrilled her. Her mind was already churning with ideas about what to teach and how to teach on the trail. She rolled onto her back and amidst the night sounds of crickets in the tall grass and bullfrogs on the river, she drifted into contented, peaceful sleep.

# CHAPTER EIGHT

The sounds of morning broke into Megan's consciousness before she was awake enough to remember where she was. Not more than five feet away, Ralph was splitting wood for the fire. Elizabeth was unpacking the iron skillet to start the bacon, and two small children whose names she had already forgotten ran squealing between the wagons. She threw her blankets aside when she realized all three of her nieces were already out of bed and gone. Elizabeth smiled at her when she scrambled to her feet, rolled up the quilts, and hurriedly stuffed them into the back of the wagon.

"Oversleep, did you?"

Megan rubbed her eyes and ran a comb through her hair. "I guess I did. Sorry. Where is everyone?"

"I sent the girls after water. Don't worry about breakfast. It's taken care of. Why don't you go down to the river and wash up some clothes? We've got a few things in that bag over there."

Megan climbed into the wagon, pulled the opening shut, and got out a shirtwaist and one of the new skirts Elizabeth had made. On second thought, she decided, she'd wait and put those on after she was done washing clothes. No sense in taking a chance on getting them wet and muddy. Her nightclothes, a worn, flannel dress handed down from her sister, would have to do. It was a little big on her but certainly nothing to be ashamed of in these surroundings.

She grabbed a few of her dirty clothes, Elizabeth's bag, soap, and scrub board and headed toward the river. Several paths led to a trampled, muddy bank where everyone had been leading their horses and oxen to drink. She made her way upstream through the brush until she found a secluded, clean, grassy area to do her work.

As she unlaced and took her boots off, her eyes scanned the edge of the river and the overhanging branches for snakes. She hiked her dress up to her knees and tucked the excess into her belt then picked up a big flat rock and hurled it into the river. Hoping that any snakes would be scared off, she grabbed the scrub board, soap, and one of Charles' shirts and stepped into the cold water and got to work.

Half an hour later, the clothes were clean and spread over the surrounding bushes to dry. The bottom half of Megan's skirt was soaked and she lay sprawled on her back in the grass with a contented smile on her face. She loved this life being outside day and night, cooking and eating outside, even doing laundry in a river! Uncle Chester and Eleanor would faint if they could see her. She had forgotten how good it felt to step barefooted onto the damp morning grass, to splash around in a river, to chase cows through the field, to ride a horse, even to get good and dirty now and then. She never dreamed she'd get such deep satisfaction from the menial chores of cooking and laundry and doing things for herself for a change.

"Megan!" Lucy's voice came drifting through the bushes. "Megan, where are you?"

"Lucy, I'm over here! What do you need?"

Lucy pushed through the thick brush and made her way into the little clearing. "Hi. Ma didn't know how long you'd be so she sent some milk and biscuits and jam for your breakfast."

"Oh, how nice! Come over here and sit down." She patted the grass beside her and gratefully reached for the food. "Isn't this nice here? You can watch the river go by and no one knows you're here."

Lucy settled down and, true to her character, looked around her in awe at the beauty, the possibilities. "This would be a great secret hideout, wouldn't it?"

"Yes, it would. In fact, I was just thinking what a great place it is to get a quick bath. How about you be a lookout for me, and as soon as I'm done eating, I'll wash up?"

"Alright, I'll stand over here and make sure no one's coming." She jumped up and posted herself where she could peek through the bushes.

Megan brushed the crumbs off her dress, unbuttoned down to her waist, and went down to the water's edge with the soap. Checking to make sure no one could see, she used a little soap and a lot of water and tried to wash herself as much as possible without undressing. By the time she was finished washing her hair as well, her dress was soaked. She buttoned up and started gathering the clothes off the bushes.

"Thanks, Lucy, honey. Could you help me carry some things?"

As they approached the wagons, Charles crossed their path. "Hi, ladies. Looks like you've been busy." His eyes traveled up and down Megan's dress as he spoke. "Have you been doing laundry, or did you decide to jump in for a swim? I'll be surprised if you got the laundry clean in that river. Looks like slow moving mud to me. Megan, Mr. Webster wants to talk to you."

"The wagon master? Me? Why?"

"He wants all the livestock owners to list their animals

and give him some way of identifying them. I guess they had some major disagreements on the last trip west over some cattle. He said they lost quite a few on the way and a bunch of men claimed the same cows. Almost had a gunfight on his hands. So, this time he's playing it safe."

"Where is he?"

"He and his crew have three wagons about five or six wagons upriver from ours. You'll find him."

Lucy helped Megan tie a rope from a wagon to a nearby tree and hang all the clothes out to finish drying. She changed into a fresh shirtwaist and skirt, pinned her still-damp hair in a loose knot, and took off to find Webster's camp.

Five wagons down the row from them, she found a group of men milling around. Attached to one of the wagons sat a small table with three camp stools around it. On one stool sat a man who Megan immediately recognized as one of the men who almost ran into her at the mercantile. This was the talkative one, she remembered, as she stiffened and tried to turn away before he noticed her.

"Can I help you, ma'am?" he drawled in a loud, friendly voice.

She turned away and answered, "No, thank you. I'm looking for Mr. Webster." Her eyes scanned a group of men on the right then locked with the steel-gray eyes of a man who stood almost a head taller than those around him; the same impudent man at the mercantile that had warned her about buying a gun!

Recognition flashed between them immediately and she tore her eyes away, cleared her throat, and in the coolest voice she could muster, she politely asked the man at the table to please direct her to Mr. Webster.

"He's right there, ma'am, looking right at you." He inclined his head toward his tall friend.

Megan glanced quickly at him and in a small voice asked, "Mr. Webster? The wagon master?"

Webster's eyes had never left her. The others had stopped talking and waited for a response. In a slow, deep voice he answered, "Yes, I'm Webster. And who are you?"

"Uh... I'm Megan O'Mally and I was told you wanted to see me about my cow," she answered, trying to keep her voice steady.

"Are you Charles Batten's sister-in-law?"

"Yes, sir, I am."

He hesitated then said, "I'll be with you when I'm finished with these men."

The man at the table locked his fingers together behind his head and leaned against the wagon, staring at her and grinning from ear to ear. Megan wanted to walk over and knock the stool out from under him.

She went over and over in her mind her encounter with these two men at the mercantile. Were they really as bad as she remembered? Had she maybe overreacted and said some things she shouldn't have? She couldn't remember. She only knew she didn't like them at all and wanted to stay as far away as possible. What an unfortunate coincidence.

She dared to look at Webster again. His shoulders were broad and well-muscled. He had thick, dark hair, almost black, with a straight nose, mustache, and a strong mouth and jaw. He was truly a magnificent specimen of masculinity, one of the best-looking men Megan had ever seen. Yet he looked unfriendly, almost angry, and that frightened Megan. She wanted nothing to do with him.

He caught her eye and she quickly looked away. When she turned her eyes back to him, he was talking to a man but watching her. Soon the last two men dismissed themselves and Webster turned to Megan.

"Have a seat, please," he said in a restrained voice, indicating the stool opposite from him. Towering over her, he picked up a book and flipped through some pages. An older barrel-chested man with a droopy mustache walked up and started asking questions. Webster set his notebook in front of Megan and gave the man his attention.

Megan's eyes scanned the page in front of her. There was a column for names, one for livestock, number, and identifying brands or other marks. Hoping to get this over as quickly as possible and avoid any conversation with these two, she reached across the table for the pen and started writing her name in the first column. Webster's hand came down and rested on the page, keeping her from writing any more.

Startled, Megan drew back and glanced up at him. He was still in the middle of answering the old man's questions and never bothered to look down, but his hand remained on the book until his guest left. Then he gave Megan a long, thoughtful look. She felt like a schoolgirl being given the eye by a new schoolmaster. She straightened and mustered all her dignity to keep from squirming. He looked away, cleared his throat, and sat in the chair opposite her. His companion was still sitting back against the wagon, obviously enjoying her discomfort.

"So, you have a cow?" Webster began.

Never had Megan felt so uncomfortable being asked such a simple question. Webster's dark eyes bored into hers with a suspicious, almost-humorous gleam. She had nothing to feel guilty for, nothing to be ashamed of.

"Yes, I have a cow," she answered with a defiant tone. "Surely that's not a problem for you." Out of the corner of her eye, she saw an appreciative nod and a widening grin on the face of Webster's partner.

Webster's features didn't soften any. "No, that shouldn't be a problem, but as soon as you fill this out, I have another matter to discuss with you."

Megan stared at him then at the page in front of her. She continued to fill out the information he asked for until she came to the brand. "Uh...I don't think she has a brand, at least I haven't noticed one yet."

"What kind is she?"

"I think she's a Jersey like Charles' cows."

"There are at least 50 other Jerseys here so far and not enough markings on them to be able to identify them, so we'll have to brand her for you. What's your name again?"

"Megan O'Mally."

He turned to his friend. "An 'M' should be easy enough for you to make. Right, Thomas?"

"Sure." Thomas let his chair fall forward with a clunk and stood up. "I'll get right to it."

"He's going to make an 'M' brand for your cow. When he's done, you take him and find your cow. Right now, I want you to go to your wagon, get that nice new Colt you bought, and bring it here."

"What?" Megan stood up.

Webster stood up and leaned forward resting both hands on the table, bringing his eyes level with hers. "You heard me," he said, staring at her with a hard determined set to his jaw.

Megan put her hands on her hips and tried to match his stare. "Why?" she demanded.

In an even, firm tone he answered, "I thought I made that clear before you bought it. This is the second train I've led west. We made mistakes on the first trip that I won't make again. We had 2 people killed and three wounded from accidental gunshot wounds. I'm not about to let a young lady like yourself haul a pistol around with her that she doesn't even know how to load, much less shoot!"

Megan's face was flushed with indignation. "That pistol is my personal property which you have no right to take from me. I am not a stupid, careless child and I *will* learn how to use my gun! Good day, Mr. Webster!" She turned and walked briskly away then stopped and turned. "And tell your friend when he's ready, he can find me five wagons down." With that, she left.

By the time Megan reached her wagon, she was

furiously wiping tears off her cheeks. Stopping at the end of the first wagon, she leaned against it to compose herself before anyone saw her. She was angry with Webster, but she was beginning to get angry with herself for the way she had acted. She tried to tell herself she was justified in the way she felt. *I didn't buy that pistol just to turn it over to someone else for the duration of the trip. Just because he leads this wagon train doesn't give him the right to confiscate personal property. I can't allow a stubborn male, whose authority has gone to his head, to intimidate me.*

Taking a deep breath and jutting her chin out, she determined she wouldn't let him get her riled up again. She'd maintain her composure and calmly let him know she wouldn't put up with that kind of nonsense. And furthermore, she'd go out of her way to avoid him. That shouldn't be too hard, given the size of this train.

Her thoughts were interrupted by Ralph walking toward her. A few steps behind came Webster's sidekick with a branding iron in his hand and the same irritating, amused look in his eyes.

"Ralph, if you're not busy, could you help this man behind you?"

As Ralph turned to look, the man tipped his hat toward Megan. "My name's Thomas, Miss O'Mally."

She nodded briefly then addressed Ralph. "He's going to brand my cow. You know where she is, don't you?"

"Yeah, she's out with the others. You want fer me to get her?"

Thomas took control. "We've got a good hot fire over there. Bring her on over. Does she have a halter on?" Their voices trailed off and Megan stepped around the corner of the next wagon to find Charles and Elizabeth enjoying a relaxing moment together, Elizabeth on a stool and Charles on the grass with his back up against the wagon wheel and his arms resting on his drawn-up knees.

"Hi, you two. Charles, don't go anywhere. I'll be right back." She went to the back of the wagon and climbed in.

In no time, she reappeared holding her shiny new Colt. "You told me you'd teach me how to use this. Is now a good time?"

Fifteen minutes later, Megan and Charles were a good distance away from any people and animals. Charles had drawn a target on a discarded board and tied it to a branch. He taught her how to load, aim, and shoot. The first results were terrible. He showed her how to steady her grip and eye down her arm and the short barrel. She tried again. They walked the distance to check their target.

"Not bad, not bad. At least you hit it this time. You missed more than you hit though. Need some serious work I'm afraid."

"A rifle would've been a better choice?"

"Easier to hit your target, that's for sure."

Megan looked up to see a horse and rider standing in the spot they'd been shooting from. The rider was watching them intently. Something about him looked strangely familiar, but she couldn't quite remember where she'd seen him. As they approached, he sat upright and waved his hat.

"Miss Megan O'Mally!" came his voice, accented with surprise and delight. He slid off his horse and started toward her. Only after taking a few steps did Megan realize who he was.

"Andrew Cunningham!" she squealed. She ran to him and grabbed his hands, repressing a desire to wrap her arms around him.

"I was hoping I'd bump into you before we left. How have you been?" Andrew asked.

"I'm fine." She turned to Charles and introduced them to each other. "This is that doctor I told you about. We sat next to each other on the train."

"Glad to meet you, Dr. Cunningham. It sure eases a

man's mind to know doctors are heading to Oregon as well as farmers." They shook hands warmly and started comparing war experiences. Cunningham's work at the prison in Chicago fascinated Charles.

"Megan, I told Stephen Sanders I'd help him butcher a cow this afternoon, so I better get movin'. If Dr. Cunningham doesn't mind, I'll leave you with him so you two can catch up on the latest."

Andrew tipped his hat and smiled. "My pleasure, Mr. Batten." He offered his arm to Megan and they strolled across the field, exchanging news of the last several days. "You sure look different than you did the first time I saw you. Here you are with a half sensible dress on, good tough walking boots, and lo and behold, the lady's carrying a gun!"

Suddenly Megan stopped and pulled on Andrew's arm so he'd face her. "Is your train full yet, Andrew? Could you take on at least two more wagons?"

Andrew looked down at Megan's eyes and smiled. "I'd have to ask first, but I'm sure we have room for several more. Why? Are you planning on jumping ship?"

"If I can talk Charles and Elizabeth into it. We've got some good families with us, but I'm sure we'd find that on any train. It's our wagon master. He's the most intolerable, arrogant, bossy, pigheaded man I've ever met."

Andrew threw his head back and laughed. "Intolerable, arrogant, bossy, and pigheaded? That bad, huh?"

Megan frowned. "I'm serious, Andrew! The trip to Oregon is going to be hard enough without having to be under the rule of a tyrant."

"All right, I'll talk to Nick. I'm sure there won't be a problem as long as your family doesn't object. You'll like Nick; he's a great man with a lot of experience. And I would be delighted to have you come with us." Then he mumbled, "So would my brother and Nick for that matter." He steered her toward a gravel bank. "See that clump of dandelions over there?"

"Yeah."

"Show me what kind of aim you have. If you can shoot just one head off in five shots, I'll be impressed."

Megan flashed a big smile at him, took careful aim, and shot. The flowers stood unmoved. She extended her arm, rested her right hand in her left to steady her gun, and tried to sight down the short barrel. Two men on horses rode up, but Megan ignored them to concentrate. She pulled the trigger and saw slight movement in the flowers. Casting a triumphant look toward Andrew, she saw him talking to the wagon master, Webster, and his partner, Thomas. Her whole body became tense as she caught Andrew's last words, "so she wants to know if her family can join us." Megan drew her breath in sharply as her hand flew up to cover her mouth.

Webster's face was expressionless as he looked at her and answered, "'intolerable, arrogant, bossy, pigheaded tyrant?' That's pretty bad. No one should have to put up with that kind of wagon master. I'm sure we can do something to help." He dismounted and walked toward her. "Why don't you introduce us, Andrew?"

Megan felt heat rise up and wash over her face. She wanted to turn and run but she couldn't move a muscle other than her eyes, which darted from his face down to the gun she held in her sweaty hands.

"Miss O'Mally, I'd like you to meet Nick Webster, the best wagon-master you'll find anywhere, and my brother, Thomas Cunningham, over there." Thomas tipped his hat, grinned, and winked at her. "And, Nick, meet Miss Megan O'Mally, the lady I told you about that I met on the train in St. Louis."

Nodding his head toward her, Nick said, "I'm glad to meet you, Miss O'Mally. I'd be more than happy to have you join us, but I need to make sure of a few things first if you don't mind."

Megan stared at his feet for a full minute trying to compose herself then looked at Andrew with imploring eyes. He looked befuddled, watching her strange reaction. Then slowly she saw understanding come over his face. "Surely this isn't..."

She smiled and nodded.

He shook his head and looked down in apology.

Finally, Megan made herself meet Webster's eyes. He raised his eyebrows, waiting for a response.

"I'm waiting," Webster said quietly.

Finally she answered, "I don't mind, go ahead," her voice barely above a whisper.

Webster continued, "I need to know that you'll be cooperative, that you'll respect the people that are in authority, and try to understand that the decisions we make we believe are the best for the whole group." He lowered his head and studied her face. "Can you do that?"

She swallowed and glanced over at Andrew. He shrugged and gave her a reassuring smile. Looking back at Webster, she whispered, "I can," then dropped her eyes to his feet again.

Nick lowered his voice so only she could hear. "And will you defy me again?"

With shame, she quietly answered, "No, sir. I won't."

She looked down and saw the gun she was holding as a glaring reminder of their last encounter. With a big sigh of resignation, she handed it to him. As he took it, he gave her a warm smile that was so unexpected she felt stunned for a moment.

"Well, I think she passes, boys," he announced loudly. "It's a pleasure to have you with us, Miss O'Mally. Andrew, I'll leave her with you to escort back to her wagon." He mounted, tipped his hat in farewell, and rode off with Thomas behind him.

# CHAPTER NINE

By the next day, Webster's train had more than doubled in size. The camp seemed to be in chaos as people rushed from one job to another. Children, dogs, and chickens were under foot everywhere. Webster had chosen a committee from among the first arrivals to inspect wagon and oxen conditions and to make sure everyone had adequate food and water supplies. If anyone failed inspection, they were told to stay behind to make necessary preparations and hook up with another train. He did his job with efficiency bordering on ruthlessness. They were scheduled to leave May 5, the next morning.

On the day of departure, the sun rose on a camp that resembled an ant's nest. Eager anticipation was written on every face, and most were scrambling to prove themselves as capable as their neighbors at working quickly and efficiently at this new life on the trail. Megan, though, couldn't get used to the early rising that came so naturally to everyone else. Her first conscious moment was of the toe of a boot gently poking her arm.

"Hey, sleepyhead, get up."

Still caught between dreams and reality, she stretched, turned her head, and drifted back into slumber. The toe prodded harder, then she felt a hand rest on her shoulder and a voice gently say, "Megan, it's me, Andrew. It's time to get up." Her eyes flew open. She looked quickly from side to side at her nieces' beds then up at Andrew with a groan.

"Aw, Andrew, I can't believe I overslept again. What's wrong with me?" She pounded her fist into the ground and crawled out from under the wagon, dragging her bedroll with her. "I guess I've lived in the city too long." She folded and rolled and poked her bedroll into a ball with vengeance. "How long is it going to take for me to snap out of it and fall into step around here? I'm certainly no help to Charles and Elizabeth until I do!"

Andrew watched her fling the bedroll into the back of the wagon and turn toward him, impatiently brushing strands of hair out of her scowling face. "Good morning, Miss Sunshine!" he greeted her.

With her hand on top of her head still holding onto unruly hair, she stopped and gave him a big grin.

"I think maybe you're being a little rough on yourself," he said.

Struggling to get a comb through her hair, she responded, "No, I want so badly to not be a burden to them...or anyone else for that matter. I want to help them, but sometimes it seems I don't have much to offer." She hastily stuck pins in her hair then with determination added, "But I'll learn. I'll unlearn these bad habits and learn how to be the best pioneer woman anyone ever saw, all the way from getting up before the sun to learning how to kill, skin, and cook my own buffalo."

A voice behind her asked, "What a woman! Will you marry me?"

She whirled around to see Thomas on one knee, his hat gripped in his hands, and a pleading look in his eyes. Despite herself she laughed then asked, "Is this normal behavior for him?"

"I'm afraid so. You'd better give him an answer; he won't move until you do."

"Sorry, Mr. Cunningham. Not now, not ever."

He stood and slapped his hat against his leg. "Not ever? That's an awful long time, Miss O'Mally."

"You're right, and my answer stays the same."

"Any lady who can kill and skin a buffalo is worth chasin' in my book."

"Well then, she should be safe from you for a long, long time," Andrew said.

The sound of horse hooves turned their attention to see Webster ride up. Glancing uncertainly at him, Megan turned and busied herself getting breakfast utensils out. She had avoided him since their last encounter, which hadn't been difficult because he'd been so busy.

"I need you boys," he growled, glancing briefly at Megan. "Can you tear yourselves away and give me some help?"

"Sure, Nick. What do ya need?"

They both headed toward their wagons and swung themselves onto horses saddled and ready. As soon as they left, Megan took the cover off the spider skillet and scooped out a helping of fried potatoes, bacon, and one last biscuit. She ate quickly and started cleaning up before she saw any of the family.

Charles walked around to the back of the wagon with Ralph trailing behind, dipped his hand into the grease bucket hanging between the back wheels, and started rubbing it sparingly on each wheel and axle. "Have a nice sleep, squirt?"

"Too nice, I'm afraid." Dropping her hands in frustration, she added, "I'm sorry, Charles. I intend to do better, but you're going to have to be a little more persistent waking me up."

Not looking up from his work, he responded, "You probably needed the extra sleep. You've been looking pretty tired the last couple of days. Elizabeth and the girls are down at the river washing out a few clothes. How 'bout you run on down there as soon as you're done here and help out? We'll be pulling out in about an hour."

By the time Megan, Elizabeth, and the girls got back to camp, Charles and Ralph had all the oxen yoked, hitched up, and ready to go. Elizabeth helped Megan string some rope up across the backs of each wagon and hurriedly hung the clothes to dry. "If we stir up much dust, these clothes will be dirtier by the time they're dry than they were when I started. Lucy! Charles, where's Lucy? She was just here. That girl can't stand still for two seconds!" She turned and looked at Megan with exasperation. "Megan, could you go find her? My guess is she's run over to Sanders' wagon to find Rachel and Meggie. We'll be getting started before you know it and I want all three girls sitting right behind me in this wagon where I can see them! With all this confusion and all these different wagon trains all getting ready to leave, I'm scared to death one of them will get herself mixed up with the wrong group of people and we'll never see her again!"

"I'll find her. Hang on to these two while you can." Megan wrapped her arms around the shoulders of Suzanne and Abigail and gave them both a wink before she left.

Over a hundred wagons had gathered under Nick Webster's leadership, but Megan had no trouble finding the Sanders' wagon. They and the McKays were doing their best to stay near the Batten's wagons. Elizabeth had found kindred spirits in Caroline McKay and Rebecca Sanders. The three women helped ease each other's uncertainties about leaving friends and home and striking out for the unknown.

As expected, Lucy had ensconced herself in the back of Sanders' wagon between the Sanders' twins.

"Hi, girls. Going someplace?" Megan asked pleasantly.

Lucy rolled her eyes and gave her a *don't be stupid* look.

"Lucy, you never told your mother you were coming over here."

"Yes, I did. She just didn't hear me."

"Well, she's pretty worried about you, so you better come with me."

"No, I'm riding here with Meggie and Rachel." She stuck her hands out to each side and grabbed the hands of each twin.

Lucy had never defied her before and Megan knew she shouldn't allow it. She braced herself. "Lucy, you are precious to me and I think I'd do almost anything for you, but don't ever, ever again tell me 'no' when I tell you to do something. I'm going back to our wagon and if you don't follow me, it will be your father that comes back to get you."

With that, she turned and walked away, not bothering to look back. Before she was half the distance, she heard Lucy's hurrying steps and short, quick breaths and felt her warm hand slip into hers. Lucy's eyes were on the ground and she was silent, but the hand in hers was Megan's assurance things were all right between them. Lucy was a strong-willed child, but her love for her family was intense. It was that love that kept her in line. Quite a struggle went on in her lively, strong-willed spirit. Trying to get her way in most everything but still wanting the approval of those she loved was an ongoing battle for Lucy, Megan realized.

With the girls tucked safely behind them, Charles and Elizabeth on the seat, Ralph at the reins on the other wagon, and Megan walking beside, they fell in line with the others and began their slow, plodding, creaking way to Oregon.

Megan chose to walk so she could be alone with her thoughts. Unfamiliar and unexpected emotions began to well up inside her, beginning with the first call to fall in and "wagons ho" and growing stronger with each step. What was this, she wondered; this strange excitement and anticipation taking root and growing? Things had been pleasant; the change in her life had been interesting and very welcome. She had been enjoying herself immensely. But this new feeling coursing wildly through her was so unexpected. She wanted to analyze it, pick it apart, be in control of it. If she were a child, had no inhibitions, let her emotions tell her body what to do, she would have whooped and hollered like a five-year-old, running wildly with her arms stretched to heaven and her head thrown back, exulting in it. But she couldn't, so she picked and analyzed away.

*A new beginning. That's it. My whole life is totally changing and these first steps with the train toward our destination represent that change. Some fear, perhaps? No. It's too positive, too wildly exciting to include fear.*

She looked up at Charles and saw an ecstatic smile plastered from ear to ear. He glanced down at her and their eyes locked for a moment, and in that short meeting of eyes, she knew he felt it, too. He winked at her and looked away. And with that, Megan stopped trying to understand and control her feelings. Instead, she let herself simply enjoy them and relish every moment while it lasted.

Early that evening, they pulled into Elm Grove and set up camp. Nick Webster sent messengers to summon all family heads for an organizational meeting.

Megan helped with supper preparations then excused herself to go listen in on the meeting. She made her way through wagons, women, children, cooking fires, and tents to find the men gathered near Webster's wagon. She settled herself down on a box within sight of most of the group, but purposely out of Nick Webster's line of vision.

He had already started the meeting, laying out the law with a firm, businesslike, not-to-be-questioned tone. Andrew had told her Webster had been a sergeant during the early part of the war and then at Ft. Klamath in Oregon. *He certainly sounds like a typical sergeant.* When she was in Independence, she had overheard a group of men talking about the chaos associated with putting a wagon train together, hiring scouts and a wagon master, setting up rules; everyone loudly declaring they know a better way, groups even splitting before they started. Nothing chaotic about the way Nick Webster did the job, she thought cynically. Although she did admit to herself, as ruthless as he seemed, she preferred a strictly run organization over a loosely organized, undisciplined one, especially when that organization included people of questionable character.

"We'll pull out every morning at seven o'clock," Webster's deep, confident voice rang out. "You're each responsible to decide when you need to rouse your families to meet that deadline. Anyone not ready will lose their place in line and will have to move fast to catch up. We won't be responsible for you. We'll stop at noon for an hour to eat and rest. Then stop again at six o'clock for the night.

"All males twelve and older will take their turns throughout the trip rounding up the livestock, keeping them moving and guarding them at night. All males eighteen and older will be put on a rotating schedule for guard duty. These schedules will be posted on my wagon. All interactions with Indians will be through the court and me first. The court," he went on to explain, "is made up of six men I've already chosen. I talked to them earlier and I'd like for them to stand and show their faces when I call their names." Among the names he called were Charles Batten and Stephen Sanders. "Any major disagreements that you can't work out in a civilized manner will go before the court. When I send a matter to the court, their decision is law. I know some of this sounds like you're under martial law. Most of you know this is my third time to lead a wagon train west. I've seen firsthand what happens when there's no discipline. After a while, people will give their right arm to have someone take control, someone they can trust. I've made mistakes that I won't make again. My job is to get you to Oregon safely, in good time and with as much cooperation from you as possible. All my rules are for this purpose. If you don't think you can live with these rules, please leave us now and join up with the next train that comes through." His voice gradually rose, sounding like a sergeant barking out orders to fresh recruits. "If there are any complaints, I want to hear them today, not when we're halfway to Oregon!"

He paused and looked around. Megan heard murmurings and embarrassed laughter, but no one spoke up.

Webster continued, "Most of you have already met Thomas Cunningham. He's our head scout. He'll be choosing some of you to help periodically. This is his brother, Dr. Andrew Cunningham, who will be on duty as our doctor for the entire trip. And Elmer Stone is our cook. These three men will be excused from livestock and guard duty."

Megan shifted her weight and adjusted her skirt. She glanced over at the fire by Webster's wagons and saw a little man that looked like a wrinkled elf with a long bushy gray beard and a round paunch protruding between suspenders. He was puttering around his pot like an artist at work, whistling, dropping in a pinch of this and a spoonful of that, stirring, tasting, savoring, and then talking to himself as he added several pinches of something else from a small crock. That must be Elmer, Megan thought, intrigued by the man's total absorption in his work.

When she turned back to the meeting, the men were drawing slips of paper from a hat. She heard Webster explain that the numbers on the papers determined the order of the wagons. As each man drew a number, Thomas wrote their names beside the corresponding number. When they were done, Thomas handed the list to Nick.

"Tomorrow morning, we will pull out in this order." He read the list beginning with number one and going on to family number ninety-two.

After a dozen or more names were read, Megan reluctantly got up and headed back to help Elizabeth. "Well, it looks like Webster's got things under control."

"Do I sense a touch of sarcasm, little sister?" Elizabeth asked as she replaced the skillet cover.

Megan shrugged and started digging plates and utensils out. "I suppose I'm being unfair, but he sure doesn't leave any room for suggestions."

"I hope you didn't go over there and offer any suggestions."

"Humph! Don't worry. I'm not stupid. I'm making a concentrated effort to not cross that man's path until we reach Oregon!"

Elizabeth stood, wiped her hands on her apron, and studied her sister. "I think you're being too quick to judge the man, Megan," she said quietly.

They both turned when they heard the loud talking and joking of the men as the meeting broke up. Charles and Stephen Sanders came around a wagon smiling and looking quite pleased with things. Rebecca walked away from her fire to join them.

"How did the meeting go, boys?" she asked.

"Great! The man sounds like he knows what he's doing."

"Yeah, he sure does. Gives a man a kinda secure feeling knowing we're in good hands."

Elizabeth grinned and raised her eyebrows at Megan. "I thought you looked pretty happy walking over here," she said.

"Well, that's not all," Charles added. "They drew names for the order of wagons and the Sanders are right in front of us."

Elizabeth and Rebecca exclaimed their pleasure and gave each other a quick hug.

"McKays are only about five or six wagons away and Webster's group is directly behind us."

Megan's body froze and she stared at Charles, hoping she hadn't heard him correctly. Apparently, Elizabeth noticed her reaction. She couldn't keep the twinkle out of her eyes as she gave Megan an exaggerated wink.

"And is this the order we stay in for the duration of the trip?" Elizabeth asked.

"Yep," Charles answered, "it sure is. Unless of course there are unresolvable problems with neighbors. But that won't happen with us."

Megan smiled and continued helping with the meal.

## CHAPTER TEN

As soon as the sun came up the next morning, Megan could tell it would be an unusually hot, humid day. When they broke camp, Thomas held the list and called off names as wagons pulled into line. Megan gathered her nieces and headed for the back before Charles' wagons moved.

By the time the wagons stopped for the noon meal, or the "nooning" as the emigrants called it, Megan was dripping with sweat. For the last two hours, there had been a noticeable decline in the chattering and laughter among those walking behind and beside the train. To save time, the wagons stopped where they were without bothering to pull into a circle. There was little need to protect themselves from Indians here in eastern Kansas.

Megan held onto Lucy and Abby's hands and dragged them over to their wagons. She quickly dug out a rag, dipped it in water, and wiped it over her face, neck, and arms. She helped the girls do the same, greeted Charles, Elizabeth, and Ralph, then poured drinks for them all before she started slicing smoked ham for their meal.

Webster's cook, Elmer, whistled and poked fun at his three "boys," Nick, Andrew, and Thomas, as if he was oblivious to the heat and humidity. Keeping her head down and eyes averted, Megan finished her work, took her meal toward the front of the wagon, plopped down in the grass, and started eating. No sooner had she taken her first bite, than Andrew appeared on her right and Thomas on her left, each settling down beside her. They both gave her a friendly nod before they started shoveling food in.

Megan took a long drink of water and let her head drop back on the wagon wheel. "If this is a typical day, I'm afraid I'm going to be a trifle wilted by the time we get there."

"Typical? Humph!" snorted Thomas through a mouthful of potatoes. "I wouldn't be counting on anything typical if I was you. Just count on gettin' blistered on the sunny days, soaked on the rainy days, and frozen on the snowy days. And when there's thunder and lightning, you can count on chasin' cattle for a few days."

While Thomas rattled on, Megan noticed Andrew's eyes on her. "It is unusually hot, especially for walking in the sun all day. Make sure you and the girls drink plenty of water, and if any of you get dizzy or weak, you'd better go on up and ride in the wagon for a while. In fact, judging by the way you look now, it wouldn't be a bad idea to start this afternoon in the wagon."

Thomas chuckled. "So, how do you like having your own personal doctor?"

Megan smiled and looked fondly at Andrew. "I like it and I think I'll take his advice. I need to save my strength for all those days of getting blistered, soaked, frozen, and having to chase down cattle."

"Humph!" Thomas snorted again and grinned. "I like your pluck, Miss O'Mally."

"According to Nick, our campsite tonight is right next to a creek that has a fresh spring pouring into it. Sounds like that'll be nice for cooling off in after a day like today," Andrew said.

Thomas threw his head back and twisted his mouth into a thoughtful grimace. "Yeah...yeah, I remember that place; has a spring pouring right out of the side of a cliff. A few of us went swimming in our birthday suits after dark if I remember correct."

Megan cleared her throat, wiped the crumbs off her skirt, and stood to go. "I'll remember to ask Charles to park our wagons a good distance away, then."

"No need to worry none, ma'am. There won't be any of that tonight 'cuz of the full moon."

"Well, I'm truly relieved. Good day, gentlemen. I need to help Elizabeth clean up." She nodded at Andrew who smiled sheepishly and gave her an apologetic shrug. Megan heard him chide his brother for his crudeness as soon as she was out of sight.

Charles and Elizabeth appeared to be in deep conversation with Webster and an older couple Megan had not yet met. The girls had gone off to join the McKay and Sanders' children. Although Suzanne was only twelve, Michelle McKay and Sarah Sanders, both fourteen, treated her like an equal. Lucy and the Sanders' twins were tormenting Todd and Abe McKay, ages twelve and ten, simply by following them around and talking incessantly. And Abby had found willing playmates in six-year-old Stephen Sanders and five-year-old Amanda McKay.

With a strong sense of pleasure, Megan let her eyes roam over the various groups of children and listened to their talk and giggles. She sighed contentedly, turned back to her work, and found Nick Webster's eyes fixed on her as if he'd been studying her for a while. Her eyes locked with his steel-gray ones for just a moment and then he looked calmly away. Heart pounding, she quickly went to work, berating herself for her reaction to him. Taking a knife, she scraped thin flakes of soap into a pan of lukewarm water,

worked it into suds, and started gathering plates and
utensils to add to it. The more she railed at herself, the
harder and faster she worked. A voice behind her caused
her to jump and turn.

"Megan, I'm sorry about my brother. I didn't realize
how upset he made you."

Andrew stood there looking so sorry Megan couldn't
help but smile. "Oh, Andrew, believe me, it's alright. I'm
not upset about that. I just didn't want to stay around and
encourage him, that's all."

"Well, I've given him a good chewing out. He can be
rather crude at times, but he doesn't mean any disrespect
toward you. He hasn't been around many civilized folks in
a long time."

"It seems he and his partner have the same problem."

Andrew looked confused. "Who, Nick? Naw, Nick's not
the same. In the first place, he's been around a lot more
than my brother. Thomas stayed on their claim up in
Oregon for several years while Nick was in the Army."

"Oh, yes, the Army's been known for its cultural
influence."

Andrew studied her for a minute. "You have a case
against that man, don't you?"

Megan's chin rose a notch. "Not really. I just find him to
be a very rude and cold individual."

"I think what you're seeing is a man with a military
background who's taking his job very seriously. He's dealt
with some problems on the other trains he's been on and
he's just making sure he doesn't make some of the same
mistakes on this trip." He rubbed the back of his neck and
paused. "He's also had one painful experience that I think
figures pretty heavily into how he treats some people. If
you want to understand the man, I'll take the time someday
to tell you about it."

"No, that won't be necessary. There's no need for me to
know." She forced a quick smile and went back to her

work.

"Megan," Andrew said quietly, "whatever you have against Nick, I hope you can get over it. I think I have more respect for him than any man I know."

Megan soon discovered she couldn't escape the heat riding in the wagon and that walking was far more relaxing than bouncing around. The afternoon sun was almost unbearable. She longed for even a hint of a breeze. Finally, she went to the wagon Ralph was driving, grabbed onto the back, and swung herself up inside. She dug out four rags, found their canteen, and filled it with water. Pouring enough water on the rags to thoroughly soak them, she jumped out and headed back to the girls. They all drank greedily then laid the rags on top of their heads, letting the water drip down their faces. Suzanne and Abby closed their eyes and stuck their tongues out to catch the drops. Lucy tipped her head all the way back until her face, draped with the wet rag, was almost parallel to the ground. She staggered along, groping with arms outstretched so she wouldn't bump into anyone. Megan directed her into the path of Todd McKay, who had his face turned to talk to his brother. They collided and fell in a heap on the grass. Meggie Sanders shrieked with glee and threw herself on the pile. The squeals of laughter drew people like a magnet. Children and many adults were bored and ready for some fun. Before Megan could stop her, Lucy snatched up her wet rag and started slapping the other children across their heads and running away, daring them to come after her. Todd reached over and grabbed Abby's rag and took off after Lucy. Soon it was a free-for-all, people trying to steal rags and chasing each other, little girls screaming as if they were about to be scalped, but running back into the thick of the game. Most of the adults just watched and laughed.

It wasn't long before they heard a horse and rider approaching fast. Megan looked up to see Webster reining his horse to a stop next to three women who were enjoying watching the game. Although she couldn't catch all his words, she could clearly detect a tone of concern. She could see the women gesture and hear them laugh as they explained the noise and screams that brought Webster over in such alarm. Then he looked directly at her as one woman pointed her direction and laughed again. He smiled, tipped his hat to the women, and walked his horse slowly toward the group Megan was walking with.

When he reached them, he turned his horse and fell into step, striking up a pleasant conversation with two middle-aged women. One of the two had a ruddy, smiling face and was very talkative. Mopping at her face and neck with her handkerchief, she asked good-naturedly why Webster didn't order better weather for them. Megan heard him tell her she'd enjoy their campsite that night and that he thought they'd get there a little earlier than expected. Glancing over at him, she found his eyes glued on her, so she quickly looked straight ahead and kept up her pace. For the next several minutes, he continued to greet different people until he had worked his way unobtrusively through the group to Megan's side. She continued to walk with her eyes forward until he greeted her.

"And how's your day going, Miss O'Mally?"

"Oh." She looked up with a smile, trying to muster up some confidence. "I'm fine, thank you."

"Are you finding things a little monotonous for your tastes?"

"Not at all! Other than being too hot, I find everything quite fascinating."

"Oh? According to what I've been hearing, you've been busy livening things up back here."

She laughed guiltily and looked at him. "That wasn't planned, you know."

He smiled down at her, the first sign of warmth she'd seen in him. "I don't have any problem with a little fun," his rich, deep voice reassured her. "Heaven knows people are going to need some before this trip is over. Just as long as it's coupled with common sense." He nodded in her direction and nudged his horse into a trot toward the wagons.

Three hours later, they pulled into a loose circle about three wagons deep. As soon as the oxen were settled and jangling yokes and harnesses were removed, Megan could hear the bubbling and splashing of the spring. She heard Thomas hollering orders for the livestock to be watered downstream, loudly emphasizing the word "downstream" until some of the older boys started mimicking him. Megan glanced in his direction and saw a good-natured grin in place. Despite her earlier opinion, she was growing to like this crude man. She suspected he was intentionally rough-mannered merely to amuse himself.

As always, meal preparations claimed their attention first. Elizabeth sent her two oldest down to the creek to get water while she and Megan gathered wood for the fire. Charles and Ralph led the six teams of oxen down to the creek before they turned them out to graze.

Andrew and Thomas joined them again for their meal. All five Battens, Ralph, Megan, and their two guests sat cozily in a circle listening to the men swap yarns, especially Thomas. No one could quite beat him at weaving a tale that kept his audience's rapt attention. Megan took her eyes off him for a second to look over at Webster eating his meal with his foot propped up on his wagon wheel and nodding at something Elmer was saying. He sauntered over to join them about the time Elizabeth and Megan stood to start cleaning up.

"Megan, why don't I stay here and take care of this mess and you take some clothes on down to the creek to wash? And bring back a bucket of clean water if you can. Take Lucy with you to help," Elizabeth said.

"Can I get wet, Ma?" Lucy begged, running over to her with hands clasped tightly under her chin.

"Me, too, Ma? Me, too?" Abby danced up and down, eyes sparkling.

"Well, I'm not surprised to hear you asking. It's certainly too hot for a body to bear very long." She pressed her lips together and studied them for a minute. "I suppose so. Just be sure it's downstream from people drawing water; and only to your knees! And take your boots and stockings off first."

Starved for family life, the three guests watched the girls and their mother with smiles. Megan stepped close to her sister and said quietly, "Me, too, Ma? Me, too?"

Elizabeth answered with a grin, "Do what you must, but please don't forget to bring me back a pail of good clean water. Get it close to that spring if you can," handing her a bucket and giving her a playful shove.

Despite the heat, the afternoon was pleasant, with the buzzing insects and silvery warbling of the birds. Megan saw two red-winged blackbirds calling to each other from the tops of black willow trees which lined the bubbling stream. A red-tailed hawk circled overhead screeching at an unseen mate.

By the time she got to the creek, the bank was crowded with people washing clothes, soaking tired feet, and playfully splashing one another. Lucy and Abby spied Meggie and Rachel already in the water up to their calves, so they started peeling boots and stockings off and throwing them carelessly in the grass. Megan gathered them and piled them neatly at the base of a tree then stood to inspect the scene. Two older boys had escalated the play by dumping buckets of water on each other. It wasn't long before more boys and a few men joined them.

Megan leaned down to scoop water into her cupped hands. She splashed it over her hot face and neck. *Oh, it feels so good.* Standing, she stretched and closed her eyes to the glare of the sun. She was tempted to go wading with the girls. Instead, she grabbed the soap and bent to scrub a shirt from the small pile of clothes. After she washed, rinsed, and shook out all the clothes, she took them up to the wagon to hang, then headed back down to the creek with the bucket.

At the edge of the creek, a young man, George Hawkins, who had spoken to Megan a few times, cupped his hand and hit the water sending a cascade of water over her. She drew her breath in sharply and suppressed a scream. Before he had a chance to defend himself, she skimmed her bucket across the water and sent it into his face, then picked up her skirts and ran laughing toward the wagons. When she turned to look back, he was gone but she saw someone else running toward her with a bucket. She managed to jump to the side in time to avoid getting thoroughly soaked.

Down at the creek, it had turned into a free-for-all. Turning to check on the girls, she was hit square in the face by a wall of water that took her breath away. Sputtering and wiping her eyes, she vowed she'd even the score before she quit, so she watched her assailant out of the corner of her eye while she nonchalantly went to the bank and filled her bucket. Moving slowly away from the bigger battle in the middle of the creek, she put two portly gentlemen between her and her target. He lost sight of her and made his way back to the creek to load up on ammunition again.

Megan was very careful to keep out of his sight. The two men she hid behind moved up the hill, so she quickly took cover behind a tree and cautiously peered around it to see her target walking slowly toward his wagon. This was going to be easy, she thought. She had the cover of several wagons as she closed in on her prey, but just before she got close enough to hit him, someone called out a warning and he turned and heaved his bucket at her. Water ran down her face and hair and weighted her skirts down so they clung to her legs, but she managed to take two labored steps toward him and hurl a gallon straight past him into the face of an elderly woman standing at the back entrance of her wagon. The unexpected force of the water knocked her backward against the wagon.

Before Megan realized what she'd done, a big hand seized her upper arm and roughly turned her around. She looked up to see Webster's face livid with rage. He glared at the dripping young man and bellowed, "That's enough! Go on back to your wagon." Without releasing his hold, he scowled at her and gave her a quick shake, his eyes hard and severe.

"Where's your common sense?" he growled.

Megan just stared back, too dumbstruck to answer. She opened her mouth but nothing came out. She could see the muscles in his jaw working.

Webster's expression didn't change. "I want you to meet someone." He turned her to face a very wet older woman with a look of tender compassion on her face and a wiry old man handing her towels and fretting over her.

"Joe and Maude, I want you to meet Miss Megan O'Mally. And Miss O'Mally, I'd like you to meet Mr. and Mrs. Davis. They'll be your neighbors for this trip. They're very dear people to me."

Megan recognized them for the first time as the older couple she had seen with Webster earlier. She stood speechless for only a moment longer as she took in the damage she had done. Her hands flew to her cheeks in shame.

"Oh! Oh, I'm so sorry! What have I done?"

Webster finally let go of her arm and walked over to look into the back of the wagon. "Looks like you managed to get quite a bit of water in here, too. This sack of flour is soaked." He picked it up and raised his eyes to meet Megan's. "Looks like it needs drying out in here."

Maude Davis put a hand out and touched Webster's arm. "It's all right, Nick. We can take care of it."

"I think Miss O'Mally needs to spend some time with you, mopping up the inside of your wagon." He looked at Megan. "I'm leaving you here with Maude. I'll talk to you later this evening about this incident." He nodded at her and stalked away.

Megan watched him go then turned back to face the Davises. She shook her head slowly. "I'm so ashamed... I...I don't know what to say."

Maude simply reached out with both hands and said, "Megan, come here," with such tenderness, Megan found herself irresistibly drawn to the woman. She placed her hands in Maude's and looked into forgiving, understanding eyes.

"Don't mind Nick. He's havin' a hard time of it right now, I think. And lands! He's been so protective of me since his ma died, I think I'm gonna suffocate! But bless his soul, he means well. It almost breaks my heart to watch him sometimes." She clasped Megan's hands tighter. "And don't you worry none about this water. I know you was just playing. There's no harm done." She glanced at her husband, eyes twinkling. "Why you know, I believe I'm feeling a whole lot better now that I'm wet. If you have any more water in that bucket, I bet Joe would be obliged if you'd dump some of it on him."

Joe chuckled and held up his hands, eyes dancing at the two of them.

Megan grinned but couldn't hide the tears that had started as soon as she looked into Maude's kind face and heard the mothering tone directed at her. She realized in an instant how starved she was for this kind of attention. No wonder Webster was so protective of her. In that instant, she thought she'd kill for this woman.

She shook her head, released her hands, and wiped them across her eyes. "No, that's very kind of you. But it was wrong of me to do this; and so stupid and careless. I'm so sorry. You've got to at least let me clean the water out of your wagon. And I'll buy more flour at the next town."

Maude started to protest, but Megan grabbed her hands and held them, firmly but gently. "No, you have to let me do something. I feel so bad about this. Mr. Webster was perfectly justified in what he said. Besides that, how do you think I could ever face him if you let me off so easy?"

Maude and Joe faced each other and nodded in agreement. "Well," Joe drawled slowly. "Here's the towel."

Megan accepted it and went to work mopping up water from the floor of their wagon. She found two other sacks of flour that were soaked through. When she was finished, she brought them out and presented them to Maude. When she offered to replace these, also, Maude put a hand out in protest.

"Megan, dear, believe me when I tell you we had more than we needed. There's just the two of us and we really don't eat that much."

"It doesn't matter. I owe it to you and I will make it up to you," Megan said with a stubborn tilt to her chin.

Maude sat back with a chuckle and threw her hands up in surrender. She sat shaking her head and pondering for a moment. "You know, Megan. Where would we be with the Lord if we took that kind of attitude with Him?"

"What kind of attitude?" Megan asked with a hint of concern in her tone.

"Oh, thinking we have to pay off all our debts even when we're told by the one we owe it to that it's all taken care of."

"Well, I've been taught all my life that's the honorable thing to do."

"Oh, it is, it is." Maude reached over and patted Megan's arm. "And I do respect that in you. But I also would have respected you taking me up on my offer, 'cause it was sincerely meant. I was just wondering how God must feel when He offers to take care of our debts and we refuse Him. He must feel mighty frustrated, especially when it's such a big offer for such a big debt."

Megan stared, trying to grasp the full meaning of what Maude was saying. The older lady was leaning back in a rocking chair they kept handy at the back of the wagon. She leaned way back and looked up at the stars that were just beginning to show. Her plump face had wrinkles in all the right places, Megan thought, a face that has done more than its share of smiling for a lifetime. She fought the urge to sit at her feet and just pass the evening away, but she knew there would be plenty of time for that later.

"I need to go now, Mrs. Davis. My sister probably needs me. In fact, I still haven't fetched the water she asked me to get." She laughed and rolled her eyes. "I'll come back and check on you this evening."

Maude caught her hand as she got up to go. "Megan, you call me Maude now, you hear? None of this 'Mrs.' business from you. You're going to be like a daughter to me on this trip, I'm thinking. Nick's my boy and now I've got me a girl." She chuckled pleasantly and gave Megan's hand a friendly squeeze before she let go.

Later that evening when Megan walked over to see Maude, she rounded the corner of their wagon to find Webster and Andrew standing on either side of her, still sitting in her rocking chair. They had obviously been discussing something funny judging from the smiles they all wore. Webster's was the only smile that faded when Megan appeared. He cleared his throat and gestured for her to follow him, but before he could speak, Maude reached her hands out to welcome her.

"Well, look who's come to see me. And looks to me you've finally got out of those wet clothes you had on." Her whole face crinkled a smile up at Megan as she squeezed her hands in welcome. "Well, dear, did you finally get that water for Elizabeth?"

Megan smiled and nodded. "Yes. I even went down to get it in my wet clothes in case someone decided to dump water on me again."

"Your sister is a jewel, just like you. I'm so happy you're our neighbors. Nick, I don't know why you didn't introduce her to me before." She glanced up at him with mock accusation. "Shame on you. I'm glad she came over here and threw water all over me if that's what it takes to get an introduction."

Nick didn't smile but his eyes danced with amusement. He raised his eyebrows at Maude as if to say, "I know what you're up to."

"You'll have to let her go for a minute or two, Maude. I still need to talk with her."

"Oh, there's plenty of time for that later. Why don't you men just go on and do what you have to do and leave us women alone so we can chat for a while. Did I tell you, I'm adopting this girl for my new daughter?" She glanced up at Nick again. "And you're my boy, you know, so I guess that makes you two almost brother and sister." She chuckled and looked from one to the other. "Well, how about that?"

Megan had to look at the ground to hide her smile.

"Run along now, boys," Maude continued. "We've got things to talk about."

"Maude, that's enough," Webster growled good-naturedly. "Megan's coming with me now. I'll send her back to you when I'm finished with our little talk."

Megan looked up quickly at him, surprised and strangely touched by the use of her first name. Somehow, watching him with Maude, she no longer saw him as a harsh, insensitive brute.

Maude gave Megan's hands another squeeze. "You be nice now. You hear, Nick?"

Nick sent her a warning look as he walked away. "I

promise I won't hurt her too bad. Andrew, go get the horsewhip out of my wagon."

Maude sat back and snorted. "Go on, Megan. He wouldn't hurt a flea. Goodness gracious! Those boys! Maybe I'll just get me a whip to use on them when they start bullying little girls!"

Megan followed Nick who had already disappeared around the corner of his wagon. She found him standing beside a rugged, beat-up, old chair tucked under a small table that was hinged neatly to the side of his wagon. It wasn't very many days ago, she thought, since she'd sat at that same table and registered her cow. The same table she had leaned over to stare Webster down just so she could keep her gun. A lot of good that did her. That same ruthless, stubborn man stood before her rubbing his hands over his face. When he saw her, he dropped his hands, smiled, and shook his head.

"I love that dear woman, but she sure does exasperate me sometimes." Quickly his expression sobered and he motioned for her to sit on a stool at the table opposite his chair. "Have a seat," he ordered.

She sat down timidly, not sure what to expect from him this time. He settled his large frame on his chair, ran his hands over his face again, then leveled a steady gaze at her.

"Miss O'Mally," he began then rubbed his thumb back and forth over his chin thoughtfully, making a rasping noise. "What I saw you do today... Do I have any reason to expect more of the same impulsive, foolhardy behavior from you?" He paused and waited.

Megan cleared her throat and offered an answer. "Well, I can promise I'll never throw water on Maude again."

Grinning and leaning back in his chair, he folded his arms across his chest and squinted at her out of the corner of his eyes. "I think you know what I'm looking for."

"I am truly sorry for what I did today. It was careless and stupid and I deserved everything you said to me. I'll try to use more common sense from now on," Megan answered with sincerity.

He raised his eyebrows. "Well, this is an unexpected surprise. That's not exactly what I expected from you." He stood, turned his back on her, and started pacing slowly. When he walked back to where Megan was sitting, he stopped and fixed his eyes on hers.

"Did you dry out her wagon?"

"Yes, sir."

"Did you offer to replace her spoiled food?"

"Yes, sir, I did."

"And will you?"

Insulted, she stood and glared at him. "Of course, I will! What kind of person do you take me for?"

He smiled and turned away. "I'm sorry," he muttered. Turning, he repeated his apology, more clearly this time, "I'm sorry, Miss O'Mally. That was uncalled for. Forgive me, please."

Megan nodded and said softly, "You're forgiven."

Nick cleared his throat. "Uh…that's all. You may go now."

Relieved it was over, she turned to leave but stopped when Nick spoke again.

"One more thing. Do me a favor and limp when you walk past Maude."

# CHAPTER ELEVEN

For the next one and a half weeks, the train wound its way through northeast Kansas toward Nebraska. They passed Lawrence, a town of 5000, and came to Blue Mound, a small mountain significantly higher than the rolling, grass-covered hills surrounding them. Several people, including Megan, Thomas, Andrew, and the girls walked to the top to look out over the panorama.

At the top, George Hawkins introduced Megan to his sister, Jessica. Panting hard from the climb, Jessica was barely able to greet them, much less to carry on a conversation, but she tried. About Megan's height and twice as wide, she had a pleasant, friendly face and hair hanging to her waist. The two Hawkins accompanied them back down the steep hill, Jessica gasping for breath and talking all the way. But she was interesting and Megan liked being with her.

Late the next day, they reached the Kansas River near Topeka, the new state capital. They crossed the river the next morning by ferry at a dollar per wagon. Megan and

Elizabeth clung to the three girls as they looked down into the angry, swollen river and thanked God for ferries.

The next river crossing was by bridge at the Red Vermilion River but still cost each wagon a dollar, charged by the builder and owner of the bridge. Webster called the train to a halt for the night earlier than usual so the livestock could take advantage of the plentiful grazing nearby. Already the men were finding it necessary to guide the herd quite a distance away from the trail to find enough good grass. Several large herds had already passed through the area ahead of them.

They continued on past Alcove Springs, where the grass was green and high and wildflowers bloomed in profusion. Megan had organized her little school, so she walked with the younger children in the morning and with those over twelve after the noon meal. At Alcove Spring, she had them collect flowers, and as they walked, they took turns using Megan's book to identify the different species. The children loved the diversion of school, and several others joined the Batten, McKay, and Sanders' children. Megan carried a slate board and chalk with her in the morning and had her young students take turns practicing writing and spelling. She used a couple of reading texts both morning and afternoon, and the children walked in a tight cluster listening to each other read and discuss the text.

A few older boys joined them but seemed more interested in talking with Megan than doing the lessons. One of these was George Hawkins, Jessica's brother, who Megan was sure was at least twenty years old. He could only join them occasionally when he wasn't driving their wagon or herding, and he was never a distraction. Joe Purdy and Bill McCullough presented a different problem though. They were loud and rude and showed no interest in the lessons. On the days they joined the students, Megan got very little accomplished. Fortunately those days were few.

On the day they crossed the Kansas-Nebraska border and pulled into the Rock Creek Station, both young men were free to follow Megan's class. In the morning, she politely but firmly let them know she was working only with the younger ones.

Joe Purdy laughed and slapped his companion on the back. "That's fine with us. We'll just walk back here behind you. The view's great back here, ain't it, Bill?"

"Yeah, we don't mind. Besides, we'll be back for the big boys' class later today," Bill loudly guffawed, digging his elbow into Joe's side as if he was impressed with his own cleverness.

Megan rolled her eyes and tried to concentrate on her few students in spite of the continuous heckling from behind. By noon, she was so angry she had tears in her eyes when she joined Elizabeth at the wagon.

At noon and in the evening, Webster had the wagons pull into small circles of eight wagons each, called "messes," which in turn were arranged in one large circle. The Batten's two wagons were in the mess with the two wagons of Webster's crew, Joe and Maude's wagon, the Sanders, the Simmons, and a quiet German family by the name of Schultz.

Megan realized she was doing a poor job of hiding her anger. She worked silently and quickly, answering only in monosyllables when spoken to. When the meal was ready, she settled herself between Maude and Andrew and looked around at her friends.

Since the beginning of their journey, Andrew and Thomas had joined them for meals, with Nick, Elmer, the Davises, and Sanders occasionally joining them around the fire later in the evening. Within a week, Nick, Elmer, Joe, and Maude were there for every meal, carrying their chairs and food over. The sense of family was strong and growing more so daily.

"Well, Megan, out with it," Charles said. "Something

happen in your school to get you all stewed up this morning?"

Her fist pounded on the arm of Maude's chair, who in turn jumped, almost spilling her plate on her lap. "I'm so mad I could scream!" she exclaimed, standing and pacing back and forth in the small circle of attentive listeners. "I think I'll strangle them both. If this was the first time, I'd be a little patient, but it's not, and every time they're worse!"

"Let me know before you do any strangling," said Thomas, stretched out on the grass, obviously enjoying Megan's display. "I want to be sure I'm there to watch."

"Who is this you're talking about, Megan?" Nick asked, his eyes searching her face.

"Joe Purdy and Bill McCullough," she answered through clenched teeth.

"Purdy and McCullough?" Nick's eyes narrowed. "What in tarnation are those two doing hanging around your class? They're too old, by a long shot."

"I'll give you three guesses what they're doing," answered Thomas, sitting up straight and no longer amused. "I figured those two would be trouble the first time I laid eyes on 'em. How about Andrew and me go over there and sneak up on 'em from behind?"

Nick gave him a quick warning glance then turned to Megan. "What are they doing, Megan?"

"Oh, they poke fun at the children and at me, they tickle the backs of their necks with grass, they used one little girl's pigtails and pretended they were horse's reins, and they won't leave when I ask them to. They say they have as much right to walk there as we do. And," she added, "they've come up, grabbed my hand, and told me to take a little walk with them. They said they'd show me a better time than that pack of kids would." Megan's anger was suddenly subdued when she saw the look in Nick's eyes.

Thomas sprang to his feet and handed his dirty plate to

Elmer. "Say no more, my damsel in distress. You'll not be seeing those two again on this trip."

Elmer chuckled loudly, his bristly whiskers working up and down. "Why, I recall hearing you say somethin' pretty close to that to this same damsel just a couple days ago, Tommy boy."

Thomas stopped in his tracks and glared. "That's different! That's entirely different! Don't even think about comparing me to those two pea-brained louts. I wouldn't trust them around my grandmother. And besides that, Megan knows I'm not serious." He stopped, thought a second about what he'd said, then turned quickly to Megan with a red face and grabbed her hand. "I'm not serious 'cuz she don't take me serious. Will you marry me, Megan?" he asked, looking down at her.

"No."

"There! See? She don't take me serious. If she'd have me, I'd marry this girl so fast you'd all be dizzy. That would put a quick stop to all these unattached men on this train with their tongues hangin' out."

Andrew cleared his throat loudly and nodded toward the women when Thomas looked at him.

"Oh! Sorry, ladies. I keep forgettin'. But it's true and you all know it. There's close to twice as many men on this train as there are women. You get an unmarried woman on a train and there's trouble. Especially when she's as pretty as Megan, here. We had two men almost kill each other over a woman on the last train, and they weren't the only ones makin' fools of themselves. The whole trip, it was one thing after another. That's why Nick didn't want to take Megan with us."

Megan drew her breath in and spun around to look at Nick. An awkward silence followed as Nick stared ominously at Thomas.

Thomas looked down and quietly said, "I'm sorry, Nick." He turned to Megan who continued to look at Nick.

"Megan, it was before he knew you."

Megan turned to Charles and Elizabeth. "Did you know he didn't want me?"

"Megan," Charles tried to explain, "he was trying to do what he thought was best for the whole train. We did talk about it and he decided to let you come as long as I'd be responsible for you."

She raised her eyebrows and in a hurt tone said, "Oh." Then with lifted chin, she turned back to Nick and said, "I'm sorry if I'm a problem for you. I don't mean to be."

His steel-gray eyes had a hint of a warning in them as he answered, "I know you don't mean to be a problem. Any trouble I've had with you so far has been pretty minor compared with some of the things I've had to deal with."

"Seems to me," Megan went on with a haughty tone, "it's the men that are the problem, not the women."

"That's true to a point," he answered patiently, leaning against his wagon and folding his arms across his chest. "It's certainly no fault of the woman that she's unattached or attractive to men."

"That's true," Thomas added, "but a couple of those women on that last train sure did a heap of encouraging."

"And is that the way you see me?" She directed her question at Nick.

"No, not at all," he answered softly. "In fact, I find you to be quite the opposite." For just a moment, his eyes held hers in a tender gaze that drained her of her haughtiness.

They were interrupted by a snort from Thomas. "Ain't that the truth, now."

"What about those two characters, Nick?" Andrew asked, walking over to stand next to Megan. "What are we going to do?"

"I won't have any trouble taking care of them," Thomas said.

"I don't want any fighting, Tom, you know that," Nick answered.

"I can't think of anything that would work any better."

Megan looked from one to the other with concern. "No! Please! I'm sorry. I didn't mean to cause a problem. It's not that bad," she said. "I...I think I can handle them myself."

Nick pulled his watch out and looked at it. "It's time to pull out." He and the others moved to go. Elizabeth and Suzanne were already packing hastily washed dishes in the side box.

"Wait!" Megan called out to Nick's back. He and Thomas were throwing saddles on their horses and Andrew and Charles were hitching their teams up to the wagon. Megan marched over to Nick and put her hand on his arm to stop him. "Aren't you listening to me? I said I think I can handle them myself."

Nick finished tightening the cinch and turned to look down at her, resting a hand on the saddle horn. "Sorry, Megan. I didn't mean to ignore you. You're not causing the problem and it can easily be taken care of."

Thomas had mounted and eased his horse over to them. Megan nodded her head toward him. "Are you going to let him fight them?"

"No, he's not gonna be doing any fighting," Nick answered, looking at Thomas to make sure he heard. "I'll take care of it. A few well-chosen words will do the trick." He turned and swung up into the saddle. "You just carry on with your school the best you can and try to ignore them. I'll be over after a while to see what's going on."

Megan was never sure what Nick said to Bill McCullough and Joe Purdy, but it sent them ambling sheepishly away. Megan sent a quick smile of gratitude to Nick who simply tipped his hat and rode off.

Late that afternoon they pulled into a field next to Rock Creek Station. Always hungry for any sign of civilization, most people on a wagon train would take advantage of every opportunity they had to visit every town and settlement on their way to Oregon. In 1865, there were considerably more settlements along the Oregon Trail than there were in the early days of the trail.

"We're close enough to town that I think you could easily walk there," Megan overheard Nick telling Maude.

"You can walk with Elizabeth and me, if you'd like," Megan offered.

"Ooo, that would be delightful, dear." Maude reached out to cradle Megan's hand in hers.

When the meal was finished, Megan walked with Elizabeth and Maude to the trading post, Megan's first escape from the train since they had started. She walked slowly and marveled at everything. Never had Megan met anyone who enjoyed life as much as Maude. Joy oozed from every pore. Although, she thought, Elizabeth didn't have far to go to match her. She couldn't think of any two women she'd rather be with. Her sister almost frustrated her at times with her incredible patience. She couldn't understand it. Megan knew she was too quick to fight, too quick to challenge anyone or any situation that didn't conform to her ideas. She thought back to her confrontation with Nick at noon. She knew she could have handled that better than she did. She remembered the sympathetic look on Elizabeth's face when she challenged Nick. If she could only learn to take life like Elizabeth and Maude did, everything would be so much easier.

They were disappointed at the lack of food supplies at the trading post. The man behind the counter apologized. "I expected a shipment of flour and other food with the last stage, but they didn't have it. There should be another stage in day after tomorrow." A bullet of chewing tobacco flew from the side of his mouth and hit a spittoon by the stove with a loud *ping*.

Just as they were about to leave, the door swung open on squeaky hinges and Nick, Andrew, and Charles walked in. "Ladies," they greeted them, briefly lifting their hats.

"What are you three up to?" Charles asked.

"Just gettin' out to enjoy this beautiful place," Maude answered. "Did you come through the field and see all those flowers, boys? They just about took my breath away."

"Well, we went through the field, but I don't recall the flowers. Sorry, Maude," Andrew said.

"I came so I could buy a couple of sacks of flour for Maude to replace the ones I ruined," Megan said, "but what they have looks pretty sad."

"If she can wait a week, you'd be better off buying some at Ft. Kearney. They've got plenty of good supplies," Nick said. He looked over at the storekeeper. "I do need a good blacksmith though. Can you recommend anyone?"

"Yer lookin' at the only one. I'd be happy to help." Out came another bullet of tobacco juice. *Ping.*

Elizabeth walked back with Charles, leaving Megan alone with Maude. The sun was setting, and cool, gentle breezes were beginning to stir. Maude reached over and clasped Megan's hand for a moment. "Megan, dear, why haven't you been coming to the services in the evenings?"

Megan swallowed a lump and tried to come up with a satisfactory answer. "Uh...I've been to some, earlier in the trip. It just seems like there's so much to do in the evening now that I have my classes."

Maude's eyes had a tender, knowing look in them. "Honey, the last thing I want is to make you feel guilty. Don't you think by now you can tell me how you feel without worrying about what I think of you?"

Megan stared at the grass, grabbing at her skirt as she tromped over it. "I'm not sure I even know how I feel." She fumbled for words. "I used to like church. I tried going to listen a few times, but I..." She shrugged. "I couldn't seem to make myself go back. I'm not sure why."

"Elizabeth tells me you were raised by very strong Christian parents."

"That's true. We were. Our Pa would make us all sit

down every evening for Bible reading and prayer. And we never missed church on Sunday."

"Did they ever teach you the importance of taking all that Bible learning and making it yours? Making that one most important decision to ask the Lord to be your own personal Savior, not just *the* Savior, but *your* Savior?"

Megan looked at her thoughtfully. "Yes. Yes, as a matter of fact they did. I wasn't very old, but I remember kneeling by my ma's chair crying my eyes out because I wanted Jesus to come into my heart."

Maude's eyes crinkled merrily and a tear slid down her cheek. "And did he?"

"Oh my, yes! Did he ever!"

"And what's different now?"

"That was a long time ago, Maude," she answered sadly.

"Well, He hasn't changed and His love for you hasn't changed."

"I guess that's your answer, then, Maude. Must be I'm the one that's changed." She walked and thought for a moment. "It's so much easier when you're a child. Nothing stands in your way."

Two horses came running toward them from behind, the sound of their hooves muffled by the tall grass. The women turned to see Andrew and Nick pull up beside them.

"Somehow, I can't quite feel right about being on this horse while these two ladies are walking," Andrew said as they dismounted to walk with them.

"Nonsense!" Maude exclaimed. "Besides, we're almost there. I don't think you boys are capable of enjoying a good walk as much as we women anyway."

"You're probably right, Maude," Nick said, putting his long, muscled arm around her plump shoulders. "Aren't you getting a little tired?"

"No, heavens, I haven't even noticed. Megan and I have been having such a good talk."

"Why don't you boys go on and be about your business.

We've only a short way to go and I'll be just fine, Nick."
She patted his arm fondly.

When they'd ridden away, Megan pointed at them.
"What about those two?"

"What do you mean?"

"Do they go listen to the preaching? I know Thomas
doesn't. He told me he stays as far away as he can get."

Maude sighed heavily. "Yes, Thomas turned his back on
God when he was a boy. I was hoping all these years with
Nick would change him. I supposed it kept him from
getting worse," she chuckled.

"So, Nick knows God?"

Maude looked at Megan with shining eyes. "My, yes.
He's a real man of God. He wasn't when he left home the
first time. He was a pretty bitter man back then. Something
happened out in California that changed him though. First
time I saw him when he came back, I could see the change
in his eyes."

"Well, I have trouble seeing it," Megan mumbled and
kept her eyes averted.

Maude tenderly responded. "Just because a person is
God's child doesn't mean they don't make mistakes."
When Megan didn't say anything, she went on, "There's a
lot of things that influence the way Nick acts. Being in the
military was one thing and you've heard the boys mention
some of the bad experiences they had on that one wagon
train. But has anyone told you about the girl he almost
married?"

Megan's head shot up. "No."

"That probably has a lot to do with how he treats you."
Maude's eyes twinkled. "Why are you giving me that
puzzled frown? Most other people would have no trouble
recognizing him as a man of God. Even Elizabeth
commented to me the other day about how good she feels
having such a strong Christian man be in charge of the
train. You and Nick though." She shook her head in

bewilderment. "You and Nick have had trouble since the day you met."

Megan stared at Maude, waiting for more, but Maude just looked straight ahead with a faint smile on her lips.

"Sometimes I think he hates me and he only pretends to like me when we're with everyone else."

"Oh, Megan, don't think that," Maude said. "I know that's not true. If you could only see the look he has in his eyes when..." She stopped herself. "Never mind. Just don't let yourself think he hates you. In fact, he thinks very highly of you. Would you like to hear the story of the girl he almost married before we get back? We're almost there. We'll have to walk slow if you want to hear it all."

"Yes, please," Megan gushed. "We can stop walking if we have to."

"I'll make it short 'cuz I don't know all the details. When Nick was eighteen or nineteen, he started courting the daughter of a fairly wealthy family that owned a couple of businesses in town. Sally was her name. She was pretty and spoiled rotten by her high falutin' mother. That family must have spent a fortune keeping that girl in fancy frocks. Well, I guess she took one look at Nick and decided she was gonna have him, so for almost two years, she did everything in her power to snag him. And Nick, of course, being young and having no experience at all, was so lovestruck he wasn't himself. He thought she was pretty wonderful. Well, they set the wedding date and he spent a lot of his time building a small house on his pa's property. He was so proud of that place. I remember him coming over to get me and Joe and taking us over to see it. You should have seen that boy's face."

Maude quickly swiped at a tear. "He was so excited and so proud, I thought he'd bust. Well, it turned out, Nick's pa was in danger of losing their farm because they had two bad seasons and he was late paying on some loans. That must have bothered Sally. Two days before the wedding,

Nick went to get her to show her their finished house, and he was met at the door by Sally hanging on the arm of a rich young banker from St. Louis. On the day she was to marry Nick, she had a lavish wedding in her parents' house and married the banker. If they hadn't left on a honeymoon that night, I really think Nick might have killed that man. Less than a week later, Nick and Thomas left town and hired themselves out to work for the government doing survey work out west."

"Oh, Maude, that's awful!"

"It pret' near broke his ma's heart, too, seeing her son hurt like that and then havin' him leave. She told me he vowed he'd never look at another woman again. Far as I know, he's kept his vow."

They had stopped walking because the wagon enclosure was no more than ten yards away. Megan just stood and stared at Maude, feeling the impact of her words.

"So, Megan, dear, if he's not too friendly with you, I think it's 'cuz he's afraid. How about the service tonight? Will you come with me?"

Megan shook herself out of her reverie and reluctantly agreed, "I suppose so. When does it start?"

"It's getting pretty late. They've probably already started."

There were two preachers traveling with the train who had agreed to take turns conducting services. Most people tried to attend a few times every week. It was a welcome relief and provided much needed entertainment. Megan had only heard one of the men and it was him that was speaking when she and Maude found places to sit near the back. She never saw much of Reverend Holt except when he got his chance to preach. A thin man with a scraggly black beard and intense eyes, he seemed trapped in one theme; that of God's anger with sinners.

Megan heard his first words and braced herself. "Sin and those who commit sin are a stench in the nostrils of the

Almighty! You've read God's holy word! You know what it says!" he hollered, waving his big, black Bible back and forth. "He will not tolerate sin in his camp! The measures God took to purge sin from among his people were severe! Did he weigh their sin and say some are lesser sins and therefore deserve an easier sentence? *No!* Sin is sin! Disobedience is disobedience! And the Holy God abhors all sin! All sinners are an abomination to the Almighty! All sinners desecrate the throne of the living God!"

As his voice rose, so did Megan's churning emotions. All her guilt and self-condemnation that she had laid so comfortably to rest weeks ago were stirred up and rising to the surface. She wanted desperately to leave but felt bound by a commitment to Maude. She looked at the older woman but couldn't read her face. Sensing Megan's eyes on her, Maude turned to give her an encouraging smile. Megan smiled back, but she was certain Maude could see the turmoil in her eyes. They both turned their attention back to the preaching.

"And don't think Jesus came to make things easy for sinners! Remember what he says about murderers! Remember what he says about adulterers! Whosoever has anger in his heart is the same as a murderer! Whosoever has lust in his eyes is an adulterer! And God's anger is even now directed at you!"

Megan very quietly stood and walked away. Gasping for air in an attempt to keep from crying out, she made her way around and between wagons until she came to an open field, and still, she continued until the grass around her stood tall and untrampled. Finally finding a refuge far from the eyes and ears of anyone else, she fell on her face and let her emotions go. She cried in great wracking sobs, trying intermittently to make contact with her Creator, to appeal for His forgiveness and His compassion on one so unworthy.

But in response, she felt only more condemnation. Why

would one such as He condescend to even listen to her? Tormenting thoughts twisted her thinking as if demons had forced their long fingers through her skull and were stirring her brain around and around. *You're no different than a whore. Look how far you went. You know you had lust for all those men. All that flirting, all the things you did to get their attention. Even your own cousin thought you wanted more. And she knows you, probably even better than you know yourself. She saw the truth in you. She saw what you were really like. No wonder the school fired you. No wonder those parents didn't want you around their precious daughters. You and your wanton ways would corrupt them. You're not fit to be around these Godly people. If they ever knew what you really are...*

A loud moan escaped her lips and she buried her face deeper into the grass and wept without hope.

# CHAPTER TWELVE

The next morning, Megan opened her swollen eyes and forced herself to go through her normal activities. Somehow in the light of day, surrounded by people who so obviously cared about her, the condemning voices faded far into the background. Her classes continued as usual, but in the evening, if Megan couldn't find work to do, she'd take a walk. Maude didn't ask her again to go listen to the preaching, but Megan often noticed her expressions of affection and tenderness.

Soon the train joined up with the Little Blue River and followed it to the Platte. The plains were still grass-covered and rolling, but the gentle swells were occasionally broken by high buttes and the steep banks of the river. In one place, called The Narrows, the trail was bordered by the steep bank of the river dropping sharply down on one side and a high rocky butte rising sharply on the opposite side. There was barely enough room for the width of a wagon.

Two nights out of Rock Creek Station, the rain started. It was nothing more than a slow drizzle at first, but it showed no sign of letting up by morning. Megan and the three girls huddled together in the wagon, sang songs, and took turns telling stories, trying to be heard above the constant drumming of the rain on the canvas overhead.

At noon, Charles set up his ingenious "kitchen roof," a large canvas tarp he hooked onto one side of the wagon box, then threw over the top and stretched out a full ten feet from the wagon on the other side to be held up by a pole at each of the two corners. It was completely waterproof, and because it went over the wagon, that side was protected from rain blowing in or running down onto Elizabeth and Megan as they prepared meals. All of their extended family managed to squeeze under to eat, either sitting on chairs or the same tarps they slept on at night.

A major flaw in Charles' invention showed itself when the first gust of wind came. The canvas snapped up and the poles came loose and fell on the dining crowd, one across Thomas' plate. Everyone scrambled to grab the flapping canvas and hold it steady while the men got rope, replaced the poles, and fastened them securely.

When they all settled down again, Elizabeth, with a flushed face and sparkling eyes, looked around her circle of friends and said, "This is so much better than I dreamed it would be! I'm actually enjoying myself on this trip! I never expected that!"

She was answered with a chorus of enthusiastic responses, but it was Charles' response that went straight to Megan's heart "You have no idea how much it means to me to hear you say that," he said with tears in his eyes as he reached out and captured Elizabeth's hand. Megan turned in time to see Nick gazing at her with such tenderness, it bewildered her.

Throughout the rest of the day, dark rumbling clouds blocked the sun, and the wind whipped the prairie into a frenzy. Nick had his train make camp early. Tents were staked down securely, horses were hobbled, and extra men were put on livestock duty.

On clear nights, Megan and her nieces slept under the wagon. On stormy nights, the girls joined their parents in the wagon. Megan slept inside Maude's and Joe's wagon so Ralph wouldn't have to give up his place in the Batten's second wagon. They tied the canvas at both ends of the wagon into tight circles, but the wind managed to snake its way in and fill up the inside. The sound of canvas billowing out then being smashed inward again by the wind, joined the pummeling sound of the rain. A couple of times, Megan woke and thought she heard pounding hoofs and men hollering, but it was quickly drowned out by the wind and rain.

By morning it was over. Megan untied the canvas and stuck her head out to see the sun peeking through clouds on the horizon and people scrambling around gathering up their possessions scattered by the wind. Charles and Ralph looked exhausted at breakfast. They had been up most of the night rounding up frightened cattle.

Most of the morning, the traveling was very difficult because the wagon wheels kept sinking into the mud. Nick directed the train out of the ruts of the trail and onto the grass. It took hours, though, to get all the wagons out of the ruts. Whenever a wagon got stuck, several men had to lift each wheel while the oxen pulled. By the time all the wagons were off the muddy trail, it was time to stop for the noon meal. The men were caked with mud and exhausted, some even too tired to eat, throwing themselves across the grass to catch some sleep in the little time they had.

Late that afternoon, the combination of wind and sun had dried the grass, and people could walk again without getting soaked. Everything around her after a rain seemed to sharpen Megan's senses. The musty smell of the damp earth, the clean air, and bright green of the new grass against the brilliant blue of the sky, the contrasting blues and yellows and violets of the prairie flowers, and the sounds of celebration from the birds all combined to overwhelm her with delight. She had just gathered a handful of interesting blue flowers when Andrew trotted up and drew his horse to a stop in front of her.

"Would you like to take a ride with me?" he asked, offering his hand.

"I'd love to!" she answered, eyes dancing. Flinging her bouquet over her shoulder, she held out her hand and swung up behind the saddle. Andrew told her to hang on tightly and took off in a smooth canter to the north.

"I've got something pretty to show you," he called over his shoulder. "I thought you'd enjoy it."

Soon they approached a rocky slope. Andrew slowed the horse to a walk and let her pick her own way around the rocks and clumps of brush. When they got to the top, he indicated with a swoop of his hand what he brought her to see. Megan shifted to her left and looked out over the wide expanse of the Little Blue River valley. Up close, the river looked muddy from all the rain, but up high with the sun hitting it at just the right angle, it looked like a sparkling blue ribbon. And beside it, like a string of pearls, was the wagon train. In either direction, the Oregon Trail was visible winding its way through the new spring grass punctuated throughout by scrub brush and the dry brown sage of last year.

"Oh, Andrew, it's beautiful!" Megan exclaimed. Grabbing the back of the saddle, she swung down to the ground and walked over to the edge of the butte. Before her was a steep drop covered with loose rocks and scattered brush. She heard Andrew's footstep behind her.

"I knew you'd like it," he said. "Sarah would've liked it."

Megan looked up at him. "Do you miss her?"

"Terribly." His eyes were moist, looking out over the valley.

She reached her hand out and briefly touched his arm in comfort. "I'm sorry, Andrew."

Andrew stood silently, his clear blue eyes scanning the horizon. Shaking himself as if from a trance, he looked down at her and smiled. "I'm all right, Megan. It only gets bad once in a while." He shrugged and added, "Like now. Nick keeps me busy though. Every time he thinks I'm daydreaming, he gives me another job to do."

They walked silently back to the horse, mounted, and slowly made their way back to the train, which was already beginning to pull into camp for the night. Most of the way, Megan asked questions about Sarah which Andrew eagerly answered. When they finally pulled into camp, Elizabeth was already dishing up supper.

"Where have you been? We were getting worried," she scolded.

"I'm sorry, Elizabeth. I had no idea it was this late."

Nick joined them holding a mug of hot coffee, with a rather annoyed look on his face. "Yeah, where were you? I start to get a little concerned when people are missing about the time we pull into camp."

Megan, surprised by his tone, started to answer but Andrew cut her off. "Sorry, Nick. I took her for a ride to see the view. I meant to have her back long before now."

Nick just gave him a curt nod and walked back to Elmer's fire to get a plate of food. Andrew looked down at Megan and shrugged then joined Nick, the two of them soon conversing in low tones.

Frowning, Megan stood and watched them for a second, then turned to help herself to cornbread and beans. Elizabeth caught her eye and quietly said, "Nick was pretty upset when he found out you were gone."

"Well, why? I see people ride off all the time. You've even done it and I don't remember him getting mad at you."

"I'm not sure why. I think he figures most of the women

and children have someone to worry about them and you don't."

"That's nonsense!" she said, raising her voice. Elizabeth immediately put her finger on her lips, and Megan, glancing toward the men, lowered her voice. "I have Charles! He worries about me plenty enough!"

"Yes, but Charles was gone. He took off as soon as we stopped to go check on the stock. Besides that, you should be flattered that Nick even noticed. There's too many people on this train for him to notice everyone, you know."

"Humph!" she snorted. "I'd rather not be noticed if it means..." Her words were cut off by the approach of Nick and Andrew with loaded plates. Megan turned and gave Nick an unabashed smile then settled into a comfortable position on the grass next to Suzanne and started eating.

The others soon joined them and the tension melted away in the midst of friendly chatter. Lucy had center stage for a while when she talked about her problems with the McKay boys. Thomas and Nick, eyes twinkling, kept leading her on with questions and advice.

After supper, the women cleaned up and went on a short walk around the perimeter of the wagon enclosure to visit with neighbors before they were chased back to the wagon by a quick rainstorm.

The next day, they were greeted by scattered showers with the sun breaking through the clouds occasionally and dazzling them with a bright rainbow. Flowers and butterflies were in abundance and Megan longed to get out of the wagon and enjoy them, but the grass was too wet to walk in with a long skirt. After another hour of bouncing around in the wagon, she and Lucy climbed out the back. The trail was too muddy so they went out into the wet grass. Within minutes, their skirts were soaked to their knees and clung to their legs with every step. Undaunted, they continued on, giggling at the sight of the other one trying to walk. It was still better than the wagon. By the time they stopped to make camp, Megan's boots were soaked through and her feet were blistered.

Everyone had been using buffalo chips for fires since they'd reached the plains, but it was almost an impossible task to build a fire out of damp fuel. Megan took her wet boots and stockings off and hung them over the smoldering chips then bent down and blew until she was dizzy, trying to coax some life into their fire. Andrew took one look at her wet boots and raised his eyebrows with a disapproving expression. She got up quickly and crawled into the wagon to dig out her extra pair of boots.

"Feet a little sore?" he asked when she came out.

"A little," she answered, then set the spider skillet over the barely smoking fuel and bent down to blow some more.

"Get your feet wet?"

She looked up and gave him an indulgent smile. "Yes, Andrew, I got my feet wet."

"Thought so." He shook his head at her then bent to help her with the fire.

# CHAPTER THIRTEEN

**M**egan sat quietly, her back against a wagon wheel, her blistered feet throbbing. She eased her boots and stockings off. Several rows of people sat on the grass between her and the dancers. Feet stomped and swished through the trampled grass. Charles and two other men sat at one end of the space cleared for dancing, fiddles tucked under their chins, grinning and winking and trying to match the strokes of their bows slicing across tight strings. "Turkey in the Straw," "Old Dan Tucker," "Irish Washerwoman," the lively notes wound their way around the tired travelers and out to the empty, lonely expanse beyond the wagons.

The dance ended with laughter, women fanning themselves and exclaiming over being winded, and single men scanning the crowd for new partners. Megan made herself small, not wanting to be noticed. She saw Thomas headed her way so she looked down.

"Would you honor me with this dance?" he asked, hand outstretched.

"Not tonight, Thomas. But thank you."

"Come on. You know you'll enjoy it."

"I'm barefoot." She felt a blush creep up her face. "My blisters are killing me."

Thomas looked out over the crowd of happy travelers. "Nothing to be ashamed of out here. You're not the only one."

To Megan's surprise, for the first time she noticed he was right. Not just a few, but many of the women were also barefoot. She laughed, stood, and accepted Thomas' hand. What freedom she thought, to be able to cast off the expectations of society.

The square dance calls forced them together then apart. Thomas smiled and winked at her. The music gripped her and she let herself move to the beat. Thomas moved toward her, took her in his arms, and swung her around. Forward and curtsy, backward and do-si-do, swing your partner, swing your corner, around and around, feet stomping, people laughing. Elmer stood next to the fiddlers, slapping spoons against his thigh and calling the dance.

Megan caught herself laughing with those around her. "Buffalo Gals" ended and the fiddlers joined Charles in "Billy Boy." Thomas caught Megan's arm and steered her away from the throng of dancers toward Andrew and Nick standing off to the side watching them.

Before Megan could greet her friends, a heavyset woman pushed her way between them. "Mr. Webster! Here you are! I've been looking all over for you. Shame on you, hiding yourself during a dance. There's a beautiful young lady that's been dying to dance with you all evening, but she's too shy and too proper to make it known." She cast a slightly accusing glance in Megan's direction.

"I'm sorry, Mrs. Simmons, but I really don't like to dance," Nick replied.

"Oh, nonsense! Sure, you do. And besides, I'm afraid her feelings would be terribly hurt if you refused. She's too young to have men start hurting her tender feelings, and I'm sure you wouldn't want to do that, now, would you?"

Nick just stared at her with his mouth hanging open. Finally, he roused himself to answer, "No, I wouldn't want that. Where is she?"

"Don't look so scared. It's just my daughter, Natalie. Over this way," she rattled as she led him away.

Andrew laughed and reached for Megan's hand. "Would you like to dance, Megan?"

Her eyes sparkled with amusement. "I would like to very much, thank you," she answered with a curtsy. "Especially if you get us in the same set Nick's in."

He offered his arm. "That's the plan, my dear. That's the plan."

Late in the afternoon of the next day, the train pulled into camp within easy walking distance of Ft. Kearney. Close by to the west lay Doby Town, a rollicking frontier settlement built to cater to the needs of the soldiers in the nearby army post.

When Megan handed plates of hot food to her three nieces then to Charles and Ralph, she noticed with relief the relaxed smile on Nick's face when he came over to join them. Before he settled his large frame on the ground, he walked over to help Maude carry her chair.

"You and Joe don't want to miss seeing this fort tomorrow, Maude. One of the nicer fort's you'll ever see in this part of the country. It was built for the specific purpose of protecting people traveling this trail. The stockade was put up just last year."

Megan listened with interest. "Why did they wait so long to build their stockade? Seems to me that's the most important part of a fort."

"Well, I'd guess just the presence of the soldiers in the

area was a strong deterrent to Indian problems at first. But things have heated up considerably in the last few years."

He took a bite of food then looked at Megan while he chewed. "Indians are a much bigger threat now than when I took my last train through here. We've been lucky, so far. I've heard the biggest problems are up ahead to the west of Ft. Laramie. Sioux, Cheyenne, and Arapaho are working together. It'll be a miracle if we get through without an attack." His voice was low enough the three chattering girls on the outside of the circle couldn't hear. It was obvious he wasn't trying to spare Megan though.

Her eyes got bigger as he talked and her fork was suspended halfway to her mouth.

"What do you figure our chances are?" Charles asked.

Nick pulled his eyes away from Megan. "If I didn't think our chances were good, I wouldn't be taking you through. I'm not saying it'll be easy though. We'll have to have a big show of force. Guns will be loaded and ready and in plain sight. We'll put a tight guard on the cattle and pull into tight circles. One of their biggest tricks is to stampede the cattle, steal what they can, then attack anyone that comes looking for them."

He looked at Megan. "We can't have any stragglers. Anyone who walks will do it close enough to a wagon to jump in quick. And on the days we're being watched, we'll try to travel in a bunch, with everyone riding except armed men."

Megan, still wide-eyed, asked, "Will it be like that all the way from Laramie to Oregon?"

"No, after South Pass, we'll be in friendly Shoshone territory all the way to Ft. Bridger, maybe farther."

Lucy walked over to Elizabeth to ask for more food so the subject was changed.

"Will the store here have flour? I still need to buy some to replace the sacks I ruined," Megan asked Nick.

"You'll have a better chance finding some here than

anywhere else," Nick answered. "Go to the sutler's store at the fort. Don't waste your time in Doby Town. It's not a fit place to visit."

While Megan helped clean up after the meal, she overheard Thomas asking Elmer if he was planning a little trip to town. Elmer snorted loudly. "It's been many a long year since I've even considered such a thing. How 'bout you, youngun? Seems like that's more to yer way o' things than mine."

"Not if I value my hide. Ol' Nick and I have this little agreement, you see, while we're working this trip."

"No wild livin' for a while, I take it." Elmer chewed and spit. "I'm surprised you stuck it out."

"I think I'm getting old, Elmer. It's not as hard as I figured it'd be. I think Nick's starting to rub off on me after all these years." He slapped Elmer on the back and walked away.

Megan finished drying the dishes and hung her towel up to dry. "Elizabeth, are you walking over to the fort this evening?"

"No, Nick said we're spending the day here tomorrow so they'll be plenty of time then. Besides, Caroline McKay invited Rebecca and me over for coffee. You're welcome to join us."

"No thanks. I'll get Jessica to go with me. I'm really looking forward to seeing this place."

She had no trouble convincing Jessica to go. Although Jessica was nineteen, her mother wanted to know exactly where they were going and how long they were staying. She patiently gave her all the information she wanted and repeatedly assured her it was safe. Her brother, George, walked by and, overhearing his mother, stopped to tell her many other people from not only this train but another one camped a quarter mile away were walking back and forth from camp to the fort and they'd be fine in the company of all those people.

"I've seen the fort, Ma. It's bigger than I expected and neat and orderly with rows of trees and flowers. They even have a hospital. You'd like it, Ma. You really oughta go see it when you get time."

Jessica leaned over and gave her mother a kiss on her cheek, flashed her brother an appreciative smile, and left.

The sutler's store at the fort was large and well stocked. Megan and Jessica were amazed and delighted. It seemed like years had gone by since they'd seen a store like this. Megan laughed to think how quickly her perspective had changed. Only a few weeks ago, she was shopping in St. Louis stores. A place like this would have seemed dirty and primitive. She glanced down at her clothes. Now she felt dirty and primitive standing in the middle of these neat rows of new merchandise. They wandered up and down and gawked. The sutler obviously catered to emigrants as much as he did to soldiers, judging by the cook stoves, buckets, civilian rain gear and boots, pots and pans, spider skillets, knitting and sewing supplies, and bolts of gingham and calico. A few blue-uniformed soldiers moving up and down the aisles stirred unwelcome memories in Megan. She moved away from them and feasted her eyes on every detail of the place, Jessica by her side, chattering away about everything she saw. At the counter, she purchased five pounds of dried buffalo strips and asked about sacks of flour.

"Sorry, ma'am. Sold out just this evening before you got here. I just can't seem to keep them on the shelf longer than a day or two with all these wagons coming through. I'm supposed to be getting a shipment in tomorrow, but I can't guarantee it."

Megan looked so disappointed that he quickly added, "There may be some down at the store in Doby Town. They don't sell out as fast as I do 'cuz they charge more. But if you really need some bad, I'd skidaddle right on down there before it's sold, too."

151

"Is it far?"

"Naw! Just a coupla miles. You can see the town from here."

"Would we have to worry about Indians?" they asked almost simultaneously.

"Naw, there's so much traffic back and forth on that road, there's nothin' to worry about. The only Injuns I've seen in weeks are here to do business."

Both women looked uncertainly at each other, thanked the sutler, and walked out the door. From the height of the porch, they could see the road to Doby Town. Sure enough, they could barely make out buildings against the brightness of the western sky. And, just as they were told, there were many people on the road, some on foot and some in wagons or on horseback. Among them were a few women.

"As long as we stay on the road, I can't see any reason this wouldn't be safe," Jessica said.

"Well let's get going before the sun goes down," Megan said as she followed Jessica off the porch. "I was hoping we'd get to see the town. Forts are interesting, but I'm so homesick for towns I could cry."

Two women from the train stepped out the door onto the porch and called a greeting to Megan and Jessica just as they started on their way.

"Would you please tell Charles or Elizabeth we're going to Doby Town to buy flour?" Megan asked. "The store here is sold out. We'll get back a little later than we expected. I don't want them to worry."

"Flour? Would you buy a sack for me?" one woman asked as she fumbled in her purse for money. "Some of ours must have gotten wet." She handed Megan twice what they figured flour would cost and thanked her profusely.

As they walked, Megan fretted at the speed the sun was dropping. She wanted to move faster, but Jessica had been out of breath since the beginning of their walk. About three quarters of the way there, an older couple stopped them to chat, asking them if they were headed to California or Oregon, how they liked their wagon master, where they came from, had they had any problems with Indians. The sun sat on the western horizon by the time they excused themselves.

By the time they arrived, it was starting to get dark and Jessica was panting.

"Maybe we should head back," Megan said. "We can come back tomorrow."

"Not on your life," Jessica gasped. "We got this far. Let's finish what we started so we don't have to do this walk again."

Doby Town was unlike any town they'd ever been in and not at all what they had expected. It was a noisy town, with lights streaming out of buildings across the boardwalks and deeply rutted street. Tinkling piano notes floated through windows and mingled with contrasting notes coming from other buildings. Loud, raucous laughter and hollering came at them from all sides.

Megan and Jessica looked at each other with wide, frightened eyes. A gunshot caused them both to jump.

"Where's that store? I want to get out of this place. It scares me." She turned and looked up and down the busy street, realizing for the first time there were no women in sight. They passed several saloons and a blacksmith shop but nothing that looked like a store. Finally at the end of the street they saw a building with "Sadie's Hotel" written in big letters over the door.

"Let's ask in here," Megan said as she opened the door and led the way into the shabby lobby. A man stood behind a makeshift counter and asked with a tinge of annoyance what they were looking for.

"We were told there's a store in this town. Could you tell us where to find it?"

Megan shuddered as his bloodshot eyes traveled over her. He tipped his head back and squinted his eyes, a discomforting grin on his mottled face.

"On the street behind this place. You can just take the alley out here. Save yerselves some time. Course, I wouldn't mind much if you hung around here a spell."

Megan drew herself up haughtily. "We'll be on our way. Thank you for the directions."

The man nodded toward a door at the back of the room. "Might be smarter for you to go out the back, closer to the street you want. Not too smart for two pretty young ladies like yerselves to be walking down an alley this time of night."

Megan hesitated and studied him. His expression had unexpectedly changed to one of respect. "Thank you," she said, walking toward the door, eying him warily all the way. She opened the door and looked out. A few steps would get them to the side alley then out onto the street they wanted. She called back over her shoulder, "Which direction do we go to get to the store?"

"When you get out to the street, turn left. Just a couple o' buildings down on the other side."

They walked down rickety steps to the ground. The noises of the street were muted, but they were reminded of the sordidness of the town when they heard glass crunching under their feet and smelled the strong odor of whiskey. There was no light left in the sky and very little light reached them from the street. Megan carefully picked her way through the debris with Jessica on her heels.

Sounds of men talking and laughing came from the direction they were going. They got louder and closer. Megan put her hand up to stop Jessica.

"Shh, I rather they not see us. Let's wait 'til they pass."

Footsteps crunched on the gravel at the end of the alley. Megan drew in her breath and flattened herself against the building as she saw the outline of three men move into the alley and head in their direction. She saw them stagger and laugh and smelled the liquor on their breath before they reached her. One bumped into her and swore then looked very carefully into her face, making her almost gag with his powerful breath.

"Well, lookie here, men. They're sendin' the girls out to us. How convenient," he slurred.

Megan heard Jessica turn and run. She moved to follow her but was roughly grabbed by the shoulders.

"No, you don't! They're gettin' away from us, boys. Better grab you one. This one's mine." He crushed her roughly against his chest and dropped his hot mouth down to hers, but not before a strangled cry escaped. When he pulled back, Megan yanked away and staggered backward away from him, gagging and wiping furiously at her mouth.

"Oh, so you want to play awhile. I got me a fun little wench this time, boys."

"Well hold her still a minute so we can get a look at her," one snarled as he stepped up beside his buddy. Megan saw with sickening realization, the blue uniforms and gold buttons gleaming in what little light was available. Numb with fear, she stepped back when all three men reached out to grab her. Her foot caught on a rock. She stumbled backward, reached out to catch herself on the side of the building, and landed with a sickening crunch on her right shoulder in the middle of broken glass. Hands grabbed for her. She shoved them away and struggled to get up. Whiskey from an open bottle in the hands of one soldier splashed in her face when they bent over and grabbed her arms, yanking her roughly to her feet.

Megan tried to holler for help, but her terror was so strong she thought she would suffocate. Only a pitiful whimpering sound came from her open mouth. All three men had firm grips of her arms. One had a handful of her hair. They breathed their foul breath on her as their bloodshot eyes swept over their catch.

"Now, ain't she a right purty little thing."

"She's mine, boys. Don't be fergittin' it, either."

"Pshaw! She don't look like one a' Sadie's girls. They send fer a new batch a' girls an' not tell us or somethin'?"

It all happened in such quick succession it was a blur. Two rifles cocked, the hard cold steel of a barrel came down across Megan's shoulder and jammed into the chest of the soldier directly in front of her and a strong arm encircled her waist from behind, almost lifting her limp body off the ground.

"Get your filthy hands off the lady and back up, or I'm putting a bullet through your heart." The tone, hard and cold, gave the soldiers no reason to doubt he meant exactly what he said. As soon as they dropped their arms and stepped back, Megan was spun around behind her rescuer and nudged away. For the first time, she realized it was Nick when he ordered her, "Move out of the way."

Backing down the alley, she saw Nick and Thomas set their rifles behind them and attack the soldiers with their fists. Frozen in place by the spectacle in front of her, she tried in vain to see who was hitting whom. She heard footsteps running, grunts and groans and threats, then silence. Finally, two tall figures moved toward her. She held her breath and stepped back, straining to identify them. Thomas! Then Nick moved around him and stood in front of her. He put his hand on the back of her head and pulled her against his chest.

"Are you all right?" came his voice, husky with emotion.

"I'm fine," she answered weakly, her head nodding up and down.

Handing his rifle to Thomas, he put both hands on her shoulders and set her at arm's length. His tone changed. "Why are you still standing here? I told you to move out of the way."

"I...I did."

"And what in God's name are you doing in this hellhole? Didn't I tell you to stay away from this place?" he asked through clenched teeth.

"You didn't tell me..." Her voice trailed away as she tried to think back to what he did say.

"I don't even want to think what would've happened to you if Mrs. Sanders hadn't told us where you were. I knew you'd be trouble on this trip, but I never dreamed you'd be this much trouble. I have a good mind to lock you up until we get to Oregon." He ranted and raved until his alarm and anger were spent. Then he was silent, breathing hard in the darkness. Leaning toward her, he sniffed, filling his nostrils with the overwhelming smell of whiskey. Megan waited, willing him to speak again, dreading the silence more than his words. He turned her and moved her toward the street.

"Let's get you out here in the light where we can get a good look at you."

Nick tried to control his raging emotions. Seeing Megan in the clutches of that drunk soldier was enough to undo him. His military years enabled him to act rationally, even though, at the moment, he wanted to kill someone.

Jessica moved to join them as soon as they stepped out of the alley. She took one look at Megan and gasped. Thomas, walking behind them, reached out and gently touched Megan's back. "Nick," he said in quiet alarm. "Blood. She's covered in blood. All over her back and shoulder."

Nick stopped her in the light of the saloon and looked down at her in shock. Blood still oozed from the deep cut on her shoulder, a crimson stain spreading all the way down her sleeve. Her hands and back were covered with a multitude of smaller cuts. Blood was smeared all over her face from her hands. There was so much it was impossible to tell at a glance where it was coming from. He looked down and saw that his hand and shirt were bloodied. "My

God," he whispered and looked up. "Megan, why didn't you tell us?"

"I didn't know," she answered, examining herself.

"What did they do to you?" he asked, his voice strained.

Jessica was sobbing quietly beside her.

"The glass. I must have cut it on the broken bottles when I was on my back."

"Thomas!" he barked. "Go inside and get some rags, something to stop this bleeding until we can get her to Andrew." He turned to her, his eyes squinting in anger, his breathing hard. "On your back? They had you on your back?"

"No!" she quickly corrected him. "I fell. When I was backing away, I fell. Then they grabbed me and pulled me to my feet and...and then you came."

"Thank God," he breathed then gently lifted her arm and pulled the already torn cloth away so he could get a better look. She winced in pain. "Now that the shock of your experience is wearing off, you're probably going to start feeling pain. Brace yourself."

Thomas crossed the boardwalk and jumped down beside them, tearing strips from a rag. Nick held her arm while Thomas wrapped it. Blood soaked through every layer as fast as they wrapped.

"We'll have to start over. We've got to get some pressure against the wound," Nick said. "We've got to get the bleeding slowed down before we move her."

Thomas unwound his work, used the strips to make a thick pad, then pressed it against the gash in Megan's shoulder. Gasping with pain, she yanked away.

"Easy, Megan," Thomas said. He looked at her with pity. "I'm sorry I hurt you, but I don't think there's any other way."

"Sit down, Megan." Nick guided her gently over to the edge of the boardwalk and sat next to her, opposite her hurt shoulder. "You're going to have to hold still. We've got to get this bleeding under control, Thomas." He motioned for him to try again. Reaching across in front of her, he grasped her elbow firmly. She shuddered against him.

"You smell like you spent the night in a saloon, you know." He sat so close to her, he could feel her warmth. She managed a weak laugh.

Thomas had to wrap the cloth around her arm and up over her shoulder. "It's not a pretty sight, but it should work 'til we get her to Andrew." He took the remaining cloth and walked over to a watering trough to pump water on it, then came back and started wiping the blood off her face and hands. Nick checked her back for heavy bleeding. Her shirtwaist had several small tears, but he could only guess the cuts were shallow because the bleeding had almost stopped.

Both men stood and looked her over. Jessica took Thomas' place and tried to clean the blood and dirt out of the cuts on Megan's hands. "I'm so sorry I ran away, Megan. Maybe this wouldn't have happened if I'd stayed."

"No, Jessica. Running was the only thing you could do. I tried to follow you. And if you hadn't run, then you wouldn't have seen Nick and Thomas."

"I hope you've given some thought to the fine fix you'd be in right now if we hadn't come along when we did," Nick growled. His anger was coming to the surface again, now that the immediate need of tending to Megan's wounds was temporarily taken care of. "You're a mess." He turned to Thomas. "We can't take her back to camp in this shape. It would scare Elizabeth and her girls out of their wits to see all the blood, to say nothing of the tongue wagging this would start. She smells and looks like she just came out of a barroom brawl."

Thomas laughed and shook his head at her. "He's right, you know. You're quite a sight."

Nick just stood there and glared down at her. "We need to get you to Andrew in a hurry so he can stitch up that shoulder. But first, I want to know what in tarnation you're doing in this place."

Megan looked at him and shrugged. "I came to buy flour. The store at the fort was out and he told me I'd probably find some here."

"Flour? Flour? All this for a lousy sack of flour?" He ran his hand over his jaw and shook his head. "So how did you end up in the alley next to the whorehouse?"

Megan's head snapped up. "The what?"

"The whorehouse. Sadie's Hotel is the main whorehouse in this town. Not the only one but by far the busiest. Those three soldiers probably took you for one of Sadie's whores standing in the alley just waiting for customers."

Megan jumped to her feet, gasping with indignation and unbelief. "How dare you?" she almost shrieked, her eyes burning with accusation. "How dare you stand there and accuse me of something so degrading," she choked on a sob. She pointed a finger at him and raised her voice in outrage. "So...so horribly disgusting!" Both hands flew to cover her face now crumpled into angry tears.

Nick's mouth dropped open and he took a step back, totally befuddled by her outburst. "Megan, I didn't mean..."

Her hands came down and she glared at him. "Don't talk to me!" she hissed then hiccupped on a sob. "Don't even look at me! No decent man would ever, ever say such things to a lady if"—she wiped furiously at her wet cheeks—"if he had any respect for her at all!" She covered her face again and between choking sobs cried, "You're just assuming something that's not true and you don't even care enough to find out what really happened!" She whirled away from him and buried her face on Jessica's shoulder.

His face ashen, Nick turned confused eyes on Thomas for help. Thomas, looking as befuddled as Nick, moved to rest a hand on her shoulder. "Megan, Nick wasn't accusing you of anything except being in some place you shouldn't be." He cast an uncertain glance at Nick. "What I meant to say is, Nick didn't mean what you think he meant."

Nick jumped in, "Megan, I'd never even think such a thing about you. I was just trying to say how it probably looked to those soldiers."

She didn't move. Jessica looked up at them and shrugged.

"We need to get her to Andrew," Nick said quietly. "I think the whole experience has been too much for her." He moved to get the horses. "Thomas, maybe you better take Megan with you. Jessica and I'll ride up ahead and arrange to have one of the officers' wives take her in for the night. Lt. Lucas' wife would be more than willing. Then we'll find Andrew." He mounted and reached down for Jessica's hand. "Meet me at the west gate, Thomas." He waited until Megan was seated behind Thomas then waved and took off at a trot. "Ride easy with her," he hollered back.

As predicted, Sarah Lucas graciously opened her home to them. Nick found Andrew near the Batten's wagons waiting with a very worried sister and Jessica's mother. He explained only that Megan had fallen on broken glass and needed to be stitched up. She'd be fine but needed to stay at the fort while Andrew tended to her.

On the way to the west gate to meet Thomas and Megan, Nick warned Andrew not to question her when he saw her. "I think she's taken all she can tolerate for one night. To make a long story short, she tripped and fell on some broken bottles trying to get away from three drunk soldiers. They must have spilled whiskey on her judging by the way she smells."

Despite the warning, Andrew was shocked when he saw her, even more so when he saw her in the light of Mrs. Lucas' parlor. He peeled the dressing off her shoulder and gave a low whistle. Megan sat on a stool and craned her neck to look. "It's a pretty nasty sight, Megan." Her eyes met his and he asked gently, "Do you want to bite a bullet, or do I need to use chloroform?"

Her eyes widened. "I don't know. What do you think?"

He studied the cut and began pulling the blood-encrusted fabric away. Megan stifled a gasp and pulled slightly away from his hand. He looked up at Nick and they both nodded and said simultaneously, "Chloroform."

Andrew stood. "Jessica and Mrs. Lucas, if you two would help her get out of her shirtwaist and have her lie down in one of your bedrooms, I'll go over to the hospital and get what I need. And when you're done, Jessica, go get a clean shirtwaist from Elizabeth."

The next morning, Megan woke with a throbbing pain in her shoulder and the sight of Elizabeth's worried face looking down on her. "How do you feel?"

Megan, reaching out and taking Elizabeth's hand, smiled weakly and answered, "I'm fine, other than a sore shoulder and a splitting headache."

"What happened last night? Nobody's giving me much information."

Megan frowned and looked away.

"Is it really that awful?"

"Yes, I mean, no." Megan closed her eyes and sighed impatiently. "It was bad, but it could easily look a lot worse than it was." She looked at Elizabeth. "That's probably why they're not saying much." She proceeded to tell her the whole story and finished with, "The worst of it is that Nick said those soldiers thought I was a whore." She bit her lip and turned her face away again.

Elizabeth sat quietly for a moment then squeezed Megan's hand. "Megan! That's awful! I'm so relieved that help got to you in time." She paused, chewing her bottom lip.

"Wait! Of all that happened to you last night, you think what Nick said was the worst of it?" She shook her head and stood.

Megan cringed at the memory.

"Megan, who knows what those men might have done if Nick and Thomas hadn't shown up. And these cuts all over you! Honey, I'll admit what Nick said wasn't the most delicate way of putting it, but it's certainly not the worst that happened and nothing to be ashamed of. It was dark and, unknown to you and Jessica, you were right next to a brothel. It only stands to reason a drunk man might think you were one of 'those' women. I just thank God you were spared from much worse!"

Megan chewed on her lip and stared at the far wall, trying to sort through the confusion of last night. Andrew knocked and entered. "How's my favorite patient? Do you think you're ready to move back home?"

"I don't know. I haven't slept in a bed this comfortable in so long, I forgot there was such a thing."

He helped her sit up and peeled back the dressing to check on his work. "It looks good. Let's pray there won't be any infection. I had to pick some glass out before I stitched you up. It was a pretty jagged tear."

He looked at Elizabeth. "You'll need to clean this and change the dressing every day. While you're at it, wash all these other cuts, too. I want to check her again in a couple of days."

He moved around in front of Megan and studied her face. "Did you tell your sister what happened?"

She nodded.

"All of it?"

"Everything I remember."

Andrew pulled a chair up close to the bed, sat down, and leaned forward. He picked up her hand, turned it over, and studied the cuts in her palm. He raised his eyes and looked at her intently for a moment. "Nick told me what happened. Now you tell me how you're really feeling."

"My shoulder hurts a little, and these cuts all feel about

the way you'd expect, and I have a headache and that's all."

"Were you afraid?" he prompted. He saw her hand clutch the sheet and draw it closer to her chest.

"Yes, very afraid," she answered quietly.

He leaned closer and very tenderly said, "I want you to tell me exactly what they did. Can you do that?"

She searched his face and nodded. "They grabbed my arms and said some awful things I can't recall." She talked slowly, trying to remember it all. "The first man hugged me and then kissed me and then I tried to get away and fell. They pulled me to my feet, then Nick and Thomas got there."

Andrew's face was livid, yet he sat very still. "Is there anything you're not telling me?"

"No, that's all of it."

"Didn't anyone warn you about this town?"

"Nick says he did, but I guess I didn't understand him."

Andrew sighed with frustration and stared at the floor for a moment, shaking his head back and forth. He finally ran both hands over his face and looked at her again. "I'm just glad it wasn't any worse."

# CHAPTER FOURTEEN

Early that evening, Megan sat alone near the fire. Charles, Elizabeth, and the girls had gone over to tour the fort after supper. A fiddle was playing in the background and Megan could barely make out the sounds of a man calling for a square dance. She sat back gently into a pillow propped against a wagon wheel and watched little Stephen Sanders tease his dog.

"Are you feeling any better?"

Startled, she jerked her head around to see Nick looking down at her. "Oh! I didn't know you were there."

"I'm sorry. I'll try to announce myself next time. How's your shoulder?"

"Sore, but I guess that's to be expected."

He moved to stand in front of her as he swung two sacks around and placed them at her feet. "I brought something for you."

Megan sat up and looked down at the sacks. "What's this? Flour?" She looked at him gratefully. "Nick, that was nice of you."

His only response was to look back at her with a faint grin. She sat back and searched his face. "So...what do I owe you?"

"Two things."

She raised her eyebrows in curious expectation.

"May I?" He motioned to the stool directly in front of her. When she nodded her assent, he pulled it closer and settled his large frame, leaning toward her with his arms resting on his knees.

"Number one," he started, not taking his eyes off her, "I'd like you to forgive me for all the careless words I said to you yesterday in Doby Town. What I think you thought I was implying is so far from anything I could possibly think about you..." He paused, groping for the right words.

"I've already forgiven you," she said quietly, dropping her head. "Actually, there's nothing to forgive. I badly overreacted. In fact, I probably owe you an apology instead."

"No, Megan, there's no need for you to apologize." His voice was gentle. He said nothing for a while.

Her eyes didn't leave her hands, nervously clutching her skirt. "What's the second one?" she asked, finally looking up.

"I'm afraid this one won't be easy for you. In fact, I ask this one of you, not just as a friend but as the man in charge of this outfit." His eyes held hers steady for a moment.

"What is it?"

"I don't want you leaving the immediate area of the wagons without checking with me first...for the remainder of the trip."

Megan just stared at him, not moving a muscle. Finally, she responded, "Seems to me you're overreacting now."

Nick studied his hands for a moment then looked back at her. "Don't make this difficult, Megan."

"You're the one that's making things difficult." Megan immediately regretted the tone she used when she saw his jaw muscles tighten and his eyes snap with irritation.

In a calm, steady voice he continued, "I will not change what I expect of you. Your only choice is what kind of attitude you're going to have about it." He stared at her for a moment in silence. "Today you got yourself into an unbelievably dangerous situation. Before this, you took off with Andrew without a word to your family. You've shown me you have very little common sense concerning these unfamiliar surroundings you find yourself in. That's no reflection on your character, it only shows a lack of experience, and that's to be expected since you've spent your entire adult life being pampered in a city. Well, this is not St. Louis, Miss O'Mally, and I won't run the risk of you endangering your life or anyone else's for the sake of a little adventure. You'll get more than your share of adventure before this trip is over. The Indian situation will get worse, there's more towns like Doby Town, and there's scores more men like those three in the alley last night."

Nick stood and raked his fingers through his hair. "I need to know you'll check with me before you take off so I won't have to waste my energy wondering what kind of scrape you've gotten yourself into."

Her eyes followed him as he paced a short path back and forth in front of her.

"You see me as nothing but a child, don't you?"

Nick tipped his head and studied her. "Is that the way you see this, Megan? If Maude had done the same, I'd deal with her as I am with you."

"How about Jessica?"

"I've talked to her father."

Megan let out an impatient snort.

Sighing in aggravation, he shifted his weight and folded his arms across his chest. He looked down at her and scowled. "Just do as I say without any trouble. Is that understood?"

"I have no trouble understanding it. I just don't like it,

that's all." She shrugged and gave him a weak smile. "There's no point in arguing with you, is there?"

He turned to go. "Not on this, there isn't."

Elizabeth was mildly disturbed to hear Megan's comments a few mornings later as they walked along the south bank of the wide, slow-moving, muddy Platte River. It wasn't exactly what she said, but the slow, expressionless way she said it.

"Thomas told me that this river is known as the most useless of all rivers, too full of quicksand to ford or bridge, too muddy to drink or wash in, and too shallow for a boat or ferry." A long deep sigh followed. "It's beautiful, isn't it? Intriguing with its string of islands so isolated in that wide expanse of brown, swirling water." Elizabeth watched Megan stare at the islands with longing.

"They seem so alone and unreachable," she said quietly.

"This concerns me," Andrew said as he checked her stitches that evening. "This whole area around your stitches looks bad." He decided to take over the job of changing the dressing and cleaning the wound each evening. Megan seemed unconcerned. She simply watched Andrew without a word.

"She's much too quiet," Elizabeth whispered to Nick who watched Andrew from across the circle of friends.

"I think she might still be protesting the restrictions I've placed on her."

Thomas joined the hushed conversation. "I'm sure she's having a tough time shaking off the trauma of that attack."

"I think Thomas is right. We need to give her more time," Elizabeth said.

A week away from Ft. Kearny, Andrew expressed his fear to Elizabeth and Nick. It was late evening and he spoke to them quietly away from the others. "She's not healing."

Elizabeth was standing next to Nick who was struggling to sew a torn sleeve. At Andrew's words, her head came up and turned with a jerk to stare into Andrew's face. "How bad?"

"I'm puzzled by it. There's definitely infection; redness, swelling, a lot of pain in the immediate area. Judging by her overall appearance and behavior, I'd say she's sick, and the infection is spreading. But there's no fever."

"Appearance and behavior?" Nick asked.

"You're not blind, Nick."

"No, but neither am I a doctor. Tell me what you're seeing."

"She's exhausted, dark circles under her eyes, listless, poor appetite, she's just not herself. The fact there's no sign of fever leads me to suspect she's not sleeping much. And that may be a factor in the slow healing. Who knows?"

"I've been watching her and you're right, Andrew," Elizabeth said.

"Well, Doctor, seems to me you and she need to sit down and have a little chat."

Andrew looked at Nick and nodded slowly. "Yeah." He turned to leave then stopped and put his hand on Elizabeth's shoulder. "Pray for her, Elizabeth, Nick."

"I have been, Andrew," Nick answered softly.

Elizabeth found Megan sitting on the ground near the fire listening to Maude explain to Lucy and Abigail how to properly sew a hem.

Elizabeth laughed. "Nick needs to sit in on this little sewing class."

"Send him over anytime," Maude answered. "I don't know how you keep up with the mending with these girls forever running and catching their skirts on the brush around here."

Andrew glanced down at Megan. "Take a walk with me, Megan?" reaching his hand down to her.

Megan's first inclination was to refuse, but when Andrew persisted, she rose to her feet and followed one step behind him. As soon as they passed a couple of wagons, Andrew turned and asked her how she felt.

"Oh, the same, I guess. It's still a little sore."

"Other than your shoulder, how do you feel?"

"I'm fine."

"You don't look fine, Megan. You haven't looked like your usual self for a week now." He stopped her and turned her to face him. "As your doctor and your friend, I'm worried about you. Are you getting any sleep?"

Megan let out a resigned sigh and looked down. "I suppose not enough. I am awfully tired."

"What's the problem? Is it the pain?"

She pulled away and started walking again. "I don't know, maybe."

"Maybe? I can't help you if that's all the answer I get!" Andrew said, trying to catch up with her.

"It's not my shoulder. It's probably other things."

"What other things?"

Megan put her face in her hands and shuddered. "I don't know, just things...things on my mind. I can't stop thinking about them."

Andrew gently took hold of her arm and pulled her to a stop. His hands slid down and held hers. "Look at me, Megan. I can understand you better when I can see your face."

"I appreciate your concern, Andrew, but there's really nothing you can do about it."

"Well, that's for certain if you don't tell me what these things are."

Megan closed her eyes and shook her head. "Please, Andrew."

"Is it what happened at Doby Town? Are you thinking

about that?"

"No. I... I'll manage just fine without talking about it. Fair enough? Just give me more time. I'll be fine." She tried to pull her hands free, but he held on and looked down into her face with determination.

"I've given you time, Megan. You only seem to be getting worse. Talk to me, please."

She yanked her hands away from his and looking him directly in the eye, said slowly and clearly, "I don't want to talk about it! Leave me alone! Please!" Then she turned and walked away, leaving Andrew behind.

Slowly Megan became more aware of her surroundings. Ever since they'd left Ft. Kearny, the landscape was increasingly treeless and barren. Sand hills lay to the north of the Platte and hard packed clay to the south interspersed with rich buffalo grass and more sand the farther west they went. The only trees in view were occasional willows and cottonwood along the banks of the river and its tributaries. Children were given the unpleasant job of carrying sacks and gathering dried buffalo and oxen chips as they walked to be used for their cooking fires. The monotony of the landscape, the heat, and the tiring adjustment to the increasing altitude took its toll on more than just Megan. Everyone seemed to be affected.

Soon the train pulled into Ft. Cottonwood where, to Nick's obvious delight, they were told the government was beefing up their military strength in the west, now that the war was over and the Indians were becoming a bigger menace. He talked with enthusiasm as they shared their meal that evening.

"Several detachments of troops are being sent out from Ft. Laramie to other forts along the trail and some trains have the good fortune of being accompanied by these troops. I'm praying that our arrival at Ft. Laramie will be timed just right to take advantage of this extra protection. The presence of an entire company of soldiers will pretty much guarantee safe passage through the most dangerous areas."

"We'll join you in those prayers, Nick," Charles said. "It almost sounds too good to be true."

A few miles west of Ft. Cottonwood, the wagons came to the fork of the North Platte and South Platte. They continued along the South Platte for another three and a half days then forded the river at the Lower California Crossing and headed northwest to join up with the North Platte.

At noon one day, Thomas reported seeing a herd of antelope about a mile to the west, so Nick had him round up a dozen men to go hunting while the train continued on. That evening, men and women, including Megan, joined in to gut and skin the carcasses, then cut the meat into long strips and hang them on frames attached to the wagons to dry in the sun for several days.

Megan's shoulder finally showed signs of healing. Since her conversation with Andrew, she'd been making an effort to be cheerful, entering into conversations, working harder to ease Elizabeth's burdens, and at least making an appearance of continuing her morning and afternoon classes. She was well aware that certain people were not fooled, though, especially those that made it their business to watch her; namely Andrew, Elizabeth, and Maude. Andrew continued to check her wound regularly, not out of necessity, she suspected, as much as to engage her in conversation. He gently persisted in reminding her she looked exhausted and therefore wasn't getting the rest she needed. She persisted in telling him she was better and everything was fine and she looked no more tired than the rest of them.

"I can tell by the strain on your face that everything is not fine," Andrew said. "As your doctor, I've decided to order you to stop walking with your classes and ride in a wagon."

"I don't think that's necessary, Andrew," she said calmly but with an air of finality.

"You're not well, Megan. I'm your doctor. I'll decide what's necessary."

"Well, then, you're fired. I don't need a doctor anymore. I'm not sick."

Andrew just laughed and looked at her with twinkling eyes. "I hate to admit it, but it's really nice to see that old fire back in your eyes. Megan, what is it that makes it so difficult for you to take orders from anyone?"

She looked at him with a puzzled frown.

"Do you want to know what I think it is?" He didn't wait for her to answer. "I think because of your ma dying and the way your pa dealt with it, you didn't get the usual dose of parental authority. Then you went to live with an overly indulgent uncle, and now you think it's so terribly out of the ordinary to have anyone tell you what to do. A good dose of military life would do you wonders."

Megan just stared at him, not sure what to think. "So you think I'm spoiled?"

Andrew chuckled. "Most of the time I think you're one of the finest, most considerate ladies I've ever met. But now and then, you're more stubborn than a jackass!"

Megan tried to look offended, but against her best efforts, a smile broke out on her face. "I'm sorry for my attitude toward you, Andrew," she said, somewhat reluctantly. "I know you only want to help."

"Well then, just for a while do what I ask."

Andrew laughed. "I can see the struggle on your face."

She sighed and looked away. "All right, I'd go stark raving mad if I couldn't be outside some of the time. So, I'll compromise. Less time walking. More time riding."

Megan soon found herself spending mornings tucked snugly next to Maude on their wagon seat. She and Joe let her know how delighted they were to have her. They spent long hours chatting about everything under the sun. Megan told them about her life growing up on their family farm, about how Charles started courting Elizabeth, about her mother dying, then her father's grief and his death. They were especially interested in hearing about the exodus of people from Springfield following the confederate victory at Wilson's Creek and about life in St. Louis during the war.

At one point, Maude put her plump arm around Megan and asked, "Why is it, dear, when you talk about your time in St. Louis you keep clamming up on me?"

"I don't," Megan protested.

"Oh, but you do. Your whole body becomes rigid and the words stop flowing."

When Megan didn't answer, Maude squeezed her shoulder and said, "I won't pry. You'll tell me when you're ready."

The land was becoming increasingly dry and desolate as they approached the North Platte, but soon they were treated to Ash Hollow, a six-mile-long plain covered with shade trees, abundant grass, and the best water they'd ever tasted. After they'd traveled along the north branch of the Platte for a way, the landscape began to change dramatically. Strange, high rock formations began appearing on the horizon. The better known were Courthouse Rock and Jail Rock then farther on, the tall spire of Chimney Rock which could be seen for three days before they reached it.

On the evening they camped near Courthouse Rock, Megan approached Nick for the first time about leaving the wagon train. Their campsite was two miles north of the rock formations, and several groups of people were planning to either walk or ride over to see them after the evening meal. As the group around Batten's fire finished eating and started cleaning up, Charles asked Nick if he thought it would be safe to take his girls.

"If there's plenty of armed men in your group, I think you'll be fine. Thomas and a few others were scouting the area this afternoon and they didn't see any signs of Indians. They're getting ready to ride out there now ahead of the crowd to check again. If there's a problem, they'll warn us before we get there."

Embarrassed to have to ask permission to go, Megan waited until Nick turned and walked toward his wagon. She quickly finished wiping dishes, hung her towel up to dry, and followed him. She found him fishing around in the back of his wagon for bullets. He held his 50 caliber, 6-shot Colt rifle under his arm and had a Remington Army revolver tucked in his holster.

When Megan cleared her throat, Nick turned quickly to see her standing next to him, fighting with the wind to keep her hair out of her face. Megan usually wore her long, dark-brown hair pulled back loosely and twisted into a knot. Back at the beginning of the trip, she wore the fashionable style of the day, hair swept back in a "waterfall" secured with a net behind her neck. But that quickly changed.

Nick turned to look down at her. The wind whipped her hair loose from its pins.

He caught his breath and stared for a moment, thoughts racing wildly through his head. Her hair looked so shiny and full of life blowing around her small delicate face. Why, she looked like a mere child. How old was she anyway? He'd never thought to ask. She'd taught school for a few years, hadn't she? But what did that mean?

Teachers often were hired as young as sixteen. Suddenly powerful feelings of tenderness and protectiveness surged through him. He wanted to reach out and cradle her head against his chest. He could deal with these brotherly, protective feelings, unlike other feelings Megan had aroused in him, feelings he had fought and denied. Putting her in the category of a little sister was very comfortable, indeed. Finally, he could end the continuing struggle with his feelings of love and tenderness and concern for this girl who stood before him. And that's all it was, he tried to convince himself. There was nothing inappropriate in feeling this way toward a little sister. Was there?

"Nick, are you listening to me?"

Nick snapped to attention and gave her a warm smile. "No, Megan. I'm afraid I missed it. What did you say?"

"I want to go see the rocks with everyone else. May I?"

He couldn't help but smile seeing the little-girl-pleading-look she gave him. Giving her nose a little tap with his finger, he answered, "There's no reason you shouldn't go. Just stay close to me or Andrew or Charles." He turned back to grab some bullets and started loading his rifle. When he realized Megan was still there, he glanced down at her with raised eyebrows. She was watching him very carefully.

"Is there something else, Megan?"

"Is that where you put my gun?" She indicated the back of his wagon where he obviously had a plentiful supply of guns and ammunition.

"And why do you want to know?"

"You realize, don't you, Nick, that if you'd let me keep my gun, I'd be much safer wherever I go?"

Nick threw his head back and laughed then went on loading his guns. "You would've shot your foot off by now!"

"If I'd had that gun with me when I was in Doby Town, things would've been different."

Sensing the anger in her voice, Nick leaned his Colt against the wagon and gave her his full attention.

"Do you really think, Megan, that you could point a gun at someone, someone close enough you could see his face, and pull the trigger knowing it would probably kill him?"

Megan was silent, looking at the ground. Nick leaned back against the wagon, folded his arms across his chest, and waited for her answer.

Raising her head, she looked directly into his eyes and said with conviction, "Yes, if I knew he meant to harm me or someone with me and that was the only thing I could do to stop him. I'd do it without hesitation."

Nick drew his head back and raised his eyebrows in surprise. "If you're ever in a situation where you have to, I hope you can. But you have no idea what it feels like to know you've killed someone, sent them off into eternity without a string of hope. It gnaws at you for a long time and you never get over it. If I returned your gun to you, it would just give you a false sense of security. Why court trouble and then be forced to use your gun to get out of it?"

"I think you're underestimating my ability to use good judgment."

Nick answered slowly, measuring his words to avoid a fight. "Uhh...I don't think so, Megan. I don't doubt you'd use good judgment in circumstances a little more familiar to you."

She started to respond, but he held up his hand to stop her. "What do you think would've happened if you'd used a gun against those soldiers? You'd be back at Ft. Kearny waiting for a trial."

Megan dropped her eyes to the ground in shame.

"I thought, Megan, that when you handed your gun to me, that was going to be the end of it."

Megan shook her head. "I'm sorry, Nick. You're right. What you said makes sense. I'm sorry I brought it up." She looked at him. "I wish you trusted me more though. I feel...well, I feel rather insulted by the way you treat me sometimes."

Nick's attitude went from astonishment to tenderness. He chuckled softly. "Megan, how do you think I'd do if I had to function in the world you've come from? Living and working in St. Louis, dressing up in a dandy suit and going to a stuffy office every morning, going to your fancy, grand balls at night? You'd have your hands pretty full keeping me from making all manner of mistakes."

She laughed at the picture his words conjured up. "Your example is a little far-fetched, but I do appreciate your perspective. Thanks."

Before she finished, Lucy came tearing around the corner of the wagon, breathless with excitement. "We're leaving now! Are you two coming?"

Elizabeth didn't know why a four-mile, round-trip walk could be so much fun when they walked fifteen or more miles every day. Maybe because the purpose of the walk was for pleasure, not necessity. Maybe it was the freedom of leaving the slow, plodding oxen and wagons behind. Maybe because the men shared it with them. Whatever the reason, it was a refreshing change to see so many people smiling and laughing. Children ran in circles around the adults, dogs barked and chased close on their heels, husbands and wives walked hand in hand, people called greetings out as if they hadn't seen each other in weeks.

Courthouse Rock and the smaller Jail Rock stood side by side, masses of sandstone and clay jutting abruptly through the prairie floor. When they reached the base, people spread out, some to climb them, some to walk around them, most to take time to carve their names. Chimney Rock could be clearly seen to the west. The variety of strange rock formations scattered along the horizon was so different from anything the emigrants had ever seen, they just stared in awe.

Dusk was quickly approaching, though, and parents started rounding children up for the walk back. Thomas and a few other men on horseback stayed behind to make sure there were no stragglers.

About a quarter of a mile from camp, Charles, Megan, and the three girls caught up to Elizabeth's group, which included Joe and Maude. Lucy and Abigail captured their hands and described the sights they'd seen, which included the daring escapades of Daniel and Todd McKay.

"They kept on getting closer to the edge an' their pa saw 'em. Yikes! Was he ever mad!"

"Well it's probably a good thing Caroline wasn't there. She'd have had a heart attack! I'm not sure I could handle having adventurous boys to worry about all the time." When Lucy galloped toward the Sanders' twins, she quietly added, "Lucy's all the challenge I need."

Charles chuckled, "Yeah, and your sister." They both looked over to see Megan walking close to Maude, their heads down in conversation. "How's she doing, Elizabeth?"

"Better. Definitely better." She sighed and gave him a sad smile. "She's still not herself, though, Charles. I'm not sure what's going on. She won't talk to me about it."

"Do you think it's Doby Town?"

"It makes sense because it seems to have started then. If I question her at all about how she's feeling, she clams up or changes the subject."

"Maybe she's just sick of everyone worrying about her."

"You know it's more than that, Charles. Since when has it ever been hard for Megan to talk about anything? Especially with me! I'm her sister, she's always talked to me about everything."

Charles chuckled softly. "I can think of a couple of times when she clammed up and wouldn't talk."

"And?"

Charles scratched his head in perplexity. "Both times she was trying to hide something she'd done."

Elizabeth turned and looked him meaningfully in the eyes. "That's what Maude thinks. She doesn't say much about it, but she told me she thinks the incident at Doby Town stirred up some ugly memories."

Charles shook his head. "Beats me how you women can take two or three pieces and think you've got the whole puzzle put together."

"Long before Doby Town, Maude told me Megan was struggling with something. The few services she goes to, she gets so agitated she has to leave, and whenever anyone talks about God, she'll listen for a while then excuse herself. She was never this way before. I'm afraid city living has really changed her."

"Can't say you can blame it on the city." Charles ran his fingers through his hair and scratched his long sideburns. "So, what should we do? Leave her alone? Or make her talk?"

Elizabeth laughed at the simple choices he gave her. "Maude's on the right track. I think we should leave it with her for now. It seems that God has given her real sensitivity for something like this. And so far, Megan's willing to listen to her, so the best we can do is pray for them both."

"The answer to our prayers might be nearer than we dare hope," Charles said, indicating with his head Megan and Maude walking with heads close.

At that moment, Maude realized she was closer than she'd ever been to the topic that seemed to bring Megan so much pain. Their conversation had gone from the fact that Courthouse Rock was named after the courthouse in St. Louis to Megan telling about the time she, her cousin

Emily, and two Army officers had a tintype done of the four of them standing on the courthouse steps.

Megan laughed when she thought of the scene. "That poor photographer was getting pretty impatient with Emily and me. We were acting like a couple of giggly schoolgirls. Emily almost fell when she twisted her ankle on the edge of a step and Lee had to jump and catch her just when the exposure started. We ended up paying him extra."

"Emily sounds like she was a lot of fun to be with. I bet you miss her."

Megan stared ahead and said nothing, just kept walking.

"Was this Lee with you or with your cousin?"

Megan shrugged and answered in a monotone, "With me."

"What rank was he?"

"Lieutenant."

Maude studied Megan for a moment. Her eyes were focused on the ground in front of her and the cheerful, carefree countenance was suddenly changed to a tense scowl. She decided this was as good a time as any to press on. They were still a short distance from the wagons and the crowd had spread out so they were as alone as they'd been in weeks.

"Did you see much of this lieutenant?"

Megan was slow in answering. Then shrugged and said as nonchalantly as possible, "Oh, we went to a few things together."

"Did you see much of other men in St. Louis, or was it mostly this Lt. Lee whatever his name is?"

Megan cast a mildly irritated look at Maude. "Johnson's the name, and I saw more of him than anyone. But it was nothing," she quickly added.

Suddenly Maude stopped walking, wiped perspiration from her forehead, then clutched at her chest. "Megan, stop please. I need to catch my breath," she gasped.

"Maude, are you alright?" Megan asked with alarm. "Do

you need me to call Joe or Andrew?"

"Oh no, honey. I'll be just fine in a minute or two after I sit for a spell in this grass over here. You don't mind staying with me, do you, Megan?"

"Of course not, Maude! Can I run and get you a drink?"

"Oh no, dear. I'll be fine." She reached up and grabbed Megan's hand and gently pulled her closer. "Just sit with me for a moment, Megan. Let's talk some more."

Megan sat next to her and anxiously searched her face. "Sure, Maude, what do you want to talk about?"

"You, Megan." Maude's voice carried so much concern it cracked. "Something happened to you in St. Louis that you're scared to talk about. Am I right?"

Megan drew her breath in sharply and stared at Maude with wide, frightened eyes. "What are you talking about?" she gasped.

Maude calmly met her gaze. "You know what I'm talking about. It's hanging on you so heavy, you've let it make you run away from God, Megan, and He's the only one that can do anything about it."

Megan seemed horrified as she stared back at her. She gulped for air and said nothing.

Maude laid a hand gently on Megan's knee. "It involves sin in your life, doesn't it, Megan? You're carrying a load of guilt that's gonna break your back if you don't get it taken care of."

Tears filled Megan's eyes as she continued to stare with heart-wrenching fear. "How did you find out, Maude? Who told you?" she whispered.

"You did, honey. Every time you talk about your time in St. Louis, your cousin, the soldiers—every time anyone talks about God—your face tells me, your face that used to show genuine joy now and then, but now is tired from the grief you're trying to hide. It took no great wisdom on my part to figure it out."

She stopped and studied Megan's face. Silently, she

uttered a quick prayer for wisdom and guidance then carefully chose her next words. "Be done with it, Megan, here and now, before you get up from this grass."

In desperation, Megan stammered, "I can't! I've tried and it's no use! God doesn't listen to me, Maude."

Finally, her face crumpled and tears poured from her eyes. So great was her despair that a muffled wail escaped before she could bury her face in her hands, then great wracking sobs shook her body. Maude rose to her knees and pulled Megan's head against her breast and made soft cooing sounds in her hair.

As Elizabeth walked with Charles, she couldn't keep from looking back at Megan and Maude as they made their way to camp. She saw them sit down in the grass. Then stopped in her tracks when Megan cried out and slumped down. Elizabeth gasped and picked her skirts up to hurry to her sister's side. Charles held her arm.

"No, Charles! She needs me!"

A large hand dropped to Charles' shoulder. Elizabeth turned and saw Nick standing next to them, watching carefully. "Let her go," Nick said to Charles. "Only good will come of this with Maude and your wife talking to her.

Elizabeth rushed to her sister's side and reached out her arms. Megan collapsed into her. "Oh, Elizabeth, I'm so ashamed!"

Elizabeth looked at Maude, who gave her an encouraging smile.

With her face buried on Elizabeth's shoulder, Megan continued between sobs, "Ma and Pa would be so ashamed of me! I've been living a life totally different from how they raised us!"

Elizabeth pulled away just enough to see her face. "What have you done that's so awful?" she pried gently.

Megan pressed her hands tightly to her face and didn't respond.

"Megan, as painful as this may be to talk about, it's something you must do." Maude said. "God's word tells us to confess our sins to each other. This shame you have is good. It's part of God's work to draw you back to Him."

For the first time, Megan looked up with a glimmer of hope. "You think God's trying to draw me back?

"Of course, He is. That's His business, to seek and save."

"If I could only be sure of that, it would change everything. It's very difficult to believe He'd want me."

"Want you? Why wouldn't He want you?" Elizabeth asked. "Megan, He loves you!"

"I've not felt His love in a very long time. I've only felt His displeasure and His anger."

"Because of your sin?"

Megan nodded weakly. "I used to feel His love but I threw it away for..." She shook her head in disgust. "It's really amazing how you can let yourself be drawn into certain behavior and not realize until later how dirty and soiled you've become."

"Well, honey," Maude said as she stroked her hand, "sin can't find a comfortable home in God's child for very long. You may not have been feeling His love, but He's been busy showing it to you by lettin' you get so stirred up inside. He finally got your attention."

Megan stared at her intently. "Tell me what I need to do."

"You need to confess your sin and ask God to forgive you. His word says, 'If we confess our sins, He is faithful and just to forgive us our sins, and to cleanse us from all unrighteousness.'"

"Cleanse. What a beautiful word." Hope began to sparkle in Megan's eyes. She looked from Maude to her sister. "I'm almost afraid because I don't want you to think badly of me." She looked down. "I'm so ashamed, but I know I should be." Raising her eyes to Maude's, she asked,

"Should I confess to you or to God?"

"You do as you see fit, but I think it's far better to confess both to God and to a trusted brother- or sister-in-Christ. We can help confirm God's forgiveness and restoration."

Megan choked back a sob as a fresh wave of tears streamed down her cheeks. "I'm ready. Will you pray with me?"

With tears, they both nodded and bowed together in the tall grass. With no more prompting, Megan lowered her face into her hands and let forth a torrent of words. "O, God, you know how I've been living these last few years; how selfish and vain I've been, how I've ignored you all this time and how I've lived to please myself with no thought of pleasing you."

She pressed her hands tighter against her face and continued, "I'm guilty, O, God, of the sin of lust. I've gone to great lengths to attract men, wearing revealing dresses, flirting shamelessly, and going places a decent lady would never even dream of. I've been such a horrible example to my students that I was fired." Maude and Elizabeth could just barely make out her words. "Oh, God, I'm so ashamed. Forgive me, please forgive me..."

# CHAPTER FIFTEEN

For days, Megan sought spiritual food like a person who'd been starving. She and Maude spent hours morning and night poring over Maude's huge family Bible. Maude started with a short lesson from Psalm 119 about the absolute necessity of immersing oneself in God's Word and making it a part of the way one thinks and acts.

"'Wherewithal shall a young man cleanse his way? By taking heed thereto according to thy word,'" she read. "'With my whole heart have I sought thee: O let me not wander from thy commandments. Thy word have I hid in mine heart, that I might not sin against thee.'"

Next, Maude reviewed the Gospels with her and together, they read through the book of John. Then they went on to Acts, where Maude explained how the disciples weren't to go and minister until the power of the Holy Spirit came upon them. Megan was fascinated. Paul's letters intrigued her; they spoke so clearly to her about how to live and act in a way pleasing to her new Master. She was especially drawn to passages on forgiveness and the price Jesus paid on her behalf. She didn't have to earn this priceless gift. It was offered freely to her. Grace, Maude called it, an undeserved gift. This was almost too incredible to accept.

Maude said, "Don't be offended by this, dear, but I'm amazed at what little understanding of scripture you have, considering you came from the same family as Elizabeth. Apparently, you've been taught the basics, but you've had very little spiritual nourishment since childhood. No wonder you struggled so long with sin and the inability to go to God for forgiveness."

"You know, Megan," she said one morning, "that ol' devil's not too happy about you right now and that's good. We don't want him to be happy. But one thing you have to be aware of is that in the normal life of a growing child of God, Satan will try over and over again to trip you up, and I'm a-guessin' he'll start soon with you. I'm not trying to scare you; I just want you to be wise to the enemy's ways so you can stand up strong when he comes at you. Remember: 'He that is in you is stronger than he that is in the world.' Don't try to fight him with your own strength 'cuz it's pretty puny. Fight him by getting down on your knees and by poring through this great book our Lord gave us. You hear me now, honey." She looked her straight in the eye. "Remember how strong His love for you is and nothing, *nothing* can take His love away from you. Satan will fill your head all full of the most outlandish lies if you let him, and the best way to fight his lies is with the truths in this book." She lovingly ran her hand over the pages opened before them.

That evening Reverend Holt had a service and again preached about man's sinful nature and about the judgment of God. Megan sat with Maude, Elizabeth, and the girls. She looked up and saw Nick and Andrew standing toward the back joining in the singing of hymns. Both caught her eye and gave her smiles that sent a shiver of joy through her.

*Amazing grace, how sweet the sound,*
*That saved a wretch like me.*
*I once was lost, but now I'm found.*
*Was blind, but now I see.*

She'd heard the song a thousand times, but for the first time, it was rich with meaning. She sang as if she felt it from the depths of her being. Her reaction to the preacher's words was totally different than before. She understood the nature of this God he talked about. She also knew he needed to balance his sermons out with some of God's love. Yet one comment he made did stick with her. She couldn't quite shake it off nor explain it away.

"How would you stand up under the scrutiny of the people of God? Is your life full of lies? Are there things in your life so degrading and disgusting that people here would be horrified to know? Are you hiding secret sin? If so, then judgment is already being sent from the hand of the Almighty God. You can't escape the anger and justice of a holy God!"

When the service was over, Megan walked quietly back to prepare for bed. She wanted to ask Maude questions but couldn't think how to begin. Surely it wasn't necessary to reveal *everything* in her past. Her stomach tightened with anxiety at the thought of it. Woodenly, she splashed water on her face, pulled pins out of her hair, and spread her bedroll out.

Throughout the night, the father of all lies worked at twisting God's truth. Megan thrashed around so much she woke herself and Lucy.

"What's the matter, Megan?" Lucy's small sleepy voice asked.

"Nothing, honey. Go back to sleep." She heard Lucy snuggle back down into her bedroll and sigh with sleepy contentment. Megan smiled and tried to pray, but instantly her mind was engulfed by conflicting thoughts. *Boy, you sure fooled them, didn't you? Sure, you confessed, but you didn't tell everything, did you? Can you just imagine what everyone would think of you if they knew it all? You'd be thrown out of this train so fast! None of the decent men here would ever want to have anything to do with you. They could never look at you the same again. No wonder those soldiers tried to take advantage of you. They'd probably already heard about you.*

The last thought was so ridiculous, Megan finally put an end to the downward spiral of her thinking. Shaking her head viciously, she sat up and ground the heels of her hands into her eyes. "Jesus, help me," she whispered. "Help me." She sat still before him and let him calm her. Finally, she drifted into a peaceful sleep with those words on her lips, probably one of the most powerful prayers ever prayed; "Jesus, help me."

A spirit of excitement swept through the camp as they prepared to pull out the next morning. This was the day they would pull into Ft. Laramie where they'd spend several days replenishing supplies, making repairs on wagons, swapping tales with other travelers, and just relaxing from the arduous routine.

At the noon meal stop, Thomas filled his plate and lowered himself to the ground next to Megan.

"Are you going to save a dance for me tonight at the fort?" he asked her.

Megan looked up with raised eyebrows and swallowed a hard lump of biscuit. "A dance? They're having a dance?"

"Anytime we've been there on a Friday or Saturday night, they've had one," Nick answered.

"Also, anytime a wagon train pulls in with pretty girls aboard. This Major Bledsoe's pretty tough on his men, but when they're off duty, he believes in showing them a good time." Thomas lowered his voice and leaned a little closer.

"And when he gets one look at you, there'll be a party every night."

Megan rolled her eyes and got up to wash her plate and fork. "You're hopeless, Thomas. Yes, I'll save a dance for you, but if you don't find a woman soon, I hope you go drown yourself. I can't stand to see you in such misery."

Thomas looked offended and shot back with, "'Course I doubt the boss will let you go."

Megan stopped then glanced over at Nick who either didn't hear or pretended not to hear.

Nick leaned in to talk privately with Charles and Andrew. "I'm counting pretty heavy on a detachment of soldiers being sent on west with us for a way. I don't like the reports I've been hearing this last week. Things are not looking good with the Indians west of Laramie."

"Can we make a request for one?" Charles asked.

"Wouldn't hurt to ask." Nick looked up and his eyes locked for just a moment with Megan's. His heart jumped. He looked away and tried to put her out of his thoughts. He'd been doing that a lot lately. He'd heard Thomas' remark and knew Megan would be coming to him soon to ask permission to leave the wagon compound for the dance. He also knew he'd say yes. It was tough to say no to her. Besides, even though he didn't like to dance, he knew he'd end up going and against his better judgment, he wanted her there, too. He shook his head, trying to snap himself out of this train of thought. He picked up his dishes, walked over, and put them in the dishwater where Megan was working and leaned down to whisper in her ear, "You can go tonight. Just use common sense and stay close to us."

As Megan turned to thank him, her hair brushed his cheek. The urge to lower his face and kiss her was so overwhelming that he abruptly turned from her and walked away.

Later that afternoon when Megan was sitting next to Maude on the swaying wagon seat, she commented, "Nick told me I could go to that dance tonight, but he didn't seem to be very happy about it."

"Maybe he just can't stand the thought of you dancing with all those other men," Maude suggested with a twinkle in her eye.

"You're really funny, Maude, you know that? He's a difficult man to figure out. Just when I think he can tolerate me, he turns around and treats me like an annoying insect. No...worse than that; he acts mad and I'm not sure why. It's very confusing."

Megan turned and let the warm afternoon breeze blow over her face. She scanned the changing panorama. A few days ago, they came upon the first timber they'd seen in the last two hundred miles. At this point of the trip, so many flowers surrounded the trail it looked like they were wading through a sea of yellow. But all around, Megan could see where the wheels of many wagons had crushed their way through.

She turned to Maude again. "Rev. Holt said some things last night..." She paused to swat at a fly then wrung her hands and shoved them into her lap.

"Megan! Megan!" Suzanne ran up even with the wagon seat, breathing hard, sweat trickling down her face. "Lucy fell on a rock and cut her knee and ripped her dress and there's blood everywhere!"

"Oh my!" Megan exclaimed as she gathered her skirt up and jumped to the ground.

"One of these days, girl, you're gonna catch your skirts and these wheels will run right over you!" Maude hollered.

Nick heard Maude and trotted up next to their wagon in time to see her shaking her head and clucking like a mad hen. "What's wrong, Maude?" he asked.

She turned her snapping eyes on him. "You should've made rules about not jumping off a moving wagon! That Megan! Every time she wants to get off, she's in too much of a hurry to wait for Joe to stop this thing. She just hurls herself over the side."

She started shaking her finger at him, and Joe shook with laughter. Nick managed to keep a straight face. "You mark my words, Nicholas Webster, she'll get tangled up and run over one of these days. And if it's not her, it'll be someone else." Having dissipated her anger and fear with those words, she calmed and seemed a little embarrassed. "And besides that, it's entirely unladylike."

Joe laughed, put his arm around her shoulder, and squeezed. "You kinda like that little gal, don't you? Well so do I, Maude. She's getting to be more like a daughter every day. And don't worry, I'm watching out for her. You keep right on doing what you're doing. God's really using you and it does my heart good just to sit here and listen." That was a lot of words for old Joe to utter at one time. He gave Maude one more quick squeeze then settled back in the seat as if it wore him out. He was a hardworking, wiry little man, but saying more than a few words at a time taxed his limit.

Nick gave them a little smile, tipped his hat, and rode off in Megan's direction. He had many things to tend to, but he couldn't resist using this as an excuse to see her. When he finally spotted her, the last few wagons were passing. A group of children were clustered around her as she squatted to attend to a distraught Lucy. Noticed by only a few, he rode close enough to hear Lucy wailing about the torn and bloody dress.

"Ma's gonna be so mad. We just fixed this dress and now I've ruined it again! And I only have one more she'll let me wear on this trip." More tears made tracks down her dusty face.

"We can worry about your dress later, Lucy. Right now, we need to take care of your knee. Can you walk?"

"No," she sobbed.

"Well, I'm going to have to carry you, then. Here, put your arms around my neck." Megan hoisted her up with a grunt and turned to see Nick behind them.

"Looks like you could use some help." He slid down to the ground, took Lucy in his arms, and effortlessly swung back up into the saddle with her. She smiled and snuggled against him. Nick adored Lucy and he suspected the feelings were mutual. He didn't have much time to pay attention to her, but he kept her happy with smiles and winks and a pat on the head now and then.

Megan watched them with a smile. He stroked Lucy's head and jokingly scolded her, "So what kind of trouble have you gotten into this time?" She pulled her dress up to expose her cut knee. "Uh-oh. I think Doc Andrew might want to take a look at that. Is that all right with you?"

Lucy nodded with satisfaction. Finally, her injury was getting the attention it deserved.

Megan, shielding her eyes against the sun, looked up at them. "Thanks for your help, Nick. Do you want me to run ahead and find Andrew?"

"Naw, I can find him quick enough. You round up these younguns and catch up before you get left behind. Make sure there's no stragglers." With that, he tipped his hat and rode ahead.

Soon after Nick left Lucy in Andrew's care, they passed through several small Indian encampments and were greeted by Indians on foot and horseback, some wanting to sell freshly killed game, others wanting to trade moccasins and lariats for money, powder, or whiskey. As they approached the fort, they saw more Indians. They pulled into camp next to the fort in a spot just vacated by a train a few days ahead of them.

The evening meal was a hurried affair with mothers trying to get everyone fed in time to prepare for the evening's festivities. After a good scrubbing, they dressed in their best clothes, dug out from tightly packed trunks. Tomorrow they would work. Tonight was the time for fun and no one deserved it more than these tired, dusty travelers.

## CHAPTER SIXTEEN

**M**egan's eyes sparkled with excitement as she and Jessica walked up the creaking board steps into the crowded room. The musicians were sitting in and around open windows overlooking the parade grounds so the dancers outside could hear the music as well. Everywhere people were talking and laughing, men clapping other men on the back as they roared at their own jokes. Women were delighted at the chance to dress up, even if their best was nothing more than a clean, crisp calico. Even the children were allowed to join in the fun, running among the adults, ribboned pigtails flying and faces pink from scrubbing.

Blue-clad soldiers stood out from the crowd wherever Megan looked. The men surely outnumbered the women here. Just then, a man's loud voice ordered silence. His command was repeated several times before the people outside responded. Soon there was a hush everywhere.

"Hello, everyone! I'm Major Bledsoe and I'd like to welcome you to Ft. Laramie. To start the night off, I want all the men to gather on my right and the women to gather on my left. Can you hear me outside?" he bellowed.

"Yes!" several people hollered in unison as everyone, inside and out, began to part down the middle.

As Megan was winding her way to the women's side, a blue sleeve brushed her shoulder. "Hello, Miss O'Mally," came a teasing voice. She looked up into a soldier's grinning face, flashed him a bewildered smile, then moved into place beside Elizabeth. *How in the world did he learn my name so fast?*

She opened her mouth to speak to Elizabeth when another soldier caught her eye. The rest of the room faded into a haze as Megan stared dumbstruck into a familiar face. He stared back and waved. Lt. Lee Johnson! She refused to believe it was really him. He whispered something to a soldier next to him, looked back at her, and laughed. She forced herself to close her mouth and stop gawking. The soldier next to him pointed at her as he said something to Johnson and they both laughed again.

Megan's heart pounded in her head.

"Is everyone ready? Good! As soon as the music starts, I want you men to go choose your partner. After this, you're on your own."

Major Bledsoe's words sounded a thousand miles away. She looked quickly for a door just as the music started. *He's coming straight for me! Oh, God! Oh, God!* She hid behind Elizabeth then quickly ducked behind two other women. Suddenly an arm reached out and grabbed her. Megan gasped, whirled around, and stared up into Thomas' amused face.

"Hey! Are you trying to hide from me? You didn't forget your promise, did you?"

Megan let him put his arm around her. "I wouldn't hide from you, Thomas." Her eyes left his face and darted frantically around. She saw Johnson standing in the middle of the room looking at her. Thomas nodded toward him.

"See that man looking this way? That's Capt. Johnson.

196

He and his men will be traveling with us all the way to Ft. Bridger. Nick's pretty happy about that news." Thomas snickered. "Looks like he's got his eye on you already."

When Capt. Johnson saw Megan with Thomas, he turned aside and asked Natalie Simmons to dance. Thomas looked down and saw the frantic expression on her face. "What's wrong, Megan?"

"I...I'm fine, Thomas, but...but I have to go." She pushed away from him, glanced toward Johnson, and started moving in the opposite direction. "I'm sorry, but I have to go. Bye," she croaked as she pulled away from Thomas' hand and made her way to the door as quickly as she could.

As soon as Megan got down the steps and out of the light cast through the door, she ran. Her mind was screaming prayers to God and instructions to herself. *God, don't let him see me. Help me get away, oh please. I've got to hurry, get away, somewhere where he won't find me, somewhere where no one knows. God, help me! Help me.*

There were soldiers near the gate. *Okay, Megan, walk slowly so they don't notice you. Don't breathe so loud, stupid.* Her breath came in gulps and her arms and legs moved like a mechanical puppet as she forced herself to walk.

She made it past the soldiers, through the gate, then to the wagons. When she reached Charles and Elizabeth's wagon, her knees felt so weak she could barely crawl up into it. She fell across their comforter, her mind screaming at her again.

*God, I have to leave. Oh, God, what can I do? Help me! I can't live with this! Everyone's going to know. My life will be ruined! I've got to get away.* She lay there panting, trying to get control of herself. Her fingers dug into the soft fabric as she gained strength from the new determination growing in her. Quickly she jumped up and fumbled around inside the clothes chest and fished out a pair of Charles' pants, a shirt, and an old patched coat. She pulled at her buttons, yanked her dress and petticoat off, and stuffed them in a cloth pouch. Then she quickly pulled on Charles' pants and shirt. She rolled up the pant legs. Her own boots would have to do; Charles' were much too big. Then she went to the food chest and began stuffing dried beef sticks and dried fruit into the pouch. Her small moneybag went deep into her pocket. Then she got out a slip of paper, pen and inkwell, and began the difficult task of explaining this to Charles and Elizabeth.

When the note was finished, she grabbed some hairpins, twisted her hair into a tight bun, and pinned it to the top of her head. She pulled on an old wide-brimmed felt hat of Charles', bringing the brim down to conceal her face in its shadow. Her confused mind continued to click off frantic instructions. *Think, Megan, think. I need a horse. Where am I going to find a horse? I can't take Charles' or Nick's or Thomas'. They can't do without theirs. Oh, God, help me think.* She grabbed her pouch, one of Charles' rifles, and a box of bullets, and slipped down out of the wagon, looking cautiously around. No one saw her. Picking up a handful of dirt, she smeared some across her jaw, chin, and upper lip.

*A horse, Megan, find a horse. I should have bought a horse instead of that stupid cow. I'll have to just take one and leave money.* Just then, she saw three horses hitched outside the gate. She walked in measured steps, looking from side to side to see who was watching. The horses were still saddled, apparently waiting for someone.

*How much money should I leave? Where will I put the note? The note! Oh, Megan, you idiot! Get some paper, quick.* She turned and hurried back into the wagon, pulled paper and pen out again, and wrote, "I'm sorry. Hope this covers the cost of your horse and saddle."

Back over the wagon seat, across the trampled grass she went again. *God, don't let anyone see me, please.* She

wrapped the note around several bills and stuffed them
under the edge of the saddle on one of the other horses.
Talking softly to the horse, she positioned her left foot in
the stirrup and swung up into the saddle. Quietly she eased
him around into the darkness of camp. When she got well
beyond the last wagon, she broke into a trot, then a full
gallop when she passed the other trains and the Indian
encampments. Three times she was greeted by people, one
a group of Indians approaching the fort, loaded with goods
to trade.

Finally, the tears came, streaming down her face leaving
muddy streaks through the dirt she'd smeared there earlier.
*Dear Lord, I can't believe I'm doing this! Where am I
going?* Fortunately for Megan, the moon was full and she
could see the shadows of wheel ruts from decades of
wagons following this same route up to the fort. In her
confused state, she reasoned that if she continued following
what tracks she could see and going the way she had come,
eventually she would make it to a trading post where she
could stock up on supplies and continue on to Missouri, or
better yet, hitch up with another train maybe headed for
California. She figured if she rode long and hard, she could
make the distance in a fraction of the time it took the
wagon train.

# CHAPTER SEVENTEEN

Dancing wasn't Nick's favorite pastime. He knew that he, like everyone else, needed the change of pace, but he would have chosen something different. But on this night, something was different. He felt a stirring inside, almost a boyish anticipation. When Megan left, he caught himself fidgeting and watching the door. He was annoyed with himself. He drank some punch and wandered out onto the grounds among the other dancers and made small talk with people milling around on the edge.

A high-pitched voice interrupted him. "Don't let on that I said anything, Mr. Webster, but my daughter's been dying for you to ask her to dance."

He let out a sigh of resignation when he looked down into the grinning face of Mrs. Simmons. "Sorry, ma'am. I don't dance."

"Psaw! I've seen you dance. And you're here, aren't you? That tells me something."

Nick did his best to hide his growing impatience. All he wanted to do was find out where Megan had disappeared to.

"Time's a wasting, Mr. Webster," Mrs. Simmons whispered.

Nick looked around and ran his fingers through his hair. "Sure. Where is she?"

"Right over there by Dick. You'd better hurry though. Those Purdy and McCullough boys haven't given her a moment's rest all evening. Land sakes! It's all a mother can do to keep tabs on a pretty daughter. You hurry on over, now."

"Yes, Mrs. Simmons." He chuckled softly to himself as he walked the distance to her daughter. Natalie was standing sheepishly by her father, glancing occasionally in his direction. It was no secret to her what her mother had been up to.

"Hello, Miss Simmons. Do you have time to dance with an old man like me?"

"Call me Natalie, please, and yes, I'd love to dance."

Taking her hand, he led her out among the others. Nick wasn't a good dancer, but he knew his steps and managed to keep his feet off others'. Natalie chattered away and he squeezed in an occasional "uh-huh" and a smile. He was bored and again caught himself looking over the crowd for Megan.

He wasn't one to analyze his feelings, but nevertheless, he questioned and scolded himself. When the dance was over, he said a quick thank-you and strode agitatedly toward the dance hall. *Enough of this.* He was ready to leave. Thomas was dancing, and Andrew was in the corner talking and laughing. He grabbed some punch and moved over to join him. The night wore on. The crowd began to thin as mothers took their children away to tuck them in for the night.

Nick looked up and saw Elizabeth walk through the door, paper in hand and a look of fright and confusion on her face. She quickly sought out Charles and thrust the paper at him, almost in tears. Nick took five long strides and was beside them.

"What's the problem?"

Charles, in shock, handed the note to Nick.

*Charles and Elizabeth,*
*I'm so sorry, please try to understand. I have to get away as quickly as possible. I'll be okay. Charles, I took your gun and some clothes. Here's some money to help pay for them and you can have my cow. I love you but I can't stay. You'll be hearing terrible rumors about me but please believe me, they're not true! I can't bring myself to stay with people who might hear and believe it. Try to understand. I love you. I'll try to make contact with you through Aunt Eleanor. Good-bye.*
*With all my love, Megan.*

"What?" Nick exploded. "This is ridiculous! Where would she go?"

"Find her, please, someone!" Elizabeth sobbed.

Andrew was reading the note now. "Dear, Lord!" he uttered. "What in God's name is she running from?"

Charles headed for the door. "Well if we're going to find her, we better do it quick before she gets any farther." Andrew and Elizabeth followed.

Nick caught up to them outside. "Slow down, everybody. It won't do any good riding all over the countryside. We've got to try to think like Megan for a minute and figure out which way she went. She was obviously very upset about something and left in a terrible hurry. She said something in her note about taking some clothes. I'm guessing maybe she's dressed in Charles' clothes."

"So, we can't expect to be looking for someone that looks like Megan," Andrew added.

"Or if she's on horseback or on foot," Nick said. "I

figure she's got enough sense to stick to a marked trail, and there are two that can be seen very well in this light; the one we came on and the one we're leaving on. There's also one headed north that might be easy enough to see. I don't know what condition it's in right now."

"If she's running away, she's not likely to go on ahead of us," Andrew said.

"Not unless she's planning on riding hard and joining another train. Most likely she followed our trail back."

By then Thomas had joined them. "If I'd had any sense, I would've followed her when she left. She was pretty churned up about something."

"Well let's saddle up and go!" Charles said impatiently.

Nick started barking orders, "I need someone to take each trail and someone else to circle around the area. I'll go east, Charles, you go west; Thomas, north and, Andrew, you make several sweeps of the area then ride out to meet me if I'm not back by sunrise." He nodded at each man as he gave his orders.

"Right, boss." They moved quickly to saddle up. Nick packed a few provisions, mounted, and rode out.

The moon was full and high in the sky. Nick could see the trail clearly, but there was no way he could track anyone. Too many wagons and horses had passed this way recently. He had ridden off the trail a few times to look for anything that would indicate a lone rider. Nothing. He continued following the wheel ruts, praying that Megan would've had enough sense to do the same. He chuckled at himself and shook his head in frustration. He knew it was useless to count on her using common sense about anything right now. The fool woman!

Looking at the moon, he calculated the time since he left camp to be about two hours. As fast as he'd been riding, he hadn't figured it would take nearly this long. He was beginning to think he'd passed her, or maybe she'd gone a different direction.

Just when he was about to turn back, he heard a horse whinny to his right. He slowed down and eased his horse off the packed ground and into the grass. As he got closer, the moon offered enough light so he could barely see one horse and what looked like a man sitting in a grove of trees. There could easily be more, but the lone horse was enough evidence for Nick that he dared approach. He slipped out of the saddle, tied his horse to a bush, and grabbed his rifle. Keeping the other horse between himself and his prey, he crept cautiously forward. Talking in low, soothing tones, he ran his hand over the flank of the strange horse. Just as he feared! A U.S. Army brand! His eyes scanned through the grove. A figure sat about thirty feet from him, slumped against a tree. No one else was in sight. Still guarded by the horse, Nick called out, "Hello."

Instantly the figure stood up and whirled around, rifle at the hip. "You stay away from me or I'll shoot!" hissed a frightened female voice.

Tremendously relieved, Nick stepped out from behind the horse. "Megan! It's me...Nick."

Her gun cracked and Nick heard the bullet whiz by over his head. Instinctively he threw himself onto his belly and pulled his rifle up.

"Megan! Megan! Don't shoot! It's me...Nick Webster. Don't shoot!"

"Nick? Did I hit you? I'm sorry, I meant to shoot it over your head."

He stood, brushing dirt from his clothes, then walked toward her.

"Don't come any closer!"

He couldn't believe it! Her gun was still aimed at him. "Put the gun down, Megan."

"No, Nick. You get on your horse and leave."

He stood dumbfounded then ran his fingers through his hair in angry frustration. "Not without you, I won't. Give me the gun," he commanded her.

"I'm serious. I'll shoot if you come any closer."

"You wouldn't shoot at me." He started moving cautiously in her direction.

"I'll do it if I have to. Stop, Nick."

"Megan, this is nonsense! Give it to me, now!" His voice came out angrier with every word.

"No!" She backed up as he got closer.

He held out his hand. "Give me the gun," he demanded slowly and firmly, with steel in every word.

She took another step back and cocked.

Nick kept moving. "Megan," he warned.

She took one more step back then threw the rifle at his face and turned to run. It didn't take Nick long to reach her. He grabbed her arm and tried to hold on, but she hit him, wrenched it free, and kept going. Throwing his gun down, he took just three long steps, grabbed her arm, and swung her until her back was firmly pressed against his chest. He brought both arms down around her shoulders, pinning her arms to her sides. She kicked and struggled and sobbed. Lifting her off the ground, he held her firmly until she drooped against him like a rag doll. The fight was over and all that was left was choking sobs. Something in him wanted to gather her up in his arms to soothe her and protect her. He checked himself. Putting her down, he turned her to face him.

"It's time for us to have a serious talk, Megan." His voice was husky with emotion. He held her firmly by the arm and steered her over to a log lying on the ground. They both sat. "I saw your note to Charles and Elizabeth."

Megan's face was a muddy mess. She kept wiping at her eyes and nose with the sleeve of Charles' old shirt. Her sobbing had stopped, and Nick could see it took a lot of control for it not to start up again.

"Before we get back to camp, I want you to tell me what's going on."

"I can't tell you and I'm not going back."

Nick rolled his eyes and stood up. "Whatever it takes, young lady, you're going back with me. Don't fight me on this, Megan," he warned. "I promise you I'll win."

She stared at her feet and didn't respond. Nick walked a few paces, stopped, broke a dead branch off a tree, and threw it down at his feet in frustration.

"I'm trying to understand why you're doing this and you're not helping me any. What's this about some terrible story about you?" Turning, he could see she'd lost the fight with her tears again. Her face was buried in her hands and her body heaved with gulping sobs.

"I'm sorry," she choked. "I can't stand for anyone to know."

Nick sat next to her again. Gently he prompted, "I'm bound to hear it from someone. Wouldn't you rather I get the straight story from you first?"

He waited a long time before she raised her head and gave a deep, exhausted sigh. "Fine, I'll tell you. But first, I want to know if you think you can believe me."

"Why shouldn't I? I've known you long enough to know you wouldn't lie to me."

Megan brought her eyes to his and studied him for a moment before she started. Despite the circumstances, Nick couldn't help but be amused at her appearance: muddy, tear-streaked face, hair hanging in strings from under the hat she had pulled low on her forehead. The clothes looked huge on her.

"When I lived with my aunt and uncle in St. Louis. I...I taught school there. I had two cousins, Julie and Emily. Emily was a little younger than me and...and very beautiful and lively and spoiled. She did whatever she wanted; no one stood in her way. And, I found out later, she had no morals." Megan paused and took a deep breath. She continued in a slow monotone, "She and I started going to a lot of parties where there were soldiers, mostly young officers. I went because it was fun." She looked up at Nick to gauge his response. "You understand, just to dance and...and, I started enjoying it so much it almost became the focus of my life." Megan stood up, slowly took a few steps, then turned around. "I'm ashamed to admit this now, but I really did enjoy the attention of all those men. And now, looking back, I realize all the things I did to get that attention; the flirting, the way I dressed, the things I said."

She dropped her face into her hands in shame then abruptly looked over at Nick. "Don't misunderstand me, please. I never went beyond being a little free with hugs and kisses and"—her voice lowered and her eyes dropped in shame—"wearing dresses so low, I'd die if any of you good people saw me in one." She looked up, fatigue making her look ill. "But beyond that, there was nothing."

Nick nodded. She went on. "I spent a lot of time with one officer in particular. I was really getting to like him. His name was Lt. Lee Johnson. Captain now, I hear."

"Oh yes. We met." Nick's eyes narrowed.

Megan took a deep breath and walked farther away until she stood under a tree. Her hand reached up to clutch at a branch. Nick could see the tenseness growing in her.

"One night, Emily asked me to go to a party with her at a house out in the country. She borrowed her father's buggy and drove us out there. Just the two of us, unescorted. I should have known something was wrong as soon as I walked in...I was so stupid and naive...and never in my wildest imaginings would I have thought my cousin would ever, ever get herself involved in such...such a horrible place."

She looked at Nick. His eyebrows were drawn together in confusion. Megan closed her eyes and shook her head back and forth in disgust. "Nick, it was a whore house! A so-called 'high-class' brothel for wealthy men and military officers. Emily had been working there for months and she actually thought I'd want to work there, too! Can you believe that? I guess it goes to show the kind of image I had."

Nick was shocked. He tried to control his reaction. "What happened then?" he asked.

"I still didn't know what kind of place it was. When I walked out onto the porch, I saw Lee. At the time, I couldn't figure out why he acted the way he did. At first, he acted confused and angry to see me there. Then he changed to being extremely friendly, then...then when he got me alone outside, he turned into a different man than I'd ever known

Nick felt anger well up inside. He wanted to hit something. "Go on," he tried to encourage her.

"I was too stupid to know what he was after. Of course, the more I resisted, the angrier he got." She hesitated. "Without going into any detail, he finally got to the point where I realized I was in danger and needed to get away. I shoved him and ran to the house, found Emily, and made her take me home." Too drained to continue, she lowered herself to the ground and rested her head in her hands. Nick looked on in stormy silence.

After a while, Megan lifted her head and continued, "The next day I found out where I'd been and what Emily had been involved in all these months. In less than twenty-four hours, it seemed as if Lee had spread the news among the whole United States Army that Megan O'Mally was a whore and they were lining the streets to be my next customer. Somehow the news reached the school board before Monday and I was fired in disgrace." The pain was evident in her voice. "I figured I'd be safe from all the gossip if I went west with Charles and Elizabeth. But now..."

"Now, you think the gossip has followed you because Capt. Johnson is here."

"I know it has. He was pointing me out to the others and laughing. Do you understand now why I ran?"

"Yes, I do," he answered.

She gave one great sigh of relief and smiled a tired smile. "Good, then you know why I can't go back."

He put his hands up to stop her. "Whoa! Slow down there. You had more than one choice laid in front of you and you picked the worst."

Megan put her hands on her hips and stared him defiantly in the face. "Mr. Webster, I saw the look in Lee's eyes. And I know exactly what he was telling his men. And then I heard he and those same men will be traveling with us. Now our train will be escorted by soldiers who think I'm a whore. And soon the whole wagon train will think that. And before you know it, all of Oregon will know. If you think I'm going back to face that, then you're crazy!"

Nick never lowered his gaze. "Miss Megan O'Mally," he spoke each word with emphasis, "are you innocent?"

"Of the charge of being a prostitute, yes. But not of all the other stuff I told you about, the flirting and immodest dress."

"And those are forgiven and in the past, right?"

"Yes," she answered confidently.

"Then why in God's name are you running away?"

She didn't answer.

"Because you're afraid of what people might think. Am I right?"

She shut her eyes and nodded.

Nick stood and put his hands on her shoulders. "Now look at me."

Megan opened her eyes, glanced up at his, then stared at his chest.

He gave her a gentle shake. "Megan, if you run now, you'll be running your whole life. You've got to face up to it, declare your innocence, and trust God to work things out."

"I can't," she whispered.

"I'll help you."

She brought her hands up and gripped his shirt just as

the tears started pouring down. He pulled her to him and nestled her head against his chest.

"Megan, it wasn't at all hard for me to believe your story. Don't you think Charles and Elizabeth will believe you?"

Her head nodded against him.

"Andrew and Thomas, Maude and Joe, they'll all believe you, too. In fact, even if you were guilty of the worst of the rumors, they'd all go on loving you. Can't you see that?"

She didn't respond.

Nick held her head against his chest and looked up through the trees at the sky. The eastern horizon was beginning to brighten. He knew he had to get her back soon.

Before he could say anything, Megan pushed away and begged him, "Nick, can't you please at least let me leave so I can get to the last trading post we stopped at?" She grabbed his arm when he turned away with exasperation.

"Please, Nick, I know I could work things out. I'll catch a wagon train headed for California. Everything will be fine."

Nick could feel his patience slipping away. "No, everything won't be fine. For one thing, the U.S. Army will be hot on your trail wherever you go."

"Why?"

"Because, little lady, you stole their horse!"

"What? I did not! I paid for that horse and the saddle."

"It doesn't matter. The horse wasn't for sale. When they find out it's missing and you're missing, they'll come after you. Wherever you are, Megan," he added.

She walked in a stupor away from him. "My God, what have I done?" Running her hands down over her mud-streaked face, she started chuckling weakly. "I'm not only accused of being a whore, I'm also a horse thief. Why don't you just hang me right here and let's be done with it."

"We better ride, Megan. The sooner we get back, the better. I figure if you go straight to the major and confess, he might have some pity and let you off." He moved over and threw the blanket and saddle on the horse's back.

"I've really made a mess of things, haven't I?"

Nick just glanced up quickly at her then tightened the cinch. "Come over here and I'll help you up."

She stopped by the horse's head. "Nick, I'm scared."

He reached out and guided her by the shoulder to the stirrup. "I know you are. Let's just pray Major Bledsoe's the man I think he is. Up with you now. Let's go."

# CHAPTER EIGHTEEN

$M$egan fidgeted with her skirt while she and Nick waited outside Major Bledsoe's office. It had taken them longer to get there than had suited him, she realized. The ride back took almost three hours then the poor man had to wait while she washed up and changed.

"Well, it's certainly not going to hurt the situation to have you looking like this," he said, as he looked down on her with appreciation. She'd pinned her hair up, her dress was fresh and clean, and she'd scrubbed all the dirt off her face. "You're not a typical picture of an emigrant who's been on the trail for months." Her face heated with his compliments.

"While you were getting ready, I returned the horse to the post livery, then I went to the major to prepare him. Bledsoe is a kind and reasonable man, but he's also a strong military man who believes in justice. I still don't know what to expect from him."

"Major Bledsoe will see you now," announced the corporal with a nod toward the major's door. Nick stood first and offered his hand to Megan. She took a deep breath to calm her nerves. The results of this meeting could change the course of her life. In the back of her mind, she entertained the faint hope that maybe she wouldn't be allowed to continue with her wagon train. Dealing with strangers seemed far easier than dealing with people she knew. But that thought was quickly replaced by a new fear which surprised her; what if she never saw Nick again? He knew her whole story and he hadn't shunned her. Instead, he'd responded with tenderness and acceptance. He was so strong, unbearably tough at times, but her growing awareness of his gentle, loving nature threw her heart into confusion. Just the touch of his hand as he helped her up and guided her toward the door made her pulse quicken.

The major stood as they entered. He waited in silence until the door was closed, then he nodded toward Nick with permission to begin. "Sergeant Webster."

"Major Bledsoe, I'd like you to meet Miss O'Mally. And Miss O'Mally, Major Bledsoe."

They nodded and made short, formal greetings, then sat at the major's command. "I'm sorry you didn't stay to enjoy the dance last night, Miss O'Mally."

Taken aback by his opening statement, she opened her mouth to respond, but nothing came out.

He leaned forward and rested his arms on his desk. "Tell me about the horse." His voice betrayed his gentle side.

Megan took a deep breath and started. He was obviously a busy man, so she tried to keep it short. Briefly she gave the background and told of the false accusations, then of seeing Capt. Johnson and hearing he and his men would accompany their train. "Major Bledsoe, I can't possibly make you understand the fear and confusion I felt. When I took that horse, I only had one thing on my mind and that was to get away as quickly as possible. I knew it wasn't right, but in my confused state, I never even considered it would appear I'd stolen the horse...because I paid for it. I'm so sorry, sir. Never in my right mind would I stoop to stealing anything, sir, especially something as important as a horse." Against her will, her voice began to take on a pleading tone.

She saw a flicker of amusement in the major's otherwise-steady gaze. "I believe I understand your explanation, Miss O'Mally." He stood and walked to the window. "I even sympathize with your plight." He looked at her and she began to relax.

"However, the fact remains that a horse was stolen, correct?"

Megan swallowed. "Yes, sir."

"And there's no one else to blame for the taking of this horse?"

"No, sir," she answered weakly.

"My position on this has to be that thievery must be punished; whether the crime was committed by male or female, or whether there's reason or not."

Megan's hopes plummeted.

"As of this day I'm putting you under house arrest."

Megan gasped and Nick started to rise in protest. With one quick motion of his hand, the major stopped any interruption and continued. "Since her home for the last month or so has been your wagon train, that will also be her prison and I'm putting her under your guard for the duration of the trip," he said to Nick, who slowly began to grin. "I don't consider this a joke, Sergeant. You will swear to me to do your duty as appointed unto you by the authorities in charge of this matter. Do you swear?"

"Yes, sir, I swear," Nick quietly answered.

Bledsoe walked back to his desk and looked from Nick to Megan. "I want to impress on both of you the serious nature of this case and the fact you're getting off extremely easy, Miss. A man in my position has the right to execute judgment on military property as he sees fit. Another man might have had you hung, and he would have been acting within his rights. So, appreciate your sentence, Miss O'Mally. You are to stay with this train under Sergeant Webster's guard until he decides your destination has been reached. If I hear that you've left the train before then, you'll be considered a fugitive from the law and I'll have you arrested and brought back here. I'll not go easy on you again."

After two days of washing clothes, fixing or replacing broken wagon parts, tending to damaged and worn hooves, and buying new supplies of every description, the wagons finally pulled out and continued on their long journey. Capt. Johnson had his men mounted and ready. He assigned three scouts to work with Thomas and had the rest of his men ride in pairs, spread out the length of the train.

Much as he hated to admit it, Nick saw that Johnson was a good officer; organized and disciplined. His men respected him and obeyed commands without hesitation.

Megan had made herself as scarce as possible since the morning she walked back to camp after her "sentencing." She fended off questions from family and close friends until she'd gathered them together that night. Tearfully she apologized and repeated the story she'd told Nick. They reacted the same as he had. Elizabeth had the hardest time dealing with it. Knowing that her cousin, Emily, was involved in prostitution was extremely hard to bear. Telling all of them was most likely one of the most difficult things Megan had ever done, and Nick's respect for her grew.

At first, the rough, rocky trail went up and down steep hills covered by pine and cedar. At night, they pulled into a tight circle and put extra guards on the cattle. Soldiers and emigrants were told to have rifles ready and in plain sight. Nick found himself admiring Capt. Johnson's military style; the two agreed on everything concerning security.

That's as far as any communication went between them. The sight of Johnson filled Nick with disgust. He caught himself watching him with suspicion, so much so that he neglected some of his duties.

Several days out of Ft. Laramie, the trail wound through steep, oddly shaped bluffs and rock formations with no vegetation. Later, they traveled through sandy hills with little feed for the livestock.

As far as Megan knew, Capt. Johnson still didn't know she was on this train. She was filled with dread at a possible meeting, so she stayed hidden. It was easier than she thought. She simply pretended to be sick. It wasn't entirely a lie, since she didn't feel at all good. After shifting things around in Charles' wagon, she made a bed for herself at the back where she could ride and still be able to see out. Elizabeth or Maude brought her meals and sat near her to visit while they ate.

Andrew dropped by every day to feel her forehead, check her pulse, and look in her eyes and down her throat. She knew he suspected all the time what she was up to. He waited until nightfall of the fifth day before he ordered her out of bed. "It's time for you to get up and get moving, Megan. Let's go for a walk."

She quickly pulled her blanket up to her chin. "I can't, Andrew."

Andrew leaned in close to her and lowered his voice. "I know what you're doing, Megan, and you know this can't continue."

"What are you talking about?"

"You can't fool me. I'm not stupid. You're hiding and it's time to quit."

"Andrew, I don't think Capt. Johnson knows I'm here. If I can stay out of his sight until he leaves us, then maybe no one else will hear anything he has to say about me."

"That's a long time for you to lay in bed. He'll be with us for several weeks. And yes, he *does* know you're here."

Her eyes widened with alarm.

"Major Bledsoe told us he had a talk with Johnson about the whole incident. He told Johnson he was mistaken about you and warned him to leave you alone."

Her eyes still wide, she asked, "And he agreed?"

Andrew shrugged. "It was an order from a superior officer. He had no choice." He took her hand. "Come on. You'll be fine. If we see Capt. Johnson, we can walk the other direction."

Megan grabbed her bonnet and reluctantly climbed out.

"Are you sure you need your bonnet? There's no sun," Andrew teased her.

She smiled back at him as she pulled it low over her forehead. "The moon's a little too bright, don't you think?"

He chuckled and shook his head. "I suppose."

They walked close to the wagons, Andrew taking care to steer her clear of any soldiers he saw. Greeting people as they passed, Andrew kept Megan's hand tucked securely in the crook of his arm. He leaned in close and spoke quietly.

"Megan, I'd like to see you hold your head up proud and be willing to face the world. You can't go on hiding like this."

"If you'd seen Capt. Johnson and his men at that dance in Laramie, I think you'd understand."

They walked in silence for a while, nodded a greeting to a family relaxing around their fire, then turned right when they saw a group of soldiers in their path, talking and laughing.

When they were out of earshot, Megan continued, "I'm terribly frightened that the rumor will get out and I'll go to Oregon branded for the rest of my life. I don't think I can live with that, Andrew. That's why I left St. Louis. 'No one would want a woman such as you to teach their young, impressionable children.' That's what my superintendent said when he fired me. Am I going to have to face that kind of reaction everywhere I go for the rest of my life? I can't do it." She felt tired and discouraged.

Andrew put a protective arm around her shoulders. "I'm sure it's been difficult, but I think it's important for you to stand up to people who lie about you. Declare your innocence. Don't let fear control you. Live in such a way that no one will believe the rumors."

"There are lots of people who will believe anything. They enjoy believing bad things about others."

"Yes, that's true. But are you going to let those people control how you live?"

Megan looked down and sighed loudly. "It's not as easy as you think, Andrew."

"I know it's not..." He stopped abruptly. They had walked a circle and were back at Charles' wagons. There were two soldiers looking into the back of the wagon where Megan had been staying. Andrew tried to turn her away, but it was too late. She froze in place as the words reached her ears.

"Miz O'Mally, you have customers," they drawled in drunken voices. "Come on out, little lady. You've been hiding from us long enough."

One of the soldiers turned and saw Andrew and Megan staring at them. "There she is, Todd. I told you we could find her. Looks like someone else got to her first."

"Are you done with her, mister?" the other soldier asked. "We want our turns now."

"Get out of here," Andrew hissed through clenched teeth. "Now!" he ordered.

They moved closer to Megan and reached for her hand. She yanked away and moved behind Andrew.

"Come on, honey. We'll be easy on you. We set up a nice cozy spot in one of our supply wagons."

Andrew's knee came up hard into the groin of the

closest man and his fist smashed the nose of the other. Both men fell to the ground with Andrew on top, both fists pummeling away. He grabbed one man's ears, lifted his head, and was about to pound it against a rock when Nick and Thomas grabbed him from behind and yanked him to his feet.

"What in tarnation is going on?" Nick hollered.

Andrew ignored him and threw himself at the two groaning on the ground. One was almost unconscious. The other rolled aside and came up on his feet, fists ready.

"What's gotten into you?" Thomas hollered at his younger brother as he grabbed him, twisting his arms and holding them firmly behind his back. "Get a hold of yourself! Now!"

Nick seized the standing soldier and shot a steely warning glance at Andrew, who had shaken loose of his brother and stood with clenched fists.

"I've gotten your brother out of countless fights in my life, but I never thought in my wildest dreams I'd have to get you out of one," Nick growled. "What in God's creation got you so riled up?" He let go of the soldier and glanced down at the one sprawled on the ground. "This had better be good, Andrew, or I'll be forced to use harsh disciplinary measures."

When Nick looked around at the gathering crowd, he noticed Megan standing to one side with both hands covering her mouth in horror. "All right, folks, it's over now. Go on back to your wagons. I need to talk to some people alone."

Elizabeth immediately went to Megan, put her arm around her, and led her away. As Nick watched them leave, he started guessing at what triggered Andrew's attack. He hoped he was wrong. His jaw muscles tightened in anger and his eyes narrowed when he turned to face the guilty party.

Andrew was in control of his temper but stared in stony defiance at anyone he looked at. Nick had never seen this side of him before.

"What brought this on, Andrew?"

"These soldiers," Andrew almost spat the words out, "decided to pay Megan a visit and be her next 'customers.'"

Overwhelming rage threatened to undo him. When he turned to look at the two young soldiers standing behind him, they merely stared, then dropped their eyes in fear.

Finally, Nick spoke in a steady, controlled tone, "I smell whiskey on your breath, private. What's the penalty for drinking?"

"Uh, we're not on duty now, sir."

"No, sir. The captain, he said it's okay to drink some when we're not on duty, sir." Their words stumbled over each other in their haste to get Nick to back off.

"Oh, he did, did he?" Nick said through clenched teeth. "We'll see about that. Also, this woman you came after? Someone has lied to you about her. You, in your incredible, drunken stupidity, have embarrassed a good woman and disgraced her name. What are your names?" he barked.

"Smith, Todd Smith, sir, and Harley Gump."

"Private Smith and Private Gump, I never want to see your faces near any of these wagons again! Do you hear me?"

"Yes, sir."

"And I want a meeting with Capt. Johnson at exactly ten tonight. Will you get that message to him, please?"

"Yes, sir."

"Yes, sir."

"Now get out of my sight! I hope I never have to see either of you again."

In their haste to get away, they almost tripped over each

other.

Nick turned to Andrew who didn't look at all satisfied.

"You were too easy on them, Nick."

Nick's eyes snapped in irritation. "Well, you certainly weren't! Wasn't that enough? Their faces are bloody. I believe one of them has a broken nose. And look." He pointed at the soldiers retreating into the darkness. "They're both limping. One's holding his head like it's split down the middle."

"Not bad, brother, not bad." Thomas slapped Andrew on the shoulder. "I knew all the lessons I gave you would pay off."

Nick looked at the two with anger. "I can't believe you! This is not how we're to handle problems on this train, at least not while I'm in charge. I won't have this again, Andrew."

Andrew quietly answered, "I didn't tell you everything they said, Nick. You would've done far worse if you'd heard it all."

Nick swallowed and ran his hand over his face. "Did Megan hear it all?"

"Yes. Every word. And they tried to grab her."

Nick's head snapped up and his eyes locked with Andrew's. Understanding passed between them. Silently, with narrowed eyes, Nick nodded his approval.

An hour later, Capt. Johnson looked up to see Nick Webster approaching. He'd been enjoying a game of cards with his lieutenant and sergeant. He made no move to acknowledge the wagon master.

He heard Nick take several deep breaths before speaking, "Excuse me, Captain. May I have a private audience with you?"

"Why, sure, Webster, anytime." Johnson stood with a

broad, confident grin that didn't match the cool suspicion he felt. He followed Nick around to the other side of the wagon and out to an outcropping of rock, mildly amused at the sight of Nick clenching and unclenching his fists. He had not reached his position in the military for cowardice or stupidity. He knew exactly why Webster came to him. He'd been expecting something like this since they'd left the fort; ever since the major had talked to him about Megan and he'd picked up a few hints about Webster's feelings for her.

Webster turned and began immediately. "Two of your men were caught insulting and making advances toward a young lady on my train. I insist they be punished. How you do it is your affair but they will be banned from any of our wagon enclosures from this day on. If I see them anywhere near Miss O'Mally, I'll not rescue them from a beating again."

Capt. Johnson's eyebrow shot up in mock surprise. "Miss O'Mally? How did she get involved in this?"

Nick studied Johnson's face. Not bothering to honor his question, he asked, "Why didn't you do what Major Bledsoe told you to do?"

"And what was that?"

"Talk to your men and get your story straight on Miss O'Mally."

"I did. I have no control over whether they believe it or not."

"On the contrary, Captain, I think you have tremendous control over what they believe. You've never heard Miss O'Mally's explanation of how she showed up at the brothel you apparently went to quite regularly; how her cousin took her there, without any clue on her part, what kind of place it was. Did you ever ask yourself why you were so shocked to see her?" Nick glared down at him. "Nothing in her character up to that point indicated she was anything other than a lady with the highest of morals. Why was she so resistant to your advances once you found her there? Why in God's name did she run off if she was there for the reason you imagined?"

Johnson stood very still in thoughtful silence, swayed by the intensity in Nick's eyes and voice.

"If you or any of your men continue acting on this horrible misunderstanding, you'll be guilty of destroying the reputation of a fine young lady who deserves far better."

Convinced for the first time of the very real possibility of Megan's innocence, Lee said, "Maybe I should talk to her and get everything straightened out."

"I think not, Johnson. You're the last person on the face of this earth she'd want to see."

"And who are you, Webster, her guardian? I have as much right to see her as anyone; more right in fact. She and I were about to be engaged."

Johnson took pleasure in the look of shock on Nick's face. He turned and walked a few steps away in thought then came back and faced Nick again. "You know, Mr. Webster, I'm greatly relieved to hear this. I wasn't convinced when the major talked to me, but now for the first time, I actually believe I was mistaken about her. I'll make sure my men understand, Webster."

He turned slightly and continued as if talking more to himself than to Nick. "Yes, Megan and I definitely need to talk. I suppose, if I'm lucky, we can pick up where we left off."

Lee thought he heard a low growl come from Webster, who stood there like a blind, lovestruck fool. "I would advise you and your men to stay far away from her. Good night, Captain." Delight filled Johnson's heart as he watched Webster strut away in anger.

As Nick approached his wagon, he rubbed the back of his neck in agitation. Why did it matter to him that Megan had wanted to marry this character? Disappointment in her? Jealousy? *Snap out of it, man! What's the matter with you?* He walked around his wagon and over to the fire. Thomas, Andrew, and Charles were sipping coffee and talking quietly. Elmer was washing pots and pans, making more noise than was necessary.

"Where's Megan?"

"She and Elizabeth took a short walk. They'll be right back," Charles answered.

"Did you talk to the captain?" Thomas asked.

"Yeah. I think he believes us this time. He'll talk to his men. Hopefully it'll make a difference." Nick ran his hand through his hair and stared at the ground. "Says he wants to talk to Megan. Sounds to me like he wants to start courting her again."

Charles got to his feet. "Not without my permission, he won't."

"Charles," Andrew interrupted. "Megan's not a child. If she wants to encourage the man, there's not much we can do about it. I don't think we have anything to worry about though. She's too smart to get involved with him again."

"You sure about that?" Nick asked.

"Of course she wouldn't!" Thomas snorted. "After what he's done to her!"

"Well, it's not beneath me to get in the man's way," announced Charles.

Nick looked him in the eye. "I won't stop you, Charles." The men all looked up to see Elizabeth walking toward them.

"Where's Megan?" Nick asked.

"She said she needed time alone, so I left her just outside camp."

Nick snapped erect. "Alone? You both know better than that. Where is she? I need to talk to her."

Elizabeth put her hand gently on Nick's arm. "I'm sorry, Nick. She's close, just over in that grove of trees."

He patted her hand then broke away and strode purposely in the direction Elizabeth had pointed. Again, he wrestled with his feelings. How could he be so weak to let himself feel like this for a woman again? Mentally he kicked himself over and over. *What a fool I am.* By the time he reached the trees, his hands were clenched in anger. It was dark and he had to feel his way through the branches. "Megan? Megan, are you in here?"

"I'm over here, Nick."

Moonlight shone through a small clearing, and Nick could barely make out Megan's form sitting on the ground. She stood as he approached and he could clearly see her features when he stood in front of her.

"Why are you out here alone?" he asked, looking down on her, anger and impatience evident in his tone.

"I...I'm sorry. Elizabeth just left me. She said she'd watch out for me."

Her face looked so tender and vulnerable in the moonlight. Streaks were still evident on her cheeks from her recent tears. Regret at his harshness brought a lump to his throat and as he looked down into her hurt eyes, he couldn't resist reaching out to put his hands on her shoulders.

"Are you all right, Megan?"

She nodded. "I'll be fine. Did you talk to Capt. Johnson?"

His face tensed and he swallowed before answering, "Yes...yes I did."

"And?" she inquired.

Nick forced an encouraging smile. "Well, for the first time, he might believe you're innocent. He's going to explain things to his men and...and, well, he says he wants to talk to you, Megan."

She jerked away from Nick's hands with a snort of disgust. "What nerve! I suppose he thinks I can act like none of this ever happened!"

Nick was relieved at her response. He decided to continue, watching her face carefully. "He told me you were about to be engaged and he mentioned something about maybe continuing your relationship."

Megan's mouth dropped and she stared incredulously as Nick talked. "What?" she hissed. "What?" Louder this time. "He's insane! We never even discussed marriage."

Feeling like a ton of bricks had lifted from him, Nick smiled tenderly and reached out to brush a loose strand of hair from her face. "That's good to hear. I figured you'd be too smart for that. I told him to stay away from you."

"Thank you, Nick."

"But that doesn't mean he will."

"I don't want him to come anywhere near me. I don't even want to see his face!"

"Then we'll see to it he stays away." He nodded in the direction of camp. "We need to get back."

As they made their way through the branches in the darkness, Megan chuckled. "If I were to look for the silver lining in this, I'd say it's discovering what Lee Johnson was really made of before I stumbled blindly into a serious relationship with him."

"If it wasn't for this, you'd still be in St. Louis, wouldn't you?"

"You're right! Oh, my! Thank God I'm not."

Nick stopped. "You mean that, Megan?"

She was slow to respond to his question and even she seemed to be amazed at her answer. "Yes, I guess I do. A few days ago...a few hours ago," she corrected herself, "I wouldn't have said that, but I really mean it. And thank God I wasn't successful at running away. I would sure like to change a few things around here, but I want to stay with you...with all of you. You're all my family and my friends.

You're all so good to me; how could I have ever wanted to leave you?"

No one saw the big smile on Nick's face as they emerged from the trees and walked toward camp.

# CHAPTER NINETEEN

"**W**ell, Megan, my girl, it sure is nice to have you back among the living," Maude said as they held on to the swaying wagon seat. She held the reins loosely and crinkled her eyes in the noontime sun.

Megan turned her eyes away in embarrassment and studied the horizon a moment before she answered. "I can't say I'm proud of the way I've been acting lately." She stretched her legs out and sighed, "You know, Maude, for the first time, I can see that things might work out after all. People kept trying to tell me to trust God with this mess, but I couldn't, I...I didn't know how. But it seems He's working things out anyway, despite me."

Maude chuckled, "You're learning, sweetie. Maybe next time it'll be easier. One of my favorite scriptures is found in Romans. It says 'All things work together for good to them that love God.'"

She squinted her eyes to see ahead. "Looks like Thomas is giving the signal for the nooning. Good! It's about time! I'm about to starve. Our breakfast burned and I couldn't choke it down, though the good Lord knows I tried." She expertly eased the tired oxen into the small circle of wagons but yanked back on the reins when Megan jumped to the ground.

"Why do you insist on doing that? You're gonna kill yourself and the blame will fall on me!" Maude climbed down still muttering as Megan went to her family's wagon and started unpacking fixings for the meal. Elizabeth soon joined her.

"Are you feeling better, Sis?"

"Much better. Thank you." Megan reached out and gently touched her sister's arm. "I'm sorry I've been such a bother."

"Megan, you're no bother to me. You've been through a lot. I'm not sure I would have handled it any differently."

Megan started to disagree but stopped herself and gave her sister a big hug. "How did I ever deserve a sister like you?"

"Oh hush!" Elizabeth held her at arm's length and just smiled. "I can't tell you how happy I am that I finally have my little sister back. Now let's get busy before those hungry men get here."

"Too late. We're here," Charles announced as he and Ralph came around the wagon. The two women quickly set out biscuits and beans left over from breakfast. Elizabeth added a little jerky to complete the meal. The noonings were the easiest and most relaxing of the meals. There wasn't enough time to make a fire and cook so they usually ate leftovers or other cold food. The men loaded their plates and found places to sit. Soon, the girls and the rest of their extended "family" joined them.

Nick walked over carrying a plate in one hand and Maude's rocking chair in the other.

"Any sign of Indians?" Charles asked quietly. His girls were sitting between their wagon and the Sanders', too occupied with their friends to hear the men talk.

"As a matter of fact, yes," Nick replied as he helped Maude get settled. "We saw a band of what looked like Sioux about an hour ago."

Megan looked up from her plate in alarm. Elizabeth's eyes were wide.

"We've been expecting this, ladies. After all, this is their home we're traveling through."

"How many?" Megan asked.

"Only about five or six. They looked like a hunting party. I'm not terribly worried. One look at the size of this train and the number of soldiers we have should scare 'em off. Every man is being reminded to have his guns ready and out in plain sight. Keep the girls close to the wagon just in case."

"So, I guess this wouldn't be a good time to start my little school up again?"

"No, you'd better wait awhile on that," Nick answered with a grin. "I'll let you know when we think it's safe."

Before stopping that evening, Nick approached Charles in private. "I just got word from Capt. Johnson that the Sioux, Cheyenne, and Arapaho in this area are banding together to get revenge for a massacre some time last year. Hopefully, we'll still look like too big of a challenge for them, but this definitely changes things."

"What do we need to do?"

"Have several guns loaded and ready and keep your family in the wagons. It'll be tough on them in this heat and with the trail as rough as it is, but their safety is our main concern. We'll get through this area as fast as we can, and we'll only stop where we can pull into a tight circle." He removed his hat, mopped sweat off his forehead, and ran his hand through his dark hair. "As much as I personally dislike the captain, I thank God he and his men are here.

They're a bunch of hardened war veterans and the captain obviously knows what he's doing."

"Kinda makes it hard to keep on hatin' the cuss, don't it?"

Their eyes met in understanding. "Yeah, it sure does," Nick answered. "But I'm a long way from liking him. He's a good soldier, but he's got the morals of a dog and I still want him as far away from Megan as possible."

Megan held tightly to her seat as the train worked its way through the deep ruts cut in the soft sandstone by thousands of wagons before them. Finally, they reached a flat expanse where they pulled into a tight circle, three wagons thick. Nick had spread the word about the Indians to the men with the help of Thomas and Andrew. The women and children were ordered to stay in the wagons or inside the circle. Extra guards were posted and the soldiers patrolled the outside perimeter of the enclosure. Despite the possible danger, they still needed to eat, so the women worked as best as they could in the crowded conditions, many of them sharing fires. A hush fell over the entire company, and mothers put their children to bed early so they'd be easier to tend to.

The next day was the same...and the next. Tensions were high. The adults got little sleep. The women and children were hot and growing weary of the incessant jarring of the wagons. Megan thought her teeth were coming loose. Every joint ached. She and Lucy rode in the wagon Ralph drove, while Elizabeth and the other two girls rode with Charles. She had tried to make it fun for Lucy by thinking up fun games and telling stories. But they were both too tired and too cross to try anymore. Both of them dozed off and on. Lucy woke with a jolt when the wheels hit a rock. She looked at Megan with huge, frightened eyes. "Are they here, Megan?"

"Who, Lucy, honey?"

"The Indians."

Megan chuckled kindly. "No, sweetie, it was just another big bump."

"Oh," Lucy said, almost sounding disappointed. "I almost wish they'd go ahead and attack just so something different would happen. I'm so sick of riding in this wagon I could scream."

Megan chuckled again. "Well, if you screamed, you'd be sure to see something different happen."

Lucy's eyes lit up. "What would happen?"

"Every man that could hear you would ride up with their rifles cocked, ready to shoot whatever made you scream."

"That sounds like fun. Let's try it."

"Don't you dare even think about it!" Megan exclaimed, believing Lucy would do it in a heartbeat just to break the monotony.

Lucy's eyes twinkled and she opened her mouth wide. Megan threw herself across the box between them and clamped her hand over Lucy's mouth just as Lucy burst into peals of laughter. She laughed so hard she had to wipe her eyes. Megan just lay there across the box and stared at her niece.

"You scamp! How could you?"

Lucy kept laughing and pointing at Megan. "That was the most fun I've had all day," she said.

"At my expense, you imp." She brushed her hair out of her sweaty face and laughed. "You're quite the scalawag, you know that?" She straightened up and invited Lucy to join her at the back of the wagon so they could look out.

Lucy snuggled close and slipped her hand into Megan's. "I like you, Megan."

Megan kissed the top of her damp head. "I like you, too, squirt."

"That's what Pa calls you sometimes. What does it

mean?"

"Oh, I guess it's a nickname for someone who's small. He started calling me that when I was littler than you, and I guess he's so used to it he can't stop."

"Oh," Lucy said quietly. "That's not very nice."

Megan hugged her. "Oh, no, Lucy. If someone calls you that, it also means they like you a lot."

"So, when you call me squirt, it means 'little person that I like a lot.' Right?"

"Right. So, little person that I like a lot, it feels like the wagons might be pulling into a circle for the night. Are you ready to get out of this rattling, shaking box?"

While fixing supper, Megan learned a large war party had been spotted that afternoon. Nick, Thomas, and most of the soldiers saw them.

"They were a good distance away. I figure they were watching us," Nick said in a low voice. Megan knew he wanted to keep the little ones from hearing.

"No sleep for the weary tonight," Charles remarked.

Megan looked around the circle of tense, tired faces.

"We won't be much good at defending ourselves if we don't get some rest tonight," Andrew said.

"The doctor's right," Nick added. "There's no reason we can't sleep in shifts. I'll have the men in every third wagon keep watch for three-hour shifts starting at eight. That'll give everyone six hours sleep. We'll be up and out of here at the usual time." He and Thomas left to spread the word.

That night, Megan couldn't sleep. The night started out with the beat of war drums then later she heard eerie, bloodcurdling screams. They seemed far away, but it still frightened them, so much that Lucy spent the night clutched tightly to Megan. Several times, Charles looked in on them and asked quietly how they were doing.

At some point, she must have dozed off because she was abruptly wakened by the noise of breakfast preparations just on the other side of the canvas. She didn't know if she could face another day in the wagon. Groaning, she shifted Lucy away from her and crawled out the back. The sun wasn't up yet, but the eastern sky was light.

Elizabeth looked about as bad as Megan felt. They gave each other weak smiles. "How's my Lucy?" Elizabeth asked.

"She slept through most of it, I think. When did the war cries stop?"

"I don't know. I must have fallen asleep. Charles is still asleep. He had the middle watch. I don't have the heart to wake him."

From under the wagon came a grizzled voice. "I'm awake. Where's my breakfast?"

The women smiled and got back to work. Soon the others join them.

"Why didn't they attack?" Megan asked after she got settled with her meal.

"If my hunches are still holding out, it's because they've seen how threatening we are. They don't want to risk it," Nick answered slowly, fatigue in every word.

"Why all the noise?"

"Trying to scare us," Thomas answered.

"Will they do it again tonight?"

"I'm hoping to put another fifteen to twenty miles between us before tonight," Nick said. "We'll be crossing the Platte today, too, which might help."

"Is it a hard crossing?" Charles asked.

"No, there's a bridge there now. There will probably be a toll, but that's a lot better than crossing through the water."

"And faster," Thomas added. "Indians have been known to attack a train right in the middle of a river crossing when the train's split in two."

"What's there to keep them from attacking us when we're crossing the bridge?" Megan asked. "We'll still be split in two."

"Soldiers, armed and ready," Nick answered simply. "There are enough trains coming through here that are a lot smaller and that don't have the military escort we do. The Indians know that. I'll be very surprised if they attack us."

"Do you think they'll attack one of the other trains?" Elizabeth asked.

"I'm sure of it," Nick answered grimly.

Megan sat in stunned silence for a while, chewing slowly, counting her blessings, and feeling a little guilty, knowing she'd probably be spared but others wouldn't; others just like her.

The train moved quickly that day with no sign of the Indians. Before noon they reached Platte Bridge Station and crossed to the north side of the river, each man reluctantly paying the toll as he crossed. They pulled into a circle for the nooning, close to the station's few buildings.

Nick couldn't hide the concern on his face when he showed up late for his meal.

"What's the latest?" Thomas asked around a mouthful of biscuit.

Nick shook his head and stared at the ground for a moment before answering. He looked around at all their faces and swallowed. "Did you notice the telegraph lines?"

"Yeah," Charles and Thomas both answered.

"Indians cut 'em?' Thomas asked.

"The station master says they can't keep them fixed long enough to send any telegraphs. They either burn the poles or pull the wires down. The army keeps soldiers posted here to protect this place and keep the lines fixed. He says he's never seen it so bad, especially here on the north side of the Platte. Says the Indians are bound and determined to keep white people from crossing through here."

"What about all the trains ahead of us? Have they made it through?" Charles asked.

"Yes, but not without casualties. Several women and children were taken prisoner not more than two weeks ago."

"Looks like we're jumping from the frying pan into the fire," Thomas said solemnly. "Is the captain aware of the situation?"

"Yeah, he knows."

Everyone sat silently, chewing slowly.

Megan wasn't hungry anymore. She set her plate down and glanced over at Elizabeth whose eyes were on her girls.

A man clearing his throat broke the silence. Nick stood just as Capt. Johnson stepped into view. "Captain, what can I do for you?"

"You've heard how serious the situation is?"

"Yes, sir. I have."

Megan squirmed. Sir? Since when had Nick called that worm "sir"?

"Fifty of the soldiers stationed here have agreed to ride out with us until we reach Independence Rock. That's about three days from here. Where the trail allows, we'll ride three rows of wagons. Keep the circles tight and three wagons deep like you've been doing. We'll probably have another night of war cries, but it's essential for the men to get some sleep. They'll be worthless without it. Understand?"

"Yes, sir."

Capt. Johnson turned and tipped his hat in greeting. "Ladies." He nodded toward Elizabeth and Maude then rested his eyes on Megan. "Megan, nice to see you again."

"I'm sorry, Captain, I can't return the sentiment." She stood and walked away.

Eight tense miles later, they pulled into camp. The night started out quiet. Megan and Lucy fell exhausted into bed and were quickly asleep. About an hour later, they woke to deafening screams. Megan grabbed Lucy and pulled a heavy quilt over them. The attack had finally come! They were both paralyzed with fear. After an agonizing period of time, she realized the screams and drums didn't change in intensity. They just went on and on without stopping. She dared to pull the quilt off her face to listen. They sounded like they had the previous night only this time they were closer. What was going on out there? She raised her head and peeked out the back of the wagon. She saw outlines of men standing guard. They weren't moving. They didn't even have their rifles drawn. Was this just another show of force by the Indians? Or did it mean they were about to attack? She thought she'd go insane listening to the demonic screams. No one could possibly sleep through this. She pulled her head back in and scrunched down under the quilt. Lucy whimpered.

"Shh, they're just making noise again. You'll be all right." Amazingly, her words had the desired effect. Lucy drifted back to sleep with both arms wrapped around Megan's waist. Megan found a pillow and buried her head in it enough to cover both ears. After what seemed like hours, she, too, fell into a fitful sleep.

In the morning, they were ordered to eat quickly, pack up, and leave. They were on the trail an hour earlier than usual. No one felt like talking. Their movements were jerky and clumsy. Everyone's faces were ashen with dark circles under bloodshot eyes. Even the animals looked exhausted.

The train passed through rough, dry territory with no water for the livestock. The nooning was cut short and the train pushed on, heading to the southwest toward Independence Rock and beyond that the Sweetwater River and South Pass.

That night, to everyone's relief, there was no more noise from the Indians. Nick and the captain didn't ease up on the security. They warned the men to be alert. This could be a trick to lull them into a false sense of security.

Morning came without incident. People were starting to look a little more relaxed.

"Does this mean they're gone?" Megan asked hopefully at breakfast.

Several pairs of tired, red-rimmed eyes turned to her, then looked at Nick for an answer.

"That would be nice," he answered without conviction.

"In other words, he doesn't know," Thomas said. "For all any of us knows, they could be waitin' around the next bend. Their strategy is to wear us all out with their screamin', then swoop down on us when we least expect them and we're too tired to fight back."

"Thomas," Andrew growled in warning.

"Sorry, ladies. I was exaggerating a little. Just trying to ease the tension a mite."

"I honestly believe they could defeat us with just their screaming alone if they kept at it a couple more nights," Megan said.

They broke camp and kept up the same pace as the day before. Megan didn't know how much more of this she could take. She knew it must be much harder on the men.

The next night was also quiet. In the morning after traveling a mile or two, Ralph called to Megan to look ahead. She crawled over crates and barrels to peer out the front.

"It's Independence Rock. I heard Nick say so. Look." He pointed ahead to a long low mound rising above the desert.

"Why, it looks just like a giant turtle," Megan said. "Lucy, come up here and see the turtle."

"I don't imagine we'll be stopping to see it. I was gonna carve my name on it, but it's probably too dangerous to wander around out here now," Ralph said with disappointment.

"I suppose you're right, Ralph. It looks like it would be a good place for an ambush."

They hadn't gone much farther when all the wagons came to a stop. Megan waited and listened. She finally stuck her head out the back to see Charles standing up straining to see ahead. He had a puzzled frown on his face.

"What's happening, Charles?" she hollered.

"I'm not sure. It looks like some soldiers are riding ahead."

Against her better judgment, Megan crawled out and jumped to the ground, telling Lucy to stay put. She saw several other women doing the same, including Jessica Hawkins several wagons ahead. *They must detest riding cooped up in these hot, dusty rattle traps as much as I do.* Jessica turned, caught Megan's eye, and waved. She'd seen very little of her good friend over the past couple of weeks. There hadn't been much time or energy for socializing. She missed her.

There were still soldiers stretched along the length of the train, but she could see most of them congregated up in front of the train. Then they rode ahead toward the Rock.

"Looks like the captain is sending out a scouting party," Charles said. "Makes sense. This would be a great place for an ambush."

Megan heard Elizabeth quietly shush him as she climbed out to join him on the seat. Charles put his arm around her, pulled her close, and nuzzled her neck.

"Here comes Nick. He'll tell us what's going on," Elizabeth said as she waved.

Megan turned in time to see Nick riding down the length of the train, pausing at each wagon. Women were quickly crawling back inside for safety.

When he reached Megan, he scowled down at her.

"What are you doing out here?"

"I'm just watching to see what's happening."

"You've been told to stay in the wagon."

"I'm sick of riding in the wagon. Are the soldiers checking for Indians around the Rock?"

Nick's scowl deepened, then he looked up at Charles. "They're sending a scouting party ahead. Have your rifles ready, just in case. When the wagons start moving, it'll mean it's clear."

He looked back down at Megan and his eyes narrowed. "Don't give me any trouble, Megan," he said quietly. "Get back in the wagon...now."

"Yes, sir," she answered. She meant to answer respectfully but failed to keep a tone of sarcasm from her voice. She regretted it immediately when she saw his face just before she turned away. *Why do I treat him that way? He's a good man who's doing a great job in horrendous circumstances. On the other hand, he doesn't need to talk to me the way he does,* she thought in her defense as she settled herself beside Lucy in the dreaded wagon. She looked out to see that Elizabeth had also gone back inside. Charles had a worried frown on his face. Megan was ashamed. Nick was only doing his job and she wasn't helping.

To everyone's great relief, the soldiers found nothing and the train started moving again. They traveled without stopping at the famous Independence Rock. The beautiful Sweetwater River was on the south side and the Rock on the north, with a twenty- to thirty-foot strip of land between for the wagons to travel on. They could see thousands of names carved or painted on the Rock. Some names were huge and easily read from a distance.

At the nooning, Megan got out, stretched, and looked around in awe. They were in what seemed like a huge bowl with mountains on every horizon. Inside the bowl ran the Sweetwater toward the east, which occasionally disappeared down deep gulches. Throughout the area were granite mounds sticking abruptly out of the ground. Ahead was a treeless terrain with more sagebrush and sparse grass.

Nick and Thomas passed them, leading their horses down to the river for a drink. Megan turned and hurried to catch up with them. She fell in step beside Nick, who glanced at her and raised his eyebrows, silently asking what she wanted. He didn't slow down. When they reached the river, he turned again to her. "Yes?"

"I'm sorry, Nick, for the way I acted earlier; the way I answered you. It wasn't right."

He looked back at his horse and said nothing.

"I appreciate the job you're doing. I know it's not easy."

He looked at her again and nodded slightly. "Thanks." His voice was tired and gravelly.

Megan turned and walked quietly back to help with the meal.

Again Capt. Johnson paid them a visit while they were eating. He told Nick they could take time for laundry and bathing that evening while they had a river close by. "I'll have my men keep a close watch. Everyone needs to be done by nightfall, though, and back in the enclosure."

He turned to greet the ladies again. Then directed his attention to Megan. "I'd like to have a word with you, Megan, if you don't mind."

"I do mind very much. I have nothing to say to you, and anything you have to say to me, I'd rather not hear."

"Well, I do have something to say and since you won't let me say it in private, I'll say it in front of these good people. I want to apologize for all the hurt I caused you. I realize how terribly wrong I was. You have every right to hate me. I'm deeply sorry, Megan." He put his hat back on, gave a little bow, and walked away.

An awkward silence followed.

"He's a snake," Megan hissed.

Maude and Elizabeth stared at her in shock.

"Megan," Elizabeth said gently. "He may have wronged you, but he's apologized. And now you need to forgive him."

Megan felt as if Elizabeth had just slapped her.

"Forgive him? Why in the world would I want to do that?"

Maude reached out and gently touched Megan on the arm. "The Bible says we're to forgive others, honey."

"If I believed for a minute he meant what he said, I

might consider it!"

Charles cleared his throat. "As much as I hate what the man did to you, Megan, I really think his apology was sincere."

Megan snorted. "You don't know him like I do!" She stood and walked away. Just before she rounded the end of the wagon, she turned and faced them. "Forgiving someone is the same as saying what they did doesn't matter. I will never, ever be able to say that to him."

The others looked uncomfortably at each other. They finished eating in silence then went through the same old routine to get back on the trail.

Later Maude came to her and said, "I've arranged for Lucy to ride with Charles and Elizabeth so you can ride with me and Joe. We need to talk." After they tucked themselves into the back and started back down the trail, Maude opened her Bible and showed Megan passage after passage on forgiveness.

"You were wrong, honey, when you said forgiveness is the same as sayin' the sin don't matter. Forgiveness doesn't excuse the sin as if it were nothin'. Forgiveness means you no longer harbor bitterness and condemnation toward that person. They may not deserve to be forgiven, but neither did we deserve to be forgiven by our Heavenly Father. How can we refuse to forgive when God so freely forgives us? Even on the cross, Jesus asked God to forgive the ones who put him there."

Megan slumped down, realizing Maude was right. But what if she couldn't do it? Forgiving him would not be easy.

"What do I do, Maude? I can't just stop feeling the way I do. It won't go away."

"God just expects you to be willing to forgive. Ask Him to help you, then go tell the captain you forgive him and start treating him like you mean it."

They rode in silence for several long miles while Megan

thought. Maude dozed off. She jolted awake when Megan said, "I wish I could do this without actually talking to the louse." Joe guffawed loudly from the front.

Maude smiled. "I agree, it won't be the easiest thing you've ever done. But who knows? Maybe if you tell him why you're forgiving him, it'll make him realize he needs the Lord, too. Soldiering is dangerous work. It would be a shame for him to get hisself killed before he gets saved."

That thought made Megan shudder. It also helped her see her way to forgiving him. She disliked the man intensely, but she realized with surprise, she had no desire to see him condemned to Hell. So, she prayed. She prayed all the way to the evening stop, asking God to help her to truly forgive, to take away her bitterness and hurt, to give her courage to talk to him, and to help her to treat him in a civil manner.

She climbed down from the wagon, resolved to do the right thing even though she dreaded it terribly.

Elizabeth called her over. "Let's get cleaned up and get some laundry done before we get the meal started. If we hurry, we can find a good spot upstream from everyone else."

They gathered up dirty clothes and soap and called the three girls to help. To Megan's delight, Jessica joined them. Soldiers and men from the train were stationing themselves up and down a length of the river. The three women discreetly removed their boots and stockings and stepped into the cool refreshing water, followed by the girls. They soaked washrags and buried their faces in them, washing off days of dirt and sweat. They took turns dumping buckets of water over each other's stooped heads then shampooing and rinsing. Rebecca Sanders and her four daughters joined them to make a circle of privacy so they could each unfasten a few buttons and quickly wash their upper bodies under the bodice of their filthy dresses.

"Ooo...I know why they call this the Sweetwater,"

Jessica said. "Taste it."

They all waded a distance away from the soapsuds and scooped up handfuls of water to test.

"It's sweet!" several exclaimed at once.

"Don't drink too much," a man's voice called from close by.

Megan glanced up to see Capt. Johnson watching them from the top of his horse. She was filled with dread at the coming confrontation.

"The water tastes sweet because of the alkaline in it. Too much can make you sick." He started riding slowly toward them. Megan grabbed some clothes and soap and started washing.

"Are you the boss of all those soldiers?" she heard Lucy ask.

"Out here I am."

"How come you haven't killed any Indians yet?"

"Lucy, mind your tongue," Elizabeth said quietly.

The captain laughed. "I hope we don't have to kill any. It would make them awfully mad, don't you think?"

"Do you think the worst of it is over, Captain?" asked Rebecca, squinting in the glare from the setting sun.

"Yes, I do, ma'am. We got word from up ahead that things are pretty quiet all the way through South Pass and on down to Fort Bridger."

"Isn't that where you leave us?" Elizabeth asked

"Yes, ma'am, we'll be stationed there for the rest of the summer."

Megan gathered up the clothes she'd hurriedly washed, grabbed her boots and stockings, and quickly walked up to the wagons while the captain continued talking to the others

# CHAPTER TWENTY

The notes of the fiddles wound around each other and danced out over the wagons and beyond to the livestock munching on the dry grass. Megan sat by herself, propped against a wagon wheel, a quilt cushioning her back. She watched dreamily through half-closed eyes as people started to gather after the evening meal and chores.

She heard the crunch of grass next to her and turned to see Capt. Johnson settling comfortably on the ground. She was annoyed at the intrusion into her peaceful solitude, but she knew she couldn't and shouldn't keep on avoiding him.

The train had traveled several days up the Sweetwater toward South Pass, and the captain and Nick were finally convinced the threatening war party was far behind them. Guards were continually on duty, but the group of tired travelers could begin to relax.

"So, you're not running away this time. What brought this about?"

Megan cringed and then breathed a silent prayer for help. Wanting to get it over with as quickly as possible, she chose to be direct. "I realized God wants me to forgive you." She took a deep breath and continued, "So that's what I'm doing, forgiving you."

"That suits me just fine," Lee said as he stretched nonchalantly then laid his long frame on the grass beside her.

Megan scooted away and looked him in the eye. "This does not mean that I consider your behavior acceptable, nor do I have any interest whatsoever in continuing any kind of relationship with you."

Lee put his hands up in defense. "That's fine. That's fine. I just want to talk, that's all." He put a piece of dry grass between his teeth and turned his attention toward the fiddler who was beginning to call out moves for a square dance. "I'm sorry for all the trouble I caused you. I was hoping there's some way I could make it up to you. You know, maybe undo some of the damage I've done."

"The only thing I would ask is for you to consider your need to ask God's forgiveness."

"God? How in the world did he get involved in this? And since when did you start caring what God thinks?"

"Most of my life." She sighed and looked away. "I guess I got distracted for a while. Then the good people here helped me remember how much God loves me and how willing He is to forgive me if I ask."

"Well, how about if I distract you again?"

Megan sighed. "I was right. You're a snake." She started to get up, but Lee quickly grabbed her hand and begged her to stay.

"I'm sorry, Megan. I was only making a joke. It was a stupid thing for me to say. Please stay."

She didn't move in either direction.

"Please, Megan. Sit down and tell me more about God's forgiveness."

Reluctantly she sat and started talking, trying to remember all Maude had taught her about forgiveness. She felt very uncomfortable in his presence, trying to communicate something so precious. Was he really listening? She couldn't say for sure. Finally, she wrapped up her little sermon with, "And if you don't repent of your sins and ask Him to forgive you and save you, you'll go to hell when you die." *There!* She'd said it all. Now she could wash her hands of this man.

He just lay there with his hands behind his head and stared at her. He looked slightly amused. Or was it interest?

Megan stood to go. Lee also stood, trying to find a way to keep her from leaving. At that moment, Nick walked by behind Megan. He stopped and locked eyes with Lee, who chose that precise moment to look down into Megan's face and say with a catch in his voice. "Thank you, Megan. I can't tell you how much I appreciate what you've shared with me. I want to talk to you some more about this. Can we get together again?"

He saw that Nick was about to step in to rescue her, but he stopped just as Megan replied, in a somewhat breathless voice, "Yes, Lee."

The look on Nick Webster's face was priceless, Lee thought with satisfaction as he walked back to his wagon. All the nonsense Megan was spouting about God and hell was worth listening to just to get to be with her and look into that pretty face. And if he feigned enough interest, he might be able to lure her back. She was definitely worth it. The icing on the cake would be watching Webster squirm. He had it bad for that woman.

Megan walked away in a daze. She could hardly believe

it. God answered her prayer far above what she had expected. Not only had He helped her forgive, but He also helped her say all the right things. Lee was truly touched! He almost cried! Wonder of all wonders.

Nick was sitting with Charles, Elizabeth, and Maude when Megan got back from the fiddlers.

"What's that smile all about, darlin'?" Maude asked.

"I just had a wonderful talk with Capt. Johnson."

"You don't say!" Maude exclaimed. "And it went well?"

"Yes!" Megan answered. She sat down next to Maude almost in a trance.

Nick looked at her and snorted with disgust. Then he stood and stalked away.

"What's gotten under his skin?" Thomas asked.

His words barely registered with Megan, who was still dazzled by Lee's reaction to her preaching.

Charles cleared his throat. "Ahem...Megan? Exactly what did you and the captain talk about?"

She snapped to attention, looked at him intently, and answered, "God! And he listened! I'm still amazed. I never dreamed he'd listen, much less take me seriously."

Charles eyes widened and he looked at the two older women to gauge their reaction.

"Megan, that's wonderful!" they both gushed at once.

"Did you pray with him?" Maude asked.

"No, we didn't get that far. But he wants to talk some more and, and he had tears in his eyes."

"Praise the Lord Almighty!" Maude exclaimed. "See what happens when you forgive? God is so good."

"I never dreamed it would turn out like this."

"Well, I don't want to douse your hopes, but this ain't the end of the story yet," Charles said.

All three women turned to him at once. "Where's your faith, Charles?" Elizabeth said.

"Of course, it's not the end of the story, but it sure is a good beginning," Maude scolded.

"I can't just ignore him, can I, Charles?" asked Megan. "He said he wants to talk some more about this. He said it with *tears* in his eyes," she emphasized.

Charles looked flustered. "No, you can't ignore him, squirt. But be careful, guard yourself."

She laughed. "From what? I'm surrounded by a hundred people or more. What could he possibly do?"

"I think he means, guard your heart," Elizabeth said quietly.

Megan sat back, shocked. "You can't be serious! My heart is quite safe, thank you."

Three days later, Nick scanned the western horizon with deep content, marred only by thoughts of Megan and the captain. The train began the gradual ascent into South Pass. It was so gradual, in fact, the emigrants would have missed this momentous occasion if the more experienced travelers hadn't taken the time to educate them. He pulled his horse up next to Joe and Maude's wagon and informed them, "Well, this is it! We're in the middle of South Pass, about to cross over the Continental Divide."

Maude looked around the broad valley in wonder.

"Couldn't even tell we were goin' up." Joe chuckled.

"No. And you won't be able to tell when we start down, either," Nick answered. "But in a little while, you'll see streams running west instead of east; west toward the Pacific," he added as he gazed wistfully ahead.

"I was expecting a narrow gap and pretty steep going by the time we got here," Maude said, still looking around at the vast panorama spread before them. "It's as if God put this here to make it easy for us."

"Most people are surprised by this pass," Nick said. He tipped his hat and trotted over to Charles and Elizabeth's wagon to share the same news. He was disappointed he didn't see Megan with them. Not wanting to appear too obvious, he rode slowly to the back of the train to look for her, greeting and visiting with people along the way.

Again, he was aggravated with himself for his strong attraction to Megan. He knew when it had started; back in that general store in Independence when he looked into her stubborn, pretty, little face. He wouldn't have admitted it then, not for all the tea in China. He chuckled. Who was being stubborn then, he asked himself. He'd avoided her like the plague at first, then a slow thaw worked its way into his heart. It had taken weeks before he would admit it to himself.

He still wasn't ready to admit it to anyone else, although he was certain a few of the more canny ones had figured it out by now. Maude especially. He chuckled again. Maude had probably seen it before he had. She didn't miss much, that sweet, old soul.

He spotted several groups walking beside the wagons, including Charles' three girls, but no sight of Megan yet. He visited with Lucy awhile. She was always ready to chat about almost anything. He suspected she was a lot like Megan at that age. He shook his head in frustration. He couldn't get that woman out of his head. Where was she anyway? If she wasn't with Maude or Elizabeth, she could almost always be found with her nieces.

Looking at the few people walking behind the last wagon, he finally spotted her. A warm gladness spread deep inside. Again, he good-naturedly scolded himself for allowing his feelings for her to grow. It was too late, he realized. He wondered if she knew. And if she didn't, how should he go about telling her.

Before he could think any further, people in front of Megan shifted just enough for him to see she wasn't in a group. She was walking with the captain. His heart skipped a beat, but he kept riding toward them. He had tried to forget the little tête-à-tête between the captain and Megan he had witnessed a few days ago. It was foolish to think she would encourage his attention. *If that were true, then why was she with him now? And why in God's name was she smiling?*

Nick nodded at the people he passed then exchanged pleasant greetings with Megan and Capt. Johnson. He told Megan about South Pass, talked to the captain about the Indian situation, then asked Megan if she'd given any thought to starting her classes again now that the Indian threat had diminished.

"I haven't even thought about it, Nick. Sorry. I guess I've been a little distracted the past few days," she said with an embarrassed laugh and glanced shyly at Johnson. When she looked away, the captain looked down at her with unashamed affection, then looked up at Nick with a big smile.

Nick nonchalantly excused himself and rode away perplexed and angry. Putting a little distance between himself and the wagons, he tried to convince himself he was reading too much into what he just saw. Megan was no fool. She couldn't possibly be gullible enough to let that man talk her into resuming their relationship. Was she? He took his hat off and slapped his thigh in frustration. Black, his horse, bolted at the sound, and Nick had to rein him in and calm him with soothing tones. Straightening up in the saddle, Nick resolved to put this nonsense out of his head and get back to work, an antidote that had been quite effective in the past.

Soon after Nick rode away, Capt. Johnson excused himself, mounted his horse, and rode off.

Megan caught up to Suzanne and Lucy. "Hello, girls. Mr. Webster just told me we're in South Pass now. We're crossing the Continental Divide."

"What's that?" Lucy asked with a wrinkled nose.

Megan laughed at her comical face. "It's where the streams and rivers all start to run west to the Pacific Ocean instead of east toward the Atlantic. It divides the continent. That's why it's called the Continental Divide."

"Wow!" Suzanne exclaimed, looking around in amazement.

"What's a continent?" Lucy asked.

"Lucy! We talked about that in our class. Weren't you listening?" Megan scolded.

"Where is it exactly? The Continental Divide, I mean," Suzanne asked.

"That's a good question. I don't know. We'll have to ask Mr. Webster. He knows a lot about this part of the country."

They heard hollering up ahead and saw the wagons begin to pull into circles. Soon they reached their wagons and started helping Elizabeth with the meal. Nick walked by and glanced quickly at Megan before cornering Thomas to discuss a problem with the livestock. They dug into their supply wagon and walked away carrying a small bucket. Megan didn't have a clue what they were up to.

"I didn't expect it would be this cold in July," Megan said to her sister.

"Me, either," Elizabeth answered. "I guess we're pretty high up. Did you see the snow-covered mountains to the north?"

"Yes, they're beautiful."

Charles was busy building a fire with cow chips and dried sagebrush. They settled the spider over the fire and started frying some salt pork. Megan got the hominy and threw it into the hot fat and began stirring while Elizabeth added seasonings and dried onions. Elmer and Maude were working over their fire just ten feet away.

By the time Thomas and Nick joined them, the food was ready and plates were full. Each person took their plate and settled down on stools, small chairs, or the ground. The three girls were on a blanket and had a second blanket wrapped around their shoulders.

"You girls look so cozy, I think I'll join you," Megan said, settling onto the blanket next to Abigail.

"Well, Megan, how's Capt. Johnson doing?" Maude asked between bites.

Megan couldn't help notice the scowl on Joe's face.

"He's asking a lot of questions. I'm not always sure how to answer. I've got a lot of thinking to do. Maybe you can help me."

"I'd be happy to any time, Megan. Ride with me tomorrow for a spell and we can talk." Maude squeezed Megan's hand affectionately.

Megan shifted her attention to a conversation she heard among the men. As soon as her eyes met Nick's, he looked quickly away. It was obvious something was wrong. Were the Indians still a threat? She didn't envy Nick's position. There was no better man for the job. Megan admired him greatly. In fact, she thought as she sat there and watched him, she couldn't think of anyone she respected more. *Too bad he finds me so annoying.* She sighed and refocused her attention on the men's talk about various problems with the livestock, a topic that didn't interest her in the least. Everyone looked tired but happy, she noticed. Again, she breathed a silent prayer of gratitude for these good people God had placed in her life. Finally, she rose to her feet and started gathering dirty dishes.

The men were interrupted by a visit from Mrs. Simmons and her daughter, Natalie. Megan couldn't hear most of what was said. Those two women were very annoying with their high-pitched prattle. Though their wagon had been close to the Batten's wagons for the entire trip, there had been very little friendly exchange between them and Megan or Elizabeth. In fact, Megan thought as she dried the dishes, the only sounds she'd heard from either of them had been complaining or flirting. Mr. Simmons on the other hand seemed rather pleasant.

For several days, the train wound its way gradually up and gradually down through the 100-mile-long valley of South Pass. They came to the Little Sandy River, the first westward flowing water. The Little Sandy led them to the Big Sandy then on to the Green River.

Nick and Thomas rode the length of the train explaining what to expect at the Green River crossing. Nick approached Maude and Joe's wagon with a big smile.

"Howdy, how are my two favorite people doing?"

"Fine, Nick. And yerself?"

"Couldn't be better. The closer we get to Oregon, the happier I get." He took his hat off and ran his fingers through his hair. "We've got a river crossing up ahead. We should get there and across it before we set up camp. The Green's current can be a force to reckon with, but if my memory serves me correctly, the water's a whole lot lower than usual. If I'm right, we'll tie ropes onto the wagons and have four or five men on horseback upstream holding on. It will be faster and a whole lot cheaper than ferrying across."

"I'm all for faster," Maude said.

"And I'm all for cheaper," Joe added.

"By the way, where's Megan? I rode by Charles' wagon and they told me she was with you."

Joe gestured with his head. "Back there someplace getting romanced by the captain."

Nick felt like he'd been shot. He recovered in time to hear Maude correct her husband. "Pshaw! Joe, I can't believe you! There's no romancing goin' on between those two! Megan's just talkin' to him about the Lord."

"Seven days straight?" Joe asked.

"Seven days?" Nick interrupted. "I haven't seen them."

"That's 'cuz the snake's courtin' her. A man doesn't court a woman out in front of everyone, does he?" Joe heaved a big sigh. "I've been watchin' him."

"Nonsense!" Maude exclaimed.

Ignoring Maude, Nick looked intently at Joe. "Does Megan encourage his attention?"

"She's with him, ain't she?"

"She goes willingly?"

Joe looked at Nick and nodded.

"She goes willingly because the captain is hungry to learn more about the Bible," Maude argued.

Joe snorted. "The captain's hungry alright, but I guarantee it ain't for the Bible!"

Nick yanked his reins around and rode toward the back of the train.

Capt. Johnson saw Webster far ahead, riding toward them. For the last half hour, Megan had been answering his questions; one question after another about the Bible and about God and Jesus and all sorts of nonsense. It was the only way he could get her to spend time with him. He'd discovered she was resolute in her decision to not renew their relationship. Any attempts in that direction were met with cold rejection. So, he'd kept up his "interest" in God. He was running out of questions. But remarkably, if he could think of anything at all to ask her about God or the Bible, she'd not only stay with him, she'd actually be enthused.

It appeared Webster was looking for someone. As he rode closer, he saw them and their eyes locked. Webster was angry and Capt. Johnson knew exactly why. He glanced down at Megan. She hadn't seen Webster yet, so Lee stopped and turned her to face him.

"Megan," he faltered, "I...uh...I think I understand."

Megan's eyes grew bright with hope.

He had to keep her attention and somehow get the desired reaction just when Webster got close enough to see her expression and maybe even hear her.

"I've been praying a lot lately," he said softly and looked down.

"You have?" Megan exclaimed and absently grabbed both his hands. "Lee, I'm so happy!" Her face was beaming.

This was better than Lee expected. But when he glanced up, he saw that Webster was still too far away. Quickly his mind plotted what to say while he held on to Megan's hands.

"Yes. Megan, I think God is opening my eyes to what you've been telling me these last few days." He put a catch in his voice. "I...I need you to pray for me. Will you, Megan? Will you pray for me?" He dropped down on one knee and looked at her with sad, pleading eyes.

Nick watched in shock as he saw Megan reach out and grasp the captain's hands with passion. Then his shock turned to horror as Johnson spoke to her and dropped to one knee, still holding hands. He would never forget the joyful tone to her voice as she gave her answer, "Yes, yes, I will! Of course, I will, Lee! This makes me so happy!" He couldn't bear to hear or see any more, so he yanked Black's reins sharply left, dug his heels in, and rode hard to the north.

*How could this be? A little over a week ago, she hated him, and now, she was accepting his proposal?* He hated himself for caring. He hated himself even more for the overwhelming pain he felt. He'd vowed years ago he'd not let another woman do this to him. *Are all men this blind? This vulnerable? This stupid?*

He rode hard and fast. He tried not to think about it. The pounding hooves eased his mind, only a little though. He turned his horse to the west and rode hard again. "God, why, why, *why*?" he asked, not expecting an answer. Then he turned his face toward heaven and hollered at the top of his lungs, "Why, God? Why?" Tears streamed down his face and he angrily wiped them away with his shirtsleeve. He shook his head, determined that no more tears would fall. Digging his heels in, he relentlessly rode Black harder and faster until his mind cleared. Then he reined him to an abrupt stop, slipped to the ground, covered his face, and cried out to his Heavenly Father.

Nick arrived back at the train in time to direct the crossing of the Green, a beautiful, clear, fast-flowing river with a gravely bottom. Normally a difficult river to cross, the Green was well below its usual level. But it was still a challenge and required time and hard work to get each wagon across safely. Ropes were fastened securely to the front, back, and sides of the wagon beds and held by several men on horseback, bracing themselves upstream from the wagons.

While the women set up camp and started the evening meal, the men tackled the job of herding the livestock across the river. Most went across willingly, but others balked at the deep, swiftly moving current. Nick stuck with the job until the last stragglers were across. Elmer kept a plate of food warm and handed it to him when he finally appeared. He took it and quietly excused himself, saying he had a matter to attend to.

Megan noticed Nick's look of sheer exhaustion and felt respect and compassion for this man who worked so hard and competently without complaining. His red-rimmed eyes gave testimony to his unyielding devotion to his job. She looked around at the other men. They, too, looked ready to drop, but none looked as bad as Nick.

Just then, Natalie Simmons walked past Megan to stand in front of Thomas and Andrew. With hands planted firmly on her hips, she announced, "My mother sent me over here to tell you we still have two cows missing." She looked around impatiently. "Where's Mr. Webster? I suppose I'll need to tell him if I want anything done about it."

"He's busy with another job right now. Perhaps your father could find your cows," Megan said as politely as she could manage.

Natalie swung abruptly around to face Megan. "I wasn't talking to you." She sniffed and tilted her nose up a little higher. "Are you his secretary, Miss O'Mally? Do I need to make an appointment with you in order to see Mr. Webster?" She tossed her head. "I think not! Since you spend most of your time with a certain captain, I would think you'd leave poor Mr. Webster alone. I can find him without your help, thank you." With that, she twirled around and walked quickly away.

Megan's mouth hung open and everyone else sat in dumbfounded silence. Finally, Thomas started laughing. Soon, one by one, everyone joined him. Elizabeth laughed so hard she had to wipe away her tears. Megan was torn between bewilderment and absolute hilarity.

When the laughter died, Megan asked, "Please be honest with me. Do you think she's the only one who's gotten the wrong idea about Captain Johnson and me?"

There was polite silence for a moment as she looked from one person to another. Elizabeth finally comforted her with, "I don't think most people pay attention to who's talking to who. Most people who know you well also know you're talking to the captain about the Lord. Most everyone else probably doesn't even notice."

"That's right, honey. You just keep doin' what yer doin'

and don't worry about anyone else," Maude said with a warning look at Joe. "Besides, I hear we'll be gittin' to Ft. Bridger in about four more days. Then yer chance to talk to the captain will be gone, so keep at it. And I'll keep on prayin' for him."

As Nick walked away with his dinner, he was certain Megan had already made her wedding announcement to her family and her friends while sharing their meal. He had purposely stayed busy at the river until there was nothing left for him to do. He would have done anything to avoid hearing her announcement. Making his way upstream, he found a quiet place to sit and eat. Fort Bridger was only four days away. Captain Johnson and the entire attachment under him were to stay there at the fort where they had been assigned. His only conclusion was that Megan would also stay and the wedding would follow shortly after. Perhaps they'd even have the wedding immediately so her family and friends could attend.

He set his plate on the ground and buried his head in his hands. *Was she so desperate to marry that she'd even consider for a moment a lifetime with the very man she'd called a snake just a week or two ago? What had happened to her in so short a time? Shouldn't he at least give Megan the chance to know how he felt? If she knew he wanted her, desperately wanted her to be his wife, would she choose him over the captain?* He groaned and slowly ran his fingers through his hair. He couldn't bear to lay his soul before her and have her reject him. In fact, the more he thought about it, he knew he couldn't bear to be near her again.

It was easy for Nick to find a way to avoid Megan. He simply traded jobs with Thomas. He told Thomas he wanted a change for a few days. It wasn't that unusual for them to share duties. So, for the next five days, he went out every morning as the guide for the hunting party. He had Elmer pack breakfast and lunch for him so he could do a little scouting early in the morning before the other men joined him. After the hunt, he volunteered to dress the game so the others could eat the noon meal with their families. By the time they were done, he had the meat cut into portions to divide among the wagons and was ready to guide a second hunting party for the afternoon.

The evening meal was a little more difficult to avoid. He couldn't work around his wagon. It was too close to where Megan usually was. Although, at one meal when he tried to slip in unnoticed to get his food from Elmer, he noticed she was missing and at another meal, he glanced over and saw the captain talking and laughing with Megan and Maude. None of the men looked very happy though, bless them. He solved his problem by getting his food as early as possible then slipping away to check on the livestock. There were always problems with the livestock, although the young men who were assigned rotating shifts guarding the stock were doing a fine job and seldom complained.

One night as Nick was finishing his work helping to doctor a lame cow, Captain Johnson rode up next to him. Nick hadn't noticed his approach so he had a hard time disguising his disgust when he first noticed the captain's expression. He quickly looked away and from years of military discipline was able to mask his emotions.

"Good evening, Webster."

Nick wiped his hands on a rag and glanced up. He wanted to pound his fist into that satisfied smirk.

"So...I suppose by now you've heard the good news from Megan."

Nick continued to stare.

"We're planning a simple ceremony at the Fort, soon after we arrive so her family can be there. Hope you can make it, too." He smiled, tipped his hat, and rode away, chuckling just loud enough for Nick to hear.

Nick stood as still as a rock, breathing deeply and clenching his fists in tight, hard balls, wanting to lash out but holding himself in check until Johnson was out of sight. Then he mounted Black and rode in the opposite direction, his worst fears confirmed.

The day the train finally pulled into Ft. Bridger, Nick scouted and hunted until nightfall. Thomas requested a one-day layover to make wagon repairs. Nick agreed and planned to wake early the next morning and leave for the day. In the dark of early morning, he quietly put some food in a pouch. He told Elmer he'd shoot what else he needed; game was plentiful and he'd join up with the train the next afternoon.

"What's gotten into you, Nick?" Thomas asked as he stretched and crawled out of his bedroll. "I've never seen you like this."

"Nothing's gotten into me. I'm just getting tired of the same old routine day in and day out. It's amazing how good it feels to be out there riding fast through this gorgeous country. It seems like it's been years since I had this freedom. Give me a couple more days of this, then we can trade jobs again."

"Good! I'm getting wore out by all the bickerin' an' complainin'. I forgot how whiney people can get. Especially those Simmons' women."

"People git that way when they're tired," Elmer added. "I don't think we've gotten over those sleepless nights with the Indians screaming nonstop."

"You're probably right," Nick said. "Hopefully a day here will help." He was expecting and dreading that someone would ask him if he was attending the wedding. Quickly he gathered his things and said, "I'll meet you sometime tomorrow."

"You be careful out there alone," Elmer said.

"He'll be fine," he heard Thomas say as he walked into the darkness.

# CHAPTER TWENTY ONE

Megan lay wrapped warmly in her bedroll and thought about the day to come with mixed feelings. Despite weeks of talking with Lee about salvation, he still hadn't come to the point where he was ready to take that giant step. She could talk until she was blue in the face, but until he recognized his sinful state and his need to ask Jesus to be his Savior, then all her talking was in vain. But she still had today. She made up her mind to press him for an answer, one way or the other. Would he admit he's a sinner and accept Jesus or would he reject him? She breathed a prayer for wisdom then threw her blankets aside to start her day.

The fort was just a stone's throw away. Beyond the fort, she could see an odd assortment of buildings and a small Indian encampment. She knew Lee had to report for duty to the commanding officer at the fort. She had no idea what his schedule would be, but she knew he'd find her, she didn't need to go looking for him. It had been that way for the last two weeks. He seemed so eager to talk about spiritual things. He asked questions as if he were trying to find his way through a confusing maze. Maude had told her to be patient; that often God used one person to plant a seed in someone and He used others to water the seed and others to help the seed finally take root and sprout. That sounded great, but apparently, she wasn't mature enough to have that kind of patience. She wanted that stubborn seed to sprout today!

"Good morning, sleepyhead. Looks like you're still lost in a dream."

Megan snapped to attention to see Charles smiling at her as he finished shaving. "Oh, good morning to you, too, Charles. Well, I guess today we say good-bye to our soldiers."

"Does that make you sad?"

"A little. I felt much safer with them along."

Charles nodded in agreement. "I won't argue about that. Although, I'm pretty sure we're in safe hands with Nick and Thomas for the rest of the trip."

"Of course, we are. I don't doubt that at all. It's just that the extra numbers were nice."

Charles studied her face for a moment then asked, "Do I detect a little sadness for a particular soldier?"

"Do you mean Captain Johnson?"

"You're going to miss him, aren't you?"

"Miss him? Charles, surely, you're joking! You really think I'd miss him? I can barely tolerate him."

"That's not what I've seen the last two weeks. It seems every spare minute you have, you're off alone with him."

Megan stared in disbelief. "Alone? Every spare minute?" She sputtered. "What are you talking about? You sound like Natalie."

"Ok, I exaggerated a little. It wasn't *every* spare minute and at least you were in sight of others when you were walking alone together. But it was starting to look like a courtship and I was getting a little concerned."

"A courtship? How could you think that? I thought you

knew how I felt about him. We were just talking about God, about salvation."

"For two whole weeks?"

"But, Charles, he had so many questions. He's so close to finally understanding and, and maybe, finally, to making a decision."

Charles' face softened when he saw and heard her earnestness. "You really believe that's all he was interested in, Megan?"

"Yes, Charles, I really do."

"Are you going to have one last talk about it today?"

"Yes. I guess that's why I have my head in the clouds this morning. I want to say all the right things because it's my last chance. After today, I'll never see him again."

"God will."

Megan just looked at him.

"No matter what you say to Capt. Johnson, no matter how eloquent or wise your words are, it's still his decision to make, not yours. And it's God's job to convict him of sin and to open his eyes before he can make that decision. God cares about the captain far more than you do and he'll not stop working in him just because you're gone."

Again, Megan stared at him thoughtfully. Finally, she said, "Thanks, Charles. You're right. I just need to trust God. I'm not very good at that yet."

"Breakfast, you two," Elizabeth called from the other end of the wagon.

Megan rushed over to her sister, full of apologies for not helping. Charles grabbed a plate full of steaming biscuits lathered with butter and a generous helping of bacon and what looked like a piece of fried chicken.

"What's this?" he asked, looking over at Thomas' and Andrew's plates to see the same.

"Pheasant," Thomas answered. "We've got an abundance of food since Nick decided to take over the hunting parties. They're finding game everywhere and he's pushin' 'em to hunt pret' near round the clock."

"Wait 'til you see what we have for dessert," Lucy said with a twinkle in her eye. "Nick found them; lots and lots of them!"

"Berries?" her father guessed.

"Pa! Who told you? It was supposed to be a surprise!"

"Nobody told me, honey. You just gave me some great clues and I guessed."

"Can you guess what kind, Pa?" she asked.

"Gooseberries?"

"No, not gooseberries," Abigail joined in, jumping up and down with excitement.

"Abigail," Lucy scolded. "It's my secret, not yours."

"Lucille, the secret belongs to all you girls. Be nice," her mother admonished.

"It's strawberries!" Abigail squealed.

Everyone laughed and exclaimed with delight over Abigail's happy revelation. Except Lucy who scowled at her sister and said, "Now you've ruined it, Abigail."

Charles grabbed Abigail and gave her a big hug. "Nothing's ruined, Lucy. We still get to eat them, don't we?"

"Of course, we do, Pa! I'll go get them."

When she walked into the circle with a big bowl full of berries, they were all truly amazed.

"Nick picked all these?" Megan asked.

"He has all the time in the world to shoot enough pheasant for the whole train and pick berries all day now that he lives somewhere out there in the wilderness and turned the wagon master job over to me," Thomas complained.

"I haven't seen hide nor hair of the boy for a few days now," Maude said. "How long is he gonna keep this up?"

"He's joining back up with us tomorrow," Thomas answered. "Then I'm getting my old job back. Nick said he needed some time off. Said he was tired of the same

MEGAN O'MALLY

routine."

"I can sure understand. I think we're all tired of the same routine," Charles said.

"It's not just the driving and the scenery, it's the bickerin' an' whinin' he hears all day."

"Poor boy," Maude said. "It's not an easy chore bein' in charge of this many people. But Nick's doin' a fine job, if you ask me."

"He's the best wagon master you'll find anywhere," Thomas said. "You folks better be happy I'm not the one in charge. I'd have shot half a dozen of these whiners by now and my list gets longer every day."

Megan walked over to the trading post with Elizabeth and Maude after breakfast. She hoped she'd see Lee, but so far, there had been no sight of him. The fort had close to thirty buildings, with a large, very nice clapboard house that served as officers' quarters. At Ft. Bridger the trail split; the Salt Lake route went southwest and the Oregon route continued to the northwest. The land around the fort was beautiful with plenty of good water and grazing. If it wasn't for the Indian problem, Charles had announced at breakfast, he'd be tempted to stay.

Megan wandered the aisles of the trading post then went out to the porch to wait for her sister and Maude. A soldier who looked familiar walked by and tipped his hat. He stopped and looked at her again.

"Miss O'Mally?"

"Yes?"

"I thought I recognized you. Capt. Johnson just rode over to the wagons lookin' for you."

"Thank you. I'll walk back and look for him. If I miss him and you see him again, tell him I'll be by my wagon, please."

"Sure thing, ma'am. I'd be pleased to."

After telling her companions where she was going,

Megan headed for the wagons. Halfway there, she saw him riding back toward the fort. He swung his horse in her direction and dismounted.

"I'm glad I found you. This will probably be our last chance to be together. I've got a full schedule for the rest of the day. Of course, I'll be free this evening if you'd like to get together then..." His voice trailed off as he looked down at her and smiled.

Megan looked intently into his eyes.

"I've never seen you look at me like this. Is it possible your feelings for me are changing?"

She chose to ignore his remark. "Lee, I have a very important question to ask you."

"Yes? What is it, Megan" He reached a hand up to stroke her cheek.

She flinched away. "I've asked you this, several times, but I'm not sure you've understood. You always change the subject."

"Well, what is it?" He sounded irritated.

She decided to be direct. "Will you admit that you're a sinner and will you ask Jesus to save you?"

He stood very still and studied her face. Then he answered with a question of his own. "Megan, if I say 'yes,' I'm a sinner and 'yes,' I'll ask Jesus to save me, will you stay here with me and marry me?" He firmly but gently grabbed her shoulders and forced her to look at him.

"Will you?" he asked again.

"No, of course I won't!" she declared, shocked by his question.

Lee glared at her for a full minute then pushed her away. "Then my answer is 'no'! And you can go to hell with me for all I care!"

"Lee! How can you say such a thing? Don't you realize you're choosing to reject God Himself, and everything He's done for you? He's your only hope!"

"Hogwash! I don't need hope from him. Besides, I don't

believe a word of it and I'm fed up to here with all your holy talk!"

"You're fed up with it? You were the one who wanted to talk about it. You're the one who asked all the questions. What do you mean you're fed up with it?"

"Megan, I declare, you are the most naive woman I've had the pleasure to know. I only pretended to be interested in all that God stuff to get close to you. Hoping maybe someday we could move past the holy stuff and pick up where we left off. It was *you* I was after, *sweetheart*, not God. And if you're not willing to be romanced, then I'd rather not see you again."

"Two weeks? You carried on with this pretense for two weeks?"

He swung back into his saddle and looked down at her with scorn. "Very cunning of me, wasn't it? But apparently it wasn't worth my time."

He took off at a canter toward the fort with Megan staring at him in shocked disbelief. She was still standing in the same spot when Elizabeth and Maude saw her on their way back from the fort.

"Megan? Megan, what's wrong? What's happened?" both women asked together.

Megan couldn't bring herself to answer or to even look at them. She bit her lower lip to keep from crying out.

"Is it Lee, child?" Maude asked gently.

Megan gave a brief nod but still made no sound. Both women wrapped their arms around her.

"He said 'no'?" Maude asked again.

Again, Megan nodded.

"Megan, remember what I said about sometimes all we do is plant the seed and someone else may reap the harvest. You planted a seed, honey, and someday it will sprout."

At this, Megan broke free from them and buried her face in her hands and groaned, "No, Maude. No!" She lifted her face and looked into Maude's face and almost in a whisper said again, "No, Maude. You're wrong. I've been wrong. We've all had the wool pulled over our eyes."

"What are you talking about, Megan?" Elizabeth asked.

"I'm talking about Capt. Lee Johnson, the snake," she answered, getting angrier with every word. "He was only pretending to be interested in God so he could win me over. The men were right. I was a complete idiot! I can't believe I fell for it. Two whole weeks! You'd think in that time I would have caught on."

She shook her head in disgust and walked toward the wagons then stopped and turned around. "I hate the man! I truly hate him!"

She turned again and walked away.

"Megan," Maude called. "Megan, I'm so sorry."

Megan stopped and turned toward her precious friend. "Maude, you have nothing to apologize for. You only knew what I shared with you. Day after day, you listened to me go on and on about how interested he was, how close he was to accepting all of it. It was me and only me who was bamboozled by the snake." She took a few more steps. "What a waste of time and energy." She chuckled and looked at the other two. "Remember the parable about the seed being sown by the wayside? Well, I guess that's where I've been scattering my seed. And it was all for nothing."

"'All for nothing?' I think not!" Maude declared with loud conviction.

Both Megan and Elizabeth stopped and turned to her.

"For two weeks now, you, dear girl, have been giving an answer for your faith. You've been coming to me every night with more questions. We've dug through God's Holy Word and found verse after verse to answer all those questions. You've memorized most of them so you'd remember what to say to the captain the next day. He might have been pretending, but he asked some great questions and you learned how to answer them all! Now you're telling me that was a waste of time?" Her eyes bore holes into Megan's, demanding an answer.

Megan looked down in shame. "I'm sorry, Maude."

"And furthermore, don't be too quick to think that seed was scattered on infertile ground. Lee may act like he didn't really care, but a man doesn't ask those kinds of questions without some help from the Holy Spirit. There's somethin' goin' on inside that man, even if we can't see it. Now, child," she said, looking directly at Megan, demanding her attention, "that ol' devil would love to have you hate the captain and hate yourself for what went on for two weeks, but I'm a-thinkin' the angels and God himself have been rejoicing the whole time. God knows what He's doin'. His ways are higher than ours. Just 'cuz you don't understand His ways, don't be fussin' and complainin' about them!"

Megan stared at Maude with wonder. She had never heard the dear lady talk like this. Even though she had been thoroughly scolded, she felt joy mixed with her shame. Then she started to laugh! She forced herself to stop. Maude's face crinkled into a huge smile and she, too, started laughing. Megan threw her arms around the old woman and surrendered. She laughed. And laughed! They all did. It felt so good, as if they were being bathed in joy. It was so like God to gently reprove his children then completely change their perspective and fill them with joy, "Joy unspeakable and full of glory."

Nick was tired and dirty. He needed a bath and a shave. He hadn't slept well the last two nights. Thoughts of the captain and Megan being married tormented him. He had so wanted to purge his mind of those thoughts but fought in vain. As he made his way back to the trail to join the train, he figured time and hard work would cure him. There were a good number of pheasants and several rabbits tied to his pack and more berries, but he'd taken no pleasure in hunting them. He was ready to turn the job back over to Thomas and resume his own duties. Knowing he must look as bad as he felt, he was determined no one would ever know how he felt about Megan. He couldn't bear their pity on top of losing her.

As he crested the hill, he saw the trail but no sign of the train yet. It was what he had expected. He dismounted and sat down to wait.

The train made its way through some of the most beautiful terrain Megan had ever seen. They were surrounded by abundant evergreens. Pine, spruce, and fir were everywhere in addition to patches of strawberries and bushes of yellow currants which she and the girls picked for the evening meal. The wagons had to maneuver up and down steep hills surrounded by deep ravines and gorges punctuated with ledges of red sandstone. In the morning, Megan had picked a big bouquet of beautiful white honeysuckles. In some places, she had to carefully find her footing around melting snowdrifts. Despite the cold temperatures and difficult terrain, Megan delighted in the lavish display of God's amazing creation. She realized this was a healing time for her; a time to reflect on God's providence and a time to drink in a fresh awareness of His presence and love.

Finally, the time came to stop and set up camp for the night. There was a sparkling, clean creek for drinking and washing. She heard both Thomas and Nick calling out orders for the wagons to pull into two tight circles. It was a relief to hear Nick's voice again. His presence seemed to give her a sense of peace. She could hear Nick dividing the men up for guard duty. Despite all the work, there seemed to be a festive spirit in the air. The rest they had at Ft.

Bridger must have done wonders, thought Megan as she started water to boil for stewing the currants. She planned to serve them over a cake that Elizabeth had managed to bake.

The meal was ready and waiting by the time the men arrived. Megan filled her plate and snuggled next to her nieces on a quilt. The others assembled one by one. Maude and Joe came carrying their food and chairs, then the men lined up to dish out their portions. Megan noticed how tired they all looked. Finally, Nick arrived, unshaven and drooping with fatigue. He nodded affectionately at Maude, who greeted him with enthusiasm.

"Nick, it's so good to see you again. Where have you been hidin' yourself?"

He smiled. "Just been hunting for a change, Maude."

"Well by the way you look, I can't say the change did you any good."

Nick chuckled as he loaded his plate. "I couldn't get comfortable last night. He took one bite of Elmer's succulent meal and looked up again. "I'm hoping after a shave and a bath and a good night's sleep, I'll be presentable again."

He looked over at Charles and Elizabeth's three girls. "So...what kind of mischief have you three been up...."

He turned as white as a ghost and stepped back in shock, his mouth hanging open. Megan froze with apprehension as he stared at her.

"Nick?" Thomas asked. "What's wrong, ol' boy?"

Everyone stopped eating and watched Nick. Had he completely lost his senses? Andrew stood and reached for his arm. "Nick, are you all right?"

Nick put his plate in Andrew's outstretched hand and stiffly walked around the wagon out of sight. Everyone sat in stunned silence.

In less than a minute, he was back. He looked at Megan again. "Why are you here, Megan?" he asked, softly.

Megan didn't know how to answer. The others looked uncomfortably at each other. No one made a sound.

"Why are you here and not back at Fort Bridger?" he asked more forcefully.

"Fort Bridger? Nick, I don't know what you're talking about," she answered slowly.

Nick rubbed his eyes vigorously with the heels of his hands and shook his head to clear his brain. He looked at Megan again and said, "Come with me, Megan. We need to talk."

Without hesitation, she set her plate aside and followed him. When they were out of sight of the others, he reached out, grabbed her hand, and led her out of the protective circle of wagons. He didn't stop until they were well out of earshot and in a small grove of pine trees. The sun had already dropped behind the mountains, but there was enough light for them to see each other clearly.

Megan felt dwarfed by Nick's tall, broad frame. He was in need of a haircut and shave, but in no way did that detract from his rugged, handsome face, she thought. Smelling of pine and wood smoke, he gently grabbed her shoulders and turned her to face him. His eyes bore into hers with an intensity she hadn't seen before.

"Megan, I need to know. Did you decide not to marry Captain Johnson?"

"Captain Johnson? Marry him? Nick…why…what are you talking about?"

"Megan, I saw him propose to you. And I heard your answer. You told him yes. Don't pretend you don't know what I'm talking about." He gave her a gentle shake. "I saw and heard with my own eyes and ears."

"How could you see and hear that? It never happened!" She yanked away from him and stared at him defiantly.

Nick leaned forward to get at her eye level and spoke slowly. "I saw the captain drop to one knee while holding your hand. It was obvious by the look on his face he was pleading with you about something. What else could that be but a marriage proposal? The next thing I hear is you squealing 'yes' over and over and telling the captain how happy he's made you. Now how else am I supposed to interpret that?"

Megan stared at him with a puzzled look, trying to remember the scene he described.

Nick watched her carefully.

Finally, it dawned on her. "I think I remember... Was it just a few days ago?"

"Maybe five or six days back."

Megan laughed at Nick's interpretation of that scene until she saw his scowl.

"I'm sorry, Nick, but when you hear what was really said, you'll probably laugh, too."

"I'm listening."

"Lee was asking me to pray for him. I can't remember his exact words. I just remember how excited I was that he finally believed everything I'd been telling him and he dropped down on his knee and asked if I'd pray for him. And of course, I told him yes. I guess that's what you saw. It's the only time I remember him on his knees in front of me. Of course, being the idiot I am, I believed the slithering, lying snake."

Nick smiled. "A 'slithering, lying snake'? Now that's music to my ears." He shook his head and continued, "Megan, the captain came to me one night and told me you were getting married at the fort and that your family was planning to attend the ceremony."

Megan gasped. *The audacity of the man! Was there no end to the conniving tricks he would pull?*

Nick had more. "He even invited me to come."

"Nick, I don't understand. How can anybody stoop so low? Why would he say such a thing?"

"I'm not sure, Megan. I think it's because he's a slithering, lying snake."

They said the last three words together, with their eyes dancing in amusement.

The amusement vanished as quickly as it had come.

"Why were you so quick to believe I would do something as stupid as marrying that lout? You knew how I felt about him. How could you? And why didn't you ask me if it was true? Why go around for days believing something ridiculous? Why didn't you come to me?"

She saw his eyes narrow and the muscles in his jaw tighten.

"Answer me, Nick."

"I couldn't."

"Why?"

"I just couldn't. That's why."

"That's not an answer. There's got to be a reason. What was it?"

He turned abruptly, ran his fingers through his hair in agitation, then looked up at the sky. After a moment, he whirled around to face her. "You want the reason, Megan?" he hollered. "Do you really want the reason?"

Megan gulped and barely managed to nod.

Nick groaned, "God, help me!" He closed the gap between them and grabbed her shoulders again. His voice was husky with emotion. "The reason, Megan, is because I'm so insanely in love with you, I can barely breathe! And I watched the captain steal you away from me before I could admit to you how I felt. I saw you accept his proposal and I knew I'd lost you forever. I couldn't face you, Megan!" He looked away from her, his face creased with emotion. "I felt like my soul had been ripped out and I couldn't bear to have you or anyone else see it. So, I left. I thought if I stayed away, it wouldn't hurt so much."

He released her and turned away. "I didn't want to love you like this, Megan. God knows how hard I've tried not to. But there's nothing I can do to stop it."

He turned back to her. "Will you marry me, Megan?"

"Marry you?" she asked, too dumbfounded to say more.

"Yes, marry me. Today or tomorrow or sometime this week."

"Nick, I can't marry you," she gently replied.

Nick stood rooted to the spot, his face turned ashen. "I…I understand, Megan. I'm sorry." He turned to leave.

Megan ran to catch him. "Don't go, Nick!" She grabbed his arm and tried in vain to turn him around. "No, you don't understand. Listen to me!"

Once she had his full attention, she smiled into his handsome, disturbed face. "I can't marry you, Nick, only because you need to court me first."

Nick's face relaxed only a little. "Court you?"

"Yes! Court me. You can't expect me to accept a marriage proposal when I just now found out you love me. I need to be courted a little while, then you can ask me."

He eyed her suspiciously. "How long will this courtship take?"

"Oh, I don't know. Maybe a month."

He smiled and turned fully toward her. "A month? That's too long."

"Too long for you, maybe. But I just now found out you love me. Now you need to show me so I'll believe you. After all, you haven't exactly been treating me like you loved me, or even liked me, for that matter. In fact, you usually act annoyed with me. It'll take some time to undo *that* damage." She smiled encouragingly.

Nick studied her upturned face. His smile grew. A deep chuckle forced its way out. He raised his hand and cupped her cheek.

"And at the end of that month of courtship, what might you say to me if I ask you to marry me again?"

Megan looked down. Nick gently raised her chin.

"I might…no, I'm quite certain I would say, 'yes,'" she whispered and looked down again.

Nick pulled Megan into a quick embrace then released

her. "Then it's settled. Beginning tomorrow after the evening meal, our courtship will begin. If it's courting you want, Miss Megan O'Mally, courting you will get." He grinned from ear to ear.

Megan's heart soared as they walked hand in hand back to the wagons.

## CHAPTER TWENTY TWO

At breakfast the next day, Nick and Thomas told the assembled group that some of the most beautiful but most difficult terrain lay ahead of them. "From Fort Bridger, the trail turns back to the northwest and crosses over the northern end of the Bear River Divide. We'll follow Bridger Creek down to the Bear River. Then the trail runs along the Bear for several more days," Nick explained.

"We'll be goin' over hills a sane person wouldn't even consider," Thomas announced. "And then we'll come to Soda Springs where water gushes straight up in the air with a loud whoosh. Kinda sounds like a steamboat. There's springs there you can drink out of. Tastes all bubbly in your mouth. Boy, oh boy, it's good." He smacked his lips and smiled at the girls who were watching with wide eyes. "There's even one spring, if you drink too much, you'll get a little tipsy."

"Thomas," Elizabeth scolded, "That can't be true."

"I swear by it, ma'am. Not that I would drink it, of course." He winked at the girls.

Megan kept stealing glances at Nick, who hadn't even looked at her this morning. He had obviously bathed and shaved. And his entire demeanor had dramatically changed since the last time they had shared a meal. She smiled at the memory of last night and looked down so no one would notice the blush she felt creeping up her neck. A shiver of anticipation passed through her when she let herself think about the coming night. He seemed very confident about courting her once he warmed up to the idea. What did he have planned for this evening?

When she had returned to her family last night, she couldn't ignore their curious stares and upraised eyebrows. So, she explained to them Nick's misunderstanding about her marrying Johnson. But that was all she said. Nick's declaration of love was too private, too precious to share with anyone yet. They'd find out soon enough. For now, it was hers and Nick's to treasure. She looked up with a smile to see Nick studying her. She almost melted at the intense look in his eyes. He winked before he turned away. Had anyone seen him? *Surely by now they can tell something is going on.* She looked around, but everyone was too busy visiting and eating to pay attention to her. Eating! She realized she hadn't taken a bite. Quickly she forced a few bites down then jumped up to help Elizabeth wash dishes.

As announced at breakfast, the terrain was breathtaking, at least for those willing to appreciate the ever-changing beauty in God's creation. Megan, Elizabeth, and Maude were among that number. The three Batten girls and a few of their friends danced circles around the women, frequently stopping to pick berries and flowers.

"I declare, these children must walk three or four times the distance we women do. Look at 'em. I don't recall ever havin' that much energy," Maude grunted, stopping to mop her forehead with the handkerchief she always had clutched in her hand.

Elizabeth stopped beside her and wiped loose hair out of

her damp face. "I sure don't have the energy I did at the beginning of the trip."

"I feel the opposite," Megan declared. "I have so much more energy now than I did when we started."

"I wish I could say the same," Elizabeth said, trying to catch her breath. "It must be the condition I'm in." She continued on ahead of the others.

Megan and Maude looked at each other then hurried to catch up. Megan grabbed Elizabeth's arm. "Elizabeth? Are you trying to tell us something?"

Elizabeth laughed. "Yes, Megan. By the end of December, you'll have another niece or maybe a nephew."

Megan almost screamed with joy. She clamped her hand over her mouth and hugged Elizabeth with her free arm. "Does Charles know?"

"Of course, he does. We've known for about a month."

"A month? How could you keep it a secret for so long? Do the girls know?"

"No. We're going to sit down and tell them tonight."

"Well then, I feel honored. You told me before you told them."

"Should you be out walkin' like this?" Maude asked.

Elizabeth chuckled. "It's better than riding in the wagon, especially when it's this rocky." She reached out to hold Maude's hand. "I'll be fine, Maude. I worked harder than this when I carried the girls."

They were interrupted by Abby, breathlessly running up to present a large bouquet of wildflowers to her mother. Stooping down, Elizabeth hugged her youngest and buried her nose in the flowers.

All day, Megan was plagued with butterflies in her stomach. How could everything change so completely in one day? She couldn't look at Nick without blushing, so she tried not looking at him. Thoughts of the coming evening had her so excited and nervous, she had a difficult time attending to anything else. Elizabeth's happy news distracted her for a while, then Nick rode by and greeted them briefly before trotting off again, leaving her with a racing heart and churning stomach. *Am I completely daft? I'd better get control of my emotions before tonight or he's bound to think he made a big mistake.*

The nooning was almost tortuous. Nick sat less than ten feet from her, but there was no communication between them. If Nick had tried to make eye contact, Megan wouldn't have known because she never looked his way. She barely touched her food and was too quick to jump up and start putting things away.

To distract herself in the afternoon, she gathered her younger students together to go over their arithmetic and spelling. Lucy and the Sanders' twins, Rachel and Meggie, were trying to outdo each other, which only made it more fun for Megan. The McKay boys didn't care that the girls were passing them in every subject. They were far more interested in running in and out of the trees and jumping over rocks. Megan usually tried to think of ways to draw them back into their studies. But on this day, she just let them run.

When the wagons pulled together for the night, Megan wrung her hands together and tried to force herself to breathe normally. She helped prepare the food then dished it out for their family. Nick was already seated by the time she finished her work. She sat down in the circle across from him. Forcing herself to take a few bites, she tried to focus her attention on the various conversations taking place around her. Maude was talking to the girls about going to school when she was young. Nick and the other men were discussing problems they were having with a few families who couldn't get along. Rebecca Sanders and Elizabeth were laughing over something little Steve Sanders had just said. Megan's attention went back to Nick. *How can he sit there and talk about everyday business as if nothing had changed? And look at the man eat! He has a huge appetite,* she thought with mild irritation.

Just then, Nick glanced at her and smiled. Her stomach fluttered again. She looked down at her plate and scolded herself. Nothing on the plate looked good, so she pushed it around with her fork and gave up.

Nick stood to his feet and stretched. He deposited his plate by Elmer's fire and walked back to the circle. "Charles, could I have a word with you in private, please?"

"Sure, Nick," Charles answered and stood. They walked around the wagon out of sight with Megan staring after them.

In a very short time they came back, both wearing big smiles. Megan got up to help Elizabeth but didn't miss the knowing grin Maude flashed her direction. She was happier and more excited than she ever remembered, but she still couldn't quell her anxiety over the whole matter. The courting was to begin soon. She wished Nick would come and get her and put an end to the waiting. She vigorously scrubbed the pots while glancing nervously at Nick. He slowly sipped at a hot cup of coffee and listened to Thomas talk about his day. When he finished, he poured the leftovers in the grass and walked away.

Megan sighed and looked up at the sky. *Was he torturing her on purpose?* Suddenly she had an awful thought. She stopped scrubbing. *What if he's changed his mind? Nonsense. He said he's had these feelings for a long time. They're not going to disappear in a day.* She, on the other hand, had had less than a day to get used to the news. No wonder her thoughts and feelings had been in turmoil. She scrubbed harder.

"Megan, I think that pot is clean," Elizabeth said with a smile and quick hug. "Would you be willing to do all the dishes so I can make biscuits for tomorrow?"

Megan blushed. "I'd be happy to, Sis. Is there anything else I can do?"

"Dry them and pack them away. As soon as I'm done with the biscuits, Charles and I are going to talk to the girls about the new member of the family."

When Megan was done, she sat down to read. After several minutes, she put the book aside and began to write in her journal. In it, she very honestly poured out her heart. She finished with, *Even if our feelings for each other die someday, I'll want always to remember this day and what a wonderful man Nicholas Webster is.* When she had finished, she sadly realized it was starting to get dark. She put her journal away and dug out her bedroll to spread under the wagon where the girls were already sleeping.

"Megan?" a deep, low voice rumbled behind her. Still on her knees, she turned to see Nick squatting next to her. "You're not turning in for the night, are you?" he asked, his voice low and husky.

"No, Nick." She smiled. "I was just getting it ready for later."

"Good." Nick stood and extended his hand. Megan took it and laughed softly when he hoisted her up. "Come with me," he said and led her away.

Fires were crackling and crickets chirping as Nick made his way past several wagons toward some rock outcroppings among tall evergreens. He led Megan to the biggest rock and up the front of it, placing his feet carefully and holding tightly to Megan's hand. When they reached the top, he turned her to look back through the sparse branches at the wagon encampment.

"Oh, it's beautiful," she murmured breathlessly.

She glanced up to see him looking at her. "Yes, it is beautiful," he whispered.

When she saw the expression in his eyes, she looked down. "Is it safe out here?" she asked as she turned and moved away from him.

Nick chuckled softly.

"I mean safe from Indians," she quickly added.

Nick sat down on the rock with his legs dangling over the edge. Patting a spot next to him, he looked up and wordlessly invited her to sit down.

Blushing and averting her eyes, she did as he asked.

"Actually, we're quite safe here. This whole area and as far as the Bear is safe because of Chief Washakie, Head Chief of the Eastern Shoshone tribe. He's been a friend to the white man for years. In fact, he's a friend of mine. I was hoping we'd cross paths, but I haven't seen any sign of him."

"How did you meet?"

"Thomas and I did some survey work for the government about ten years ago. We were hunting near Ft. Bridger and came across a group of young bucks from the Ute tribe. We were outnumbered and they didn't look very friendly, so we talked and did some trading and about the time they pulled their rifles out, another party comes swooping down from nowhere. They were Shoshone led by Chief Washakie. He gave those boys a tongue-lashing and sent them away. Then he invited Thomas and me to join him at his village for a few days."

"Did you go?"

"We didn't dare say no. He was our protection. Those Utes would have been hot on our trail if we hadn't gone. Washakie treated us like royalty, especially when he found out we were working for the U.S. government."

"And he's still the Chief around here?"

"Yep. And he's proved himself faithful to the white man over and over through the years. We've seen him two times since then and he's never forgotten our names. Pretty impressive."

"I'd love to meet him."

"I promise you, if I see him, I'll introduce you."

Megan smiled up at Nick but quickly averted her eyes when he looked at her.

Nick was quiet for a moment before asking, "Megan, are

you all right?"

"I'm fine."

"Then why are you acting so skittish? You'd think we'd just met. We've been through a lot together. I would think by now you'd be comfortable around me." He waited for an answer, but Megan only wrung her hands and bit her lip.

"Have you changed your mind about me?" he asked quietly.

Megan spun her head around and looked up at him in alarm. "No, Nick! Please don't think that!"

"Then what is it, Megan?" he gently pried, running a finger down her cheek.

She'd had all day to think and she knew the answer to his question. But as she sat there so close their arms were touching, she couldn't clear her head enough to think how to put it into words. "Uh, Nick, ...I...uh," She sighed in frustration and dropped her face into her hands.

Nick slipped his arm around her shoulder. When she relaxed, he brought his other arm around to embrace her.

Megan leaned in to the warm comfort of his strong arms. Why talk when this felt so right? Oddly she had the strange sense that she was finally, truly at home.

They sat that way for several minutes when Nick, mouth against her hair, asked again, "Can you tell me what's wrong?"

She sat up straight and Nick dropped his arms. Brushing hair out of her face, she looked up at him and tried again. "I...uh...you..." She shook her head in frustration and scrambled to her feet, with Nick watching in concern.

"I can't talk with you looking at me that way!"

"What way?" Nick asked as he, too, stood.

"Oh, Nick, you know. Looking at me like you love me."

Nick chuckled helplessly. "I can't help it. I do love you. I hope that's fine with you."

"Yes, Nick, it's more than fine," she answered softly, daring to briefly meet his eyes before she turned away again.

"The problem is that you've had weeks to get used to loving me." She paused and smiled when she heard him correct her.

"Months," he said.

"Months?" she asked incredulously. She studied his smiling face.

"Months," he repeated. "It started back at the mercantile in Independence."

"Independence? At the mercantile? Nick, you hated me!"

"First of all, I don't hate anybody," he said evenly, stepping closer. "I didn't want to love you, Megan. I didn't even want to like you. But, despite my efforts and prayers, I couldn't get you out of my mind. That little spark of love kept getting bigger and bigger until I just couldn't fight it anymore."

"Why were you so mean to me sometimes?"

Nick groaned. "I'm so sorry, Megan. I guess it was my way of keeping my distance from you." He looked away. "Frankly, Megan, I was scared to death of my feelings for you. I just couldn't let you get close. At least not at first."

Nick's expression tugged at Megan's heart. "Why, Nick?" she asked gently.

Nick looked at her with uncertainty and pain. "I've been hurt, terribly hurt by a woman and I'd vowed it would never happen again."

Megan was the one who closed the gap between them. She wrapped her arms around him in a brief hug then pulled back to look up at him, gripping his hands. "Maude told me what happened. Nick, I'm nothing like that girl. I hope you know that by now."

"Maude," he chuckled and shook his head. "I suspect the dear lady has been playing cupid."

He brought his attention back to her. Cupping her cheek in his hand, he said, "You're nothing at all like her, Megan.

But you still haven't told me what's wrong."

She pulled away and said, "That's because you interrupted me."

"I'm sorry, please continue."

"Now you're laughing at me!"

"I'm not laughing, I'm just smiling. Please, tell me."

"As I was saying, you've had weeks...months to get used to the idea of loving me. I, on the other hand, have had a day; one day," she emphasized, holding up a finger. "I'm somewhat overwhelmed by it. What you told me yesterday, Nick, changed everything, everything! Before yesterday, you were a dear friend, nothing more. Now, all of a sudden, you love me! You're courting me! You want to *marry* me!" She looked at him. "Nick, my whole future has changed! Everything is different and I'm trying to get used to it. When you look at me now, it's not Nick, my friend, looking at me. It's Nick, the man who loves me, looking at me. It's the man that wants to marry me looking at me. All of a sudden, I'm shy around you. I'm embarrassed. I'm even scared."

Nick reached out in the darkness and grabbed her hand. "Come here," he said, huskily, pulling her close. Wrapping her in his long arms, he spoke softly, "You have nothing to be afraid of." He kissed the top of her head. "Of course, it's going to take time. I understand, Megan. If it helps, I'll stop looking at you."

Megan laughed but didn't pull away from his embrace. "I love it when you look at me, Nick. It's just that it makes me all fluttery inside like I'm a silly schoolgirl. It's just going to take time for me to get used to this."

Nick stepped back and with his warm, firm hand raised her chin. "Maybe this will help." He lowered his face to hers and kissed her gently on her lips.

Megan gasped softly but didn't turn away. Nick brought both hands up to cradle her head and kissed her again, this time longer. He slowly pulled back and drew her into his arms.

"Oh, Megan, girl, a month is far too long," he groaned. "Maybe it's best if we tell the others. I'm tired of trying to hide my feelings." He gently stroked her back.

Megan thought she could stand there forever. "Mmmm," was her only response.

"I asked for Charles' permission to court you."

"What did he say?" she asked, barely above a whisper.

Nick chuckled at the memory. "He said it was about time."

Megan drew back and tried to see Nick's face in the dark. "You're joking."

"No, that's what he said. He was happy about it."

"I could tell by the big grin on his face when he walked back."

"So, you knew what we were talking about?"

"Yes. And I'm quite certain Maude knew."

Nick took Megan's chin in his hand again and asked, "Do you want to tell the others or wait? I'll do whatever you like."

"Let's tell them. Not a formal announcement, please; just privately, one by one, to the people we're closest to."

"What date should we set?"

Megan pulled back and looked up at Nick with alarm. "Date? We're not announcing our wedding, Nick." Then she saw the teasing in his eyes and playfully slapped his arm.

He grabbed her shoulders and pulled her back into his arms. "It's getting late and we both need our sleep."

Hand in hand, they walked to the edge of the rock, where Nick jumped down, then reached up to help Megan. When Nick lowered her to the ground, she found her face almost buried in his hard, muscular chest. Before she could move, Nick gently kissed her again. This time, she brought her arms up to circle his neck. Reluctantly they broke apart and walked slowly toward the wagons.

Two days later, the tired travelers went over the Big Hill, the steepest, most difficult hill they had yet seen. Going up was hard, tedious work, but when they saw the hill descending to the plain below, they were awestruck. It was an abrupt descent of almost a mile.

Megan loved watching Nick work. He was knowledgeable and confident. Few challenged his authority. The safety of every person on the train had always been a major concern of his, but Megan noticed he seemed overly concerned about her safety. Had he always been this way, she wondered, and she was only noticing it now?

When it was time for the Batten's two wagons to descend the Big Hill, Nick rode up next to them to make sure everyone was obeying his command of no passengers. Everyone but the driver had to walk well to the side. Megan watched him give Charles a nod, sending him down. Then he looked around with alarm. He gripped his reins and barked, "Where's Megan?"

Hearing the fear in his voice, Megan quickly showed herself. "I'm here, Nick."

The relief on his face moved her. "You stay well out of the way, you hear me?" he said gently.

"I hear you, Nick." His smile warmed her to the tips of her toes.

Soon after conquering Big Hill, the train stopped for half a day at Smith's trading post, giving the women time to do laundry and restock supplies. From there, they continued down the Bear River valley, aptly named for the frequent sightings of black bear. One morning, the hunting party rode proudly into camp with two bear carcasses slung over the backs of their horses. That evening the men butchered the bears and distributed the meat among the camp.

For days, they were surrounded by a sterile landscape,

with little vegetation other than sagebrush and prickly pear. Dust coated everything; their wagons, their skin and hair, even their food.

By the time they reached Soda Springs, most were desperate for a bath. Nick decided to make camp an hour early so they could be within walking distance of the springs. He posted several men with rifles in the area around the springs to watch for Indians. Several groups ventured out with washrags and buckets. Almost every group had a cup so they could taste for themselves the soda-flavored water.

Nick walked with Megan, again daring to hold her hand in front of the others. It raised a few eyebrows, most over twinkling eyes, though some over disapproving stares. Megan couldn't miss the disgusted glare of Natalie Simmons and her mother before they turned away in a huff. She glanced up to see Nick chuckling and shaking his head.

A hissing sound could be heard as they approached the springs. Megan could finally see several springs bubbling out of the ground. Cedar trees surrounded them. She carefully got as close as she dared and saw clear water coming up in continuous effervescence. "Oh, Nick, it's beautiful," she said breathlessly, dropping to her knees by the spring.

"Careful, some of them are pretty hot," Nick warned.

Megan reached out and dipped her cup in and brought it to her lips. She took a careful sip then looked up at Nick and downed the whole cup. "It's delicious!"

Nick laughed. "This better not be the intoxicating spring. I don't want to have to carry you back."

She scooped another cupful and handed it up to Nick. "Here, you try it."

She dipped her rag into the hot water, buried her face in it, rinsed it out, and did it several more times, then offered it to Nick. "Here, wash that dust off your face so I can see you," she said, laughing at his grizzled, dirty face.

Nick scowled, dipped the rag in the water, and wiped most of the grime away. "Mmmm, that feels good."

"You missed a few spots, Romeo," came the loved but unwelcome voice of Thomas. "No decent gal would kiss that ugly, dirty mug."

Nick dipped the rag in the spring, stood, and flung it, hitting Thomas squarely in the face.

"Thanks, it's exactly what I need." He rubbed it vigorously over his face then up and down his arms. He squatted at the spring and rinsed it out several times then handed to Megan. "Clean enough for m'lady," he announced.

Holding it delicately between two fingers, Megan inspected it with a grimace.

"Would you care to see Beer Spring?" Thomas asked.

"I'd love to!" Megan answered then looked at Nick for his response.

"Lead the way," he said to his old friend.

On the way, they saw several springs with water of a variety of colors spewing out of the ground. "Different minerals give the water those colors," Nick explained.

Suddenly they heard a forceful whooshing sound a distance away. "There goes the Steamboat!" Thomas said, searching for the geyser. "There it is! Look quick, over there." He grabbed Megan's shoulders and turned her just in time for her to see the last of the geyser with steam spraying out in all directions.

"Over here," Thomas called out a moment later, pointing at a spring where several people were dipping their cups. Thomas dipped Megan's cup and handed it to her. She smelled it, hesitated, and looked up at Nick uncertainly. He smiled.

"Go ahead. One sip won't do you any damage," Nick said, his eyes dancing with amusement.

Megan took a sip then pushed the cup into Nick's hand. "Your turn."

Thomas and Nick laughed at her expression. "What's the matter?"

"It's terrible," she answered with a wrinkled nose.

Nick took a sip and handed the cup to Thomas who drained it and went back for more. Smacking his lips loudly and wiping his mouth with his sleeve, he noticed Nick's serious expression. "Don't get yerself worked up," he said with annoyance, "I haven't forgotten the rule. Although, I think it's a cryin' shame to ignore this bountiful blessing provided by the Maker himself."

"Take a day off and drink yourself silly, Thomas," Nick said quietly and slapped him on the back.

"Thanks, I will!"

"Just don't come back to the train 'til you're sober." Nick turned and walked away, Megan close behind.

"See ya tomorrow," Thomas called after them.

"Nick, he won't be safe out here alone, will he?" Megan asked.

"He won't stay. We've been through this before. He loves to get drunk now and then, but he's never yet gotten drunk in the middle of an assignment like this."

They walked a little way away from the springs and settled on the ground with contented sighs, their backs resting on the trunks of two big cedars.

"Thomas is a lonely man, isn't he, Nick?" Megan asked softly with a trace of sadness.

Nick gazed tenderly at her before he answered. "Yes, Megan, he is. I'm surprised you noticed. He hides it well."

"What he needs is a good woman."

"No," Nick said thoughtfully. "What he needs is God."

Megan studied Nick's face, waiting for him to say more. Finally, she asked, "Have you talked to him about God?"

Nick picked up a short stick and, resting his arms across his knees, started to fiddle with it, spinning it slowly between his thumb and fingers, now and then peeling some bark off. He chuckled softly. "Yeah, I've talked to him…a lot, especially right after I got saved."

"And?"

"He wanted nothing to do with it. In fact, he gave me a pretty hard time over it, told me he felt like he was losing his best friend."

"Why?"

"Oh, I suppose it was because I was different. I stopped drinking and cleaned up my language. We didn't have as much in common anymore."

"Somehow, I can't quite picture you drinking and using foul language," Megan said.

Nick snorted. "It wasn't excessive." He looked at her. "I wasn't a drunk, Megan, in case you're worried about it." He leaned back against the tree and looked off at the horizon.

"Everything was different though. It's hard to explain to someone unless they've experienced it for themselves. One day, the loneliness and darkness seemed magnified, almost as if it was strangling me inside. I knew there was something else, or I should say, *Someone* else, and as much as I had tried to deny Him in my past, I knew that 'Someone' was God. I was desperate to find Him, but I wasn't sure what I needed to do. All the sermons, all my parents' teaching, all the Bible verses I'd heard just seemed like a confusing, tangled mess in my head. So, I just prayed in frustration for God's help. Over and over for days, I kept praying that one simple prayer, 'Help me, God. Please help me. I don't know what to do.' Then one morning, when I first woke up, a Bible verse came to me as clearly as if someone was standing there and saying it to me. 'There is none other name under heaven given among men whereby we must be saved.' It was a verse my mother made me learn as a child, and that morning, it seemed to find its way to the front of my brain, through all my tangled confusion. And I knew without a doubt the name the verse mentioned was the name of Jesus."

Nick looked at Megan and smiled. Just saying the name, Jesus, seemed to calm his spirit. "I saddled up Black and rode out to the high pasture where I'd been mending fences. I got on my knees and asked Jesus to save me. At that moment, I was almost overwhelmed by all the sin in my life." He glanced up at Megan. "By man's standard, it wouldn't have seemed so bad, but in the presence of God...it was pretty overwhelming. It was as if God shone a bright, piercing light over my past and exposed everything for what it really was. I was so ashamed I bawled like a baby. And, for a while, I was very afraid. I begged Him to forgive me and to save me."

Nick looked at Megan with tears in his eyes. She was softly weeping but smiled at him through her tears.

"It still amazes me when I think about it, Megan. The most amazing sense of peace poured through me like...almost like a river. The fear was gone. The shame was gone. I felt so clean and so in awe. I still didn't understand what was happening to me, but all day I felt His presence. He was there beside me, all around me, *in* me! I couldn't wait to tell Thomas."

He looked at Megan again and shrugged. "Thomas just laughed, told me I must've gotten whacked on the head. So that evening, I rode to a neighbors' place. I figured they were godly people and would understand. I was right. They loaned me a Bible and invited me to drop by as often as I wanted to so they could help me learn more."

Nick chuckled at the fond memory. "I think I made quite a nuisance of myself the first week. I dropped by every night! There was so much to learn. I just couldn't get enough."

He looked at Megan and sighed. "Sorry I went on so long. I hope I didn't bore you."

"Bore me? How could I possibly be bored with what you told me, Nick? It's so wonderful."

"I hounded Thomas for weeks after I was saved. I finally

backed off when he threatened to leave. It's still a sore point between us. But he seldom says anything disrespectful about God or about my faith anymore. I keep praying. Maybe someday…"

Megan sat in comfortable silence snuggled against Nick for several more minutes, quietly praying for their friend. Then she got up and brushed twigs and sand off her skirt.

"I need to get back to help Elizabeth. She works too hard. I need to give her all the help I can now that she's in her condition." She smiled down at Nick, hating to leave.

Nick rose to his full height and looked down, studying her face. She blushed and looked away when she saw the smoldering intensity in his eyes. "Tonight, Megan," he breathed as he softly kissed the top of her head then took her hand and led her back.

# CHAPTER TWENTY THREE

After traveling for five days through mountainous terrain, they passed the old Fort Hall area, where they joined the turbulent Snake River. The trail turned southwest to follow the river across flat, desolate land with mountains far in the distance. Although they followed the Snake River, it was mostly inaccessible to the travelers and their stock. In fact, most of the time they couldn't see the river unless they walked over to the edge of the deep gorge cut through the rock by the raging water far below. Occasionally, men were able to pick their way down the steep cliffs to fish and haul water for the stock.

After several days, they approached an area known as The Gate of Death. The trail dropped down into a canyon carved by the river and passed through a narrow break in the rocks. Nick and Thomas led a group of armed scouts ahead of the train to check for Indians. Once safely through the Gate, the wagons stopped for the nooning.

"Why do they call this place 'The Gate of Death'?" Megan asked the men while they were all eating.

"There was an Indian massacre here three years ago," Thomas answered. "Nine or ten white men killed by either Shoshone or Snake, not sure which."

"Actually, the battle was back a few miles to the east," Nick added. "This place has been feared ever since because it looks like the perfect spot for an ambush." He noticed the fear in the eyes of the women and quickly added, "But we're past the danger point and we've scouted the area, so there's nothing to be afraid of."

Later, as they were walking in the wide canyon next to the Snake, Megan was overwhelmed at the number and variety of birds she saw. Seagulls, herons, even pelicans swooped overhead and covered the edge of the water or bobbed on the wind-driven waves. On the far side of the river rose dark cliffs punctuated occasionally by small, trickling waterfalls. The three women walked together in silent awe. Megan stumbled several times, not wanting to take her eyes off the amazing scene.

Soon they were passed by Mrs. Simmons and her daughter, Natalie, who trudged along with their eyes on the ground only looking up to continue an argument.

"Well, Mother, just because you think I should go doesn't mean I have to. After all, I am nineteen."

"Well, you're being an absolute ninny!"

"Why?"

"I've told you a thousand times why! You never listen to me, Natalie Katherine!"

"Oh, I listen. Although sometimes I wished I hadn't!"

"What are you talking about? You ungrateful, little snip!"

Their voices drifted away as they moved farther ahead.

"I was just thinkin' that nothin' could spoil a day this beautiful," Maude said.

Elizabeth and Megan laughed.

"Where are the girls?" Elizabeth asked suddenly, looking around. "I've been too busy looking at the birds I completely forgot about my girls."

Megan saw all three of them upstream with five or six other children throwing rocks in the water and chasing seagulls. "There they are, Sis. They're fine."

"Oh, thank God!" Elizabeth said with a hand over her heart.

Megan saw her friend Jessica ahead, waiting for them to catch up. When Megan reached her, she couldn't help notice the troubled expression on Jessica's face.

"What's wrong, Jessica?"

"Can I talk to you in private?" Jessica asked, breathlessly. Jessica always seemed to be out of breath, although, Megan noticed, she was much thinner than she had been when they first met back in Nebraska.

Jessica took Megan's arm and steered her off to the side. She stopped and moved to face her.

"Megan, I hate to tell you this, but I think I need to."

Megan looked into Jessica's pain-filled eyes and, knowing her good friend was not a loose-tongued gossip, braced herself for bad news.

"Natalie Simmons and her mother have been spreading some awful lies about you."

Fear stabbed Megan's heart. "What? What have they been saying?"

"Well, they know better than to try to say those things to me. I've just heard other people repeating it and when I ask where they heard such nonsense, they tell me it's the two Simmons' women."

"What is it?"

"Basically, they're saying you are a loose woman and can't be trusted around any of the men."

Deep dread began to form in the pit of Megan's stomach. She couldn't move.

"They said you were fired from your teaching job in St. Louis because you were a loose woman. You flirted with Capt. Johnson until he proposed to you, then when he realized what kind of a woman you were, he broke off the engagement. They saw the two of you doing 'unspeakable' things together."

"What?!" Megan's mouth hung open in disbelief, anger taking root and growing fiercer with every word.

"That's not all. Now they're telling everyone you're turning your wiles on Mr. Webster. And they've seen you two doing things you shouldn't."

Jessica hung her head in shame at having to repeat such horrid news. Megan reached out and brushed her hand down Jessica's arm.

"Jessica? You don't believe any of this, do you?"

She looked Megan in the eye. "No, Megan, not a word." She chuckled weakly. "Except the part about you being fired from your teaching position."

Megan smiled sadly. She had kept none of her past from Jessica, one of the few trusted friends who had heard her whole story.

Her fists clenched in fury, Megan said, "I think it's time the Simmons and I had a showdown!"

"Megan, remember what the Bible says to do if people spread vicious gossip about you?"

"No, I don't remember. What does it say?" Megan asked, trying to control the anger in her voice.

"I can't recall the exact words, but we're supposed to live in such a way that no one will believe the lies."

"Don't you think I'm living right, Jessica?"

"Yes, Megan, of course I do. I think it means not to fight back. Just keep on doing what's right and eventually the rumors will die. Besides, most people don't believe them. They know what kind of people Natalie and her mother are." Breathing hard, Megan stared at the ground and listened.

"The Bible also says to pray for your enemies," Jessica said quietly.

Megan looked at her in astonishment and grinned.

"Since when have you been such a spiritual pillar?"

Jessica looked down in embarrassment. "I've been praying for you ever since I heard the lies. I knew this wouldn't be easy for you." She looked back up and said, "If it makes you feel any better, I wanted to go right up to the two of them and slap their faces so hard their heads would spin."

Megan laughed and hugged her dear friend then pulled back and studied her face. "Keep praying for me, Jessica. I'm so mad I could spit!"

"I will, Megan. Just promise me you'll stay away from them."

"I'll try, but their wagon is only three away from ours."

"And I'll do what I can to kill the rumors."

"Thank you, Jessica," Megan said with feeling. She hugged her again before they parted.

Throughout the day, Megan wrestled with her feelings. She went from seething anger to the awful fear that her reputation would be destroyed. No matter how she tried, she couldn't bring herself to pray a benevolent prayer for those two. She debated whether to tell anyone about the rumors. Her emotions were in turmoil over it.

When they pulled into camp, she still had no peace. She went about her duties and over-salted the stew and spilled Charles' coffee just as she handed it to him.

"I'm so sorry, Charles," she cried, grabbing at a towel and clumsily mopping his shirt. "Are you burned?"

Charles grabbed the towel out of her hand with a growl. "I'll be fine when you quit flopping this dirty towel in my face!"

"Oh! I'm sorry!"

Charles looked up at her with a puzzled frown. "What's wrong, Megan?"

"What's wrong? *You're* the one who got hot coffee spilled on him."

"I'm fine. It wasn't that hot. Just get me a new cup, and all will be forgiven."

Megan poured a new cup, delivered it carefully, dished up a bowl of stew, and sat down next to Nick. She played with her food and tried to listen to the others.

Nick gently nudged her with his elbow and asked in a quiet, deep voice, "Not hungry?"

Megan, lost in her thoughts, quickly shifted her attention to her food. "Oh...yeah, I'm hungry." She picked up her spoon and pushed her food around then took a small bite. Again, the awful words that Jessica had reported to her crowded their way into her thoughts. She gripped the spoon and stared blankly into space.

Nick leaned close and quietly said, "Megan, you need to eat or you're going to waste away to nothing."

She forced herself to smile at him and dutifully started taking small bites and forcing herself to chew and swallow.

When dishes were done, Nick walked over to her. "Let's go for a walk, Megan."

Gratefully, she hung up her dishtowel and took his outstretched hand. They walked leisurely around the circle, as Nick told her about his day. Megan noticed several people watching them. *What are they thinking?* she wondered. Who did Natalie and her mother talk to? Everyone? Many people greeted them with a friendly nod and smile. Or were they only greeting Nick and perhaps feeling sorry for him? She shook her head in agitation, trying to stop the negative flow of her thoughts.

"Megan?" Nick stopped and turned her toward him. "What's wrong?" He gently lifted her chin with his finger.

Megan tried to look from side to side to see who was watching them, but only her eyes could move.

"Megan," Nick said more firmly. He grabbed her shoulders. "Look at me." She did.

"You haven't heard a thing I've said, have you?"

"Yes, I have," she answered.

"I asked you a question and you didn't answer."

"You did?"

Nick nodded and grinned.

"I'm sorry, Nick. What was the question?"

"It doesn't matter." He took her hand again and started to lead her away from the wagons. "Let's go someplace where we can talk."

On their way to a private spot, they passed a few people who greeted them warmly. Then to Megan's horror, she saw Natalie and her mother approach. She averted her eyes as her anger rose quickly to the surface. It threatened to boil over when she heard a haughty sniff as they grew closer. Nick greeted them politely and to Megan's dismay, they stopped. Megan continued to keep her eyes on the ground.

"Mr. Webster, good evening," they both said pleasantly. Megan looked up just in time to see them glaring at her.

"I can certainly understand, Miss O'Mally," said Mrs. Simmons with a smirk at her daughter, "why you wouldn't look at us, much less greet us."

Natalie gleefully picked up where her mother left off. "Yes, after all, we are ladies and you're...oh, how should I put it? A rather loose woman, I hear. I'm surprised poor Mr. Webster dares to be seen with you."

Before Megan could think, she walked over to Natalie, brought her hand up, and slapped her face. Natalie gasped and stumbled back. Mrs. Simmons screamed.

Nick lunged and grabbed Megan and swung her around to face him. "What has gotten into you, Megan?" he said, his voice harsh and angry.

Mrs. Simmons moved so close that Megan could feel her hot breath. With a loud, shrill voice she cried, "Now you've seen for yourself, Mr. Webster, just what class of woman you've allowed to ensnare you!"

Megan, still seething with anger, yanked herself free from Nick's grasp and turned toward the sneering woman. Nick wrapped his arms around her and spun, putting himself between them.

"Enough!" he hollered. Arms wrapped tightly around her, he continued in a hard, stern voice that silenced everyone. "You, Mrs. Simmons, and your daughter will appear before the council in exactly one hour!"

"Us? Why us?" she asked with a hand pressed to her chest, her expression filled with scorn. "What have we done, I'd like to ask, Mr. Webster? And what about that little strumpet you're holding?"

"Silence!" Nick bellowed.

Soon a small crowd gathered, including Thomas and Andrew. Megan was crying so hard she was almost choking. Nick eased his grip so she could catch her breath. Andrew moved over and Nick released her into his arms so he could turn and face the obstinate Mrs. Simmons.

"You will hold your tongue or I'll have your husband deliver a well-deserved flogging. As for Miss O'Mally, she, too, will appear before the council, but not when you are present. You have already inflicted enough damage."

"Damage? Mr. Webster," she said in a wounded tone. "We have only been trying to protect the families on this train from her influence."

"Katherine Simmons, hold your tongue!" Everyone turned to see Mr. Simmons standing amongst them with a livid, beet-red face. Mrs. Simmons' face turned white and she opened her mouth in protest, but nothing came out. Natalie shrank back into the crowd.

"Go to the wagon!" Mr. Simmons ordered his wife. She obeyed, her nose tipped in the air as she maneuvered through the assembly.

Mr. Simmons turned to Nick. "I'm sorry, Mr. Webster. I'll see to it she and Natalie appear before the council."

Nick nodded his appreciation. "They're each allowed to bring two other people to testify on their behalf."

"Thank you," he said, then turned to Megan who was weeping softly into her hands, which were clamped tightly over her face. "Miss O'Mally," he said softly, "I can't tell you how sorry I am."

He waited a moment then turned to follow his family. Nick stood for a moment, breathing hard, obviously trying to gain control over his emotions. "Go back to what you were doing, everyone," he ordered the growing crowd. "The council will handle this."

He continued to stand there, watching them leave until only Andrew, Thomas, and Megan were left. His jaw muscles bulged with aggravation. Megan's soft weeping was the only sound.

"Leave us, please," he said, looking at the two brothers. "Assemble the council. Tell them I want to meet with them in 30 minutes." Andrew released Megan and the two walked away.

Megan wiped her eyes and looked at him. He stood motionless, staring at the ground, his expression hard and unyielding.

"I'm so sorry," Megan croaked.

He looked at her, a mixture of pity and anger evident on his chiseled face.

"What were you thinking, Megan?"

"I wasn't thinking," she answered, tears streaming down her face.

"Come here," he said, reaching an arm in her direction. He pulled her into a quick embrace then held her shoulders and looked intently into her eyes. "You physically attacked another person on this train. You know there will be consequences."

She only nodded and looked down in shame.

"Megan, don't you realize how serious this is? The sentence could be severe. I've seen men banned from a wagon train for offenses like this."

She looked at him. "Even when the attack was provoked?" she asked in a shaky voice.

"You were provoked verbally, not physically. I heard

them. What they said was inexcusable, Megan, but you didn't need to hit her! What got into you?"

He stood to his full height and raked his fingers through his hair. He looked down at her again. "Help me understand, Megan," he said quietly. "Help me understand before I have to report to the council."

Megan cleared her throat and wiped her sleeve across her eyes. "Jessica told me today that the two Simmons' women were spreading vicious lies about me. Several people told her what they were saying and it was awful. Some of it was about us." She kept her head down while she talked. "I got so angry, Nick, and afraid that people would believe them. I thought all the rumors about me were over, and now they've started again, thanks to those two." She looked up. "I was so mad I wanted to strangle both of them. But Jessica calmed me down. I tried so hard all day to keep my anger under control."

"Was that why you didn't eat and why you didn't hear a word I said to you earlier?" Nick asked.

Megan nodded and looked down.

"I'm so ashamed, Nick. I can't believe I actually hit her." She wiped fresh tears away with the back of her hand. "What I did was so wrong. Please forgive me."

He pulled her into his arms again and sighed helplessly.

"Oh, Megan, what am I going to do with you?" he whispered against her hair.

The six men, appointed at the beginning of the trip to serve as the council gathered in a private spot near Nick's wagons. He looked at those men with confidence. Stephen Sanders and Charles were among the six. Nick was asked to be in attendance at both sessions since he was the only witness to the fight. They first met with the two Simmons women. Mr. Simmons sat with them. Although they were each allowed to bring two others to speak on their behalf, neither had been able to convince anyone to do so.

Mr. Piper, an older, much respected man, presided. He cleared his throat and began. "Katherine and Natalie Simmons, charges have been brought against you. They are…"

"Excuse me, please, Mr. Piper," Mrs. Simmons interrupted. "Who, exactly, brought these charges?"

Mr. Simmons glared at his wife.

"Mr. Webster witnessed these events and spoke with other witnesses. He is the one bringing the charges."

"Well that alone should bring suspicion on the truth of the events, wouldn't you say?" she asked sweetly.

"Katherine, sit down!" her husband commanded and pulled her down next to him. "We're sorry. Please continue," he addressed the council.

"Thank you, Mr. Simmons. As I was saying, the charge against you is slander, bearing false witness against your neighbor. Both of you have been heard making false and malicious statements about Megan O'Mally. Every member of this council, with the exception of Mr. Batten, has heard at least one of you making these accusations. You've also been heard verbally attacking Miss O'Mally with these false accusations."

Rising in indignation, Mrs. Simmons asked, "And who, pray tell, is the judge of whether or not these statements we made are false?"

"We are," Mr. Piper said quietly and confidently, never taking his eyes off her.

She sat down again with a loud, "Humph!"

"Miss O'Mally is not, nor has she ever been guilty of being a 'strumpet' as you, Mrs. Simmons, accused her."

Mrs. Simmons squirmed when her husband looked at her aghast.

"Miss O'Mally was never engaged to marry Capt. Johnson. According to several witnesses, she spent time with him to convince him of his need for salvation."

"And you believe that?" Mrs. Simmons asked.

"I believe it," Mr. Simmons announced. "And you be quiet!"

"All of the members of this council and many others we questioned have never witnessed Miss O'Mally behaving in an unseemly manner with any of the men. She has conducted herself as a fine Christian woman, except…"

"What about…"

"Sit down, Katherine!"

Mr. Piper held up his hand to silence the council so he could continue. "Except in her behavior today. She will be appearing before us when this session concludes. Do either of you have anyone here to speak on your behalf?"

Mrs. Simmons looked expectantly at her husband. After some hesitation he stood.

"Mr. Piper, I…ah…I do have something to say. The charges you brought against my wife and daughter are…well, from what I've witnessed, they are guilty of all charges."

His wife gasped and grabbed his arm.

"It's true and you know it, Katherine! You need to own up to it, both of you do!" He turned back to the council. "I…ah… I have just one request. I…I humbly ask for you to go easy on my daughter. She's guilty, but she has been influenced by her mother. And that's hard for a daughter to resist. Thank you. And…I… I'm so sorry I let this behavior go on. Maybe I should be on trial as well. I beg your forgiveness." He looked at Nick when he said those words. Nick nodded his understanding.

Natalie watched her father and bowed her head in shame.

"Do you have anything to say in your defense, Mrs. Simmons?"

She sat silently with her mouth hanging open.

"Miss Simmons, do you?"

Natalie looked up with tears in her eyes and answered clearly, "No, sir."

It pained Nick greatly to stand in the next council session and hear Mr. Piper state that the charges filed against Megan were brought by him. He hoped Megan would look at him, but she kept her eyes on the ground. When asked if she had anything to say in her defense, she answered quietly, "No, sir."

"Then you do admit you struck Natalie Simmons on the face?"

"Yes, sir."

"Do you have anyone to speak on your behalf?"

"Yes, sir. Maude Davis and Jessica Hawkins." She looked at both of her friends who nodded sadly.

"Were either of you ladies witnesses?"

"No, sir," they both answered.

"What do you ladies have to say, then?"

Jessica stood and cleared her throat. Her hands shook and her voice trembled when she spoke. "I was with Megan not long before she...uh, before she hit Natalie. I told her about all the vicious lies the two Simmons women were spreading. She hadn't heard anything about it until I told her and now, I wished I'd kept my mouth shut. But it hurt her terribly to hear what they were saying to everyone. It was ruining her reputation. And of course, she was angry. Wouldn't you be? She was going to try to stay away from them because she was afraid she'd say something she'd regret. Before I left her, she told me she was angry and asked me to pray for her. So, she was trying terribly hard to do the right thing under the circumstances."

Jessica turned to Megan with tears in her eyes. "I'm so sorry, Megan. If I hadn't said anything, none of this would've happened."

Megan reached out and squeezed her hand.

Maude stood. "Mr. Piper, even though it was wrong for

309

Megan to strike Natalie, it wasn't without provocation. And I'm a witness to that provocation. I've heard on more than one occasion both of the Simmons women spreading false rumors about Megan. An' more than once I rebuked 'em. I can't tell you how close I've come to doin' just what Megan did. It's wrong, I know. I'm just sayin' they needed someone to set them straight. I'm sorry it ever got back to this dear, sweet, innocent girl. She shouldn't have to fight those two alone. If the rest of us had done our jobs, we could've silenced them long ago. And that goes for you men, too! Shame on you! Every one of you! Lettin' this malicious gossip go on like it did. I'm ashamed of all of us!" With that, she sat down.

Nick raised his eyebrows at the five red-faced men, all squirming under Maude's scolding. Charles, the only one who hadn't heard the gossip, looked at them accusingly. Mr. Piper cleared his throat several times before he could speak.

"Ah... Mrs. Davis has raised an interesting point. I'm ashamed to admit I did hear this gossip, knew it to be false, and did nothing to stop it." He paused and looked at the other men. "How many of you can say the same?"

All but Charles sheepishly raised their hands.

"Then I think we all owe Miss O'Mally and her family an apology." He looked at the men and waited. They all in turn nodded their assent.

Mr. Piper turned to Megan. "Miss O'Mally, I speak for myself and these men. We are deeply sorry for allowing this slander to continue. And we will commit ourselves to seeing to it that it's not continued. Charles, our apology is also extended to you and your family for allowing your sister-in-law's name to be maligned. Will you accept our apologies?"

Both Charles and Megan indicated they did.

"However, the matter before us now is the physical attack of Miss Simmons, of which you, Miss O'Mally, are guilty. Mr. Webster, did Miss O'Mally approach the Simmons women or did they approach her?

"They approached her."

"So, from what you observed, Miss O'Mally was in no way seeking a confrontation."

"No, sir. From my observation, Miss O'Mally was trying to avoid a confrontation."

"Did her actions seem to be premeditated?"

"Not at all."

"Miss O'Mally, how do you feel about your actions?"

"I am very ashamed of what I did. It was wrong and I will always regret it," she answered sincerely.

"Would you be willing to apologize to Miss Simmons?"

"Yes, sir."

"Does anyone have any further questions for Miss O'Mally?"

He waited. "Then this council session is adjourned. We will call for you, Miss O'Mally, when we've decided what the consequences of your behavior will be."

An hour later, Katherine and Natalie Simmons were told by the council to make a public and written confession stating they spread malicious and false rumors about Megan O'Mally. If they refused or if they continued slandering Megan, they would be asked to leave the train. They were also to apologize to Megan.

Mrs. Simmons stood and glared at the council. "We will have no trouble finding another wagon train. It will be my pleasure!"

Mr. Simmons stood also. "You will do it alone, Katherine, and you'll go without the wagon!" he said with finality.

She turned and looked at him aghast, her hand pressed to her heart. "You...you'd leave me?"

"No, Katherine, you'd be leaving me."

Her face turned white. "Horace Simmons, I can't believe

my ears! You want me to…to write that confession? I won't do it!"

"I will, Pa," Natalie said softly behind him.

He turned and laid his hand gently on her head.

"Natalie!" her mother exclaimed in a hurt tone.

When her daughter didn't respond, Mrs. Simmons looked from her to her husband, then at the council with her mouth frozen in speechless indignation.

Finally, she recovered enough to exclaim, "Well, I never!" With that, she sat down, her back as stiff as a board.

Later, Megan was summoned. Her eyes darted quickly to Nick, the only other person present besides the six men of the council. His face was unreadable. She took her seat quietly, dreading what she would hear but ready to do whatever they asked of her. After praying with Maude and Elizabeth, she knew that whatever came, God would be with her.

"Miss O'Mally," Mr. Piper addressed her gently, "taking everything into consideration, we have reached a verdict. Your brother-in-law has chosen to withhold his judgment because he's a relative. The rest of us have decided that you must apologize to Miss Simmons."

Megan nodded.

"Also, for seven days, when the wagons are moving, you must walk by yourself at the back of the train. You may not speak to anyone or walk near anyone. You may rejoin your family whenever the train stops." Megan was surprised to see tears in Mr. Piper's eyes when he looked at her. "Miss O'Mally, with the council's permission, I'd like to talk to you as a father." He swallowed and looked down at his hands. "I do understand your actions this evening. After spending time in Mrs. Simmons' presence, I almost wished you'd slapped her instead of her daughter."

The tension broke and everyone laughed.

"However, we can't let an offense go unpunished. Mr. Webster has managed to run this train in such a way that there have been few altercations, and from what I hear, that's a rare thing on these trains. If we allow your offense to go unnoticed, it would set a precedent for the rest of the trip and we can't take that chance. I hope you understand."

"I do understand, Mr. Piper. Thank you for your kindness to me, under these circumstances. I'll do my best to not disappoint you."

# CHAPTER TWENTY FOUR

The next morning after breakfast, Megan made her way to the back of the train with a canteen of water and her Bible. Seven days alone with God and his word could only do her good, she'd decided.

After she had left the council the previous evening, she had gone directly to the Simmons and apologized. Two members of the council accompanied her. Natalie hung her red face and stammered an awkward apology in turn. Mrs. Simmons on the other hand looked her boldly in the face and uttered a flippant, insincere, "I'm so sorry."

Megan looked uncertainly from her to her husband's scowling face. When no one challenged her, Mr. Simmons stepped forward and took Megan's hand.

"Miss O'Mally, please accept my sincere apologies for allowing this to continue. I'll do what I can to undo the damage caused."

Megan answered softly, "I forgive you, Mr. Simmons. Thank you. And please, would you forgive me for slapping your daughter? It was so wrong of me."

"Horace!" his wife screeched from behind him. "For pity's sake!"

"It was probably a well-deserved slap," he answered with a wink.

"Horace!"

Megan's mouth opened in surprise. "Oh, no, Mr. Simmons. It was wrong of me. I've never slapped another woman. I still can't believe what I did. I'm so ashamed of myself."

"You're forgiven," he answered with a quick squeeze to her hand before he turned back to his family.

Megan kept dropping farther back to escape the dust from a hundred moving wagons. The dust, combined with the wind and heat, was almost unbearable. It was only midmorning and she already missed her usual companions. She heard hoofbeats coming her way and looked up to see Nick emerge from the swirling yellow sand. He trotted up to her and dismounted.

"You can't fall back this far. It's not safe," he said, concern in his eyes.

"I can't breathe if I'm any closer."

"I know. The wind is bad today." He looked uncomfortably at her then at the ground.

They walked together silently for a while. Then Megan laid a hand on his arm and said, "You're not supposed to be here with me, remember?"

He smiled. "Actually, I convinced them to make an exception."

"Oh?"

He glanced at her with pain in his eyes. "I reminded them it wasn't safe, especially for a woman, to be out here alone. They told me I could ride near you as often as I thought necessary."

He stopped and turned her to face him. Their eyes locked. "And right now, I think it's necessary."

Megan swallowed nervously. His eyes were so sad. What could this possibly mean?

"Have...have you changed your mind about us?" she asked with dread.

Nick's eyebrow's shot up. "No, Megan. Why would you think that?"

"Because...because of what I did. I was afraid that maybe you..." Her voice trailed off and she looked down.

"Megan, look at me," Nick said softly. "I came back here to apologize."

"For what?"

"For bringing a charge against you before the council."

"Nick, that's your job."

He hung his head. "I know. I hated doing it, but I would've done the same to anyone else." He locked eyes with her again, the pain less evident. "I couldn't make an exception in your case just because I'm madly in love with you and plan on being your husband someday." His eyes began to twinkle.

Megan smiled and laughed with relief. She stepped into his outstretched arms and laid her head on his chest.

"Thank God for this infernal dust storm. No one can see us," Nick laughed.

He continued to walk with her until the nooning. She kept reminding him this was supposed to be a punishment so maybe they shouldn't talk. Finally, he agreed that she wasn't supposed to talk, but he wasn't being punished so he could talk 'til he turned blue.

After the nooning, the wind died down. Nick saw to it that either he, Thomas, or Andrew, all on horseback, rode beside Megan to assure her safety. They continued their watch over her for the next six days.

Megan was resolute in her determination to obey the council. She hushed the men if they spoke to her and for most of the six remaining days kept her nose buried in her Bible or her eyes lifted in prayer. It was time well spent.

She read the story of Joseph in Genesis, of how his brothers sold him as a slave. Later he spent years in an Egyptian prison for a crime he didn't commit and yet he continued to serve and trust God. Through an amazing series of events, Joseph was awarded a position second only to the Pharaoh. Later in Genesis 50:20, Megan read words Joseph spoke to his brothers, *But as for you, ye thought evil against me; but God meant it unto good.*

*Even in this situation, the Simmons meant to do evil to me, but perhaps if I'm truly repentant, and I think I am, then God can somehow turn this into good.*

She read in Psalm 62,

*Truly my soul waiteth upon God; from Him cometh my salvation.*

*He only is my rock and my salvation; He is my defense; I shall not be greatly moved.*

*My soul, wait thou only upon God; for my expectation is from Him.*

*He only is my rock and my salvation: He is my defense; I shall not be moved.*

*In God is my salvation and my glory: the rock of my strength, and my refuge is in God.*

*Trust in Him at all times; ye people, pour out your heart before Him; God is a refuge for us.*

Megan's heart thrilled at the words as she applied them to herself and her situation. *God is my refuge! He invites me to trust in Him, to pour out my heart before Him.* She basked in His glorious presence. She asked God each day to forgive her for her actions and to enable her to truly forgive Natalie and her mother, to forgive even when Mrs. Simmons was so obviously not sorry. She reminded herself over and over of the words from Psalm 62, that God is her rock and her defense. Even if Mrs. Simmons continued her hateful gossip, Megan knew she needed to continually forgive her and let God be her defense. Let God be her rock, her strength.

Later, on the hottest day of the week, she read in Psalm 63, *O God, thou art my God; early will I seek thee: my soul thirsteth for thee, my flesh longeth for thee in a dry and thirsty land, where no water is.*

Megan chuckled and looked up as if sharing a private joke with her Father.

She read on,

*To see thy power and thy glory, so as I have seen thee in the sanctuary.*

*Because thy loving kindness is better than life, my lips shall praise thee.*

*Thus will I bless thee while I live: I will lift up my hands in thy name.*

*My soul shall be satisfied as with marrow and fatness; and my mouth shall praise thee with joyful lips:*

*When I remember thee upon my bed, and meditate on thee in the night watches.*

*Because thou hast been my help, therefore in the shadow of thy wings will I rejoice.*

*My soul followeth hard after thee: thy right hand upholdeth me.*

*But those that seek my soul, to destroy it, shall go into the lower parts of the earth.*

*They shall fall by the sword: they shall be a portion for foxes.*

*But the king shall rejoice in God; every one that sweareth by him shall glory: but the mouth of them that speak lies shall be stopped.*

Halfway through Megan's week of solitary walking, the Simmons', somewhat reluctantly by Mrs. Simmons, publicly confessed their wrongdoing in word and on paper, which was passed from one family to another.

"Megan, you seem so quiet and...and subdued,"

Elizabeth whispered to her the following morning when they were fixing breakfast together. "I'm worried about you. This can't be easy for you."

Megan wrapped her arm around her sister. "Oh, Elizabeth, don't give it a thought. I'm doing just fine. Better than fine," she added as she realized others must be concerned as well. She was simply enjoying the peace God had so unexplainably wrapped around her like a warm quilt. Later that day, she read in Philippians, chapter 4, verses 6 and 7, *Be careful for nothing; but in everything by prayer and supplication with thanksgiving, let your requests be made known unto God. And the peace of God, which passeth all understanding, shall keep your hearts and minds through Christ Jesus.*

She couldn't understand this peace that enveloped her. She didn't try. She simply accepted it gratefully from the hand of her Father.

Megan gathered her class around her on the first day she was free. She had grown to love and cherish her students. On that particular morning, she had a heightened sense of appreciation for each one of them. Besides her three delightful nieces, she continued to teach the McKay and Sanders children. Fifteen-year-old Daniel McKay was tending the stock, but his four younger siblings tagged along beside Megan, repeating arithmetic facts with their other classmates. The Sanders twins, Rachel and Meggie, talked incessantly while their little brother, Stephen, stopped to turn over every rock. Their older sisters, Amy and Sarah, took turns grabbing his hand and steering him back toward Megan.

The day was hot and dusty. Everyone needed frequent drinks. Despite the enthusiasm at the beginning of the morning, spirits lagged by the nooning because of the relentless heat. It was all they could do to put one foot in front of the other, much less talk.

Late that afternoon, they pulled into Rock Creek Station,

a welcome sight to man and beast. The cattle swarmed to
the creek's edge and drank deeply then moved to the
abundant green grass. Nick declared a half-day layover for
repairing wagons. After replenishing food and other
necessities at the well-stocked store, the women quickly got
busy doing laundry and bathing themselves and their
children.

Megan stood in the middle of a circle of women and
took her turn to shampoo her hair and scrub the dirt and
sweat from her tired body. She quickly rebuttoned the front
of her shirtwaist and straightened her skirt then rejoined the
circle to help provide privacy for the other women. There
was much happy chatter as the women stood together
combing tangles out of each other's hair and spreading it
out to blow freely in the breeze and dry in the hot sun.

Megan noticed Nick watching her and Elizabeth walk
back to their wagons with their damp hair still hanging
loose. He'd stopped in the middle of repairing a broken
wheel to stare. Megan blushed. She stopped and, gathering
her hair, held it firmly in one hand.

"What are you gawking at?" she asked him with a
scolding look.

"You," he answered boldly and stood, his job forgotten.

"This isn't the first time you've seen me today."

"It's the first time I've seen you with your hair blowing
in the wind and your face so fresh and rosy."

"Nick, hush. People will hear you." Her blush deepened
and she looked around to be sure no one had heard.

Nick chuckled deeply. "I don't care who hears me."

"I do, Nick." She looked at him with pleading eyes.
"You know how quickly people can get the wrong idea."

He moved closer and lowered his voice. "What idea?
That I love you? That I've claimed you for my own? Let
them think that. It's true!"

*Confound it!* She couldn't stop her blushing! "Nick,"
she beseeched softly, "please."

"No one is listening to us, Megan. And if they're looking, they won't see anything other than a man keeping his distance from the woman he loves."

She looked up at him and in spite of herself, she smiled. "I swear, Nicholas Webster, if I didn't know better, I'd think you were *trying* to embarrass me."

"I'm not," he said huskily. "There's just times I can't keep my eyes off you, Megan."

She caught her breath. Oh, how she loved to hear him say her name in that tone.

"Will you go for a ride with me this evening after our chores are done?"

Megan nodded and turned to go to her wagon. Would she ever get used to that man loving her? Her heart pounded as she crawled into the wagon to change out of her dirty, wet clothes and into a fresh, clean skirt and shirtwaist. The skirt she selected was the only one she had left that hadn't been shredded at the hem by sagebrush. She loosely twisted her hair and pinned it in place at the back of her head. Looking in a mirror, she tried in vain to tuck in stray tendrils.

The conversation at the evening meal reflected the long-needed refreshment the tired travelers were enjoying at Rock Creek. The little girls looked delightful with their clean hair and freshly scrubbed faces. Elizabeth and Elmer had both taken extra time to prepare a special meal complete with dessert.

Megan sat contentedly between Nick and Andrew. She relished the feeling of being clean for a change. As Nick reached forward for his mug of coffee, he brought his head close to hers.

"Mm, your hair smells delicious," he muttered softly.

She shot him a warning glance then looked away and tried to hide her smile.

"Do you two need a chaperone?" Thomas asked,

grinning wickedly.

"I think they'll do just fine without your interference, young man," Maude said, then quickly changed the subject. "Are we still following the Snake? I haven't seen it in a while."

Nick stretched his long legs out in front of him before he answered. "The river's a few miles to the north of us. We're pretty close to Shoshone Falls. I'm planning on taking Megan out there to see the falls if we can leave in time to get out there and back before dark." He added, "Anyone's welcome to come with us as long as you're on a horse."

He grinned when no one asked to join them. "Well, Megan, I guess it's just the two of us," he said with a teasing wink.

"If you're going to look at me like that, I might just insist on a chaperone," she said as she got up to start her chores.

Nick chuckled behind her. "You all know my intentions are nothing but honorable."

Andrew laughed. "I'm not so sure about that," he ribbed his friend. "Thomas, you're on duty this evening, I'll take tomorrow."

Megan shook her head at their comments. Thankfully her nieces had finished eating and were with the Sanders children. She caught Andrew's eye and saw immediate regret there.

"Megan, I'm sorry. You know I was only teasing."

She continued to vigorously wash dishes.

Andrew looked helplessly at the small gathering and tried again. "Megan?"

She looked at him.

"I meant nothing by it. I have absolute faith in you two."

She nodded and forced a smile then continued working.

Maude again had the wisdom to shift the focus away from Nick and Megan. "Will the trail take us back to the

Snake?"

Nick cleared his throat. "Yeah, a little more than a day's travel from here, we'll get back to the Snake."

"Won't we be at Fremont's Fishing Falls by then?" Thomas asked.

"Yep." Nick nodded. "There used to be an Indian settlement there. If they're still there, we should be able to do some trading for a considerable amount of salmon."

"And after that we'll come to a place called Thousand Springs. It's quite a sight," Thomas said. "Water gushin' out of black cliffs all over the place."

"When do we cross the Snake?" Joe asked, leaning forward so he could hear the conversation.

"At a place where there are three islands right across the middle of the river like stepping stones," Nick answered, raising his voice slightly for Joe's sake. "The river's more shallow there. It's still not an easy crossing. I don't look forward to it."

"Can we drive the wagons across?" Charles asked.

"We'll check the depth first," Nick said. "The gravel shifts over time. It's usually shallow enough to drive across though."

"Dessert, anyone?" Elizabeth asked, carrying a pan of steaming, fragrant gingerbread. Elmer followed with a gooseberry pie. All conversation ceased as they lined up to get helpings of both desserts.

As soon as Megan finished her last bite of gingerbread, Nick asked Elizabeth if she could spare Megan for a couple of hours so they could make it to Shoshone Falls and back before dark.

"She's already finished most of the dishes, so there's not much work left for me," Elizabeth answered. "Go, but please be careful. I still worry about Indians."

"We won't be alone," Nick assured her.

A few minutes later, they rode north, Nick on Black and Megan astride Andrew's horse. They cantered comfortably

most of the way then slowed to a walk to give the horses a
rest. Nick eased Black up next to Megan.

"Stop your horse, Megan, and listen."

She stopped and strained to hear above the horses' loud
breathing. Soon she could hear a faint roar in the distance.

"That's the falls," Nick explained. "If you look closely,
you can see the spray." He pointed ahead.

Megan looked over at him. "How many times have you
been through this area?"

Nick thought a moment. "A few. First time when I did
survey work for the Bureau of Topographical Engineers.
Then I passed by here on my way back to Missouri. Then I
led a train through here in '60. Passed here again going
back to Missouri to fight in the war. After two years in
Missouri, I got reassigned to Fort Klamath in southern
Oregon. A little over a year ago, I headed back to Missouri
again to take care of my sick ma." He cocked one eyebrow.
"I've lost count, I've crisscrossed through here so often."

"I thought you and Thomas had claims in Oregon. How
did you have time to take care of them?"

"Thomas took care of both claims during the two years I
fought in the war. While I was on duty at Ft. Klamath, I
was a half-day's ride from our claims, so I put in some time
whenever I could get away."

"Who's working your claims now?"

"We hired two men. They served under me at the fort.
And we hired a couple of Indian friends to help them.
When we get back, we plan on laying claim to a big chunk
of adjoining land."

The roar of the falls was getting louder and the spray
more evident. Megan caught her breath at her first sight of
over two hundred feet of cascading, churning water. They
quickly dismounted and led the horses to a hidden spot
among large boulders and trees. After tying the reins to a
sturdy branch, Nick reached out and grabbed Megan's
hand. He led her to a path that wound through the canyon

wall and out close enough to the falls to feel the spray. Megan was entranced. She moved along the wet rocks as close as she dared with Nick right behind her. Water trickled down her face and onto her clothes, but she didn't care. It felt heavenly. She laughed in delight and looked up at Nick. He pulled her to his chest and lowered his head to capture a wet kiss. They pulled apart and laughed like excited children then shared another kiss, this time longer. Nick looked down at her and smoothed wet tendrils back from her face. Never had Megan seen a look so loving. She swallowed and laid her face on his chest, barely able to contain her joy.

# CHAPTER TWENTY FIVE

Nick wiped sweat from his face and replaced his hat. The heat was unbearable, easily hovering around a hundred degrees. The travelers stumbled rather than walked. Those driving the wagons and on horseback fought to stay awake. Everyone was covered in a fine dust that stuck like glue to their sweat-soaked skin and clothes. Dehydration was a constant threat. The stops at Fremont's Fishing Falls and Salmon Falls were blessed reprieves. At both places, they replenished water supplies and traded for fish.

Three Island Crossing, where they would cross to the north side of the Snake, was only a day's travel away. Nick's heart sang. He had officially been courting Megan for a month. As soon as the last wagon pulled onto the north bank of the river, he planned to drop to one knee and propose again. He was sure of her answer. He wanted the wedding to take place soon, although he knew a wagon-train wedding wouldn't provide the ideal setting for the wedding night and honeymoon period. He'd witnessed several of those and didn't want to subject Megan to the embarrassment of a chivaree, where people celebrated by cheering and shaking the wagon where the poor newlyweds had bedded down for their first night together. Perhaps he could turn his job over to Thomas again and take Megan ahead to Ft. Boise where they could rent a room for a couple of nights.

He wiped the sweat from his face and looked over to where Megan was walking with her nieces. He chuckled at the sight of her; dust coating her face and dress, making everything the same yellow-brown color. She was still beautiful, he thought with a smile. She glanced up and caught his eye. Her teeth looked especially white when she smiled, surrounded by her tanned, dirty skin. He couldn't stop the laugh that escaped. What a sight she was. The next day, they finally arrived at Three Island Crossing, one of the shallowest parts of the Snake, with three islands across the width of the river, providing three stopping places for each wagon as it crossed. Nick, Thomas, and a few other men crossed the river several times to determine the depth and current. In spite of the strong current, they came to the conclusion the wagons could cross safely, one at a time. The riskiest part of the crossing was after the third island where there was a firm but narrow sandbar. Nick set two barrels on the north bank as markers to guide the wagons.

"As long as you aim for the middle of those barrels, you'll stay up on the sandbar," Nick announced to each driver before they crossed. "If you go too far to the left or right, you could tip over."

Because of the danger of tipping, Nick ordered all women and children to be taken across on horseback. He also had extra oxen yoked to each wagon, enough that at least some of the oxen would be on firm footing at every stage of the crossing.

The Battens and Joe and Maude were close to the back of the train, so they took time for their noon meal, then lounged by the river's edge and watched the wagons cross. Megan watched Nick ride over to them several times, always wearing a boyish grin. He told them to make sure they waited for him and Thomas to get the women and girls across safely.

"I don't remember seeing that boy so happy," Maude said. "What do you suppose he's got up his sleeve?" She glanced at Megan who only smiled and shrugged.

"He's up to somethin', that's fer sure," Joe said just before he spit into the water.

Megan was quite certain she knew. She also had been paying close attention to the passing of time and knew exactly what this day meant. She looked down at the pebbles she sat on to hide her smile. Grabbing a few pebbles, she tossed them one by one into the swirling water. *Would he ask her tonight? Or maybe sometime tomorrow?* She shivered with anticipation.

Glancing over at her sister and Charles, she saw them cuddled together on the bank watching their three girls frolic up and down the edge of the river. The girls were competing to see who could throw stones the farthest. She loved to see Charles and Elizabeth in their closeness, whispering and giggling like two youngsters.

Joe and Maude were also a delight to watch. Joe was swishing mosquitoes away from Maude's face and laughing at something she had just said. He grasped her hand and squeezed then held on while he spoke softly to her. Megan strained in vain to hear him. Then she heard them both chuckle and gaze out across the river. Her heart constricted with longing. This was what she wanted; this close, intimate bond with her husband, not just at the beginning of their marriage but in the years ahead. Would she and Nick have this? It was an intimacy that grew and matured over time. It seemed to rival what even newlyweds possessed. This kind of bond could only come from years of selfless giving to one another. She sighed with yearning then gathered a handful of stones and stood to her feet to join her nieces in their competition.

Hours passed before it was time for the Batten's wagon to cross. Nick and Thomas helped Charles take the three women and three girls across. Megan rode across on Black with her arms wrapped tightly around Nick. Between the third island and the north bank, the water was deep enough to get her skirt wet. Nick had instructed her to remove her boots and carry them. Her modesty kept her from hiking her skirt up to her knees, so it was soaked by the time Nick lowered her to the ground. He smiled down at her.

"Stay out of trouble, at least until we get these last few wagons across." He winked and squeezed her hand before he rode off.

Megan sat down on a grassy spot next to Elizabeth and Maude to put her stockings and boots on.

"Thank the dear Lord that's over," Maude exclaimed. "I heard that was one of the most dangerous places to cross, and so far, everything's gone fine."

"There's Charles!" Elizabeth said. They all stood so they could see more clearly. Charles drove his wagon into the first of four short crossings. They watched as he maneuvered the oxen up across the first island. Behind him, they saw Ralph drive the Batten's second wagon into the water. Soon Charles was approaching the second island and Ralph was driving across the first one.

"Where's Joe?" Maude asked. "He should be right behind Ralph."

"I think they're still hitching up the other team of oxen," Megan said as she strained to see. "Here he comes, Maude. I see him."

As soon as Charles approached the north bank, the women walked down to greet him with cheers. He guided the oxen slowly and carefully along the sandbar and up the bank between the barrels. Ralph, with a terror-stricken face, managed to do the same. He and Charles pulled their wagons up onto a grassy area well out of the way before they got down and congratulated each other. Megan stayed at the riverbank with Maude to wait for Joe. They watched as he lowered the wagon into the water from the third island. When the wagon dropped into the deepest water, they saw a look of panic on Joe's face as he looked down into the raging water. Nick's loud voice hollered to their right, "Joe, keep your eyes on the barrels!"

Joe couldn't hear him over the noise of the river. Nick threw himself onto Black and plunged into the river to help his old friend. But it was too late. Before he could reach him, Joe's oxen had strayed too far off course and the wagon tipped, throwing Joe into the raging current.

Megan watched with horror as Maude ran to the water's edge and plunged in after her husband. Megan ran after her to stop her, but she was too slow. As soon as Maude stepped off the gravel bar, she, too, was swept downstream and out of sight. Megan was close behind her, grabbing Maude's skirt. As soon as Megan's face went under, she scrambled to get her footing. She kicked and paddled furiously. Her boots filled with water and her skirt wrapped around her legs. She gasped for air when her face came to the surface then she was sucked under again.

Nick was horrified to see Joe struggle and go under. He galloped down the river then dove in when it got too deep for Black to move quickly. Thomas and several other men were beside him in seconds, but no one could find Joe. Nick looked frantically downstream but saw nothing. He turned when he heard screams behind him. Just upstream, he saw a submerged body rushing toward him. He realized with dread that it was a woman. Lunging toward her, he managed with another man's help to pull her face to the surface and start swimming downstream angling toward the bank. He hollered at Thomas to continue the search for Joe.

When he dragged the limp body to shore, he looked at her face. Dropping to his knees beside her, he cried out, "Maude! Maude! God no, no!" The other rescuer moved in quickly and helped Nick turn Maude over. Nick pounded her back until she heaved and spewed water out her mouth and nose. Coughing and choking, she desperately gasped for breath.

Downstream, Nick could see a group of people working over another person. Thank God he thought, they've found Joe. He left Maude with Charles, who had just arrived on the scene, and ran to help tend to Joe. When he was within a few yards, the group of men parted and he saw with dismay it was another woman. Andrew was bent over her giving mouth-to-mouth resuscitation.

Seeing that both women were in good hands, he again plunged into the water to rejoin the search for Joe. Several men rode downstream on horseback. For an hour, the men looked in vain. Then their heads came up when they heard three gunshots from farther down the river. Breathing hard from their work, they crawled up on to the banks on both sides and ran in the direction of the gunshots. On the south side of the river, they could see several men dragging a body out of the water. Nick plunged back in and swam across. When he reached them, he knew without asking that it was too late. Nevertheless, he grabbed his friend by the waist and lifted and shook him, trying desperately to empty him of the river's water. Thomas gently took hold of his arm and helped him lower Joe's lifeless body to the ground.

Nick dropped to his knees beside his old friend and groaned in agony. "No, no, no! This can't be! Not Joe. Oh, God, please, not Joe!" He frantically brushed Joe's hair off his face and stared at him in shock. Finally, he dropped his head in resignation and whispered, "I'm so sorry, Joe."

Nick went ahead of the others so he could break the news to Maude before she saw the body. He found her and the other woman in Andrew's wagon stripped of their wet clothes and wrapped in several blankets. Andrew and Elizabeth hovered over them. Maude was still unconscious. The other woman moaned softly and kept repeating in a raspy voice, "I'm so sorry, I'm so sorry."

Nick was heavy with grief and fatigue. "Will they make it?" he asked Andrew after he pulled his large frame into the wagon.

"It's too soon to tell, Nick," he answered sadly. "How about Joe?"

Nick looked at Maude and quietly shook his head. Their eyes met and Andrew got his answer. Joe had been as close as a father to Nick, Andrew, and Thomas when they were boys. Nick's pain was mirrored on Andrew's as they sat silently together. Elizabeth didn't miss anything. Tears streamed down her face as she stroked Maude's head and tried to soothe her.

Finally, Nick said, "I've got to go talk to Megan." He crawled through the opening and lowered himself to the ground.

Andrew jumped out of the wagon and ran to catch up to Nick. "Nick, wait!"

Nick stopped and turned, running his hand through his wet hair.

Andrew caught up to him and took his arm. "Nick, the other woman in my wagon is Megan."

Nick stared at him and blinked a few times, not comprehending what he'd just heard.

"You...you mean...Megan was the other woman they pulled from the water?"

"Yes, Nick. That's Megan in there," he answered, gesturing toward his wagon.

Nick stood rooted to the spot.

"I think they got to her in time, but they both took in a

lot of water."

Nick's face went from fear to anger. "What in God's name was she doing in the river?" he hissed.

"Probably trying to save Maude."

"In a dress? She probably can't even swim, the little idiot!" He took a few steps toward the wagon until Andrew grabbed his arm and yanked him to a stop.

"Nick, she reacted the same way any friend would! Ease up! And don't you dare go into that wagon mad! It won't help one bit in her recovery."

Nick shook off the anger when he realized her life was in jeopardy. He felt as if everything that mattered to him was being snatched away. Grasping Andrew by the shoulders, he pleaded, "Save her! Please save her, Andrew! Whatever it takes, just don't let her die."

"She's young and strong, Nick. Her chances are good...better than Maude's."

Nick pressed both hands to cover his face then looked up, agony threatening to choke him. "May God forgive me! Andrew, I'm to blame for this. If I had ordered the wagons to be tied together, Joe would still be with us."

"Nick, Joe is to blame for this. Over a hundred wagons made it safely across because they followed your orders. Joe is the only one who didn't. Don't blame yourself. It won't do you or anyone else any good."

The two grieving friends stood silently, not fighting their tears. Thomas joined them and laid a supporting hand on Nick's shoulder.

After several minutes, Thomas asked, "What are your orders, Nick?"

Nick cleared his throat. "We'll camp here for the night to give the women time to recover."

"What about Joe?"

"There will be no burial until Maude wakes up. Did they save their wagon?"

"We got it pulled out, but most everything in it washed

downstream."

"Is it still drivable?"

"Yeah. About the only thing they managed to save was a big dresser with blankets and clothes. McKay and Sanders pulled a couple of pots out of the water. But all the food and everything else is gone."

Nick stared at the ground for a while. Then he looked at Andrew. "The main thing now is getting those two ladies well. Can they stay in your wagon?"

Andrew nodded. "As long as they need to."

"I'd like to see Megan, now."

He followed Andrew to the back of his wagon and crawled in again. Elizabeth sat between the women and wept into her hands. She looked up briefly when the men entered and excused herself, saying she needed to check on her girls. Nick moved to Megan's side. Her eyes were shut. Every few seconds, rattling coughs shook her body. Nick brushed his hand gently across her forehead and whispered her name.

Megan's eyes flew open. Her hand came up to grasp Nick's. "Nick, oh, Nick, I'm so sorry," she moaned then coughed convulsively. She struggled to sit up, but Nick gently pushed her back down.

"Shh, be still, Megan. You need to rest."

"I want to see Maude."

"She's right here beside you. She's still sleeping."

Megan struggled to see her. "Is she going to be alright?"

"If she rests and listens to her doctor, she should be just fine."

"I'm so glad someone got to her in time, Nick. I tried, but I couldn't hang on."

The coughing started again and escalated into gagging and choking.

"Nick, sit her up and pat her back!" Andrew ordered.

Nick quickly obeyed, frightened he might be losing her after all. He laid her limp body down when the coughing subsided and looked at Andrew, panic filling him.

"Coughing is good," Andrew reassured him. "She still has a lot of water in her lungs. It's her body's way of clearing it out. Maude's the one I'm worried about most. After she rests some more, I need to try to rouse her so she can get to coughing."

"Nick."

He turned in response to Megan's raspy whisper.

"How's Joe?"

Nick glanced at Maude's still form before he answered. He took both of her hands in his and cleared his throat. "Megan, Joe didn't make it."

She looked at him as if she hadn't heard correctly.

"They found his body downstream. It was too late, Megan." Two tears made their way down his cheeks.

Megan covered her mouth and looked away. Then her whole body responded to the awful truth. She turned to her side away from Nick, drew her knees up, and wept with deep, wrenching sobs. Nick rubbed her back then turned her and drew her into his arms. Andrew silently left the wagon.

That night, Megan heard Maude wake from her coma. Elizabeth called for Andrew to come quickly. After asking how she felt and determining her state of mind to be sound, Andrew looked up at Elizabeth for support in revealing the dreadful truth about Joe. Megan thought her heart would break.

Before Andrew could speak, Maude looked at him intently and asked, "Joe didn't make it, did he?"

Andrew reached for her hand and shook his head. "No, Maude, he didn't make it."

She stared up at the canvas covering and said with a weak, strained voice, "As soon as I saw him go in, I knew

I'd never see him alive again. He can't swim, Andrew. He was scared to death of deep water." She turned back to Andrew. "Did they find him?"

"Yes, Maude. They did."

"Have they put him in the ground yet?"

"No. Nick said to wait until you're ready."

She waited a long time with her eyes shut and her lips pressed firmly together. Megan was afraid she'd fallen asleep again.

Maude then opened her eyes and looked at Andrew. "Tell Nick I'm ready. I don't want to see his body. I want to remember him alive with his eyes all lit up and happy. He's with Jesus now and I know he's smilin'." She closed her eyes and grinned with quivering lips. "Yep. I know he's smilin'."

Maude was too weak to get up, so they arranged to have a short service and burial just outside Andrew's wagon so she could watch. Megan sat with her, cradling her in a sitting position.

The next morning the train moved out. Dust poured in through the openings in the canvas and made breathing even more difficult. Maude and Megan were jarred and jostled so much they got no rest. During the nooning, Andrew and Charles rigged up two hammocks attached at the front and back of the wagon bed. They hung sheets at the openings to cut down on the dust. Most of Andrew's belongings had been moved to Maude's wagon to make room for the two women and their swaying hammocks.

Megan insisted on sitting beside Maude, bathing the sweat and dust off her face and reading portions of scripture to her. Andrew checked on them frequently, waking Maude and encouraging her to cough. Every time he stopped by, he scolded Megan for not resting.

"She has no one, Andrew, now that Joe is gone," Megan pleaded. "I'm her family now. She needs me." She looked at Maude's unresponsive body and added, "She told me I was like a daughter to her."

"You won't be anything to her if you don't get your rest and get better."

"I'm already better."

"I'll be the judge of that."

He climbed into the wagon and looked at her sternly. "To bed with you. Now."

She reluctantly obeyed and stayed there the rest of the afternoon because Andrew wouldn't leave.

By nightfall, Maude took a turn for the worse. Andrew put his hand on her forehead and announced that she was burning with fever. Despite everything he did over the next several days, her fever continued to rise and her breathing became more labored. Megan watched with dread as she saw Maude slip away. She clung to her and begged God to spare her life.

One night, Nick went to check on them and found Megan asleep, sitting on the hard floor of the wagon with her arms wrapped around Maude. In the faint light, he could see where tears had left tracks down her face. He reached under her to lift her into her own hammock but jerked back when his hand brushed against her searing-hot flesh. With mounting dread, he lay her gently down, then stepped out to find Andrew.

Andrew felt Megan's head and listened to her chest with his stethoscope. He looked at Nick with concern. "She has pneumonia, same as Maude."

Nick sat back on his heels and groaned. "What needs to be done?"

"She'll need lots of water, clean water, and lots of rest. And we need to try to get her to keep coughing. If Maude doesn't start coughing this garbage up, she'll die."

"Tell me what I can do, Andrew. I'll ride in here for the

rest of the trip if I need to."

Andrew looked sadly at his friend. "That won't be necessary, Nick. You can help by making her stay in bed and getting her to drink her water. Also, two or three times a day, we need to get Megan up to move around; a very short walk outside in morning and evening when the dust has settled. That and patting her back will help loosen up the stuff in her lungs so she can cough it up."

He paused and studied his two patients' faces. "I'll put cornmeal poultices on both of them and set pots of boiling water in here when the wagon's not moving. They need to breathe in some moist air."

Turning to face Nick, he put a hand on his arm. "Nick, you've got a job to do; a big job, getting this train to Oregon safely. This is my job. Trust me, I'll do everything in my power to save them."

"I'll help you. I'll have time." Nick said it with enough conviction, Andrew simply nodded.

Andrew decided to sleep on the floor of the wagon between the two hammocks. Nick checked on them frequently. Megan's breathing was punctuated with coughing and gagging. Maude breathed shallowly with short wheezing sounds. Their fevers continued to rage. By morning, Andrew quietly told Nick that Maude was beyond help. "I've tried several times to rouse her, but there's no response."

Despondent, he made his way out of the wagon and over to fill his plate for breakfast. Everyone there turned to him with apprehension.

He let out a long sad sigh. "It's Maude. Andrew doesn't think she'll make it."

Andrew walked slowly over to join them.

Elizabeth asked through her tears, "Is there anything we can do to make her more comfortable, Andrew?"

"She's not responding to me at all, but I suppose it wouldn't hurt to read to her from scripture. She might be able to understand and you know how she loves God's word."

Just then they heard an awful wail. "Nooo, Maude! Maude! Nooo."

The four men and Elizabeth scrambled frantically for the back of the wagon. Nick, the first to climb in, found Megan with her arms wrapped tightly around Maude, wailing continuously, "No, Maude, no!"

Andrew quickly checked Maude's pulse while Elizabeth tried unsuccessfully to pry Megan's arms loose. As soon as she pulled one arm free, she yanked it away and clung to Maude more fiercely.

"She's gone," Andrew announced sadly. He sank to his knees and dropped his head to his chest.

"She's with Joe, now," Nick choked out, in an attempt to bring comfort to anyone listening.

Megan stopped her moaning to stare at him. He took that moment to pull her arms free and hug her. Together they slumped to the floor.

"She can't be gone! She can't!" Megan wailed again. She struggled free from Nick and threw herself at Andrew. "Andrew, do something! Quick! You can still save her."

Andrew wrapped his arms around Megan, and Elizabeth wrapped her arms around them both. "I'm so sorry, Megan," Andrew whispered. "She's gone. I can't do anything to save her now."

"Megan, honey, you know she's with Jesus and with Joe," soothed Elizabeth. "Just think how happy she is."

Megan's wailing stopped and her body went limp. Nick noticed Megan's slack-jawed face and alerted Andrew.

"Andrew, I think she fainted."

Nick scooped her up and laid her in her hammock.

"Her fever's still high," Andrew said with alarm. "Elizabeth, could you get a cool wet cloth for her? I'll make another poultice. First, let's move Maude out."

He and Nick detached Maude's hammock and passed

her through the opening to Charles and Thomas.

Nick stayed by Megan's side all that day, only leaving for Maude's burial. Megan remained unconscious until dark. Then she woke enough to whimper and call for Maude. Through the night, her fever rose and she thrashed from side to side as if trying to escape an unknown terror.

For days, Megan's fever was high. She was delirious most of the time. Her family and friends took turns sitting with her and praying for her, never leaving her side. Andrew offered no hope when Nick questioned him.

Nick was beside himself. He wouldn't allow himself to think of the possibility of losing her. As much as he grieved for Joe and Maude, his fear of losing Megan eclipsed any grief he had ever known.

# CHAPTER TWENTY SIX

Megan kept dropping deeper and deeper in the swirling muddy water. Strong hands gripped her legs and pulled her down. Desperate for air, she tried to kick free, but claws dug into her flesh and dragged her relentlessly away from the surface. Her body convulsed as she gasped for breath and got only a mouthful of thick muddy water. Choking and gasping for air, she made one final, frantic effort to break free and propel herself to the surface.

Gentle hands helped her sit up in her hammock as her body convulsed with deep, wrenching coughs. She was pulled into an embrace and felt a warm hand pat her back. A deep voice tried to calm her before she was lowered back to her bed. As she drifted off to sleep, the soothing voice and warm, tender fingers stroking her head replaced her dreams.

Megan's head rolled from side to side with the rocking of the wagon. She tried to wake herself from the dizzy, whirling nightmares. Strong hands lifted her and forced her to drink warm broth. She tried to open her eyes to see who held her, but she dropped into restless slumber as soon as her body was released.

Confusing images assaulted her. She couldn't see them nor understand them. Thrashing from side to side, she whimpered pitifully, trying desperately to escape. She could feel them as they clamped their strong claws onto her arms. She screamed as her eyes flew open. Nick's face appeared in front of her, a worried frown creasing his brow. *Can he see them? Nick, help me!* She tried to scream. Then she heard his soothing voice and felt his warm calloused hands stroking her face and head. Slumping down into her blankets, she forced herself to focus on his voice as he read in soft deep tones.

*The Lord is my shepherd; I shall not want.*
*He maketh me to lie down in green pastures.*
*He leadeth me beside the still waters.*
*He restoreth my soul.*
*He leadeth me in the paths of righteousness for His name's sake.*
*Yea, though I walk through the valley of the shadow of death,*
*I will fear no evil: for thou art with me.*
*Thy rod and thy staff, they comfort me.*
*Thou preparest a table before me in the presence of mine enemies.*
*Thou anointest my head with oil.*
*My cup runneth over.*
*Surely goodness and mercy shall follow me all the days of my life,*
*and I will dwell in the house of the Lord forever.*

Megan woke one morning to birds chirping and cows bellowing. She sat and rubbed the sleep from her eyes. Turning, she saw good, old faithful Andrew sitting next to her. "Well, look at you," he said with some astonishment.

She smiled at his surprised expression.

"You look like your old self. How do you feel?"

"I feel fine, thank you."

Andrew laughed. "That's the best news I've had in weeks!"

He placed his hand on her forehead and took her pulse.

"Would you like some breakfast?"

She smiled and nodded. "Yes, I feel like I haven't eaten in days."

Andrew's smile widened. "Actually, it *has* been days since you've eaten."

"Days?" she asked, in confusion.

"Yes, days. Many days, I'm afraid." He pressed the stethoscope to her chest and shushed her. Sliding the stethoscope under her shirtwaist to hear more clearly, he smiled again. "Megan, I believe the worst is over."

"The worst?"

"You've been very sick for a very long time. We thought we might lose you. Do you remember crossing the Snake River?"

Megan stared at the canvas overhead for a moment before she nodded.

"What happened after that, Megan?" Andrew asked softly.

Before she could answer, Nick's face appeared at the back opening.

"How's our patient?" he asked quietly.

Andrew turned to him with a smile. "Much better, Nick. Come on in. I have a feeling she'd love to see you."

Nick's eyes lit with relief as he jumped in to join them, jarring the wagon with his weight. "Megan!" he gasped in a voice husky with emotion. He wasted no time as he gathered her frail body into his strong arms. "Will she be alright?" he asked, his eyes seeking Andrew's.

Andrew nodded. "She still has many days of recovery

ahead of her, but she's past the danger point."

Nick slowly released her so he could look into her face. Confusion clouded her thoughts.

"How long have I been sick?" she asked.

"A little over two weeks, Megan," Nick answered.

"Two weeks?" Her eyes absently traveled around the interior of the wagon. She tried to shake off the fog in her brain.

"Where's Maude?" she asked as she looked to where Maude's hammock had hung.

Megan turned from Andrew to Nick as the two men just looked at each other. Finally, Megan gasped and said, "Oh," as the memory resurfaced. She stared blankly into space then swallowed her tears and whispered, "I remember now."

Settling back down into her bed, she covered her face with her blanket and said, "I'm not hungry anymore, Andrew. Maybe later."

"You've got to start eating again, Megan, or you'll shrivel up and blow away," Andrew said. "Besides, your family misses you."

At that, she lowered the blanket. "Are they all doing well?" she asked.

Nick smiled and nodded. "They're all fine, Megan, just fine. But they do miss you." He lowered his face to hers and quietly added, "And so do I."

Blushing, she put her hands on both sides of his face and stroked her thumbs over his rough cheeks.

"Have you been in here with me while I was sick?"

"Of course," he answered.

"I thought it must have been you." She smiled dreamily before her hands dropped down weakly to her blanket.

"We'll come back for you when breakfast is ready," Andrew said. "Lay quietly for a while. And don't try to get up by yourself. You're still too weak."

Megan found out just how weak she was when they

came to get her. Andrew slipped his arms under her, lifted, and carried her to Nick who was waiting with outstretched arms outside. When Nick lowered her to a chair, she tried to put some weight on her feet and collapsed against him. Elizabeth and her three girls flocked around her, giving hugs and kisses and welcoming words. Megan was perplexed by all the attention.

After Elizabeth hugged her for the fourth time, she dropped to her knees and squeezed Megan's hands. Through happy tears, she exclaimed, "Megan, I was afraid I was going to lose you! You have no idea how relieved I am to see you like this. Thank God!"

Megan stared at her sister and asked, "Was I really that sick?"

"Yes, you scared us out of our wits!" Elizabeth answered. "For the past two weeks, you've been delirious with fever. You wouldn't eat. You hardly ever responded to us when we talked to you. But look at you now! Your fever is gone and you're sitting here talking to us!"

Charles bent down next to them. "Megan, we're in Oregon."

Megan's eyes flew open. "Oregon?" She looked around, noticing for the first time the drastic change of scenery. Evergreen trees surrounded them. Birds flitted overhead from tree to tree, their songs filling the air. And stretched out before them to the west was a beautiful valley with huge mountains far in the distance.

"We've just come through the Blue Mountains," Nick informed her.

"Some of the roughest but most beautiful terrain we've seen yet," Charles added.

"Those are the Cascade Mountains," Nick said, pointing west. "We should reach them in a little over a week."

Megan stared in wonder, overwhelmed by the trees and the greenness and the sounds. "Oregon?" she said again in awe.

Suzanne placed a plate of eggs, biscuits, and bacon in her lap. Megan grabbed her fork and started eating. It tasted so good. She closed her eyes and savored her first bite of real food. She stopped halfway to her second bite when she noticed all eyes were still on her.

Elizabeth laughed. "Sorry, Megan. It's just such a relief to see you eating. I was afraid if the pneumonia didn't kill you, starvation would."

"Don't eat too much too soon," Andrew advised.

Megan nodded her head and took a few more bites.

Lucy walked over and held out a hand full of berries. "See what I picked for you, Megan. You need to eat a lot 'cuz you're startin' to look like a skeleton."

Megan laughed when the others shushed her impetuous niece. "Just how bad am I?" she asked.

Elizabeth handed her a mirror. Megan took one look at her gaunt, skeletal face and gasped in horror. Then she looked down at her arms and legs and realized for the first time how much she had wasted away.

"We tried to feed you, Megan, but you'd only take so much before it all came up," Elizabeth said.

Megan turned to Nick. "I don't want you to look at me again, Nick. Not until we reach those mountains. Maybe by then, I won't look like a 90-year-old hag."

Nick tossed his head and laughed. "Just try and stop me. Besides, you're still beautiful to me." Megan shook her head in disgust as she looked again at her reflection and tried in vain to rub away the dark circles under her eyes and smooth her tangled hair.

Throughout that day and the next, Andrew showed Megan exercises she could do in her hammock to strengthen her arms and legs. He warned her repeatedly of the need for continued rest when he saw how determined she was to exercise. Too weak to stand, she remained in her hammock while the train wound its way through the

Umatilla Valley and then the Columbia Plateau, where again the land was dry and desolate.

At Four Mile Canyon where they crossed the John Day River, Megan took her first wobbly steps. They had stopped to camp for the night. After the meal, she took her usual walk propped on the arms of two strong men. This night she was between Nick and Charles.

"Stop, please," she said. "I want to try to walk without you."

"Fine, but I'm staying close enough to catch you in case you go down," Nick said.

They both stepped back and Megan, with a determined scowl, took four steps, stopped to rest, then took four more. Elizabeth and Suzanne, watching while they washed dishes, both cheered. Megan scowled harder.

"What's gotten into you?" Charles asked. "You should be happy."

She stopped and reached for his arm. "How long has it been? A week since my fever stopped?"

Charles nodded.

"And this is all I can do? Will I ever be able to walk normally again?"

Andrew overheard her from his seat near the fire.

"I told you it would take time, Megan," he said.

"Well at this rate it'll be a year!" she said, wiping away tears of frustration.

Nick wrapped an arm around her and helped her back to her chair. "Actually, you've made amazing progress. Right, Doc?"

"Right, Megan. It's easy for us to see your progress because for weeks, we saw how sick you were."

Elizabeth added her support. "Megan, I cheered for you because I'm truly amazed at how well you're doing. Please don't get discouraged."

"You'll get a little better each day," Andrew said, "unless, of course, you try to do too much too soon."

Megan forced her tears to stop and tried to believe them.

Another week passed. Her eight steps had increased to twenty. She could get herself out of bed, climb out of the wagon, and walk to their campsite without assistance. By the time she crawled into bed, she shook with weakness and fatigue. She was still confined to the wagon when they were on the move. Several times, Nick rescued her and took her on the back of his horse. One day, he showed up with a small, gentle mare that belonged to the Sanders and let her ride alone. It delighted her beyond words.

When they reached the Dalles, most of the weary travelers went to the town's few stores to restock their dwindling supplies. Megan, left behind at the wagons, sat alone and watched her family walk away. She stared at the fire and struggled with depression. Shaking off her negative train of thoughts, she stood and walked slowly over to Andrew's wagon. She climbed in, found her Bible, and made her way back to her chair by the fire.

Vaguely, she remembered some verses Maude had shared with her. Where were they? Thumbing through the New Testament, she stopped and read several passages. In Romans chapter 8 she read, *Likewise the Spirit also helpeth our infirmities: for we know not what we should pray for as we ought: but the Spirit itself maketh intercession for us with groanings which cannot be uttered. And He that searcheth the hearts knoweth what is the mind of the Spirit, because He maketh intercession for the saints according to the will of God. And we know that all things work together for good to them that love God, to them who are the called according to His purpose.*

Megan sat back and clutched her Bible to her chest. *Amazing! The Spirit, the Holy Spirit of God, intercedes for me. He helps me in my infirmities. And His Word says that all things work together for good for His children.*

She read more and quickly was amazed at the number of passages that encouraged Christians to trust God, to cast all their cares on him, to rejoice in him no matter what the circumstances. Finally, she came to the verses Maude had shown her in Thessalonians Chapter 5, *Rejoice evermore. Pray without ceasing. In everything give thanks: for this is the will of God in Christ Jesus concerning you.*

Three short verses. Three clear commands from the Word of God. She remembered Maude telling her if a person would obey those simple commands, it would change their life.

She didn't have to ask if she had been obedient. She knew she hadn't. Glad to be alone, she allowed herself to weep in shame. But on the heels of shame came joy. She looked up toward heaven, marveling at the road God called His children to walk. A road paved with joy, with a casting aside of worries, and of trusting the One who not only created her but called her to be His own. And as His very own cherished daughter, she was to commune with Him and trust Him to care for her and lead her down the path He had chosen. The joy of it all almost choked her as it welled up in her throat. She laughed. Thanksgiving and praise poured from her lips as tears streamed down her face. *God is so good!*

When the others returned, Megan greeted them with a genuine smile of welcome. Nick had a suspicious grin when he took her hand and asked her to go on a short walk with him. Leading her through some trees, he stopped, sat down on a boulder, and patted the spot beside him. She sat and with dread began to fear he was going to propose. Standing abruptly, she said, "Nick, I think I know what this is about."

Puzzled and amused, he watched her wring her hands. "Oh, you do, do you?"

"Yes," she said and turned to him with eyebrows drawn together. "Please don't ask me now. I'm not ready. I want to remember this time as a happy time." She paused and shook her head. "I *am* happy, mind you, but...Nick, I'm still an invalid. For the rest of my life, I'll look back on this day and, and I don't want to be an invalid in my memories of this day." She gave him a pleading look. "Do you understand?"

Nick's eyes twinkled. "No, Megan, I don't understand."

"Nick, you don't want to propose to an invalid! I may never fully recover. You'd be stuck with me until I died!"

Nick finally let loose with hilarious laughter. He doubled over and slapped his hat on the rock. Megan was not at all amused as she watched through narrowed eyes. Raising his head to look at her, he said, "I'm sorry, Megan. I think I'd better explain." But he couldn't stop laughing. Megan let out an angry huff and turned to stalk away.

Nick jumped up and grabbed her arm. "Slow down there, Megan, and listen."

She whirled around and glared at him. He couldn't seem to wipe that silly grin off his face.

"Megan, in the first place, I wasn't going to propose."

Thoroughly embarrassed, she could only say, "Oh."

He took her in his arms and quickly added, "But I plan on proposing soon, just not today."

Megan shook herself free of him and walked away. "What makes you so sure I'd say yes?"

He lunged for her and grabbed her arm again, turning her to face him, all humor gone. "You wouldn't say yes?" he asked, his eyes serious.

"I guess you'll just have to wait and see."

He pulled her roughly to him and lowered his mouth to hers. It was the first kiss they'd shared since the Snake River crossing. "Megan, I love you." His voice husky and insistent.

She lowered her head, ashamed of her hurtful words. *How quickly I fall from your plan, Lord,* she prayed.

Nick held her. "I won't let go until you answer me."

Finally, she looked up with eyes full of tears. "Nick, I'm so sorry."

"Sorry for what, Megan?" His hands gripped her arms.

"For saying what I said. For making you doubt what my answer would be."

He shook his head, confusion in his eyes. "What will your answer be, Megan?"

Megan hesitated but she smiled. "I want to be able to say 'yes,' but I don't want you to be stuck with me if I'm still an invalid."

Nick threw back his head and beamed, "Hah, invalid? You're not an invalid. You have more determination and spunk in you than any woman I've ever known." He kissed her again, a long, slow kiss. "And furthermore, Miss Megan O'Mally, I'd take you as my wife if all your arms and legs were cut off! So there! Enough of this invalid talk!"

Megan smiled and laid her head on his chest. How good it felt to be here wrapped in his arms. She didn't want to move. Neither did he, apparently, as he cradled her head with one hand and stroked her back with the other.

"I do have something to show you," he murmured against her hair.

"What is it?" she asked, in no hurry to move.

"You know how much you like riding Sanders' little mare?"

"Mm-hmm."

"Well, I bought you a horse in the Dalles."

Megan didn't move. Had she heard correctly?

"What did you say?" she asked, looking up at him.

"I bought you a horse."

"What?"

"A horse," he said very slowly and loudly as if she were hard of hearing. "I bought you a horse."

"A horse? Nick, you didn't need to do that!" she exclaimed, her eyes dancing with excitement. "How much did it cost?"

"None of your business. And it was worth every penny

just to see your face."

"Where is he?"

"He's a she and she's tied to a tree on the other side of those rocks." Megan started to run in the direction Nick pointed. She quickly stopped when she realized her legs were not ready for running. Slowly and carefully, she made her way around the rocks. Sure enough, tied to a tree was a beautiful little mare with a red-brown coat and black mane and tail.

Megan gasped, "She's beautiful, Nick, absolutely beautiful!" She eased up beside the horse and offered her hand to be sniffed. Then she ran her hand slowly up and down the mare's nose and on to her neck. "She's so gentle. What's her name?"

"That's for you to decide."

Megan held the horse's head between her hands and gazed into her eyes. "What do you want to be called, baby?" She untied the reins and looked up at Nick. "You bought her at the Dalles; maybe I should call her Dalles...or Columbia for the river, or Cascade for the mountains we still have to cross." She continued to chatter about names all the way back to camp. "Umatilla, Pneumonia, Invalid." She laughed at the look Nick gave her. Finally, by the time they reached camp, she'd decided. "Patience, because everyone here needed so much patience to get this far, and it will take patience to go the rest of the way."

Just before they stepped around the wagon in view of the others, Megan stopped and hugged Nick. "I've never owned my own horse before, Nick. I don't know how to thank you."

"I'll be able to think of a few ways," he mumbled, his eyes twinkling with mischief.

Patience was adored and fawned over by Elizabeth and the three girls. Nick had also bought a saddle.

"I won't have you riding side saddle out here in this rough terrain, it's not safe. The true western woman rides astride with no shame," Nick declared. Megan was happy with that. She had ridden both ways and far preferred riding astride the horse. She quickly became aware of the fact that not all females felt the same when she heard Mrs. Simmons sniff her disapproval. The fact she didn't add any comments showed how much she had changed over the last month.

Instead of riding in the wagon all day, Megan could spend a few hours riding Patience. What freedom! She could ride next to Nick or join Elizabeth and the other ladies. She could even resume her classes. She quickly gave up that idea when she dropped with exhaustion into her chair one evening after three hours in the saddle.

Andrew studied her face from where he sat then walked over and laid a hand on her forehead. "Your fever's back," he said, a scowl on his face.

"I feel fine. I'm just a little tired."

The doctor held her gaze, "You are running a fever, Megan. That means you're sick."

The others stopped and listened.

Megan's eyes remained locked with Andrew's. "Why are you frowning at me?" she asked.

"This is not good. I suspect you're not getting the rest you need."

"You don't expect me to lay in that hammock all day, do you?"

"How long did you ride your horse today?"

Nick stood behind her chair and answered for her. "She rode a few hours this morning and another three or four this afternoon."

Andrew shook his head. "I can see I'll need to keep a closer watch on my patient."

"Sorry, Andrew," Nick said. "She just looked so much stronger. I wasn't thinking."

"I am so much stronger. And would the two of you please stop talking about me as if I'm not here?"

Andrew turned an exasperated look at her. "Back to bed until the fever drops." He stood and walked away when Megan started to protest.

"Andrew, I despise that bed! I'll be fine, I promise," she hollered after him.

Nick sat down next to her and placed her supper in her hands. He gave her a disapproving look.

"What's wrong?" she asked.

"You're giving your doctor a lot of trouble. He's done everything in his power to pull you through your pneumonia. Worked day and night doctoring you, and now he's worried and he has every right to be." Nick took a few bites and chewed, looking straight ahead. Then he turned back to Megan. "Frankly I'm worried, too. If you don't do as Andrew says, you could get seriously ill again. We've got some tough going ahead of us on this Barlow Road through these mountains. It'll be cold up there; probably some snow and ice up high."

"But, Nick, I'll be on Patience. That's not the same as walking."

"True, but it's sure not the same as laying in a hammock. You're not resting when you're on horseback."

"I think I can be the judge of that. When I'm tired of riding, I'll crawl back into bed."

"There will be no riding, Megan," Nick said with steel in his voice, "not until Andrew says."

When Megan didn't respond, Nick added, more gently, "We just want you to get well. And I trust Andrew's judgment." Megan continued to eat in silence. Nick watched her for a while. "If I can trust you to stay in bed, I'll tie Patience to the back of Andrew's wagon so you can talk to her. I know she'd like that. She's really taken to you."

Megan pushed her remaining food around and fought her stubbornness and the overwhelming fatigue that was beginning to take hold of her.

"I think you may be right. I'm tired," she said. "Could you help me to the wagon?"

Megan remained feverish and weak along most of the Barlow Road through the magnificent Cascade Range. Surrounded by a rugged wilderness filled with wild animals and crisscrossed by raging rivers, it was difficult to find decent grazing for their stock. Since Megan's fever wasn't high and she was no longer delirious, Andrew asked Elizabeth or Jessica Hawkins to take his place sleeping in the wagon with her. At night, the yowling and high-pitched screeching of panthers caused the women to sleep fitfully. In the mornings, they were wakened by howls of wolves and coyotes. Patience's eyes showed white and she strained against her tether at the frightening sounds. Often, Elizabeth and Jessica were wakened by Megan's voice soothing her little mare.

"I swear, Megan, if you could have your way, that horse would be sleeping in your hammock with you," Jessica whispered one night as she watched the two of them nuzzling each other nose to nose.

Lucy ran excitedly to the wagon one morning and climbed in while it was still moving. "Megan, Guess what? We saw a bear!"

"A bear? Don't tell Patience. It'll scare her out of her wits."

Lucy laughed and settled in to share the rest of the morning with her beloved aunt.

Morning, noon, and night, Megan joined the others outside, but she was still confined to the wagon during the traveling hours. She was too tired to argue with Andrew. Begrudgingly, she admitted she was sick and needed to listen to his voice of experience. And she desperately wanted to be well when they pulled into Oregon City, the end of the trail. She knew Nick and Thomas would leave them to ride up the Willamette River to their ranch, many days ride to the south. Would she go with him? If she didn't recover, they wouldn't be getting married and he'd have no choice but to leave her behind with Charles and Elizabeth.

The two weeks to travel from the Dalles to Oregon City seemed a lifetime to Megan as she lay in her swaying hammock, drifting in and out of sleep. When the train reached Laurel Hill, fabled to be the most dangerous place on the entire trail, Nick insisted on walking beside Megan every step down the hill. No one was allowed to ride a wagon down, not even the drivers. Each wagon was tied to a tree and lowered inch by inch down the long, steep hill. Walking down through the woods was hard enough. Nick held onto Megan with each step. She clung to him, realizing she was constantly in danger of tripping and hurdling down the side of the mountain. When they reached the bottom, he deposited her on a rock well off to the side and climbed back up the hill to get Patience.

"I think I gave her the wrong name," Megan said to him when he put the mare's reins in Megan's hand.

"Why's that?" he asked, pulling her to her feet.

"Because, I have absolutely no patience left. I want to be over this fever, I want to walk, and I want to be done with this trip."

He laughed. "Well, you don't have much longer. We're only a few days from Oregon City. Think about it, Megan! We started way back in April."

"I know. If I wasn't so tired, I could get excited."

Nick held her and kissed the top of her head. Reluctantly he left to help the others.

A few days later, Megan woke to the sounds of cheering and laughing. The wagon she rode in sped up. Struggling to see out the front, she called to Matthew, Andrew's driver for the day. Before he could answer, Nick appeared at the back.

"Megan, we made it! Come on, jump on behind me."

Nicks strong arm supported her as she flung herself over Black's back. She wrapped both arms around Nick's waist and looked ahead to where he pointed. Oregon City! She couldn't believe her eyes. There it was! Finally, they had come to the end of the Oregon Trail!

"Thank you, God. Thank you, God," she said over and over. Tired or not, she was excited and ready to celebrate. She squeezed Nick with all the strength she had. He clasped her hands in his own as they cantered toward the front of the train.

# CHAPTER TWENTY SEVEN

In the rush of wagons and the tearful good-byes, Megan had lost sight of Nick. Tucked securely behind him on Black, they had ridden into Oregon City and over to see the magnificent Willamette Falls. Then he deposited her next to Thomas, Jessica, and Elizabeth in front of a boarding house.

"I promised Charles I'd meet him at the federal office to help him pick out some property in a good farming area."

"Charles is still inside with Andrew," Elizabeth said, pointing at the three-story, white clapboard building. "But Mr. McKay and Mr. Sanders should be there by now."

Giving her a brief farewell, he rode off with Thomas. With a strange sense of abandonment, Megan watched until Nick disappeared in the crowd. *Well, this is it. Will he propose? I told him not to if I was still sick. I have no one to blame but myself.* Her mind roiled with doubt.

Jessica laid a hand on Megan's shoulder. "I've got to go join my family. I'm not sure when we'll see each other again, Megan."

Choking back tears, the two young women threw their arms around each other and said good-bye. When they stepped back, Megan noticed with surprise how beautiful her friend was. Over the course of the trip, she had changed from a plump young woman who always seemed to be out of breath to a slim, vibrant beauty, with rosy cheeks and eyes sparkling with excitement.

"Thanks for everything, Jessica," Megan said. "You've been a true friend."

"I'll find out where your family is homesteading," Jessica called as she walked away with long robust strides. "I promise I'll come see you."

As Megan watched Jessica leave, she was again struck by her own frailty. She looked around uncertainly at her surroundings. It was the middle of September and the weather was beautiful, definitely warmer than the mountains. Thankfully, they had made excellent time. Many people passed them on the boardwalk, some as dirty and tired as she was, but others wore clean, crisp dresses and their faces glowed with health. Megan looked down at her filthy, torn skirt. She put her hand to her head and felt stringy, dirty hair shaken loose from the hair clasp. She knew she looked like a street urchin.

Elizabeth had her three girls gathered around her skirt, with warnings to stay close. Other wagon trains had arrived in the past week, and by the number of people crowding the streets, it was evident many had not yet moved on to their land. Often, the tired travelers chose to winter in Oregon City, but Charles was determined to get his land and have a log cabin built before bad weather hit.

"Charles and Andrew are in there getting rooms for us," Elizabeth announced with pleasure.

"Rooms?" It sounded heavenly to Megan.

Before Elizabeth answered, Charles stepped out onto the porch with a big grin. He handed Elizabeth a key. Andrew gave Megan a smile and a subtle nod when he emerged behind Charles.

The two men rushed off to meet their friends at the land office while Elizabeth turned to Megan to explain. "The Sanders and McKays parked their wagons at Abernethy Green to camp. They'll stay there until the men find the land they want. Andrew insisted we get a room so you would have a better chance to rest and recover."

Megan said quietly, "Elizabeth, I'm sorry. I'm afraid I've been quite a bother."

Elizabeth just laughed. "Megan, if you had any idea how thrilled I am to be able to stay here, you wouldn't be apologizing."

"But, the money, Elizabeth!"

"We have more than you might think. Charles even has a little inheritance that will tide us over for several months."

"Well, nevertheless, I insist on paying part of the expense."

Elizabeth squeezed Megan's arm. "Just think, Megan; we'll be in a room in a real building! Maybe we can even take a real bath!"

Megan's eyes lit up. "A hot bath?"

"Let's go on in and find out."

Megan searched the crowded street one last time for Nick before she followed her sister into the boarding house.

Sure enough, baths were available. There was a bathhouse for men only. For the ladies, a metal tub was hauled to their room and then filled with hot steamy water hauled up the stairs by a sturdy young boy making several trips lugging a wooden bucket in each hand.

Elizabeth insisted Megan go first so she could dry off and crawl into bed for a nap.

When Elizabeth was finished, she helped each of her girls bathe in order by age. Poor Abigail was last and when she looked into the water, she drew back with disgust.

"It's black! I'd rather take a bath in a cold river, Ma!"

Megan giggled under her soft warm covers. She had forgotten how good a bed could feel. Her eyes were drowsy and about to close when she heard a knock at their door. Instantly she threw the blankets back and jumped to her feet. Dressed in a clean but slightly ragged dress, she crossed the floor. Elizabeth wrapped Abigail in a big towel and the other two girls scrambled to finish dressing.

"Who is it?" Megan asked.

Charles answered, "It's us." So Megan swung the door open to reveal Charles, Andrew, Thomas, and Nick. She froze as soon as her eyes met Nick's. His admiring gaze swept over her, from her loose damp hair down to her clean bare feet. Blushing, she looked away and moved to the other side of the bed to put her stockings and boots on. In her discomfort, she almost missed what the men were so excitedly chattering about.

"We found what we wanted!" Charles said as he wrapped his arms around his wife. "Unsettled area along a branch of the Willamette with enough land for all three families. We each get 160 acres free as long as we live on it and make improvements over a five-year period. Then we get the title to the land. And there's a bonus! There's adjoining property I can buy! I already made a down payment on 80 acres."

He whooped and spun Elizabeth around. "We're heading out there first thing in the morning. If we don't like what they gave us, we can come back and pick another. As soon as we get the cabin up, I'll come back for you. Sanders and McKay are going to help me with mine first so Megan can have a place to rest indoors."

Megan's eyes teared up at this news. Charles looked at her and smiled.

"Don't fret about it, squirt. It's partly because of selfish reasons. We all decided to build a school and we want you to get well so you can be the teacher."

Megan glanced quickly at Nick, whose face was

unreadable. She looked down to hide her dismay. Wiping tears away she finally looked up and said, "I'd be honored. Thank you so much."

"Andrew, have you decided where you're going?" Elizabeth asked, oblivious to the turmoil in Megan's heart.

"I've asked him to stay here with you," Charles said, "until I come back to get you."

"After that, I plan to set up practice where they need me most," Andrew added.

"We've been trying to convince him to come our direction," Nick said. "There's a couple of growing communities not terribly far from us."

Megan could barely focus on the voices around her. Staring ahead as if listening, she avoided looking at Nick.

Andrew spoke again, this time with a smile so big it threatened to split his face. "Have you heard the news about my brother taking a wife?"

All heads spun to gape at Thomas.

"Who is she?" several voices asked. "Someone from the train?"

"As a matter of fact, yes," Thomas answered.

Megan was dumbfounded. Come to think of it, he had made himself pretty scarce the past few weeks. And he had been uncharacteristically quiet. How had she missed this?

"After I say my good-byes here, I'm headin' to the bathhouse, then ridin' over to get her and take her to the justice of the peace. We're getting married today!"

"Who is she?" Elizabeth asked, about to burst.

"Jessica Hawkins," he answered with pride.

"Jessica?" Megan said in shock, plopping onto the closest chair. "She was just here and she never said a word!"

"We agreed to keep it to ourselves," Thomas admitted sheepishly. "You know how meddling some people can get."

"Good choice, Thomas. You couldn't have done better.

362

She'll make a fine pioneer bride," Charles said.

As the others slapped Thomas on the back and offered congratulations, Megan watched quietly from her chair. She didn't know if she was happy or disturbed by this news. She should be happy, she told herself, but there was a shameful gnawing of envy deep inside. It was supposed to be her getting married and riding off to their ranch, not Jessica! Catching sight of Nick's gaze, she stood and started to rummage around in her valise. She pulled out a small silver frame and carried it to Thomas.

"Please, Thomas," she said, trying to keep her voice steady. "Give this to Jessica as my wedding gift."

Thomas clasped her hands in his. He seemed to understand the awkwardness of the situation. Swallowing back his emotions, he said, "Thank you, Megan. You're like a sister to both Jessica and me. We'll be seein' you soon, I hope."

With that, he turned and left the room.

"Well, boys, I don't know about you, but that bathhouse sure sounds like a good idea to me," Charles said, running his fingers through his dirty hair. "A haircut and shave sound good, too."

Andrew and Nick heartily agreed. Just before he stepped out the door, Nick turned to Megan and asked, "Do you mind if I come back and take you for a little stroll and out for dinner?"

Megan felt dazed. "Fine, Nick, if you want," she answered.

Releasing the doorknob, Nick walked around the bed and gently took her chin in his hand. "Megan," he said softly, "are you alright?"

She nodded and looked down.

"Maybe you should get some rest while I'm gone."

"I will."

When Nick closed the door behind him, Megan crawled under the blankets and stuffed her fist against her mouth to keep from bursting into tears. Elizabeth sat down on the edge of the bed and put her hand on Megan's head.

"Megan, what is it, honey?"

Turning to smother her crying in the pillow, Megan's shoulders heaved with the intensity of her weeping. Grief and sadness and a deep sense of loneliness and confusion poured forth. She couldn't make sense of it. She only knew it had her in its grip. Suzanne and Lucy climbed onto the bed and cuddled against her. Feeling the girls next to her comforted her, but despite her best efforts, she couldn't stop the tears.

After several more minutes, Elizabeth put a cold wet cloth in her hand and helped her sit up. Megan draped the cloth over her hot face and pressed it against her bloodshot eyes. "I'm so sorry," she said with a shaky voice. "I don't know what's wrong with me."

"I think I do," Elizabeth said, her voice gentle and patient. "First of all, you're exhausted, and that makes everything look worse than it is."

Megan nodded, her face still covered with the cloth.

"And I think you're still grieving over Maude and Joe."

Megan nodded and started crying again. Soon, all three of her nieces were on the bed with her and all three began to cry at the mention of Maude and Joe.

Elizabeth wiped tears from her face as she continued, "And I think maybe, now that we've finally arrived, you're a little disappointed at how things have turned out."

Megan nodded and wiped her eyes. After a moment she said, "More than a little disappointed. Terribly disappointed. It was supposed to be different than this, Elizabeth. Joe and Maude were supposed to be here with us, and Nick and I were supposed to get married and then ride off to his ranch together. But here I am, too sick and weak to even consider such a thing. I really won't blame Nick if he's changed his mind about us." She pressed the wet cloth against her face and cried some more.

Elizabeth smiled. "Megan, I don't think there's much chance of that."

"I have to think realistically, Elizabeth. Life on a ranch in the wilderness is not for a weak, sickly woman. Nick knows that." She blew her nose and looked at her sister. "He's not even mentioned anything about marriage for a long time. I'm sure he's having second thoughts."

"Give him time, Megan. He has a lot on his mind now."

"We don't want you to get married," Lucy said between sniffs. "We want you to come with us."

"Oh, Lucy." Megan pulled her into a hug. "Thank you. I *would* miss all of you terribly."

Suzanne and Abigail joined their sister in a big family embrace.

"Think about it, Megan," Elizabeth said. "When you first started on this trip, what were your plans?"

Megan thought for a moment. "I planned on staying near you and Charles and the girls and hoped to get a teaching position."

"Sounds like your original plans are working out perfectly."

Megan smiled and shrugged.

"I think so much of our discontent is because we have a certain set of expectations for life, and if life doesn't happen according to our expectations, then we can't enjoy the good things that God puts in our path." Elizabeth shook her head in frustration at her attempt to express herself clearly. "Does that make sense? God's plans for you could be to live with us for a while and help start the new school. But because that's not exactly what you have in mind right now, you're not happy."

Megan studied the wrinkles in the blanket stretched across her knees.

"I'm not trying to tell you what God's plans are, Megan. I'm just saying we need to be ready to accept whatever God brings us." She reached out and took Megan's hand. "I think he wants us to not just accept it but embrace it and rejoice in it. I also believe we need to surrender to God the things in our life that cause us the most anxiety. Sometimes we have to surrender the things or the people that are most precious to us."

The words Megan had read in First Thessalonians just two weeks ago came back to her. *Rejoice evermore. Pray without ceasing. In everything give thanks: for this is the will of God in Christ Jesus concerning you.*

How quickly she had forgotten. She closed her eyes and prayed silently. *Be at work in me, O Lord. Forgive me for my impatience and my lack of trust. I give you my sickness and I give you my future, whether it's as Nick's wife or as a teacher. I am yours and my future is yours. Help me to trust you and to give thanks to you for whatever comes. Please, Lord, I can't do this without you.*

Two hours later, Nick knocked on the door. Megan had slept and fixed her hair and tried in vain to rid her eyes of the redness. He tucked her hand into his arm and walked slowly down the stairs and out into the cool evening air. They passed several other couples. The one glaring difference Megan saw in those couples was the liveliness and energy in the women. She, on the other hand, clutched Nick's arm for support as she took one feeble step after another. People looked at her with curiosity and pity. Several single women smiled warmly at Nick after glancing quickly at her. Nick kindly diverted attention away from her weakness. He talked about Charles' and Elizabeth's plans, about Andrew's plans, about the McKays and the Sanders; about everyone's plans except theirs. Nick seemed to be hiding something, and the more Megan thought about it, the more obvious it was.

Nick took her to eat at a small restaurant near the government office building. What a treat it was to sit at a table and have someone waiting on them hand and foot. At first, Megan had a hard time looking Nick in the eye, but as she sat across from him, she saw the unmistakable look of love mixed with regret. She was afraid to think what it meant. When the meal was done, he escorted her back to her room and gave her a brief kiss and a promise to see her in the morning before he left.

She quietly changed for bed and crawled in next to Elizabeth. Repeating the words from Thessalonians over and over, she finally drifted off to sleep.

Charles knocked softly in the morning. Elizabeth sat up with a jerk, waking Megan. Charles, Andrew, and Nick entered, loaded down with supplies from the wagon, things Charles' family would need until he returned for them.

"Nick's going to stay and help us get the cabin built before he rides on to his place," Charles said.

Nick chuckled. "Yeah, it'll give those honeymooners a little more time before I barge in on them."

Again, Megan's heart twisted with envy. *So much for all my prayers.* "Andrew's going to stay and watch out for you ladies. The Sanders and McKays have decided to take their wagons and families with them today. Nick and I are riding on ahead so we can pick the cabin site and start cutting trees." Charles' eyes danced with excitement. Some of the old enthusiasm came creeping back in to Megan's soul as she watched him.

"Well, it's time to say good-bye," Charles said as he went over and gave each sleepy girl a hug then turned to his wife.

Nick reached out and captured Megan's hand. He pulled her into the hall and into his arms. "I don't want to say good-bye, but I have to, Megan." He smoothed her hair and kissed her head. She looked up and saw tears in his eyes.

"I'll be back for you, Megan. It may be a while, but I will be back." With that, he lowered his face and kissed her forehead, her cheek, and then her mouth. Then he walked away.

Megan silently watched him go. When she heard his feet reach the bottom of the stairs, she managed to whisper, "Good-bye, Nick."

Charles and Andrew came through the door and after giving Megan a quick good-bye hug, Charles left, leaving Andrew and Megan alone. Megan slipped down to sit on the top step. Andrew quietly joined her.

After a moment of silence, she turned to Andrew. "Be honest with me. Will I ever get well?"

Andrew studied her face. "I can't lie to you. I honestly don't know, Megan," he answered softly. "I've known of people who have bounced back from something like this." He looked down at his hands clasped together between his knees. "But many don't ever completely regain their health. I was sure you were going to be fine until your fever started up again. Then I didn't know what to expect. It's been a long time."

He sighed and looked at her again. "I'm not encouraged by what I see. I'm certain you'll get better, Megan, but I'm doubtful that you will ever be as strong and healthy as you were when I first met you."

Megan sat in stunned silence, trying to digest his words.

"If you get rest, eat healthy food, and get plenty of fresh air and sunshine, you will get stronger," he added. "Don't give up. It will take time."

Megan nodded but the only words she heard were, *I'm doubtful that you will ever be as strong and healthy as you were when I first met you.*

After she crawled into bed and pulled the blankets up to her chin, she let Andrew's words sink in. Throughout the next several nights, she tossed and turned, harassed by the realization she'd be nothing but a burden to Nick. In the middle of the fourth night, she crawled out of bed and paced the floor. Catching a glimpse of herself in the mirror, she turned to study her reflection, bathed in moonlight.

What she saw shocked her. The lack of sleep and loss of appetite had taken a terrible toll on her already-emaciated face. This woman she saw was certainly not the woman Nick had fallen in love with.

Suddenly, the truth of the situation hit her with severe clarity. In horror, she stood rooted to the spot as thought after thought coursed through her mind. She stumbled back at the power of the conclusion she had reached. Not wanting to wake the girls, she opened the door and slipped quietly out to the hall and sank with despair onto the top step.

*What had Elizabeth said about surrender? Sometimes we have to surrender the people that are the most precious to us. Haven't I done that?*

She buried her face in her hands and wept. *No, no, I haven't. I'm hanging on to Nick like a parasite. And that's all I am to him now, a parasite, a clinging, life-draining parasite. He needs a woman who can help him, care for him, cook his meals, and clean his house. He needs someone who can work beside him and bear his children. Not someone he has to care for! What was I thinking? How could I have been so selfish, so blind?*

Megan rocked back and forth in her grief, begging God to help her surrender the one thing that mattered most to her. Before she could change her mind, she found paper and a pen and by the light of the moon, she wrote her thoughts to Nick, trying her best to release him without crushing him.

*Nick, I have come to the very difficult decision of releasing you from your commitment to me. This has nothing to do with you and everything to do with me. It has been an honor that you considered me worthy of being your wife. But I realize how unrealistic and how terribly selfish it is of me to cling to you. You fell in love with a vibrant, healthy woman, well suited to join you on the frontier. I am no longer that woman and after talking to Andrew, realize I probably never will be.*

*Watching Jessica leave with Thomas and watching several other women ride out of town to join their husbands in their homesteading ventures made me realize afresh, how cheated you will be if you pursue a marriage with me.*

*I will see you again, but please don't try to change my mind. I'm quite certain this is what God would have me do and I finally have peace about it. I insist that you accept my decision. Find another, more worthy woman and go without regret or guilt to your new life. I will be fine. Being a teacher has always been my dream. And to get to teach my nieces is beyond what I ever hoped for.*

*Your friend,*

*Megan*

In spite of saying she was fine, she sobbed uncontrollably as she folded and sealed the letter.

## CHAPTER TWENTY EIGHT

**A** week later, Charles rode back to Oregon City to get his family. Nick was with him. Megan had asked Andrew to deliver her letter. "Please tell him to take some time to think and to pray after he reads it."

Andrew raised his eyebrows. "This sounds serious."

Unbidden tears came to her eyes. "Tell him I'll meet him at the church on Second Street in an hour."

From the window, she watched as Nick received the letter and unfolded it, but she couldn't bear to watch him read it. She slipped out the back, down the alley, and made her way slowly to the church. Inside the dark interior, she walked between the pews and sank to her knees on the hard floor and cried. She knew she had to hold firm to her resolve to release Nick. If she truly loved him, and she did, this was the only way.

Knowing Nick couldn't wait a full hour, she wasn't at all surprised to hear him burst through the doors early. He strode to the front, breathing heavily. From her place, she could tell he was pacing and slapping his hat against his thigh, something he often did when angry or frustrated, she thought with tenderness. Oh, how she hated hurting this precious man. She stood and cleared her throat.

Nick turned to her. He held her letter up and declared loudly and firmly, "No!" Then he walked to her, grabbed her hand, and gently pulled her into the aisle. Again, he held the letter up. "Did you hear me? I said no."

"Nick." She reached up to hold his face. "I've made up my mind. You need to be free of me."

He pulled her into an embrace. "I don't want to be free of you. Ever! You are my life. Megan, can't you see that?"

"This is how you feel right now, but a few months from now when you're dividing your time between farming and caring for an invalid, you'll have regrets."

"That's nonsense," he declared as he took her face in his and kissed her soundly.

Megan's knees threatened to buckle. She took a step back. "Nick, I love you. I've never loved anyone as fiercely as I've loved you, But I know without a doubt that the most loving thing I can do for you is to let you go."

He moved toward her, weeping unashamedly. She held up her hand to stop him. "Find a woman that's strong, who's capable of working with you, one that can bear children for you. Chances are good that I won't be able to." She kept moving farther away from him. "And if I can bear children, I'll probably be too weak to take care of them. You'll have to do it."

"You're being ridiculous, Megan," he said eyes narrowing, still walking toward her.

"No, Nick. I wish I was wrong, but I have to do this." She again held her hand up to stop him. "I've prayed and prayed and prayed. God has convinced me this is the right thing for both of us." With a sob, she turned to go. "Don't stop me, Nick. Please don't stop me." With that, she stumbled out the door and down the steps.

The next day, she rode out of town with Charles, Elizabeth, and the girls. Nick stayed away. Her heart broke as she watched Oregon City shrink behind them. As they jostled along the trail, her heartache threatened to destroy her, but never once did she question her decision. She was unwavering in her desire to do what was right for Nick. On the other hand, she realized, she would also be a burden to Charles and Elizabeth if she continued in her depressed state of mind, so she forced herself to look around at the scenes unfolding before her at every turn. It was breathtakingly beautiful. She also immersed herself in the reading of scripture. By the time they reached their homestead, she was able to see a glimmer of hope for the days to come.

Within the next month, the hardworking men managed to build two cabins for the McKay and Sanders families. Soon they added lean-tos and corrals for the horses and started work on the school.

As Elizabeth continued to grow with the baby, Megan kept getting healthier and stronger, much more so than she had expected. Each morning, she woke with a renewed sense of awe and gratefulness for health. She took great joy in the simple act of walking with strong steady strides.

In the middle of November, she started teaching. Helping Elizabeth with household chores and teaching several hours each day occupied her hands and mind. And she found herself delighting in her work. Three other homesteaders lived close enough to send their children to Megan's school, which the McKays and Sanders had decided would be forever named the O'Mally School.

"We can't pay you enough for what you've done for our children," Dan McKay said one afternoon when he and Stephen Sanders were standing on the school porch. "So, our two families decided to honor you by naming the school after you. My oldest is making a sign to hang over the door."

Thoughts of Nick continued to disturb her peace. She was afraid she had dealt him such a devastating blow, that there would be no hope of reconciliation, even as friends. When she let him go, she had intended it to be forever. *So, she told herself over and over, don't look back.*

In the middle of December, Elizabeth went into labor. With fat snowflakes drifting slowly down outside, little Russell Batten made his entrance into the world. Charles was beside himself with joy. Proudly he strutted around the cabin, holding his only son for all their visitors to see.

As Christmas approached, Megan and her students worked furiously on a Christmas program to present to their little wilderness community for Christmas Eve. Elizabeth agreed to let Russell play the part of baby Jesus. Suzanne had the privilege of being Mary, and with it the responsibility to see that no harm came to her little brother. Megan assigned various parts to every one of her eighteen students. She decided to save the parts of the three wise men for Charles, Mr. Sanders, and Mr. McKay. The plan was for them to walk in at the end of the program and surprise each child with a small gift.

Christmas Eve finally arrived. Neighbors crowded into the one-room school, greeting each other and laughing over the costumes their children wore. Little Stephen Sanders and Abigail were both dressed as lambs. Lucy was proudly strutting around dressed as an angel. Charles had raised a doubting eyebrow at that assignment. One of the larger boys wore a ridiculous donkey costume. He would carry Mary, crawling on his hands and knees, from the back of the schoolroom to the platform at the front. Joseph elbowed a friend when he was teased about being sweet on Mary. The tables at the back of the schoolroom were groaning under the weight of all the food the mothers had brought.

Finally, people took their seats and a hush came over the audience when Megan stood at the front, full of excitement. She introduced each student and the two fiddlers who would accompany the pageant. "Please join us in singing the carols whenever you see the two fiddlers stand," she instructed. "And now we will begin with prayer." She nodded to a father, who stood and thanked God for his provision and mercy. He ended by inviting everyone to join him in the Lord's Prayer.

The pageant was a delight for all to see and hear. The adults sang with gusto; the children remembered most of their lines. The McKays' oldest son read from the Bible with a strong clear voice, the little lambs were adorable, and baby Russell only cried once.

When it was over, Megan had trouble quieting the hungry crowd. "Please, take your seats. We're not quite finished. I promise, this next part will not take long. Then we can all line up for some refreshment. Children, you may all sit up here on the platform."

After they were settled, Megan gave the signal for the wise men to enter. They came through the door, each wearing a beard and carrying a bulging sack. Megan was surprised at their costumes. She had a hard time telling who was who. Their wives have been working hard, she thought with admiration.

*Ooos* and *ahhs* came from the audience as the men made their way down the aisle to the platform where the children sat. One by one, they drew small packages from their sacks and distributed them to each wide-eyed child.

When they were finished, the tallest wise man turned and looked around until he found Megan. His eyes bore into hers with intensity as he made his way to her. Perplexed by his actions, she looked into his face as he reached down into the bottom of his sack and withdrew a small package wrapped in gold paper and tied with a red satin ribbon. He put the package in her hand and stood watching while she just looked at it.

"For me?" she asked.

He only nodded.

Carefully she removed the beautiful ribbon and paper. Inside was a hinged silver box with a little clasp.

"Open it, Miss O'Mally," several students urged.

She looked up again, filled with curiosity. "Who is this from?"

"Open it and see," her students again answered.

Flipping the clasp up, she lifted the lid. Inside was a piece of paper carefully folded so it would fit in the tiny box.

"What? What is it?" the children asked, pressing in from all sides so they could see.

Megan looked quizzically at the bearded face bending over her. There was something disturbingly familiar about those sad eyes. Carefully she unfolded the paper and read the words.

*My answer to your last letter is still, "no." It will forever be "no," because one day you said, "yes" to me and I will never release you from that "yes."*

Megan gasped and clutched the letter to her chest, not daring to look up into the face she knew so well. Tears filled her eyes. She cleared her throat and managed to speak to the audience. "It's time to eat." The children all rose as one and made their way to the food-laden tables. Parents quickly joined them. Only a few stayed and watched Megan as she stood and bolted for the door.

In the clear, crisp night with a sprinkling of snow on the ground, Megan stood between two tall pines and listened to approaching footsteps. Nick stopped behind her. His breathing was steady but loud.

"Read the letter, Megan," he demanded.

She held it in front of her and turned slightly so the moon could provide light. But it wasn't enough. Nick took her arm and steered her to the porch where two lanterns hung on each side of the entrance. Megan's knees almost buckled at the touch of his hand. With shaking hands, she gripped the paper and read on.

*I thought I made it abundantly clear how I felt about you. Your sickness made no difference to me. Didn't you know, Megan, you had become my very life? How could you think I could live without you? I know you intended to do this as an unselfish act, but the pain I experienced was far, far worse than having an invalid for a wife, even if she was someone I didn't love. And you, dear girl, I love with all of my being. I told you once, if all your limbs were cut from your body, I would still want you over any woman God has created. And that is still true.*

*You have done me a grave injustice in thinking my love was so shallow. But how can I hold that against you, when you were so firmly convinced it was the right thing to do?*

*I love you, Megan, and always will. There has never been and never will be any woman for me, but you. If you won't have me, I'll go to my grave a single man.*

*Yours forever,*

*Nick*

She looked up from the letter in awe. "You'd go to your grave a single man?" she managed to ask with a smile.

He nodded and smiled back.

An anguished cry tore through her as she threw herself into Nick's waiting arms, throwing him off-balance. He clung to her tightly as he grabbed for the railing.

"I'm so sorry, Nick," Megan blubbered, her face buried in his chest. "I'm so sorry! Please forgive me!"

Nick's arms tightened around her. He rested his cheek on the top of her head and wept. They stood that way for several minutes, Megan interrupting the sweet silence with an occasional whisper of "I'm so sorry."

Finally, Nick took her face in his hands and looked down at her. He wiped her tears away with his thumbs and smiled. "I forgive you, Megan." He kissed her forehead and pulled her to his chest once again, stroking her back and whispering, "Shh, it's all right," in response to her continuing sobs.

Again, he pushed her gently away so he could see her face. "Do I dare hope, Megan, that this means we can start over from where we were when we first got to Oregon City?"

"Yes, Nick," Megan sniffed, "if I haven't messed things up too badly."

Nick smiled. "I find that my broken heart is healing quite rapidly."

Megan smiled through her tears.

"If your answer is 'yes,' I need you to give me the box."

"The box?" she asked, thoroughly confused.

"The box my letter was in."

"Oh, I think I left it inside."

"Stay here. I'll be back." With that, he disappeared into the schoolhouse.

Moments later, he emerged with the box. He took her hand and led her out into the moonlit schoolyard. Tiny snowflakes drifted slowly down around them. Nick turned Megan to face him. "Open it," he said as he handed the box to her.

Again, she lifted the tiny lid. This time, Megan looked down at the most beautiful ring she had ever seen. It wasn't large or gaudy but tiny and dainty with a small ruby surrounded by ivy, intricately crafted in gold.

She looked up to see Nick kneeling in front of her. He took her hand in his and asked, "Miss Megan O'Mally, will you be my wife?"

Megan covered her face with her free hand. This couldn't be happening! It was too good to be true!

"Well?" he asked, looking up with hope.

Megan laughed. "What was your question again?"

"You heard me," he growled good-naturedly and rose to his feet.

"I want to hear it again! And again, and again, and again! I've waited long enough, Nick Webster."

They were oblivious to the crowd that had gathered on the porch watching them and laughing.

"Will you marry me, Megan?" Nick asked again, running his finger down the side of her face.

Megan grabbed his hand and pressed his palm to her cheek, her eyes closed and her mouth curved in a blissful smile.

"Will you marry, me?" he whispered softly, his lips against the top of her head.

"Yes, Nick," she whispered. "Yes, yes, yes, I'll marry you." Her voice got louder with every "yes."

Suddenly the crowd burst into cheers and came toward them. Megan and Nick looked at the dozens of smiling faces, people they loved who seemed to want to catch every word they spoke to each other. The other wise men pounded Nick on the back and congratulated them both. Megan laughed and hid her blushing face against Nick's hard chest.

With a smile and a wave at their audience, Nick guided Megan farther away into the darkness. He moved to shield her from a blast of cold wind that hit them as soon as they stepped around the corner of the building. Wrapping his big, warm arms around her, he whispered into her hair, "Oh, Megan, I've missed you. I don't think I can live any longer without you."

He tipped her chin up so he could study her face. "You look good." He smiled and kissed her briefly. "Mmm, very good," he murmured, and then lowered his face for a longer kiss.

When they parted, Megan studied his eyes with tender concern and asked, "Nick, how...how have you been doing?"

"I've had to keep myself busy." He smiled down at her upturned face, as if drinking in every precious feature.

She smiled sadly, wondering if she'd ever forgive herself for the grief she'd caused him. "Busy doing what?"

"Building. I wasn't too keen on sharing our cabin with newlyweds, so I built a new one for us."

"Oh," Megan sighed just before Nick smothered her with another kiss.

"How about having our wedding tomorrow?" he asked.

"Tomorrow? Tomorrow's Christmas."

"I know. What better way to celebrate?" he said, grinning from ear to ear.

"It sounds wonderful to me," Megan answered, as Nick wrapped her up in his arms and lifted her off her feet. "Absolutely wonderful!" They laughed with unrestrained joy as he swung her in a big circle.

# ABOUT THE AUTHOR

Ava MacKinney formerly taught American history and Art. She is a lover of the outdoors, artist, history buff, blogger (thecrazycrookedpath.com), mother to five, grandmother to nine and wife to her amazing husband, Steve. They enjoy life on their small farm in the Ozarks, surrounded by dogs, cats and endless wildlife. Raised on a sheep farm in the mountains of Vermont, her parents gave her free reign to explore and to dream. Today she delights in dreaming up stories filled with adventure, romance, and spiritual growth.

If you'd like to follow Ava on Instagram, go to @avamackinney

Facebook, The Crazy Crooked Path.

Website: thecrazycrookedpath.com

## *If you enjoyed Megan O'Mally...*

You will also enjoy the other two books in this series. Two of Megan's childhood friends, Eliza and Maddy, experienced their own adventures during and after The Civil War.

I can't begin to tell you what a fun adventure it was for me to get their stories out of my brain and into print. Dig in and enjoy.

# Eliza Long (Book One)
*Available now through Amazon, Barnes and Noble and other online book retailers*

The War Between the States hits southwest Missouri in August, 1861, with all the ugliness and horrors of war in the homeland.

Eliza is consumed by the need to avenge her father's death. Presented with the opportunity to be involved in espionage, she foolishly says yes and is catapulted into a world of lies, play-acting and danger.

Lieutenant Jonathan Monroe is furious when he discovers her occupation. Before Eliza's father went to battle, he charged Jonathan with the job of protecting his daughter. It was an easy job to accept, since Jonathan had known and loved little Eliza since she was a baby. Against his better judgement, his feelings for her evolve from his guardian role to one of strong romantic attraction.

Will Eliza listen to reason when Jonathan begs her to stop spying? Will she be able to overcome the driving force of her anger and hatred? Anger that also extends toward God. In a pivotal moment she is faced with an unexpected choice. What will her answer be?

# Maddy Malone (Book Two)

*Available now through Amazon, Barnes and Noble and other online book retailers*

Maddy dreads the day her neighbor, Silas, will return home from war to claim his two little children. Two motherless children that have lived with her and worked their way into her heart after four long years. Yet she knows they need their pa.

How can she maneuver through the days ahead as she tries to release them into the care of their father? How can she avoid the unwanted and threatening attention from her other neighbor, Sam Potter, who is determined to marry her and add her acreage to his?

As Silas rebuilds his neglected farm, he becomes more and more aware of Maddy's dire and dangerous predicament. He wants to help her but isn't sure how. His attraction for her is strong, but he denies it in shame, because he's sure his petite neighbor is far too young for him.

In a bold and desperate move, Maddy backs him into a corner. What will Silas do?